I0646455

The Angler War

Rise of the Giants Series: Book 7

Theo Mann

The Invisible Publishing Company

Rise of the Giants Series

Contents

Chapter 1

H angman raised his hand, caught his cousin Viking's eye, and pointed sideways. Viking nodded and the two men separated to go in opposite directions.

Their band of Godless warriors separated, too. Banjo, Feather, Hangman's younger brothers Lock and Bantam, Grizzly, Kuvik, and Butch came with Hangman. Some of the others went with Viking and the rest went with Shadow.

The three groups spread through the jungle treetops to surround a herd of Stalkions grazing in an open field. A single enormous bull stood guard over his harem of cows and a bunch of calves of different ages.

Hangman and his comrades circled the field on the left side and the men put more distance between themselves. Shadow's party covered the far end of the field at an angle from Hangman. Viking's group circled to the right.

The Godless surrounded the Stalkions in silence. The bull kept snorting and tossing his head, but he didn't see any threat. He did it out of habit and to signal his dominance to his cows and the older male calves who came too close to him.

Hangman pulled his kukris, squatted on a branch, and checked left and right. The warriors of his father's group would drop out of these trees, attack the Stalkions at the center, and block them from getting out of the field.

That would be the least of the men's worries. The Stalkions wouldn't try to run away. The bull would attack the men to protect his harem. The females would attack the men to protect the calves.

Even the older male calves wouldn't attack the Godless just to practice attacking something. The Stalkions wouldn't be stuck in the field with a band of murderous Godless. The Godless would be stuck in the field with a herd of murderous Stalkions.

Hangman could see a few better ways to carry out this hunt, but he didn't say so beforehand and he didn't say so now. He didn't say much in his father's band these days. He'd learned the hard way to keep his mouth shut.

He glanced the other way and found Kuvik at his side. No one had stopped calling him Kuvik after his initiation. Hangman didn't understand why. It just seemed so much more appropriate to keep calling him Kuvik.

He didn't grow his hair out, either. He kept shaving his head bald, but no one seemed to notice that, either. He actually didn't look that much different from some of the other men who tied their hair up in tiny knots or twists all over their heads.

He let one small, thin lock of hair grow from the side of his neck behind his ear. He tied the Ridgebeak feather from his initiation to this piece of hair as a trophy and a sign of his status as a fully initiated Godless man.

He never changed his clothes, either. He kept wearing the same pair of tattered pants he'd been wearing since he came home from his five-year absence.

They were the same pair he'd been wearing before he left—the pair Hangman had given Kuvik at the artillery battery in the northern mountains.

He didn't take them off after his initiation. He didn't start wearing loincloths like the other men. The men teased him about what he would wear when these pants got too threadbare, wore holes in the seat, and disintegrated around him.

He joined in these jokes and told them that his wife Yoa was already planning to make him a new pair of pants out of hides instead of this thin cloth. He didn't want to go around in a loincloth for some reason.

Everything else about him seemed the same as Hangman remembered from before Kuvik disappeared—apart from all the scars all over his body, of course. He never talked about how he got them. He never talked about his absence at all—to anyone.

His closest friends still saw how troubled he was by his past, especially in the mornings when he woke up from nightmares. That and everything else about him were still the same old Kuvik that Hangman knew so well.

Kuvik glanced over at Hangman at the same time and Kuvik's eyebrows came together in the middle. Hangman looked away. Of course Kuvik would pick up on Hangman's tension.

Hangman couldn't explain anything to his friend right now—not without tipping off the Stalkions. Hangman craned his neck to look farther to the left. He tried to spot his father in the undergrowth over there to see when Shadow would give the signal to attack.

Hangman could see scattered men here and there all around the circle. Red and his men had integrated into Shadow's band without a hitch. They, their wives, and their children had settled in and became part of this band like everyone else.

Red's men still held a special loyalty for Hangman, though. Their connection and experience with each other bled through in subtle ways anyone could pick up.

Shadow was too smart not to notice—along with everything else about Hangman that Shadow had a problem with. Shadow had a problem with Hangman's existence.

The tension between the two men had only gotten worse in the four years since Hangman and his family had returned from the Angler Valley.

Hangman tried for the millionth time to push those thoughts out of his head. He was always trying to push them out of his head nowadays because they always had a way of intruding no matter what else he was doing.

Trying to appease his father and trying to maneuver around Shadow's constant hostility was becoming a full-time job for Hangman.

It consumed his every waking minute and distracted him when he should have been thinking about more important things—like right now. The situation especially worried Mora. She saw firsthand how much it bothered him.

Neither of them could do anything about it. His constant dwelling on it interfered with his ability to interact with and relate to his family. The situation couldn't go on this way for much longer—not without coming to some kind of breaking point.

Hangman shook his head in a hopeless effort to clear his thoughts. His gaze darted from one man to another on Shadow's side of the field.

Hangman picked out Wildling, Baron, Breaker, Devil, Prodigy......and then, for some reason Hangman couldn't figure out, they all disappeared. Their faces vanished from the undergrowth.

He stared at the spot with his heart in his mouth. The whole band waited for Shadow to make the first move. He and his men would enter the field first to draw the Stalkions' attention that way. Then everyone else was supposed to attack.

Now what was Hangman supposed to do? He told himself to turn his head and point out the situation to Kuvik and the others. They would have to decide whether to enter the field on their own or ......

That was the moment when a commotion broke out in the undergrowth on Shadow's side of the field. Hangman caught a single glimpse of Prodigy fighting someone—someone not Godless.

Hangman didn't wait to see or hear anything else. He vaulted to his feet, yelled, "Come on!" to the men nearest him, and took off at high speed through the canopy. All the men came with him. They didn't hesitate or ask any questions.

The party rushed around the field without returning to the ground. They overtook Shadow's party in the middle of a pitched battle against another group of men unlike any Hangman had ever seen before.

He didn't check his advance to find out who they were. They attacked Shadow's group with frightening power and bloodthirsty intent. Hangman dove right in and started fighting the enemy, too.

Viking's group must have heard the noise. They closed on the opposite side and his and Hangman's parties locked the enemy between them.

The enemy brought twenty men. They had the same straight black hair and dark eyes as everyone else in this country, but they didn't look like anyone else Hangman had ever seen.

These attackers painted their faces and bodies black with some kind of clay pigmented with soot. The strangers cut their hair the length of a man's hand and used the same black clay mixture to stick their hair out in spikes from their heads.

The hair spikes formed a complete spherical halo around each man's head. Their appearance looked even more otherworldly and surreal than the Bounty Hunters or the Hungry Ghosts.

These people didn't go naked like the Hungry Ghosts. The strangers wore almost knee-length pants like Kuvik's. The strangers plastered the same black clay on their pants to make them the same color as the rest of their bodies.

The strangers didn't fight like anyone Hangman had ever seen, either. These people fought with the same combination of weapons as the Godless and these people had the skill to use them effectively.

It very quickly became obvious that the strangers possessed all the Godless Clan's skill and agility in the treetops, too.

Hangman's and Viking's pincer maneuver trapped the strangers between all three Godless groups.

The Godless would have slaughtered the strangers right there, but they reacted by springing away into the branches, using them to swing back around, and attack the Godless from multiple directions.

The Godless had to fight their hardest to counter this enemy. The strangers turned out to be incredibly fast, agile, ferocious, and creative in their use of the surrounding branches.

Hangman had never fought any enemy as skilled in the treetops as the Godless. None of the other enemy Clans used the treetops at all. The jungle canopy had always been the Godless' ace in the hole for launching ambushes and surprise attacks.

The Godless could also get away into the branches whenever the situation turned against them. The Godless had always been able to rely on their enemies to stay behind on the ground while the Godless got away, retreated, and regrouped elsewhere.

None of the Godless could do that now. Hangman rushed three of the strangers, but they scattered, scampered through the branches to circle him, and came back at him from two different directions. He couldn't fight them all, so he attacked one of them.

His own speed and agility were nothing to sneeze at, so he used the strangers' tactics against them, feinted onto a different branch, and hit his enemy from the side while the guy was still facing in the other direction.

He chopped his kukri into the side of the guy's skull, spun around, and landed on a different branch just as the remaining two attackers closed from either side.

One of them fought with two small axes. The other used long rectangular metal blades like they might have been stolen from the Renegade Clan. Both strangers struck at once and would have impaled or dismembered Hangman between them.

He crouched beneath the first man's axe swings, seized him by the waistband of his pants, and flung him off the branch while Hangman drove one of his kukris into the other attacker's sternum.

The first stranger plummeted through the canopy, slammed into a branch, and fell the rest of the way to the jungle floor. Hangman's victim folded into a heap, but Hangman paid no attention.

He leapt off the branch, vaulted down a dozen more branches, and sprang clear just as the third attacker was picking himself up off the ground.

Hangman didn't wait to land on the ground to engage the guy. Hangman twisted backward, let gravity steer him behind his enemy, and impaled the bastard through the spine behind his neck.

Chapter 2

The force of Hangman's weight falling against his blade and driving it into his victim's body broke Hangman's fall.

He landed straddling the body, pulled his blade clear, and looked up to see his brothers, cousins, and comrades driving the rest of the strangers out of the area. They left dozens of bodies hanging in the branches.

The strangers shot away through the treetops swinging from branches, using the trees' elasticity to propel themselves on their way, and jumping from trunk to trunk across wide gaps in the canopy.

Hangman and his comrades all stayed where they were and watched these strangers out of sight. Hangman didn't understand them.

He didn't know who these strangers were, where they came from, or what they were doing here. He'd never seen or even heard of them before.

He didn't understand anything about them—not one single thing—except that they had attacked the Godless totally unprovoked.

They must have traveled a long, long way to get here. They must have traveled through country infested with Renegades, Bounty Hunters, deadly creatures, and who knew what other kinds of enemies.

These people would have been able to handle all of that. Hangman was certain of it. These people could handle anything. They were as brave, skilled, and cunning as the Godless if not more so.

Shadow broke the spell by turning around, walking over to one of the dead strangers, and squatting down next to the body. He and every man here dripped with sweat. Most had sustained some injury.

They got busy stopping the bleeding, applying leaf paste, and cleaning up the blood as soon as Shadow made the first move.

He rolled his dead opponent over. The man's arms and legs flopped off the branch into open space and his head rolled to one side so everyone could see his face. He was definitely human.

"Who are they, Father?" Lock asked.

"I don't know, my son," Shadow muttered. "I've never seen or heard of them before."

"Spider Clan," Kuvik interjected. "They come from the far north-west."

"That's impossible," Legacy countered. "The ocean is to the north-west."

"The land curves around. There's another landmass there attached to this one." Kuvik used his hand to demonstrate what he meant. Then he turned to stare down at the stranger. "I've never heard of them coming this far south before."

"Are you telling me these freaks fought their way through Renegades and Bounty Hunters so they could come after *us*?" Grizzly demanded. "I'll never believe that."

"It's true that we haven't seen as many Renegades and Bounty Hunters lately as we used to in the past," Red pointed out. "They may have been too busy fighting these people."

"Did you see the way they moved through the trees?" Carnage murmured. "They were incredible."

"They're known for their skill in the treetops," Kuvik went on. "They don't shy away from going down to the ground, though, so be careful of that. They nest in the trees, too. They mimic spiders. They weave nests in the trees where they keep their females and children safe from creatures. They don't make camps on the ground if they can avoid it."

"How do they build fires, then?" Breaker demanded. "They must come down to the ground to cook their food."

"I don't know what they eat or how they do it," Kuvik replied. "I'm just telling you what I know."

Shadow straightened up. "Let's move out. Fall back to the gorge camp. We'll move the band farther east away from this threat."

"We can't keep moving around all the time," Hangman pointed out. "We'll never establish a secure territory if we keep running from everyone the first time someone threatens us on our own land."

Hangman realized his mistake as soon as he said those words out loud. His father shot him a death glare—but only for a second.

"I said move out," Shadow snapped. "We'll hunt farther east after we get the women and children moving. We can't waste any more time."

Shadow took off through the branches. He hadn't lost any speed as he aged. He was as strong and sturdy in body as he had ever been.

The other men exchanged glances and then followed him. Hangman hung back. He would have preferred to leave last, but Red and Kuvik both stayed with him. He appreciated their support, but it didn't make his life any easier.

He caught his younger brothers giving him searching looks, too. They were the main reason he mostly kept quiet around his father—and every other time.

He'd grown up following his father's example of never challenging Butcher's authority. Hangman wanted to give his younger brothers the same example now. He wanted to model for them what obedience to one's Kral really looked like.

Hangman had spent the last year making an almighty effort to keep the hostility between himself and Shadow entirely one-sided on his father's part. Hangman never harbored any animosity against Shadow—not ever.

Hangman couldn't imagine what he might have done to make his father hate him so much—except that Hangman was the next most obvious possibility of someone who might challenge Shadow's leadership.

Hangman had spent almost five years as Kral of his own band. Most of the people in Shadow's band had once considered Hangman their Kral. Some still did, but they did it silently. They never said so out loud.

Red and his men belonged to this group. They followed Shadow because Hangman followed Shadow and because Hangman wanted them to follow Shadow.

Red and his men would never consider Shadow their Kral—not the way they considered Hangman their true Kral. That was just never going to happen.

Hangman didn't stick around to exchange words with his friends. He took off to follow the others. Red and Kuvik came with him. The three men caught up with the rest of the group and traveled back to the gorge camp in silence.

The men couldn't travel through the branches once they entered the gorges because there were no branches in the gorges. The Godless had to walk the rest of the way. They encountered women and children in the gorges before they got to the camp itself.

The women fell in with the men and tried to engage them in conversation. The women picked it up right away when the men didn't bite and only answered in short words when they answered at all.

The children ran ahead, so everyone in the camp knew ahead of time that the men were coming back. All the women and families gathered to welcome the men home.

"We'll pack up and move on tomorrow morning," Shadow announced once everyone assembled. "There's a new threat coming toward us through the jungle. We'll fall back to the east....."

An outburst of groans and protests broke through the crowd. "No!" someone yelled.

"Why do we have to go?" Katha demanded. "We were gone for four years and we're settled here. We thought we could stay here. Now we have to leave again?"

"There has to be a better way," Yoa added. "Why did we come back at all? We should have just kept moving around forever. It would have been easier."

"You heard what I said!" Shadow snapped. "Start packing up! Don't wait until tomorrow morning. The sooner we leave, the better. I don't want to wait all day for everyone to finish packing. Get it done tonight."

He stormed off to his own shelter. Katha met him there and immediately started talking in his ear even when he snapped at her.

Hangman watched them disappear inside. The other women grumbled—a lot. Moving away from this camp was the absolute last thing anyone wanted to do.

The men stood around exchanging glances with each other, their wives, and then the women finally started getting to work. Hangman spotted Mora watching him from across the camp. Her eyes spoke volumes.

He also became aware of his brothers and all of Red's men watching him again. They all waited for Hangman to do or say something. He set an example for all of them—but some part of him still considered himself responsible for them.

He just couldn't shake that feeling—not even after all this time of living under Shadow's authority. Hangman would always consider Shadow his Kral—and at the same time, Hangman still considered himself the true Kral of this band.

The safety and protection of everyone in this band stopped with him—not Shadow. That was the final bottom line. It would have been Hangman's responsibility to step in and overrule Shadow if he did anything to put the band in danger.

Wasn't Shadow doing that now? Wasn't he jeopardizing the band's safety by making everyone move? Hangman couldn't think that. Shadow had made the decision to leave to protect everyone from the Spider Clan. He was trying to act in the band's best interest.

Hangman waited a little longer. More women went back to work. Mora ducked inside her shelter. Was she packing up in there? Would she wait to see if Hangman intervened? Should he?

Half the men left, too. They either went to help their wives, or at least went to sit down somewhere. Hangman's brothers left—each man to his own shelter. They had lived alone ever since their initiations.

Hangman took a firm grip on himself, crossed the camp, and entered his father's shelter. He and Katha sat on their bed talking while he ate.

Katha looked up and her face drained of all color when she saw Hangman standing there. Hangman gave her a look and she left immediately. Shadow didn't look up, not even when Hangman squatted opposite him.

"Let me go scout this new Clan, Father," Hangman murmured. "We don't know how many of them there are. They may not have brought enough men to threaten us. We could at least find out how strong they are. They may have only brought a small band of warriors."

Shadow's head shot up. "You heard my decision!" he snapped. "How dare you undermine my authority?!"

"I'm not trying to undermine your authority, Father. I would never do that...."

"You may have been Kral of your own band once, but you aren't here! You heard my decision. Your only job is to carry it out. Don't ever let me hear you contradict me in front of the men—or in private. Now get out of here and go help your wife pack up. The men need to see you following my orders. Don't make me tell you a second time."

He bent over his bowl and went back to eating to dismiss Hangman from his presence. Hangman left the shelter and discovered his mother standing ten feet away waiting for him to come out.

She gave him one of those pained, sympathetic, understanding looks he had been getting from almost everyone lately. He shared a moment of eye contact with her, walked away, and returned to his own shelter.

Twelve-year-old Zaedi, ten-year-old Thena, and eight-year-old Maeno worked outside. Zaedi had been moving with a mob of boys trying to grow up extra fast. Thena had her own friends who played house and took care of the younger children.

None of the three children had been near their own shelter before. They must have been watching for Hangman to come out. They both ran over when he returned and followed him inside.

Mora sat on the floor wrapping up some of her sewing tools in a length of hide. She startled into getting to her feet when Hangman walked in.

She overturned all her needles and floundered between trying to pick them up and give him her attention at the same time.

"Are we really moving out, Father?" Zaedi asked. "Where will we go?"

"Let your father get something to eat before you start bombarding him with questions." Mora stepped in and handed Hangman a bowl of food. She sat down next to him and started handing out food to everyone else.

"I'm not staying," Hangman told her. "I have to go back out."

Her head shot up. "Do you have to? Please don't leave me to do all the packing up by myself."

"Yes, I have to," he replied and didn't explain any further than that.

"Where are you going, Father?" Zaedi asked.

"I'm going hunting."

Mora gaped at him. "The sun is going down."

"Do you remember the installation at Jeweled River?" he asked.

Her jaw dropped even further if that was possible. "Why do you ask about that now of all times?"

"You said you found out about it from books and ancient military pamphlets. You said you found out about the ancient weapons by reading about them. Was that true or did you find out some other way?"

She gasped out loud. "Of course it's true! How else would I have found out? Did you think I lied to you about it? Why would you bring it up now? That was years ago. I would have told you then if I had found out another way."

"Are you sure? Are you sure you never saw anything like that in person? You said your family band traveled all over the south country. You could have seen another installation like that."

She shut her mouth with difficulty and looked away. "No, I never saw anything like that."

"What about the artillery we found in the battery?" Hangman insisted. "Had you ever seen anything like that in person—or only in books?"

"No, I never saw anything like it in person—not even from a distance," she mumbled under her breath. "I'd only seen pictures of them before that."

"What's artillery?" Zaedi asked.

"Never mind," Mora told him. "Eat your food and then I need all three of you to help me pack up."

"What is there to pack up?" Thena asked. "We don't have anything."

Hangman put his bowl down. "I better go. I'll see you all later."

He ignored Mora's pained expression. She understood his situation better than anyone, but he couldn't deal with her right now.

He left his family where they were, walked out of the camp, and paused at the head of the gorge to look back. Everyone worked to pack up their possessions and deal with their remaining food supplies to prepare for the journey.

The men either helped their wives or worked with each other. No one guarded the camp or kept watch on the surrounding area.

Hangman turned away, burst into a run as soon as he passed out of sight in the gorges, and took off as fast as possible heading back to the spot where Shadow's band had first encountered the Spider Clan.

Chapter 3

Hangman crouched in the branches and looked down at the bodies of all the dead strangers who had attacked Shadow's hunting party. Kuvik had called these strangers the Spider Clan.

Hangman supposed he could start thinking of these people as Spiders if they mimicked spiders the way Kuvik said.

Hangman jumped down through the branches and squatted next to the body Shadow had examined. Hangman studied the man in much more detail this time. The Spiders or whatever and whoever they were didn't wear shoes. They went barefoot.

They must have gone barefoot their entire lives. The soles of their feet had developed a thick pad of callused skin almost as hard as bone. It even made a clicking sound when Hangman tapped a stick against it.

The Spiders also let their fingernails grow long. He found out why when he searched the area more closely.

He didn't think he would find any track or trace of them moving through the branches. That was one of the main reasons the Godless moved through the branches. They didn't leave tracks on the ground for their enemies to follow.

The Spiders did leave tracks—just not the same kind. The callused skin on their feet left distinctive scratches on the softer bark of a certain tree.

The Spiders used their fingernails to help them grip when they swung from branches or vaulted from one tree to another. Hangman couldn't see the scratches as clearly in the dark as he would have been able to see them in daylight, but they were still there.

He searched the bodies more closely and took their weapons. He didn't find anything else of value.

He followed the trail through the jungle. It took a long time because he had to search a wide area for each and every trace and scratch. He could have run the distance in a matter of minutes if he'd been tracking someone on the ground.

He was still following the track by the time the sun rose. The process went more quickly after that. He spotted the scratches from farther away and made it to the Spiders' camp within an hour.

They camped in the treetops and squatted on the branches the way the Godless did. The Spiders were already awake and talking by the time he found them. He approached slowly and made sure to stay hidden so they wouldn't see him.

He only saw a dozen men sitting here. He didn't see anyone else around. Was this really their whole party? These must be the survivors of everyone who had attacked Shadow's band. Why did the Spiders bring so few people?

They all talked in husky, scratchy voices for some reason. He couldn't figure out why.

"This is a good country," one of them rasped. "It will make a good territory for us."

"We have to eliminate the other local bands first," another pointed out. "These Godless will be tougher than the others."

"They use the trees well, but they camp on the ground," a third countered. "That's their weakness. They don't defend their camps well enough to stop us. We can strike their women and children and drive them out that way."

"We should go after the other band down on the southern river first," the first suggested. "They had fewer fighting men and not so skilled."

"You're right," the third man agreed. "We should travel there tonight and strike them tomorrow."

"Why tonight?" the second man asked. "We should leave now."

The others shrugged and agreed. Hangman followed them when they moved out. They traveled through the treetops, but they didn't hurry the way they did when they fled from Shadow's band. The Spiders took their time.

Hangman saw his chance, followed them, and then raced ahead. He kept thinking about the ambush techniques Mora had used against the phony Godless band on the way back to rejoin Shadow's group.

She had been able to kill almost an entire band singlehandedly by using these techniques. He should have been learning from her all this time instead of fearing how different she was.

He diverted far away from the Spiders, spent some time amassing his resources in the canopy, and then caught up with the Spiders later.

He had no problem outpacing them. They stopped often, took their time to relax along the way, and they didn't keep much of an eye on the surroundings.

He climbed a tall sapling, lashed a length of twisted vines around its topmost crown, and used his weight to bow it all the way down.

He tied the tree in that position, found a comfortable spot for himself in the fork of a different tree, made a noose at the end of his rope, and waited.

The Spiders gave him all the time in the world to drop the noose over one man's head when he paused in the branches below Hangman's position. He pulled his anchor rope, the sapling snapped up, yanked the rope tight, and whipped the Spider clean out of the trees.

He sailed high into the air before any of his friends saw what happened to him. Hangman pulled another rope when the sapling got to its highest point and released the Spider with the noose still around his neck.

The tree's momentum flung the guy a thousand feet into the air. The other Spiders heard him screaming in the distance, but they didn't see what happened to him.

They traveled somewhat faster after that. Hangman didn't get another chance to ambush them until they stopped for the night.

They traveled a long way and camped a dozen miles away from a different Godless band farther south from the gorge country. Hangman hadn't known there was another Godless band here. Shadow wouldn't appreciate Hangman informing him about it, either.

Hangman waited for nightfall. The Spiders stayed watchful and they did post a guard this time, so maybe they weren't as stupid as Hangman originally hoped they would be.

Two men stayed awake while the others went to sleep. He'd already reduced their numbers to eleven. He planned to reduce them as far as possible before he returned to his own band.

Shadow might have left the gorge camp by then, but Hangman didn't think so. Shadow had a way of springing these moves on his people, telling them they had to be ready to leave in the morning, and then getting delayed by unforeseen circumstances.

Hangman could always catch up with them if they did leave. Eliminating these Spiders would be better than leaving his or another band exposed.

He spent the time braiding some more rope while he waited. The moon didn't rise and the Spiders camped in a dense part of the jungle where very little light made it through the canopy.

Hangman found another branch he liked and watched the two guards patrol the area. They patrolled by climbing from branch to branch around their sleeping comrades. All the Spiders slept in a squat with their heads resting on their arms.

He waited until one of the guards passed down a branch ten feet below Hangman and ten feet in front of him. The man looked up and around in all directions, but he still didn't see Hangman.

Hangman didn't move until the guy looked away. Then Hangman launched himself off his branch, plunged his kukri into the guy's neck, and twisted while they both hurtled off into open space.

The guy made one loud choking noise that got his friend's attention real quick, but it was already too late. Hangman rode his victim to the ground and rotated the guy onto his back so Hangman landed on top of him.

Both men slammed down hard on the ground. Hangman froze there to listen. He strained his eyes upward into the dark trying to see any sign of the other guard. Hangman couldn't see anything. Hopefully the other guard couldn't see him, either.

Hangman pulled his kukri out of the guy's neck and climbed slowly, silently back up to where the rest of the party slept. His victim's death rattle set the other guard on edge. He woke up one of his friends.

They squatted close on the branch exchanging a rushed, whispered conversation in the dark. "I heard him choke and now he's gone!" the second guard hissed. "I'm telling you something is out there!"

"Nothing could be out there except creatures and you already said it wasn't that," the other man countered. "What happened to him if a creature didn't get him?"

"How am I supposed to know what happened to him?!" the guard demanded. "I say we wake up the others."

"And tell them what—that he disappeared without a trace and you don't know how?"

"We're supposed to put two men on guard. If he isn't here, then we need to appoint someone else."

"I'm not standing guard. It's your turn. You do it."

"Then I have no choice but to wake up everyone."

The second man folded his arms, mumbled, "Go right ahead," and put his head back down. The one guard stared at him and then glanced around at his comrades. He didn't wake anyone else up.

He was still sitting there trying to decide what to do when Hangman dove off his branch, tackled the guy exactly the same way, slashed his throat instantly, and brought that body down to the ground, too.

He left it in a pile with the other one, climbed up, and stared at all the remaining ten Spiders sleeping in front of him. Ten men—all totally oblivious to the danger they were in. Some of them even snored.

He went from man to man, grabbed them by their stiff, spiky hair, yanked their heads back before the men fully woke up, and slashed their throats one after another. He killed all but four of them and took all the bodies down to the same pile on the ground.

The others didn't wake up until daylight. They looked all around them in confusion and held a hasty conference about where their friends might be. Then one of them saw the blood splatters on the nearby branches.

Hangman had made sure to leave them a perfectly obvious blood trail to their friends' bodies. The Spiders went into a frenzy when they saw their friends dead.

None of the survivors could deny anymore that a person must have ambushed and killed these men in the middle of the night.

The remaining Spiders only exchanged a few hasty words before they took off heading northwest. The four survivors traveled much faster this time—almost too fast for Hangman to keep up with them.

He followed them all day until they eventually returned to a much larger camp exactly like Kuvik had described. The Spiders used ropes to pull branches together to make giant nests in the treetops.

Hangman didn't have to go near the camp to hear women's and children's voices and even a few babies crying. This band had brought everyone into the new territory. The Spider Clan was serious about taking this territory for themselves.

He stopped at a distance and surveyed the Spider camp. They must have sixty nests up there. The men swarmed the area outside. They went back and forth between the streams and the nests to bring their families water.

He didn't see how they cooked their food or even if they cooked it. He didn't see the men bringing in food at all, but they must have brought it in one way or the other. The women and children didn't leave the nests. He only saw men outside.

He watched for a little while before he turned around and took off running back toward the east. He'd seen enough. Now he had to figure out what to do about it.

Chapter 4

Mora stiffened when Hangman returned to the gorge camp. He'd been gone for three days with no explanation. She shouldn't have been surprised and she wasn't—not really.

She had to fight herself not to get annoyed at him for disappearing at the worst possible time. He had left her to pack up their belongings and deal with the three children at the same time.

He walked into camp like he'd never been gone and flopped down on the ground in front of their shelter. He squinted at all the Godless in the surrounding camp. Shadow hadn't moved everyone out yet.

He kept saying he was going to and then delaying. He never explained himself to women, not even his own wife, so Katha couldn't tell the women anything they didn't already know.

Mora sat down next to Hangman and served him some of the food she'd been giving Maeno. She didn't try to talk to Hangman. She didn't trust herself not to demand answers about where he'd been and why he wouldn't help her when she needed him to.

He thanked her when he took the bowl, but he didn't eat. He stared down into the fire in front of their shelter. He got that scowl on his face that he always got when he was brooding about his father.

Mora didn't see how that was possible when Hangman hadn't been near his father in three days. She already had a pretty good idea of what was coming.

She definitely was not surprised when Shadow came out of his shelter and spotted Hangman sitting in front of his own. Shadow veered off immediately and stormed over to them.

"Where the hell have you been?!" Shadow demanded. "We're in the middle of an evacuation here and you just up and vanish when we need you most?! I've never seen such irresponsible behavior in my life! What am I supposed to do with you—and you're my own son! I should punish you ten times worse than anyone else. Is that what you're pushing me to do? You keep provoking me every chance you get. What do you think—that I'm just going to stand by and let you thumb your nose at my authority like this?"

Hangman barely looked up. He kept his voice down so only Mora and Shadow could hear him.

"I didn't leave to thumb my nose at your authority, Father. I've supported you since the beginning—as much as you support-ed Butcher. You gave him your suggestions and that's all I've ever done—exactly the same way all the rest of these men give you sugges-tions."

"Where were you?!" Shadow snapped. "Answer me right now! Tell me what was so all-fired important that you had to abandon our band in the middle of a dangerous evacuation."

Hangman sighed heavily, put the bowl aside, got to his feet, and finally faced his father head-on. "I went to scout the Spiders exactly the way I told you we should. I consider it a matter of personal honor that I don't leave the band exposed to any kind of threat whether you believe the threat is real or not. I just went to see how many there were. They had twelve men—the same men who escaped after they attacked us at the field. I eliminated all but four of them and followed them back to their nest camp—the kind Kuvik told us about. That's where I've been."

"So?" Shadow fired back. "How many do they have at their nest camp?"

Hangman shrugged. "It's a lot. I won't lie about that, but I still think we can defeat them. We can't overcome them with numbers or strength, but we have other options. We can use a combination of strategies to reduce their numbers, scare them into retreating, and drive them out of the area."

Shadow waved that away. "We can't do it now. We're too close to moving out." He spun away and called to everyone else around him. "Move out! Everyone move out! We're leaving! Get your possessions and let's go!"

It still took a long time to get everyone moving. The women and children resisted a lot more, now that they'd had three whole days of not moving out the way Shadow said they would.

They didn't really leave until late in the afternoon. Hangman brooded in silence more than ever. Mora didn't dare to ask him for help, but he came out of his dark thoughts long enough to notice when she needed him to do something.

He wound up keeping Maeno with him and taking almost all of Mora's burdens to leave her free. Zaedi and Thena understood traveling well enough after the family's many months of trekking across country alone. The older two children didn't need any help at all.

Zaedi carried around two good-sized knives with him everywhere and kept a close watch on the surrounding country the same as the much older boys.

He left the family a few different times, met up with his friends, and they ran their own patrols around the column to keep the band and the terrain under surveillance.

Hangman did the same thing. The other men came over to ask him to come with them to check certain things. He always agreed when they asked him to and he took Maeno with him. That left Mora freer and more relaxed than she'd been in years.

She felt grateful to him, but none of this really solved their fundamental problem. Nothing could solve it but an open confrontation between Hangman and Shadow. It was coming. Everyone knew it. No one could deny it.

Hangman always returned silent, distant, and on edge. He was always silent, distant, and on edge these days. He never came out of it—ever. It couldn't last. He wasn't made for this. He would do something about it soon. He had to.

The band only traveled a few hours through the gorges and left them before night fell. Shadow called the first halt at the edge of a stream. A bunch of the men went hunting, brought back an adolescent Ridgebeak, and divided it between everyone.

The men retired to one side of the camp after everyone finished eating. Mora lost sight of Hangman and turned back to the job of getting the children ready for bed.

Zaedi and Thena still slept with their mother, but they didn't come in until later. Maeno still spent more time around his family and her in particular.

Mora sat up after her children went to sleep. She worried about Hangman even though she knew she couldn't help him. The other men came back and returned to their families, but Hangman didn't return. Where was he? Did he leave the camp again?

She couldn't sleep, so she got up and went to look for him. She didn't find him in the camp. She didn't find him anywhere until she heard his voice drifting on the wind from down by the stream.

She also heard Shadow talking. The two men were holding one of their tense undertone conversations—the kind where they both tried to get through to each other and couldn't.

She walked around one of the band's makeshift shelters and stopped when she saw father and son squatting by the water's edge. The other men stood around nearby listening to the two of them.

"Would you please let me see the pictures of the ancient weapons, Father?" Hangman asked. "The ones you got from Butcher. I would like to see them."

"What do you want to see them for?" Shadow fired back. "It's useless. The weapons aren't here. They aren't anywhere—certainly not anywhere we'll be able to find them."

"Please just let me see them," Hangman insisted. "It can't hurt if you think they aren't here."

Shadow rummaged in his shoulder bag. "I should have thrown these away a long time ago. Don't ask me why I keep carrying them around. I suppose I only do it to remind me of Butcher."

He pulled a stack of papers out of his bag and handed them over. Hangman laid them out on the ground in front of him and pointed to the pictures. "This one says, 'Fairchild Airforce Base'. I wonder where that is. This one says, 'McNary Army.....' something or other. I'm not sure what those words are."

Shadow's eyes fell out of their sockets. "What witchcraft is this?!"

"It isn't witchcraft, Father," Hangman replied over his shoulder. "Mora taught me to read these symbols while we were stranded away from the band. It's a perfectly simple system even a child can understand if you know how to do it."

"This is criminal!" Shadow choked. "It's against Godless law!"

"There's no law against it," Hangman returned. "We could have found these weapons years ago if we had only been able to read these words. We should get Mora to read these. She knows of maps in the south country that show all the surrounding cities and weapons storage places. She could probably find them for us. I should have asked her years ago instead of being so afraid of Follower ways."

"This is madness!" Shadow fired back. "You would betray our band by showing her these pages. Our men have fought and died to keep this secret?! You're as much a traitor as Boxer and Zyria ever were!"

Hangman looked up. "You just said it's hopeless and the weapons aren't in the country. What difference does it make if she sees them? The worst that can happen is that she tells us where the weapons are. You should let me call her to look at these. She knows a lot more than we do about this part of the country. You should use some of her techniques for ambushing and booby-trapping her enemies. We could defeat the Spider Clan easily if we only did it that way instead of running away."

"That's cowardice!" Shadow snapped. "Killing an enemy from behind instead of engaging in open warfare—that's the coward's way."

Hangman shrugged. "And running away is so much braver? Protecting our families and defeating our enemies isn't cowardice. It's our responsibility and any tactic is fair game if it gets the job done."

Hangman went back to reading the pages. Mora shrank behind the nearest shelter so the men wouldn't see her eavesdropping on their conversation.

Shadow looked away. He didn't snap or snarl anymore. "You should know better than to talk like that, my son."

"The band is alive right now because of me—because I used other tactics against our enemies. It's the only way to win. I would rather see my family safe and unharmed than leave them in danger while other men call me brave after I'm dead." Hangman looked up. "Let me call Mora here to read these papers. She may be able to tell us where these bases are. These weapons could tip the balance in our favor."

Shadow didn't answer. Mora hustled away so Hangman would find her back at their own shelter when he returned to the camp to get her.

"What's happening?" she asked him.

"Come with me. I want to show you something."

He took her hand and led her back to the river. He sat her down next to him and showed her a bunch of old, tattered glossy photographs of heavy military hardware. Most of it was big artillery pieces like the ones the band had found in the northern mountains.

Hangman pointed to the writing. "Do you know where these bases are? Did you ever see them on maps in the south country with your family? Are they nearby—anywhere we could get to them and maybe get some firearms?"

She picked up the first picture and read through the caption. The pages came from ancient military recruiting pamphlets.

"I've never heard of these bases or seen them on any map, but I wasn't really looking for them," she told him. "We mostly just checked out the local area to find any resources we could use."

"Do you know if there are any military bases in the area—or even as far south as your people's territory?"

"I couldn't tell you that," she murmured. "I'm sorry. I wish I could help you."

Hangman turned to his father. "We should travel south to get the maps from the ancient cities. Mora knows where to find the maps. They can tell us where to find more firearms and ammunition. We can use these weapons against the Spider Clan—and anyone else who comes against us.

"We can't spare any warriors right now," Shadow countered. "We need you here."

"We could go alone," Hangman suggested. "Mora and I won't make any difference to the band's defense. We're only two people. We can travel much faster alone, get the maps and....."

"I said no," Shadow fired back much more harshly. "It's hopeless. Just forget about all of this foolishness. I never should have let you see these."

Shadow grabbed the pictures and even snatched one out of Mora's hand. He almost tore them when he shoved them into his bag.

Hangman stared at him for a minute. Mora expected Hangman to argue back more vehemently, but he didn't. He didn't say another word.

"I think it's a good idea," Red interjected into the uncomfortable silence. "We've all seen what these weapons can do and we all know by now to rely on Mora's information. These weapons could make the difference so we don't have to keep moving around all the time."

Shadow glared out at his men. Mora didn't lift her head to see which of them he was glaring at like that. She didn't want to know.

"Fine, you can go," Shadow grumbled, "but only if you go alone. Go and come back as quickly as you can. The rest of you better go take care of your families. We've spent enough time on this tonight."

The men left. Mora and Hangman got to their feet to leave last. Shadow waited until all the other men departed before he grabbed Hangman's arm, spun him around, and got in his face.

"If you want to challenge me, my son, then go ahead and do it," Shadow snarled low.

"Challenge you?!" Hangman gasped. "I never wanted to challenge you."

"Don't lie!" Shadow snarled. "You've been trying to drive me out ever since you came back as Kral of your own band! You embedded these men in my ranks....."

"No, Father!" Hangman choked. "I would never do that!"

"Do you think I'm so stupid that I can't see what's right in front of my face?! You've been trying to weaken me all along. You openly contradict me in front of the men—and now the men you brought back with you are doing exactly the same thing!"

"I swear I didn't, Father!" Mora heard Hangman's voice shaking. "I spent years thinking of nothing but coming back and being your subordinate again. I swear it. I only wanted to return to my own band. That's all."

"Your own band!" Shadow raged. "I swear to God, if you don't challenge me, then I will challenge you!"

Chapter 5

Hangman couldn't bring himself to move with those words hanging over his head. His father really thought Hangman planned to challenge him as Kral of this band. That could only end one way—in a battle to the death. The victor would take over as the new Kral.

Hangman shuddered when he thought about it. *If you don't challenge me, then I will challenge you.*

He'd never thought once about challenging his father. Hangman didn't want to take over as Kral—especially not like this. He'd been bending over backward for four years to support Shadow in every possible way.

All his efforts had come to nothing. Shadow saw malice in all of Hangman's actions no matter what Hangman did.

Shadow never would have suspected anything like that before. Hangman had made suggestions and offered contradictory information countless times while Butcher had been Kral.

Shadow had never thought anything about it then. No one did because everyone else did it, too. All the men in the band offered their opinions. Everyone considered it normal.

Shadow only saw a threat in Hangman's actions because Hangman would be the next in line to take over as Kral—that and the fact that Hangman had brought all these men back with him.

Shadow already knew the men supported Hangman. That on its own made Hangman a threat whether he ever used the men's support or not.

He finally heaved a deep, shuddering breath, turned away, and came face to face with his wife standing behind him. Her eyes darted all over his features reading every shade of meaning in his father's words. No one knew better than she did what Shadow meant.

Hangman read so much in her eyes. She represented his family, his children.....What would happen to them if it really came to a challenge between him and Shadow?

Hangman, Mora, and their children might have to leave this band after all. They might have to go out on their own again.

Something snapped in his mind right then. He wouldn't take his family out on their own again. He would rally all the men behind him and depose his father before he took his family out like that. Why the hell should he when his father was being totally unreasonable?

All the men knew it. That's why they kept expecting Hangman to step out against his father or at least stand up to him. All the men knew Shadow was being unreasonable. He would rather protect his ego than the band.

Hangman had worked hard to win these men's trust. It had taken him years of careful negotiation and coordinating all their personalities.

Never in a million years would he have stomped someone under his heel the way Shadow stomped Hammer—and now Shadow was trying to do the same thing to Hangman—for what? Shadow couldn't even claim to be doing it to protect the band. He wasn't.

All of Hangman's years appeasing his father blew away in the breeze the minute Hangman looked into his wife's eyes. She needed him. The children needed him. The whole band needed him to step up and be the Kral they needed him to be.

He didn't want to challenge his father, but which would be worse—challenging Shadow or for Hangman to take his family out on their own? Which would be worse—challenging Shadow or putting the whole band in danger? It really did come down to that.

Hangman found himself smiling at Mora for the first time. He couldn't even remember when he'd smiled at her last. He couldn't remember the last time he'd reassured her that everything would be okay.

When was the last time he took the burden of worry off her shoulders? When was the last time he showed her that he would handle everything so she didn't have to?

He took a step forward and slipped his hand into hers. "Everything will be okay," he murmured. "I promise."

She gulped. Her eyes overflowed with so much aching, pleading care—for him. She only cared for him. She didn't care about appeasing Shadow. Nothing could be worse for her than to see Hangman suffer like this under his father's heel.

No more. It ended right here and now.

"Let's go back to the camp," he murmured. "I'll ask Kuvik and Yoa to take care of the children while we're gone."

Mora's eyes darted sideways. "What about....?" She didn't say it.

Hangman turned her around and led her back to the camp. They returned to their own shelter where Mora had left the three children asleep.

"Stay here," he told her. "I'll go talk to Kuvik now. I'm sure he and Yoa will be happy to help us. The children won't need too much taking care of anyway."

She didn't argue. He slipped away and found Kuvik and Yoa sitting near one of the fires. Hangman drew them both away and explained what he wanted. Kuvik must have already told Yoa about the meeting because she didn't act surprised.

"Let me come with you, Hangman," Kuvik insisted.

"Shadow would never agree to that and I need you to stay here and help defend the band," Hangman replied. "He's right that more than one warrior leaving now would put the band at unnecessary risk. Mora and I will be able to travel fast. She can lead me to the maps and we'll come straight back and catch up with you."

"You know your children will be safe with us, Hangman," Yoa told him. "It would be an honor for us to look after them for you."

"I know—and thank you," Hangman breathed. "It makes me feel so much better that I'm leaving them with people I can trust."

He returned to Mora and they sat together in the darkness. The camp noise started to die down as more and more people went to sleep for the night.

"What are you going to do about him?" Mora asked after a while.

"It isn't really a question of what *I'm* going to do," he replied. "What he does will be more important."

"Do you really plan to wait until he challenges you?" she asked.

He shrugged. "He's my father. I can't challenge him outright—not without something much more serious to provoke it. I know we're coming to a breaking point, but it can't come from me—not like that. Following him and obeying him is all I've ever known. This whole thing was his idea. I would have been his most loyal supporter if he'd only let me. I *am* his most loyal supporter. I'm practically the only man left who does support him after the way he's been acting."

"Then why is he still Kral?" she asked. "How *can* he be Kral if no one supports him?"

Hangman found himself smiling at her. "He's still Kral because I love him and I can't challenge him. He'll have to challenge me if he really hates me so much and considers me so dangerous."

She looked away. "He's completely irrational."

"Maybe he has a point. Maybe the other men never subordinated themselves to him at all. Maybe I've been their Kral all along and I'm the one who is just waking up to the fact that the territory can't support two Krals."

Her head shot up. "You can't be serious! You aren't Kral! You haven't been Kral since we came back from the northern mountains."

"You don't think so? If I told Red and his men to join me in challenging Shadow and taking over this band, don't you think they would do it in a heartbeat? I bet you the others would do the same thing. Even Bantam and Lock would do it and they're Shadow's sons, too. Shadow wouldn't stand a chance if I really wanted to be Kral. He's only Kral because I say he is."

Chapter 6

M ora put her arms around Zaedi, hugged him, and had to blink back tears when she pushed him back to hold him at arm's length.

"You be good for Yoa....." she choked. "Help her take care of the others....and help Kuvik protect the band....okay?"

"I will, Mother," Zaedi mumbled. "You know I will."

She forced herself to turn to Thena. "Father and I will be home in a few days. We won't be gone long. You'll be safe with the band. Okay? Be good. I love you both."

She stopped in front of Maeno, but she couldn't speak well enough to say goodbye to him. She just hugged him. He was growing up so fast. They all were. They weren't babies anymore. They hardly needed anyone to take care of them at all.

Mora shared one glance with Kuvik and Yoa standing next to the children, tore herself away, and hustled across the camp to where Hangman waited for her to join him. She wanted to hurry up, travel south to check the maps, and get back to her children.

This would be the first time she'd ever spent any time away from them. She'd been in constant body contact with at least one of them all day every day for years since Zaedi was born.

They didn't need that kind of attention from her anymore. They spent all their time away from her.

She dreaded leaving and at the same time she couldn't wait to leave. She wanted to feel what it would be like to spend just one day as a normal adult without constantly thinking about what her children needed.

She'd spent years without a minute's rest from some child clinging to her, demanding her body, colliding with her, screaming in her ear, and invading her personal space whenever they wanted to.

Her children didn't invade her personal space like that anymore, but her life still revolved around them. She still had to be on call around the clock whenever they needed her.

She and Hangman met up at the edge of the camp. Shadow had found some reason to stay in this camp even though he kept insisting that the Spider Clan threat was so imminent. The band had barely left the gorge country before he called another indefinite halt.

She couldn't think about that. She nodded Hangman and they passed the rest of the way out of camp on their way south. He planned to go through the gorges instead of the jungle.

She was out of practice from running. She was about to get back into practice. Hangman insisted that they could run until she got tired and then walk for a while so she could catch her breath. Then they would run some more.

They would cover more territory that way. Maybe her lung power would get good enough in three days for her to run all the time like he could.

She hated being the one to slow the journey down. He could have traveled there and back in a day or two, but he hadn't been raising three children for the last twelve years the way she had.

Hangman and Mora both paused at the edge of the camp to look back—and that was the moment when a swarm of black bodies poured out of the gorges in front of them. Mora didn't understand what she was seeing at first.

She at first mistook the attackers for some kind of creature. Dozens of them clambered over the clifftops while more poured from the gorge opening through which the Godless had traveled yesterday.

The creatures or whatever they were ran in a strange bent-over gait, used their hands and arms to support themselves, and manipulated all their limbs in a scuttling motion. The creatures could move impossibly fast that way. They overwhelmed the camp in seconds.

She didn't realize until they got closer that they were actually people painted all over in some kind of black clay. It covered every inch of their skin and clothes and stuck their hair out of their heads in a sphere of pointy spikes.

Hangman reacted first. He and Mora stood closest to the gorge opening—right in the path of all those creatures—or people—or whatever they were.

She wouldn't have recognized who or what they were if she hadn't heard the men talking about the Spider Clan so much in the last few days. The men had described the Spiders' strange way of moving and fighting.

Hangman drew his kukris, sprang in front of Mora, and went into a frenzy of slashing, stabbing, and hacking the Spiders as fast as he possibly could.

They would have brought him and Mora down immediately if the Spiders hadn't been so bent on getting into the camp as quickly as possible.

Most of the Spiders ran past Hangman and Mora. Some fell to his blades. The others raced by and went after the camp instead.

His quick thinking triggered her to do the same thing. She pulled her blades and stood her ground, but none of the Spiders attacked her. They didn't come near her.

Hangman didn't wait for them to attack him first. He leapt from one Spider to another and fought his way back into camp killing every Spider he came to. He slaughtered any Spider that attacked another person.

She recovered from her shock and copied him. She went from skirmish to skirmish and conflict to conflict. The Spiders offered plenty of targets. They attacked the Godless everywhere.

She ran up behind the Spiders, stabbed, slashed, and chopped them down with vicious fury, and worked her way to the other side of the camp—or she tried to.

The Spiders' surprise attack sent the Godless women and children into a panic. They screamed and ran, but they didn't know where to scream and run to. They ran every which way, collided with each other, and brought each other down right in front of the Spiders.

The Spiders killed at random. They killed men, women, and children wherever the Spiders could find someone exposed and undefended. Mora spotted Kuvik in the distance. He stood alone against five Spiders.

Yoa, Maeno, Zaedi, and Thena backed against the shelter wall behind him while he tried desperately to hold the enemy at bay.

Seeing her children in danger ignited Mora's fury. She charged across the camp and attacked the Spiders from behind, hacked at their legs and necks, and brought down two of them before the others turned around to confront her.

Kuvik struck without mercy, chopped his jawbone kukris together to implode the Spiders' heads, and dropped another two.

The last man turned back and forth between Kuvik and Mora trying to decide which of them was more dangerous. At that moment, Zaedi darted out from behind Yoa and stabbed his knife into the Spider's leg.

The guy bellowed, spun around to destroy the boy, and both Kuvik and Mora struck at the same time. Mora impaled her blade through the Spider's chest. Kuvik had affixed his Demonex tooth blades to the butt handle of his kukris.

He slashed across the Spider's throat and brought the enemy to the ground. The friends turned outward to face their next targets.

The Godless men and most of the women and older children fought back, but not before the Spiders brought down ten Godless men, women, and children.

Kuvik and Mora advanced through the camp, but the men were already driving the Spiders back toward the gorges. The Spiders turned and fled the same way the men said the Spiders had fled the first time.

The Spiders abandoned their dead on the field and took off scampering and scuttling out of sight. That left the Godless to pick up the pieces. Bodies lay in pools of their own blood all over the place.

Carnage bent over the body of his fallen brother Baron in the very center of camp. Baron's wife Golira charged over there, attacked the body, and tried to pick Baron up by the shoulders.

She shrieked, raged, and screamed at Baron to get up, but his weight flopped back onto the ground. Carnage watched for a minute and then stepped in. He wrapped his arms around Golira's shoulders and pried her away from the body.

Prodigy and his wife Sida bent over their dead daughter. Sida howled in anguish while she picked up the girl, hugged the dead body against her, and rocked back and forth in misery.

Red collapsed onto his seat next to the body of his wife, Ena. She lay sprawled on her back with multiple stab wounds all over her chest and sticking through her big, round, pregnant belly.

Maeno collided with Mora from the side. "Mother!" he gasped.

She put her arms around him and then Thena and Zaedi grabbed her, too. She crushed them to her. She never wanted to let go of them—not ever. She never should have agreed to leave them behind.

Scenes of heartbreak, devastation, and slaughter assaulted her senses from all over the camp, but most of the dead were Spiders. Shadow went through the camp still holding his drawn blades.

"Everyone get ready to leave!" he barked. "We have to withdraw from the area immediately! We've delayed too long already!"

"We can't leave now!" Golira roared. "Are you insane?! We're totally exposed—and now Baron is gone! Look!! Just look at that!!"

She pointed across the river toward the open country beyond the gorges—the open country Shadow had been planning for the band to cross on their way farther east.

"You want us to travel across *that*—*now*—with women and children and babies?!!" she bellowed. "You're out of your mind, Shadow!! We aren't going anywhere! The Spiders would cut us down in seconds out there!"

Carnage grabbed her away, but she burst into a fresh fit of hysterical roaring when she passed Baron and realized Carnage was taking her away from her dead husband.

She tried to fight Carnage to get back to Baron. Carnage had to pick her up off the ground and physically carry her away. Her enraged, heartbroken shrieks echoed through the camp.

No one else said a word. Hangman came around a few other shelters from somewhere. Blood splattered his face and body, but it was all other people's blood.

Blood soaked his kukris and his hands halfway up his forearms. He looked menacing and furious. He stopped next to Mora. "Are you all right?" he husked between heavy breaths. "I lost you in the confusion."

"I'm fine." She glanced behind her.

Shadow stood there fuming and glaring at everyone. He didn't tell anyone else to pack up and leave. At least he saw when his position was totally untenable.

He finally compressed his lips and walked away out of sight. Mora hugged her children tighter. She didn't want to leave, but she couldn't exactly say so out loud.

A few other people started to move around, either to go back to their shelters or to pick up their fallen loved ones. Mora had never been more grateful to have her arms around her children and Hangman's arms around all of them.

He steered them back to the place where they'd spent the night last night. The family didn't have its own shelter. They hadn't realized they were going to be staying here.

She sat down and pulled her children toward her. They sat extra close on either side of Mora. None of them made a sound or tried to go anywhere or return to normal. Mora didn't even know what that was anymore.

She kept catching glimpses of dead Spiders all over the camp. How strange they looked. She'd overheard Kuvik telling the men as much as he knew about these people—which wasn't very much.

He knew more than anyone else and now everyone in camp knew everything he knew. None of that helped the band combat this new enemy.

A group of men came up to Hangman, Mora, and their children just then. Viking, Bantam, Wildling, Butch, and Banjo lined up in front of the family. Hangman got to his feet to meet the other men.

"It's time, little brother," Viking rumbled. "You've known for a long time that this was coming. It's time for you to challenge Shadow and become Kral of this band."

"No, brother," Hangman insisted. "I can't do that."

"You have to," Wildling countered. "He's putting all of us in danger. You know it as well as we do, Hangman. You're our only Kral. You have to set him aside. You don't have to kill him outright. He isn't right in his mind. He isn't making decisions for the band."

"We want to make a stand and confront the Spider Clan," Bantam added. "We want to do it your way and take the fight to them."

Hangman turned to his brother. "Are you in on this, too? You're supporting a challenge against your own father? Where's your loyalty?"

"Our loyalty is to our families and our band," Butch fired back. "You say you know a way to defeat these people—if they even are people. We can't keep running every time someone comes against us. This is our land. We never should have left the gorge camp in the first place."

"We'll back you all the way," Banjo added. "All the men are behind you."

"Red, Prodigy, and Carnage are behind you, too," Wildling added. "You know that. All of us are. You're the only Kral we've ever had in this country. Say the word and we're with you."

Hangman shook his head. "He's my father. I can't challenge him openly, but I'll make sure he doesn't take us away from the gorges. I appreciate your support, but there's a better way to do this."

"What better way is there than to remove him?" Viking asked. "He's a danger to us and himself the way he is."

"We can't do it that way," Hangman insisted. "Just ride with me a little longer. It will work out in our favor without bloodshed between me and my own father. We can avoid that."

"Have it your way, brother," Viking replied. "We're behind you if you change your mind."

Chapter 7

Hangman squatted in front of his shelter and tried not to listen to Shadow talking to the other men across the camp. They stood in a cluster on the river side away from the women and children, but everyone could hear them as plain as day.

"We should go back to the gorge camp and make a stand there," Prodigy insisted. "We should confront this enemy instead of running away like cowards."

"Are you calling me a coward?!" Shadow fired back. "I should feed you to the ants for that."

"The Spiders don't use the same fighting style as our other enemies," Carnage pointed out. "We have to use different styles against them, too. We can use our past experience with the Renegades....."

"Are you Kral of this band?!" Shadow demanded and turned to Wildling and some of the other men. "Are you?! Are any of you?! I am Kral of this band! I make the decisions."

"Maybe your decisions aren't what's best for this band," Red muttered from the place where he squatted on the ground. "Maybe you're thinking about yourself instead of what's best for the band."

"How dare you?!" Shadow bellowed. "You have no place in this band if you can talk to your Kral like that! You've all become too insolent even to...."

Red pulled himself up smoldering with barely suppressed rage. He kept his head down and his eyes up in a murderous glare at Shadow.

"I just watched those fiends slaughter my wife in front of my eyes!" Red husked. "I've fought and bled and sweated for you. Now you'll stand and listen to what I have to say, or by God, I swear I'll gut you myself. The Spiders attacked us here because of you—because of your decision—your cowardly, stupid, selfish decision! My wife is dead because of you! My children are motherless because of you! We're all in danger here because of you—because we listened to you! Now you will listen to us if you know what's good for you!"

Shadow opened his mouth to argue, but he stopped himself when he saw the black fury in Red's face. Hangman couldn't remember ever seeing Red mad—not even a little bit. He was always so solid and calm.

Even Hangman would have felt scared confronting Red right now. No one made any move to rein him in. The others all stood behind him in open confrontation against Shadow.

Right in that moment, Butch, Bantam, and Prodigy all glanced across the camp at Hangman. He saw written all over their faces that they wanted him to get involved and step forward.

He got to his feet, slung his bag over his shoulder, and turned to Mora. "Let's go," he murmured and they headed back toward the gorges to go on their journey south.

Red gave Shadow one last disgusted look and turned his back on him. The other men followed Red and did the same thing.

Hangman couldn't wait any longer. The band would either return to the gorge camp or continue eastward. He would know where to find them either way. He couldn't stand around waiting for this situation to resolve.

It wouldn't resolve, not with the men in open conflict against Shadow now.

Bantam was the last straw. Hangman saw it all clearly now. Shadow wouldn't stay Kral of this band for long—not when his own sons abandoned him and spoke openly against him.

Hangman didn't question what Lock thought. Lock would follow Bantam and Bantam would follow Hangman. All the men would.

He took off running through the gorges. He didn't run as fast as he could have. He kept pace with Mora for an hour before she tired and had to slow to a walk. He kept pace with her then, too.

"I'm sorry I'm slowing you down," she panted.

"You aren't slowing me down," he replied. "The purpose of this trip is to take you south so you can read the maps. I wouldn't be able to go at all if not for you. I wouldn't even be able to find the maps on my own."

She made a face and looked away. "Maybe this trip isn't such a good idea."

"Why isn't it a good idea?" he asked. "We wouldn't have to flee from the Spider Clan if we found some firearms to fight them with. Of course the trip is a good idea."

"I mean maybe you should be back there with the band. Maybe what's happening with the band is a bigger threat than the Spider Clan."

Now he was the one who looked away. "I'm sure it is, but I'm not the solution to that threat. I *am* the threat."

She slipped her hand into his. "You aren't the threat. You're the solution."

He didn't want to listen, but he appreciated her support too much to let go of her hand. He squeezed it. "I'm sorry I haven't been much good to you these last couple of years. I'm sorry this situation has to weigh on you as much as it does."

"It's your problem so that makes it my problem and our problem. I don't care how it gets resolved as long as you're okay. That's the only problem I have with it—that you aren't okay."

He found himself smiling at her. "I'm going to be okay. We all are. I'm certain of it."

"How will we be okay as long as Shadow is Kral?"

"He won't be Kral forever. I'm certain of it after this morning."

She fell into a thoughtful silence and they started running again. She held up much better than he expected. She ran farther and longer each time before she had to stop and walk.

They left the gorges pretty soon and returned to the jungle where they traveled through the treetops. She started out hesitant about traveling through the branches, but she picked it up pretty soon and the two of them traveled faster.

They covered a lot of distance and camped in the treetops that night. Hangman sat close to her—close enough to put his arm around her. "This is nice," he murmured. "This is the first time we've spent alone together since we first got married."

"It's kind of nice not to have the children around just for one night," she remarked. "I keep looking around and trying to find them."

"Thank you for coming with me," he told her. "I know it's hard on you."

"What are you going to do if we can't get to the weapons—or if we can't bring the weapons with us? You remember how big that artillery was. We would never be able to move those."

"I wasn't planning to bring artillery. I was planning to bring the smaller handguns. They would be enough to swing the battle our way."

"And if we can't find them?"

"Then we use your killing techniques to eliminate the Spiders. We ambush them, lay traps for them, reduce their numbers, and frighten them into retreating. We've done it before. We can do it with them, too. Besides, I know where their nests are. We can strike their camp if we have to."

Her eyes widened. "You would kill women and children?!"

"No, no. Of course not. I'm saying the men always return to the nests. I watched them. The women and children don't come out. The men carry water to the nests, take all the food to the nests, and stand guard all around the nest camp. The women and children would have no choice but to withdraw without the men there. I'm starting to think that's their one crucial vulnerability. The men always have to go back to their nest camp. They send out raiding and attack parties, but the men always leave a certain number to guard the nest camp. They have to because the women and children can't fend for themselves. So we could ignore the raiding parties and just concentrate on eliminating the guards. The raiding parties would have to return to guard the nests and then we could eliminate them, too. Eventually, they wouldn't have any men left and the rest would have to withdraw."

She gazed up into his eyes. "That's brilliant."

He couldn't bring himself to look away from her. He hadn't talked to her like this in years—or maybe ever.

He would have liked to make a quip about how his father wouldn't think it was brilliant, but Hangman didn't say that. He leaned in and kissed her.

That kiss carried him back to his first months of being married to her—but it didn't feel the same. Years of experience and shared hardship made it mean even more. He lifted her onto his lap, put his arms around her, and swayed in all those memories washing over him.

Fate had smiled on him when it brought her into his life. He couldn't imagine any woman who would have made a better wife for him.

He couldn't imagine any woman acquitting herself as well as she had these last several years. She made him proud to call himself her husband. She had risen to every challenge and come through it with more grace and honor than he ever imagined possible.

He elevated her above every other Godless woman he knew. He would rather be married to her than any Godless woman, including his own mother. Mora turned out to be stronger, smarter, and more resourceful even than most of the men.

He clasped her in the moonlight feeling what a priceless treasure he was holding in his arms. The idea of anything threatening him set his nerves on edge, but he couldn't do anything about that—or rather he was already doing everything he could about it.

He couldn't protect her from everything, so he just had to cherish her while he had the chance. He might not get another chance like tonight. He planned to make the most of it, but he didn't even care too much about ravaging her body all night long.

She would need sleep so she could travel tomorrow. He wanted to take care of her more than anything else. He wanted to hold her while she slept and feel this flood of memories and emotion.

He wanted to dwell at least for one night in all the memories of all the times when she had exceeded his expectations and came through for their Clan in unimaginable ways.

He wanted to dwell in the memories of all the times she'd saved their band from a terrible fate by using all her wits and resources in their favor.

He wanted to dwell in the certain knowledge that he never had to doubt her. He never had to question her or suspect her. She was hands down the one person he trusted most in the world.

He trusted her more than Viking, more than Red, more than Kuvik—more than anyone. He trusted her more than his own family. She *was* his family. She was his true family—the family he shared with her.

That was the family that mattered—the band he needed to protect. Everyone and everything else fell away to nothing.

Chapter 8

Hangman and Mora raced across the countryside, passed down broken paved roads leading into the city, and ducked into one of the crumbling buildings.

Crushers rampaged across the city, but Hangman and Mora couldn't wait around for them to leave. The Crushers saw them coming, walked around the building to find them, and Hangman pulled Mora into the open.

They sprinted up the street, hid in another building until the Crushers turned a corner to search for them, and the pair ran to another hiding place.

They kept darting from one doorway and building to another before Mora held Hangman back. "The maps are four blocks that way." She nodded toward a side street heading east. "Follow me."

Now she was the one who stuck her head out, glanced left and right, and sprinted out of hiding.

She turned one way and then another, dodged behind a few different buildings to hide herself and Hangman from the Crushers, and finally took refuge in a dark, windowless warehouse.

"There," she breathed. "It's right across the street. That's where I saw the maps."

Hangman followed her gaze to a different building. Broken windows covered the front wall. A bunch of clothing, shoes, and other goods stood propped in the front window, on racks and shelves, or lay on the floor.

Mora didn't see any maps from here, but she knew they were there. She'd seen them in that store on the way to the gathering.

No one but the Followers would have been looking for those maps. She and Hangman were inside her old family band's territory and she already knew they weren't looking for those maps.

Hangman checked the Crushers' position and the couple dashed the rest of the way across the street. They entered the same room full of all different kinds of ancient goods.

Hangman looked around him like he didn't understand what he was seeing. Mora went to the aisle against the wall. The crumbling remains of books lined the shelves.

She stopped at a rotating rack and turned it around on the central rod. "This section of the rack has all the maps of the local area and the surrounding state," she told him.

"What's a state?" he asked.

"It means this part of the country. This section has maps of the wider country all up and down the coast. See?"

She took a bunch of maps off the rack and laid them out on the floor. She positioned four maps together to make one much larger one. A thick, hard plastic coating covered each map to protect it from corrosion.

She pointed to one part of the map. "This is Seattle. We're in one part of the city right now, but it's a complex of cities that covers this whole area. This map shows all of Washington State. That's what the ancients called it. See? Seattle is here. All of this territory is Washington State. This map shows the western coast of the country."

"So can you tell where the military bases are?" he asked.

"Just a minute." She picked up the map of Seattle and read the index printed in tiny writing on the back. Then she did the same with the others. "They aren't listed here. Just give me a minute and I'll see if I can find out."

She crossed the room to the bookshelves on the wall, hunted around until she found a certain book, and flipped to the index in the back.

She consulted a dozen books before she found what she was looking for. "Fairchild Airforce Base is on the opposite side of the state," she told him over her shoulder. "It's hundreds of miles away across enemy territory. McNary Army Aviation Hangars is even farther away to the south. It's south of Portland. Not even the Followers have traveled that far south. It would take us too long to get there." She turned away, returned to the maps, and squatted down next to him. "What do you want to do?"

"It's all right." He gathered up the maps. "At least we found out. We'll take these back to the band. The maps could come in handy someday."

He tapped them into a stack and tried to stick them into his shoulder bags, but the stiff maps wouldn't fit.

"Wait a minute." She took them away from him. "I have a way you can carry them."

She returned to the store counter and came back with a pair of scissors. They weren't the sharpest after all this time, but they worked to cut the maps in half so they fit into his bags.

He smiled at her. "Thank you. This is perfect."

"Do you want me to look around and see if I can find a base that's closer?"

"No, we've spent too much time on this already. We should go back."

They left the store and went through the same series of dodges to get out of town. The Crushers must have gotten distracted by something else. They didn't stick around to chase the pair.

Hangman and Mora returned to the jungle and traveled north for the rest of the day. They spent another night sitting close with their arms around each other.

"What will you tell your father when we get back?" she asked.

He shrugged. "I'll tell him the truth. I suppose it will make him feel better to rub it in my face in front of everyone that he told me so."

"What will you do if he challenges you in front of everyone?"

"I'll have no choice but to meet the challenge, but I won't take it to that on my own. These men....they don't seem to realize how serious a challenge is. I don't want to become Kral through a challenge—not for something like this. Challenging a Kral is a serious matter. I want to do everything possible to avoid it if I can. I don't want anyone to think or say that I challenged my father because I couldn't or wouldn't subordinate myself to him."

"I don't think anyone is in danger of saying that," she returned.

He didn't pick up the conversation, so she let it go. They traveled the rest of the way back to the gorge country. Hangman took much longer to navigate through the gorges back to the spot where he and Mora had separated from the band.

The Godless had left a clear trail away from the river heading farther southeast. Hangman and Mora caught up with the band two days later.

Shadow had established another semi-permanent camp in a different canyon. The women had all built shelters for themselves and their families. Hangman and Mora bumped into Kuvik first. He stood guard on the northern end of the camp.

He and Hangman embraced. "Did you have to come back so soon?" Kuvik teased. "Your children are delightful."

Kuvik led them back to his shelter where they found Yoa with Maeno and Thena. Zaedi was out with his friends.

Kuvik and Yoa had two children—a three-year-old boy and a brand-new infant baby girl still in her mother's wrap. Kuvik and Yoa couldn't be happier with their family.

Hangman and Mora rejoined their children with hugs and kisses. Kuvik and Yoa sat down with Hangman and Mora while they all talked and caught up.

"Everyone is keeping their heads down," Kuvik reported. "No one is saying anything on either side. Everyone is tiptoeing around each other pretending nothing is wrong."

"How's Red?" Hangman asked. "And Prodigy and Carnage?"

Kuvik shrugged. "Red is a disaster. That's the truth. He doesn't even try to hide it that he blames Shadow for Ena's death. Red says so right out loud. He's said it in front of Shadow more than once and to his face at least twice when I've been there. Shadow doesn't respond. He treats it as Red's way of grieving, I guess."

"Is it?" Hangman asked. "Is it his way of grieving."

"I don't think so if you really want to know the truth. I think Red is just finished playing games with Shadow. Red doesn't plan to keep his mouth shut about anything ever again. Prodigy isn't doing much better, but he keeps it quiet. Carnage is as steady as always, but he agrees with Red. Carnage just doesn't say so out loud—not in front of Shadow. Carnage is with the rest of us. Both he and Prodigy are. The deaths didn't change anything except to entrench everyone even more deeply against Shadow."

"How is Shadow dealing with it?"

"He pretends it isn't happening. Red is the only one coming out in open conflict with Shadow—except that Shadow isn't picking it up on his side. He lets Red say and do whatever he wants without contradicting. Shadow doesn't try to assert his authority with Red—or anyone else. Shadow just goes on as if everything is fine."

Hangman looked away. "Wow. That's bad."

Kuvik glanced around at his wife and the children. Mora's children acted as at home here at Kuvik's house as they did in Mora's.

"Listen to me, brother," Kuvik murmured. "I have to tell you something. I never told you before because I didn't want to rock the boat, especially not after I returned from my journey and saw how strained the situation was between you and your father."

Hangman looked up and frowned. "What's wrong?"

"Do you remember how I got separated from you? We were trying to ride the Ashtaws for the first time. They stampeded and I got tangled in the ropes we were using to try to control them. The Ashtaw I was riding ran off with me tied around its body. It ran a long way before I fell off."

"I remember. What about it?"

Kuvik cleared his throat. This was the first time he'd ever spoken about his journey or what happened to him after he disappeared.

"My first thought was to return to the Ashtaw Valley so I could pick up your trail and track you down from there. I knew which direction you planned to travel from the valley and I knew I could recognize the mountains surrounding the valley if I saw them from a distance. Anyway a lot of other things happened, but that is in fact how I found you. I went back to the valley. You weren't there. Hammer's band was there. They're living there now. The valley is Hammer's territory."

Hangman's jaw dropped and even Mora and Yoa gasped. "Really?!" Mora exclaimed. "They are?!"

Kuvik nodded. "They're doing very well. They have their own camp. They're all married to their wives with a bunch of little children running around." Kuvik turned back to Hangman. "They've domesticated the Ashtaws and trained them to carry riders in combat. Hammer's band uses the Ashtaws to defeat their enemies. That's how they established their territory—by using the Ashtaws. Don't you see? We could do the same thing. We could take Shadow's band back to the valley, rejoin with Hammer, and use the Ashtaws against the Spider Clan. The Spider Clan wouldn't go near the valley because the Spiders always stay in the trees. We would be safe there. It's just....." He faltered. "Shadow would have to subordinate himself to another Kral."

Hangman looked away and murmured under his breath, "I knew Hammer would do well. I knew he and his men would thrive. They're too smart and determined not to."

"He and his band are very happy and prosperous. I've rarely seen a band doing so well." Kuvik hesitated. "He's doing a lot better than we are. We could leave the Spiders where they are. They can have the territory. We wouldn't need it anymore."

"Shadow will never go for it," Hangman murmured. "He'll never concede to Hammer—not in a million years."

"Shadow wouldn't have to hear it from you," Kuvik suggested. "I could suggest it myself and leave you out of it. I could tell Shadow about Hammer....."

"You don't understand," Hangman interjected. "Shadow cursed Hammer when he left. Shadow would consider it an act of war if Hammer or his men set foot in Shadow's territory. Shadow hates

Hammer with a passion. Shadow would never go over to Hammer, not even to save the band."

Now Kuvik was the one who looked away. "That's what Hammer said."

"Does he feel the same way? Would Hammer consider it an act of war if we went back?"

"He doesn't feel that way about you. He admires you as much as ever. He misses you and regrets parting from you. Shadow is a different matter. Hammer feels it would be a matter of his honor as Kral to demand that Shadow acknowledge him. War is the only other alternative."

"I would have no problem subordinating myself to Hammer for the good of the band," Hangman went on. "Shadow would never do it. He would never even put himself on an equal footing with Hammer."

"Do you want me to suggest it?" Kuvik asked. "Shadow can't have a problem with that."

"I won't tell you not to," Hangman replied. "You're free to tell anyone about your journey. That's none of my business. I already know what he'll say."

"Maybe there's another reason to tell him," Kuvik suggested.

"What other reason would that be? What's the point of telling him if he doesn't take it?"

"The other reason to tell him would be so the other men can hear about the idea. They can understand that we have that option—and they can see Shadow's reaction. The other men will see that Shadow won't go over to Hammer, not even to save the band. It's another example of Shadow making decisions against the band's interests just to protect his position."

Hangman made a face. "The men don't need another example of that."

"Isn't that the problem?" Kuvik asked. "He isn't Kral if he can't make decisions in the band's interest even if it means subordinating himself to another Kral. That's what you did. You said you didn't care about subordinating yourself to him or Thunder or any other Kral if it meant the band would be safe. Every move you made was for that purpose—to get your people to safety."

Chapter 8

H angman squatted on the ground to make himself lower than all the other men of his band. He would have preferred to make himself totally invisible, but that wasn't an option.

He had predicted that Shadow would rub it in his face that Hangman and Mora hadn't been able to locate any weapons close enough for the band to get to them.

Shadow did rub it in Hangman's face, but then Shadow dropped the subject. He had much bigger problems. "Viking, you keep Grizzly, Devil, Breaker, Bantam, and Lock, here with you to guard the camp. The rest of us will go hunting before we move on."

"The band will eat whatever we kill in one night," Red pointed out. "We'll be stopping every night if we stop every time the band needs food."

Shadow spun around in a rage. "Did you hear what I just said?! I said we're going hunting. Let's move out! Don't let me hear any more of these mutterings."

Hangman got to his feet. He made sure to stay near the back of the group where Shadow would be less likely to see him.

Hangman tried not to notice Red staying near him. All the men seemed to try to stay near Hangman. None of them went forward to travel with Shadow.

Hangman cringed at the situation. He kept thinking it couldn't possibly get any worse, but it always did. It would get worse if it really came to open mortal combat between him and Shadow.

Hangman was really starting to think it would come to that. He had to prepare himself for that. He wouldn't be able to take it easy on Shadow just because he was Hangman's father.

Hangman would have to treat Shadow as an enemy—a dangerous enemy. Hangman would really have to kill Shadow to stop him from threatening Hangman again.

Hangman would have preferred to just subdue Shadow and make him a subordinate, but Shadow wouldn't let that happen. He would try his hardest to kill Hangman first. Shadow would leave Hangman no other option but to strike and strike hard.

Hangman made the decision for the thousandth time to delay that moment as long as possible. He wouldn't be the one to drive his father to it. Hangman would give Shadow every opportunity to back down and be reasonable.

Shadow should have known better than to flex his power over Red. Red could easily have taken over as Kral.

Hangman wouldn't have stood in Red's way. Red was practically Kral of his own band anyway. He always had been—just like Hammer and Hangman had always been.

Red would make a good Kral. Hangman would have supported him.

Hangman saw Red hurtling toward a mortal collision with Shadow even faster than Hangman was. Red didn't hold back and try to delay it. He really seemed to be pushing for it. He didn't have Hangman's reasons to take it easy on Shadow.

Hangman didn't know where Shadow planned to go to hunt. Hangman didn't ask. He fell back into his old silence.

Shadow traveled a long way through the jungle before he spotted a cluster of five Gorlocks in the distance. He gave orders to surround the creatures and cut one large male away from the others.

The hunting party moved into position. It was exactly the same position they had been in when the Spider Clan attacked the first time.

Hangman scanned every inch of the jungle for them—and he wasn't the only one. The other men did the same thing, but the Spider Clan didn't attack. Shadow gave the signal and the men moved in on the Gorlocks.

They isolated their prey by itself. The Gorlock spun around screeching and roaring, swiping its wings to try to hit the attackers, and diving at them to snap its beak.

Hangman took advantage of one of these turns to tuck and roll close to the Gorlock's foot while the creature's back was turned. Hangman slashed one of the Gorlock's ankle tendons.

The creature whirled around with a frightful shriek and lunged for Hangman to snap him in half with its beak.

Red and Wildling both reacted in a split second, charged the Gorlock from behind, and Red dropped on one knee. Wilding raced up behind him, stepped on Red's back, and then on his shoulder.

Wildling took a flying leap just as Red launched himself back upright. Their combined efforts propelled Wildling all the way up the Gorlock's back. He landed on the ridge of spines running behind its head and chopped across the back of its neck.

The creature went down with a colossal thud. Wildling rode the Gorlock to the ground and jumped off just as the other men moved in to congratulate him. Only Shadow looked annoyed by the stunt.

"Let's butcher this creature and take it back to camp," he ordered. "We can celebrate when we get there."

The men surrounded the Gorlock to cut it up. Hangman positioned himself on the opposite side of Shadow, but Shadow made it easy by staying on the opposite side of him—and on the opposite side of Red.

Hangman found himself on one side of the Gorlock with Red, Wildling, and the rest of Red's men. How strange that Hangman and everyone else still thought of them as Red's men even after all this time.

Hangman found it fascinating how all these much smaller bands formed and survived within the larger band. He'd been living like this for years with all these little splinter bands living together as one.

He must be the only Kral in history who would tolerate that. Any other Kral would have found that threatening—exactly the way Shadow did.

He considered Red's band a threat simply because of their history and experience with each other. Their cohesion and loyalty to Red threatened him.

Hangman had to shake his head over Shadow's hostility. Hangman had never stood against Red's leadership. Hangman valued Red's position and encouraged it. It was one of the band's greatest assets.

Red talked and joked with the others the way he always used to, but his attitude toward life had taken a turn after his wife's death. His sense of humor and his tone became more cutting.

He almost snapped at people even when he said the most innocuous things. His sense of humor became drier, harsher, and more caustic even though he was as funny as ever.

He never outright insulted anyone. He never did it passively or underhandedly, but it snuck into his tone and the short, hard way he pronounced every word.

Hangman caught Shadow shooting sidelong glances at Red while the men worked. Red posed a much bigger threat to Shadow than

Hangman did. Did Shadow even realize that? Did he even realize just how far he'd pushed Red over the line?

Hangman tried to pay attention to his work instead of dwelling on all these interpersonal issues. He should have felt grateful that Shadow considered someone else a threat.

Hangman only felt responsible for it instead. He would have liked to smooth things over between the two men. Hangman was the one who had brought Red and his band to join up with Shadow.

The men worked to butcher the Gorlock. The others teased Kuvik about taking different parts of the creature to make weapons. Kuvik kept blushing and insisting that he had enough already.

He turned the tables by asking if any of them needed him to make weapons for them. His weapons had become a running joke among the men. He was the only one who used weapons made from animal bones and teeth.

The men cleaned the blood off their arms and weapons and got ready to leave. They were just picking up the haunches of meat when another group of Spiders dropped out of the trees overhead and landed on the Godless unawares.

Another fight broke out right there around the Gorlock carcass. All the Godless men locked with the Spiders in another raging battle.

The Spiders surrounded the Godless first and backed everyone against the Gorlock carcass. Hangman found himself engaged against four Spiders. They fought with the same frantic energy with which they moved through the branches.

They fought with two weapons each—one in each hand. So did he, but that gave them six more weapons than he had. They slashed his arms and stabbed him in the legs twice. He barely held them at bay.

His cousins and friends weren't faring much better. The Spiders would wipe out the party and then not enough men would remain to defend the band.

Hangman cast around in desperation for some way to defeat this enemy. He couldn't use strength or force or numbers. The Spiders had all that. He needed something else.

That was the moment he heard a clicking noise in the canopy above him. He didn't give himself an instant to hesitate. He dove past his opponents, somersaulted across the ground, and came out behind them.

They spun outward to confront him, but he didn't stick around to fight them. He vaulted into the branches and started climbing.

Those four Spiders stayed on the ground to help their friends subdue the rest of the hunting party. Maybe the Spiders thought he was running away to save himself.

He scaled into the canopy as fast as he could go and followed the sound to a massive Krakelow moving toward the fight. The noise and Gorlock blood must have attracted the creature.

It picked up speed heading straight for the spot. Hangman couldn't wait for the Krakelow to attack first.

He grabbed a dry, dead limb from a tree, threw his weight against it to snap it off, and took off at a dead run for the Krakelow. The creature saw him coming and hurled itself at him to wrap him in its coils.

He collided with the creature, but he positioned his branch between himself and the Krakelow to stop it from wrapping him up.

Their weight tore them out of the air and they both plunged to slam on the ground. They landed at the edge of the clearing where the Godless and the Spiders still battled in bloodthirsty combat.

Hangman rotated onto his stomach, landed on top of the Krakelow, and pinned his branch down hard on top of its body. It responded exactly the way he expected it to and shattered into a million squirming segments.

He sprang clear and used his kukris to impale the segments and throw them at the Spiders. The segments latched onto the Spiders' bodies and the attackers staggered away from the Godless to deal with the new assault.

Three Krakelow segments hit Hangman in the body—one on his thigh, one on his side, and one on his shoulder. He fought through the pain and ignored the segments digging into his flesh.

He worked through the remaining segments until he threw them at each of the Spiders attacking the Godless. The Spiders backed off and the Godless finished off their enemies in no time.

Chapter 9

The Krakelow had enough to eat trying to finish off all the dead Spiders. The Godless men retrieved their Gorlock meat and retreated into the branches, but they didn't leave. Hangman wasn't the only injured man here.

He collapsed against a tree trunk gasping and flinching from the pain of all these segments still attached to himself. He could barely hold onto his kukris.

Red came over to him, squatted next to him on the same branch, and pulled Hangman's hands away. "I'll do it, little brother," Red growled. "Lie still. You aren't going anywhere for a while."

Hangman was too grateful for his friend's help. Hangman really didn't think he had it in him to cut these segments away.

Red clamped his powerful hand around the top of Hangman's thigh above the first segment, dug his blade under the segment, and cut it out. Hangman roared and struggled, but Red held him down until the wound bled freely.

Red flicked the segment off his blade and flung it back down into the clearing. Then he put his blade aside to spread leaf paste on the wound before he started on the segment attached to Hangman's shoulder.

Hangman wilted against the trunk and submitted to his friend's treatment no matter how bad it got. Hangman couldn't do it himself. He couldn't face it.

Cold sweat broke out all over him when Red picked up his blade again.

"That was cowardice," Shadow muttered in the background.

"He just saved all our lives!" Red snapped over his shoulder. "Would you have liked it better if he left us all there to die?! Don't you say a word against him!"

Shadow kept his mouth shut after that. Hangman wouldn't have been able to hear Shadow's comments over his own yelling. Hangman didn't even try to be quiet, especially not when Red dug out the segment attached to Hangman's ribs.

Hangman collapsed after that. He barely registered when Red spread leaf paste on Hangman's injuries and then dumped gallons of Gooji juice down his throat.

He woke up in a camp on the ground somewhere. Half the men from the hunting party sat, stood, or squatted around the remains of a fire. The sun was just coming up. They must have stayed here overnight.

Hangman dragged himself off the ground and looked around. "Where's......?" He stopped himself from saying the name.

"Your father took half the men to carry the Gorlock met back to camp," Prodigy explained. "We stayed behind to guard you."

Hangman slumped and passed his hand across his eyes. "Thank you, brothers."

"Can you walk on that leg?" Red asked. "We should head back ourselves. I'll carry you home to your wife if you want walk."

Hangman snorted. "You know how to motivate me, don't you? Just threaten me with public humiliation and I'm your man."

Red gave Hangman one of those crooked, wry, sarcastic grins. That was Red's smile now. It wasn't his old, warm, friendly, glowing smile of open friendship.

Hangman hauled his aching body into a sitting position. Kuvik squatted next to him and handed him a bowl full of roasted meat from the Gorlock the men had killed yesterday.

Hangman would have liked to tell Red not to antagonize Shadow anymore, but Hangman didn't say that. Red had his own reasons to stand up to Shadow. Hangman wouldn't get between them. That would be idiotic.

Red held out his hand. Hangman took it and Red pulled him to his feet—or onto one foot. Hangman balanced there and rested his injured leg on the ground without putting his weight on it.

He really didn't look forward to the trip home. "You should go ahead of me," he told the others. "You don't have to wait for me."

"We'll wait," Wildling replied. "We owe you for yesterday."

Hangman waved that away. "It was nothing."

"It was brilliant," Kuvik exclaimed. "It worked perfectly—all except the part about you getting injured—but you couldn't exactly get that close to the Krakelow without getting some of the segments on you. It was perfect."

"You say we could fight the Spiders like that all the time?" Red asked.

Hangman shrugged again. "I've done it before. It works better when you don't have strength and numbers on your side. You ambush your enemy, reduce their numbers, weaken them, frighten them, and attack them when they aren't looking. It works."

"I've done it, too," Kuvik added. "You can kill a lot more of them this way than facing them in open battle."

Wildling looked up. "What did you do?"

"Just what Hangman did. We used jungle creatures against the Bounty Hunters. We killed hundreds of them."

"Who's we?" Prodigy asked.

Kuvik squirmed and looked away. "I'm just saying I agree with Hangman. We should be going on the offensive instead of waiting for the Spiders to always ambush us first. That can't end well. They've already driven us out of our territory and they keep attacking us here. They'll never stop until we stand up for ourselves."

Almost as if his words made it happen, Shadow came out of the canopy just then. Bantam and Lock returned with him.

Hangman thanked the stars he was meeting his father and brothers on his feet even if Hangman wasn't in the best shape of his life.

Shadow might have thought his other sons would be his most loyal supporters. He probably didn't know that Bantam had already turned against him.

Shadow descended to the ground and surveyed this little camp. Then he turned his hard eyes on Hangman. "Are you ready to travel, my son?"

"Yes, Father," Hangman murmured.

Shadow nodded. "Let's fall back to the band. The women are dividing the meat. Then we can move out."

"We should stay here," Red countered. "We should stand our ground the way Hangman says. We should fight these Spiders and retake our territory from them. We can use these ambush techniques to destroy them so they don't threaten us and our families again."

Shadow glared at him and then at Hangman. "Did you put him up to this, my son?" Shadow snapped. "Did you tell him to challenge me so you wouldn't have to?"

"No one put me up to anything!" Red fired back. "I'm a grown man. I can speak for myself. Your judgment is failing, old man. You run and hide from your enemies and then you have the nerve to call him a coward when he's the only one fighting our enemies with any weapon strong enough to defeat them. What's the matter with you? When are you going to listen to reason? We shouldn't run anymore. We should fight back until we win."

Shadow took a threatening step forward. "I will be the one to decide when we fight the Spider Clan and how we fight the Spider Clan! I will be the one to decide if we fight them with blades or Krakelows or any other weapon! I am Kral—not you! None of you is Kral! I am!"

"You don't fight the Spider Clan at all," Wildling interjected. "They're the ones who decide when we fight them, how we fight them, and what we fight them with. They're the ones who choose the time, place, and manner where we have to fight them. They'll continue to do so as long as you keep running from them."

Shadow spun around to confront him and wound up facing the whole group. "Which one of you will be the one to challenge me?! Which one of you is the traitorous bastard who will challenge me to take over as Kral—or will you all do it? I don't explain my decisions to you or any man. Either challenge me or bow to my authority."

He stormed off through the trees and left his three sons there with the other men.

Wildling heaved an almighty sigh as soon as Shadow passed out of sight. "You really should just go ahead and challenge him," Wildling murmured under his breath. "Do it for the good of the whole band."

"He's right, brother," Prodigy added. "He's incapable of listening to reason."

Hangman took a few limping steps forward. "We won't do that here. Let's get back to the band. We've been gone for too long already."

Chapter 10

H angman dragged himself off the ground again the following morning. He had barely made it back to camp. He didn't have the energy even to go inside the family's shelter. He just crashed where he was on the ground by the fire.

Now he had to stand up and do it all over again. He didn't stand up. His legs and body hurt too much, but he would have to function pretty soon. He didn't plan to lie around in camp—and Shadow didn't plan to let him lie around.

Shadow and the other men gathered in the center of camp to discuss what they would do today. Shadow started out by ordering everyone to pack up to continue their journey.

He went through the group of men assigning each person to a position where they could defend the band. Shadow didn't comment on Hangman not attending the meeting. Hangman could hear everything perfectly well from here.

Kuvik piped up and told Shadow all about Hammer and how his band had taken over the Ashtaw Valley as their territory.

The men gasped and exclaimed when they heard about Hammer's men riding the creatures in combat and using them against their enemies to reclaim the territory for the Godless Clan.

Kuvik finished by suggesting that Shadow take his people to the valley, either to join up with Hammer's band or to use the Ashtaws against the Spider Clan.

Shadow refused this, too. Grumblings and outright protests answered him. Hangman expected Red to launch into another argument about how Shadow only refused because of his old resentment against Hammer, but Red didn't say anything.

Hangman watched the whole interplay from a distance. Kuvik's story produced exactly the result he said it would.

It fired the men and turned them even farther away from Shadow. It made him look petty, vindictive, and spitefully bent on shunning Hammer even at the band's expense.

Hangman got to his feet and crossed the camp in an instant. He limped over to the edge of the group close enough to Shadow for Shadow to see him.

Shadow treated Hangman's arrival as ordinary. "You can take your position near the back of the band, my son. You'll be able to protect the band from the Spiders coming up behind us."

"I'm not going with the band, Father," Hangman replied. "I'm going out into the jungle to scout the area on either side and behind the group. I want to make sure no Spider raiding parties are moving in on us. I want to be able to see them coming and intercept them before they get near us."

Shadow's features turned to granite. "I told you where to go, my son. You can't go out. We need you here."

"I'm sorry, Father, but I won't leave my family exposed by staying with the group. I'm sorry if you don't like it, but I won't follow any order if I see it putting my family in danger."

He turned around and walked away without looking back. He didn't explain himself to Mora or anyone else. Any of the men would have heard him. They would all understand.

The band had camped in another stretch of jungle for the night. He got out of sight of the band before he realized how many of his comrades had come with him.

He jumped into the trees, pushed his pain aside, and climbed up into the canopy. Plenty of men stayed behind to guard the band. Shadow got them moving out and they headed away heading southeast.

Hangman could never figure out why Shadow wanted to take the band there. None of the Godless knew anything about that country. It was probably crawling with hostile Clans.

Hangman started sweating again from the pain of his injuries. He tried to ignore Red coming over to him at their first stop and reapplying leaf paste to Hangman's wounds.

The men perched in the canopy and surveyed the area, but they couldn't see as much up here. The Spider Clan's habit of staying in the treetops made them much harder to detect.

The men kept traveling all day until they discovered a much larger group of Spiders moving in on the band.

The Spiders made a lot more recognizable noise when this many of them traveled together. They rustled the leaves and branches and their fingernails and callused feet made a distinctive scratching sound on the bark.

The Spiders trailed Shadow's band and Hangman's group trailed the Spiders for a long way. They didn't attack and they had brought too many men for Hangman to launch any attack of his own.

Shadow eventually stopped the band for the evening. The Spiders stopped, too. They gathered in the branches to discuss something—probably to outline their strategy for attacking the band.

Hangman was just thinking about a way to ambush these people when Kuvik bumped his elbow. Hangman glanced over and Kuvik held his finger to his lips. Hangman frowned. He didn't understand.

Kuvik held up his palm and pointed straight down at it. He tapped his palm twice and then climbed away into the branches. Hangman didn't understand what Kuvik wanted, but he climbed too fast and left his friends sitting there in one spot.

Hangman could only guess that Kuvik wanted the men to stay where they were. Kuvik climbed a long way and then climbed sideways to position himself directly above the Spiders.

Hangman didn't see why until he noticed a giant ball of foliage positioned right above the Spiders' heads. Kuvik did something to the surrounding branches. They sprang apart and an absolute torrent of Coffincreep poured out right on top of the Spiders.

They shrieked loudly enough for the Godless to hear them in camp, but the Godless didn't see what happened. The Coffincreep enveloped the Spiders. Half of them got away in time thanks to their speed, agility, and quick thinking.

The others went down under the rain of snakes. Some of the bigger Coffincreep carried their victims to the ground. Even the smaller Coffincreep slashed their way through dozens of Spiders before the snakes ran out of victims to kill.

Kuvik climbed down to rejoin his friends. They all clapped him on the back and shook him in friendly affection. "You're the man, Kuvik," Butch exclaimed.

"It isn't that hard," Kuvik remarked. "I'm surprised the Spiders didn't see the danger. They shouldn't have sat there."

"The survivors are all heading back to the nest camp," Hangman pointed out. "Let's ambush them along the way and reduce their numbers as much as possible."

Chapter 11

The hair stood up on the back of Mora's neck when Hangman hobbled into camp with the rest of his men. Shadow had been seething all day ever since Hangman took half the men with him into the jungle instead of guarding the women and children on the march.

Hangman buckled into the dirt next to the fire. He didn't even sit up. He sprawled all the way over onto his back.

Mora passed her hand across his sweaty, fevered forehead. "We should give you some more Gooji juice," she told him. "You need it."

"Do whatever you want to me," he mumbled. "I won't be able to resist anyway."

She chuckled and placed a bowl of the leftover Gorlock meat in his hand. Then she went to see Neia, borrowed a packet of Gooji sap, and returned to the fire to make the juice.

Some of Hangman's men came over to squat by the same fire. She tried not to read too much into both of Hangman's brothers coming over with the others.

Bantam and Lock had both left with Hangman this morning before the band moved out. All three brothers had openly defied their father in sight of the whole band. This couldn't end well.

Hangman barely raised his arm to put the food in his mouth. Mora would have put more leaf paste on his injuries, but she saw right away that one of the men had already done it. She could well imagine who it was.

Shadow glared across the camp from his own fire. Katha sat next to him talking to him endlessly. She'd been trying to calm him down ever since Hangman and Mora had returned from the Angler Valley. Katha's efforts always came to nothing.

Shadow finally got to his feet and started forward to confront Hangman. Katha jumped to her feet and tried to hold Shadow back, but he shook her off and stormed over to Mora's shelter anyway.

All the other men stood up when Shadow approached. Hangman didn't move. He barely opened his eyes to acknowledge his father.

"I suppose you're happy with yourselves," Shadow snapped. "You talk a big line about not leaving your family in danger and then you leave the band exposed with half the men while you go off doing God knows what. You should be ashamed of yourselves."

"Did anything happen today?" Hangman asked.

"No, but it could have," Shadow countered. "Then where would we be? We wouldn't have been able to defend ourselves because you weren't here. None of you were here."

Hangman heaved a broken sigh and pried himself off the ground into a sitting position. He didn't look up from the bowl while he put the food into his mouth.

"Nothing happened today because the men and I intercepted the Spider raiding party that planned to attack you. Fifty of them were watching you from right over there." Hangman pointed to the trees behind the camp. "We attacked them. We ambushed them, killed half of them, and followed them all the way back to their nest camp. We reduced their numbers to seven—so you're welcome. You all are."

"Do you think that excuses you openly defying my orders?!" Shadow countered. "Anything could have gone wrong. You go where I tell you to go. You don't go off on your own again—not without my approval."

Hangman looked up and locked eyes on his father. Mora had never seen Hangman confront Shadow like this before. Hangman wouldn't have dared.

He didn't outright glare, but he didn't look away or try to change his fierce expression.

"I'll do it again whenever I think it's necessary, Father," Hangman murmured. "I've been going out on my own since I was six years old and I'll continue to do it now. I won't follow any order of yours that puts my family in danger. There is no law anywhere in the universe that you can call on that will make me do that—and I encourage any man here to do the same thing. You don't have the authority to tell us to deliberately leave our families exposed to enemy attack or to hold back on defending our wives and children in any way we can. You would be making a big mistake by asking any of us to do that."

Hangman bent his head and went back to eating his food. He didn't look up again, and a minute later, Shadow stalked off somewhere else.

The men didn't talk afterward. They didn't say a word. They just stood or squatted around the fire, but the hidden subtext couldn't be clearer.

Shadow really didn't have any authority to order the men to put their families in danger—or to neglect to do something to guard and defend them. Shadow would be breaking the law by doing that.

He was already breaking the law by suggesting it. A Kral who broke the law was no Kral at all.

The men eventually drifted away and Hangman stretched out on the ground again. "Why don't you go inside?" Mora suggested. "Then you wouldn't have to move to go to bed."

"I would have to move to go inside," he mumbled. "I don't have to move as long as I stay here."

She laughed at him. "I have to pick you up to give your Gooji juice."

"My tormenter," he grumbled and made her laugh again.

She helped him sit up and drink the juice. Then she laid him down again and left him there to sleep. She'd seen him worse. He could still joke about his condition, so he must not be too bad.

The air of tension, resentment, and explosive hostility only got worse the next day when everyone woke up to Shadow's announcement that they would be moving on again.

The men stayed with the band this time. Hangman and the children stayed near her. Hangman barely looked at the countryside around him.

He barely seemed to maintain the energy to keep walking at the same slow pace as all the women and children. He sweated a lot and his skin took on an ashen pallor, but he stayed upright until evening.

Shadow stopped everyone in another valley full of jungle. High hills flanked it on both sides. Hangman sat down as soon as the band stopped moving.

Shadow paced up and down and all around the rest of the band. "We'll stay here for a while," he decided. "This valley will be more defensible than anywhere we've seen before. We can make camp here and defend the valley."

Hangman's eyes darted along the hillsides flanking the valley. They didn't look very defensible, but he didn't argue. None of the men did. None of them answered.

The women started to make camp. The men left again as soon as Shadow turned his back on them. None of the men explained themselves to him and Hangman went with him regardless of how injured he was.

Mora sighed and got to work making camp, too. She put Hangman out of her mind as much as possible. He always went out on his own. This time was no different just because he got injured. He had gone out injured enough times. He could handle it.

The women worked for hours before it got too dark to work anymore. The last light was just going out of the sky when a commotion broke out in the canopy on the western side of the valley.

Everyone stopped what they were doing and watched Hangman and the other men in another pitched battle against the Spiders. The conflict didn't come close enough to put the camp in danger, but anyone could see the truth.

The Spiders could get close to the camp. They could get inside the valley. The place was no more defensible than any other.

Even Shadow stopped what he was doing to watch. He didn't go out there to help his men. He didn't acknowledge the conflict at all except to watch. It was still going on when he walked off and went back to his business.

The fight migrated up the hillside and the Godless men eventually drove the Spiders back out of the valley. The men didn't return until well after dark after all the children were asleep. They reassembled and Shadow acted like the fight had never happened.

"We'll stay here another month," he decided. "Then we have to go south to take Bantam, Chiva, Ganni, and Yonna to the gathering. Hangman, Bantam, Lock, Mule, Creed, Maniac, and I will be enough to guard the two families on the journey. The rest of you can stay here and defend the band. Then we'll know where to find you when we come back."

No one argued. Mule was one of the older men in the band. He and his family had joined Shadow's band while Hangman and Mora had been isolated from everyone else.

Chiva and Ganni were Mule's twin daughters. Yonna was his niece who had grown up with him after her parents had died. Creed was Mule's older son. He was married with a family of his own. Maniac was Lock's age—not old enough to get married yet.

Bantam was the only man going to the gathering. It would just be the two families this time. Mora didn't look forward to the journey—not with Hangman and Shadow in such close proximity to each other. Bantam and Lock would be there, too.

Mule had been staying out of the whole conflict. He didn't declare himself for or against anyone. Creed and Maniac definitely sided with Red's band and supported Hangman.

Maybe Shadow would calm down on the journey once he realized he couldn't throw his weight around with these men. He would be totally without support.

Then again, he was already totally without support now. Not a single man in camp supported him. They only went along with him because the hostilities hadn't completely erupted into open warfare.

Chapter 12

Zaedi, Thena, and Maeno squatted on the ground nearby with Creed's children. Zaedi drew in the dirt with a stick while they waited for the two families to leave for the gathering.

Mule and his wife, Celera, Creed's wife, Etiri, and the three girls going to the gathering stood around waiting, too. Shadow and Katha came over and Shadow scowled at the group. "Where are the other men?" he demanded.

Mule shrugged. "They left this morning. They didn't say why."

"Don't you even have control over your own sons?" Shadow smacked his lips in annoyance. "Now we have to wait for them to show up."

Mule didn't react and neither did anyone else. Mule didn't point out that Shadow's sons weren't here, either.

"Maybe something happened," Katha suggested.

Shadow opened his mouth to say something else just as Hangman, Bantam, Lock, Creed, and Maniac came down one of the valley's side hills. The men dropped out of the trees and walked the rest of the way to join up with the two families.

Hangman had recovered from his injuries in the month since the band had come to live in this valley. His leg and shoulder still sometimes hurt him, but he didn't let them slow him down.

He complained more to Mora in the privacy of their own shelter when no one else could hear him. Old injuries caused him pain or made him stiff. He wasn't as young as he used to be and took longer to bounce back when he got hurt.

He made sure not to show it around the other men. He could still run as fast, climb as well, and fight as hard as he could when he was young.

"Where have you been?" Shadow barked. "We're all waiting for you."

"We're ready to go, Father," Hangman replied. "This is the time when you said you wanted to leave. We're here and we're ready."

"Where were you?" Shadow rounded on Bantam. "You don't seem to be taking this matter very seriously considering your whole future could depend on this trip."

"We repelled another Spider Clan incursion—from the head of the valley this time," Hangman interrupted. "They're getting bolder. This is the eighth confrontation we've had with them in the month since we started camping here."

"This is a good place," Shadow countered. "We're as safe here as we're going to be. Now let's go. We have a long way to travel."

The rest of the group followed him out of the valley. The rest of the band stayed behind. Viking would take over the band while Shadow was away.

Hangman had already told Mora behind closed doors that the men had made their own decision about who would take charge in Shadow's absence. Viking agreed to Shadow's face that Viking would take over.

Red would take over the minute Shadow left. Red would become de facto Kral until either Shadow or Hangman returned.

All bets would be off after that. Hangman said and Mora agreed that Red might not hand back the authority once Shadow returned. Red might decide to just stay in charge. Both Hangman and Mora could think of worse outcomes.

Red might turn out to be the one man here with the nerve to challenge Shadow and actually follow it through. Hangman would be the first to admit he probably wasn't the right person for the job simply because he cared about Shadow too much.

The other men respected Red too much not to let him take over. Even Hangman respected Red enough to let him take over.

Shadow fell into a thoughtful silence on the way south. All the men did. They didn't talk much. The group camped around a fire that night and met up with another Godless band the following morning.

Shadow and the other Kral talked about the Spider Clan invasion. Shadow took credit for Hangman's repeated forays into the jungle to repel the enemy. Shadow made it sound like he was the one successfully holding the enemy at bay through his own cunning and determination.

Hangman, his brothers, and Mule's sons didn't interject to contradict Shadow's remarks. The men let him take the credit for it. Mora saw the five men sticking close together. They didn't mingle with the other band's warriors.

Hangman and the others took extra care of Bantam. He was an exceptionally tall, good-looking young man with fine, strong features. He wore his long hair in tight braids that hugged his scalp and hung together in a mass off the back of his skull.

He had an exceptionally straight, dignified carriage and almost regal poise that set him above and apart from everyone around him. He had a heart of gold and he adored his young niece and nephews.

Mora had also seen Bantam being extremely kind, caring, affectionate, and playful with the other children in camp. Part of him still had a child's heart even though he was several inches taller even than Hangman.

Creed and Maniac stayed with the men. The three girls stayed close to Celera and Etiri. Katha wound up with that group a lot, too. That left Mora on her own most of the time.

The other Godless band had mothers with children, so she wound up spending time with them, but she didn't get close to them.

The party made it to the gathering ground three days later. The two Godless bands got there first. It was still late afternoon, so they camped and Mule lit a fire. He kept it small, but the gathering Clans would build it up later when night came.

Shadow pulled Bantam aside. "I want you to know everything will work out, my son. You'll find a wife and get married tonight. Then we'll go home."

"I'm going to marry Yonna, Father," Bantam blurted out. "We've already decided."

Shadow's head shot up. "You are?! When did you decide that?"

"We talked about it maybe six months ago," Bantam replied. "She doesn't want to go to another band and I don't want to marry a stranger from another Clan. We agreed we would marry each other and I would bring her home."

"But....you aren't even sweethearts!" Shadow exclaimed. "You don't spend any time with her! This is completely out of left field!"

Bantam shrugged. "Does it matter if we're sweethearts or not? I wouldn't be sweethearts if I married a stranger from another Clan, either. We both want this and we're going to do it. You can't stop us."

Shadow choked. "I wasn't planning to stop you, my son....I'm just surprised."

"You don't have to be surprised. It's already decided. You don't have to do anything—not where Yonna and I are concerned. We'll stand up and then sit down together. You can worry about Chiva and Ganni if you want to—but I think Ganni might marry Boogie."

Boogie was a young man from the other Godless Clan the group had been traveling with. Mora hadn't noticed Ganni and Boogie spending time together or getting closer on the journey here, but stranger things had been known to happen.

Shadow was still opening and closing his mouth in amazement when three other bands showed up. One was a Chosen band and the other two were Whisperers. Then two Follower bands arrived.

They built up Mule's fire and everyone settled down in their places. The assembled bands were just about to start the gathering when a third Godless band appeared out of the darkness.

Goosebumps erupted on Mora's arms when she saw Hammer, Vina, Cross, Sema, Scarecrow, and a bunch of other people Mora didn't recognize. Almost all the couples had children.

They brought Scarecrow's younger brother, Thuron, Hammer's younger brother, Lonion, and Ziti—or the boy once known as Ziti.

All three of the young men had been uninitiated boys when they left Shadow's band. Now all three came to the gathering to find wives.

All three of them must have initiated—which meant their names weren't Thuron, Lonion, and Ziti anymore. No one in Shadow's band knew these men's real names.

Everyone on that side of the fire looked amazingly healthy. The young men of gathering age looked handsome, strong, upright, and battle-hardened. They looked like the proudest, most powerful Godless men anywhere.

"What the hell are they doing here?!" Shadow snarled. "They have no right to be here!"

"They're Godless men," Creed interjected. "They have as much right to be here as we do."

"They're outcasts!" Shadow snapped. "They're shunned! No one will marry into their band. It's forbidden."

"Why is it forbidden?" Mule asked.

Shadow didn't get a chance to answer before some unspoken signal passed through the assembled bands. All the young people and Krals stood up. Hammer and Scarecrow stood up with their three young men.

Shadow and Mule stood up with Bantam and the three girls. A bunch of other young people stood up all around the circle.

Bantam and Yonna moved out of place first and sat down next to each other immediately. Neither of them waited around to negotiate anything.

Boogie and Ganni exchanged glances. Neither of them moved to come together. Then Chiva and Ganni glanced the other way toward Hammer's band.

Some of the Followers paired off with each other. Then two Chosen paid off with two Whisperers.

Chiva and Ganni looked at each other—and they both stepped out of the circle at the same time. They had to step over their nearest relatives. Both girls turned to cross the circle to Hammer's side.

Shadow lunged forward and grabbed both girls to hold them back. "No!!" he hissed. You can't go over to them! You don't understand! They don't follow the law!"

"They're Godless!" Chiva yanked her arm out of his grasp. "I'm not going to a strange Clan. I'm going with Godless men and that's final."

Mule squinted toward Hammer and his group. Hammer, Scarecrow, and everyone in their band watched the exchange with unwavering intent.

"What's wrong with them?" Mule asked. "I don't see anything wrong with them."

"I don't care what you say," Ganni fired back. "I'm going with them and you can't stop me. You either negotiate with them or I will, Father."

"I'm your Kral!" Shadow countered. "I can forbid you to marry into their band."

Hangman stood up to intervene and stuck his arm between Shadow and the others. "Hammer is a good man and we all know his people. His men will take good care of your daughters, Mule. You don't have to worry about them."

"See?" Chiva snapped.

"How can you betray me like this?!" Shadow snapped at Hangman. "You know he's a traitor and an outcast!"

"So he's a traitor and I'm a traitor." Hangman moved between Shadow and the girls. "Go talk to them, Mule. They're good, honorable men. They'll treat your daughters well."

Shadow lunged forward one more time and practically yelled out, "NO!!"

Hangman threw all his weight against his father and pushed him back into the group. "Sit down, Father," Hangman snarled under his breath. "This doesn't concern you anymore."

Shadow gaped at him in shocked horror. Hangman didn't back down. He stood there nose to nose with his father while Mule and the girls crossed to talk to Hammer.

Hammer and Scarecrow both stepped out to meet Mule. The three men stood there talking for a minute. Then Hammer and Scarecrow led the two girls over to Hammer's group.

The girls met up with the three young men. All five talked for a minute until Ziti pointed at one of the girls who had come to the gathering with Boogie's group.

Hammer and Ziti stepped out and approached to negotiate with the girl and her father. Chiva and Ganni stayed there with Thuron and Lonion. The four young people talked for a minute and then sat down together.

Scarecrow sat down apart from them while Hammer and Ziti concluded their negotiation. They returned with a wife for Ziti and all of them sat down. Mule came back and sat down. Shadow had no other option but to sit down, too. His gathering was over.

The rest of the young people went through lengthy negotiations with everyone. Boogie wound up with a wife from the Chosen Clan.

Three Follower girls had to go with strangers they'd never met and had no interest in. Four young men left alone.

Shadow fumed in barely suppressed rage until the bands separated and went off in separate directions. Hangman paused to look back and so did Hammer. The two men both raised their hands in friendship before they separated.

The party trekked a few miles into the dark until they returned to the jungle where they made camp.

Mora glanced across the fire and around at all the faces. Shadow stared into the flames and didn't engage with anyone. Bantam and Yonna sat side by side on their side of the fire holding hands.

They occasionally looked up into each other's eyes. So much meaning and unspoken questions fired back and forth between them. Mora got wistful watching them. That would have been a nice way to get married—much nicer than the way she got married.

She glanced over at Hangman at the same time he glanced at her. They shared one of those moments of eye contact with each other.

Those moments had been becoming more common with every passing year.

Mora remembered everything so vividly from the night she had met him at the gathering and every nightmarish confrontation that happened afterward.

She would go through it all again if she knew she could share this moment with him right now. All that trouble and conflict had been worth it in the end. She had married the right man. She never would have wanted it to be any different.

Mora caught Katha smiling at her across the fire. Katha remembered everything, too. The women had become bonded in unimaginable ways.

Mora saw all the years ahead for Bantam and Yonna. They had so much going for them. They had family around them on both sides. They knew each other and they knew each other's families. Neither of them had to live with strangers.

They shared a lot more open affection and heartfelt understanding in that gaze than either of them had ever shared before. They would build their marriage on a solid foundation. Mora couldn't be happier for both of them.

Chiva and Ganni would live good lives, too. Hammer and his people would take good care of both girls. Mora never doubted that.

Vina, Sema, and the other women would welcome the girls, make them feel at home, and Lonion and Thuron would make good husbands for the girls. Hammer would help his brother and so would Scarecrow. They would become family because they already were.

Mule tried to lighten the mood by talking about life back in the band.

"We should mount a party to go get the girls back," Shadow blurted out without any introduction.

Mule's eyes popped. "That would be against the law! You can't take women back once they've gone to the gathering. Everything that happened was perfectly legal. They're legally married now."

"We can't let them go with Hammer's band," Shadow insisted. "He and his people are outlaws."

"We aren't going anywhere near Hammer's band," Hangman interrupted. "He is not an outlaw. He and his men are all legally married. They're as entitled to bring their young people to the gathering as anyone."

Shadow glared at him. "You don't make that decision. I'm Kral of this band."

"Hammer and his men did nothing wrong. He's Kral of his own band. Lonion is his brother and we all know Thuron and Ziti. They aren't outlaws. You only want to go after him out of your own vindictive need for revenge. Leave him alone."

Mora cringed at the harsh, cutting tone in Hangman's voice. He didn't even try to keep the threat out of it. What would he do? He'd already restrained his father to stop Shadow from intervening at the gathering.

Was tonight the night? Would Hangman challenge Shadow right now—to defend Hammer?

No one else made a sound, but she sensed Bantam, Lock, Creed, and Maniac all stiffening and getting ready for the showdown of a lifetime.

Hangman diffused the tension. "I want to talk to you about something, Father. Mora and the children and I got isolated in a valley to the north while we were separated from you. It's a steep valley with sheer cliffs all around it. There's no way in or out except to scale directly up or down these cliffs. I think our band could establish a safe territory there. I think we should consider taking the band there."

"It will be too far away if it's to the north," Shadow muttered.

"It would be worth the journey if the Spider Clan and none of our other enemy Clans could get into our territory. We would just have to eliminate the Anglers...."

"What's that?" Bantam asked.

"They're a different kind of creature," Hangman explained. "They're exceptionally dangerous and intelligent, but we can eliminate them all and then none will be left to bother us. No other creatures will be able to get in or out, either, so it won't be a problem."

"We don't have time to go on a long journey like that," Shadow cut in. "We have enough to worry about just defending our band the way it is."

Chapter 13

A collective sigh of relief went through Shadow's party when they came over the hills and spotted the Godless camp in the distance. Hangman recognized Viking, Butch, Carnage, and Kuvik standing guard around the perimeter.

Everything else looked the same. The valley looked so peaceful with women working and children running around playing.

Shadow started down the hill. Zaedi, Thena, and the other children shot away from the group to meet up with their friends. The tension started to melt away as the party got closer to home.

The men noticed the party approaching and gathered on that side of the camp to meet up with the two families. Kuvik and Carnage stayed farther away to keep an eye on the surroundings.

"What's been happening here?" Shadow asked when he met up with Viking.

Viking opened his mouth to answer only for a smash of breaking branches to get everyone's attention at that moment. A whole mob of Spiders came swarming out of the trees right next to the camp.

The men and even the women and children must have been prepared for this. They all dropped what they were doing, charged across the camp, and met the invaders in a clash of weapons.

The women and anyone old enough to carry a weapon rushed in to join the fight. Hangman, Shadow, Bantam, Lock, Creed, Mule, and Maniac all got pulled into the battle, too. Even Mora and the other women helped out.

Hangman heard babies screaming in the background as their mothers abandoned them and raced away to defend the camp. The place emptied in seconds.

The Spiders' strategy seemed to be to throw as many people as they could at the Godless and try to overwhelm everyone. Hangman had never seen this many Spiders in one place before.

He fought his way through the mob killing with reckless abandon. He didn't try to be careful or strategic about it. He used the same tactic as last time and attacked any Spider who attacked someone Godless. This made the Spiders much easier to kill.

Hangman didn't like to leave women and children in danger, but their presence made this strategy so much easier. The Spiders went after the women and children, cornered them, and pinned them down in isolated places.

Hangman rushed up behind any Spiders and cut them down quickly and easily. He didn't have to waste time fighting them. The whole band seemed to follow the same strategy. Only Shadow tried to fight the Spiders out in the open.

The women and children seemed to understand their role in the battle. The women and children drew the Spiders to them so the men could cut down the enemy more quickly.

The men marauded through the camp killing dozens or maybe even hundreds of Spiders. The men killed so many more of them and more quickly than the Godless ever had before.

"It's getting worse!" Kuvik panted when it was all over and the last straggler Spiders had run off as usual. "They're escalating their invasion. Each attack gets bigger and stronger."

"That makes no sense," Shadow countered. "They should have slowed down when we moved farther away from their nest camp."

"They're obviously trying to take over the whole territory," Grizzly pointed out. "They obviously don't plan to back down until they wipe us all out."

"Which means we won't be safe no matter how far away we run," Viking added. "We should stand our ground and mount open warfare."

"No!" Shadow countered. "We won't do that. We already have too few men."

"We wouldn't have too few men if we rejoined with Hammer," Wildling pointed out. "We would be a lot safer there than here—and we do have women and children to protect. Keeping them here is the last thing we should do."

"We should at least call in all our available resources." Everyone turned around to see Neia joining in the discussion. "We aren't even trying to fight back. We're barely defending ourselves—and the Spiders attack almost every day now."

"This is none of your concern," Shadow snapped over his shoulder. "You women go back to work."

"This is all of our concern now," Yoa added. "Our safety and our families' safety depends on whatever you decide. We have as much right to at least hear what you have to say."

"We could at least contact Hammer," Yonna suggested. "We just saw him at the gathering. We could have talked to him then."

"You saw him?!" Butch gasped. "He was there?!"

"He brought his brother and two other young men with him—Thuron and Ziti. We don't know their real names," Hangman interjected. "Mule's daughters went with Hammer's band."

"This is great!" Nagana exclaimed. "So our bands are bound by blood now. That makes us family. We should ask him if he would help us...."

"I already said no!" Shadow bellowed. "We aren't going to ask Hammer for anything!"

"He already offered to help us," Kuvik interrupted. "I talked to him on my way home from my journey. He told me I would always be welcome there and he would always think of me as a brother. He thinks fondly of all of us. He would help us in an instant if he knew we were in this kind of trouble—and he has the Ashtaws."

Excited talk broke out through the whole band. Even the women talked about it. Hangman didn't get involved.

He really would have liked to. He ached to sit down with Hammer and find out everything he and his men had been doing since they split from Shadow's band.

Seeing Hammer at the gathering and hearing Kuvik's story made Hangman long for Hammer's company. Hangman would have left for Hammer's territory right then and there if Hangman could have his way.

Shadow didn't answer all these excited voices. He must have sensed the tide turning against him because he didn't overrule the decision again.

Everyone else kept talking about how they could do it, how they would send a party to the Ashtaw Valley to visit Hammer and get his opinion, and how the band would travel there through all the Spider Clan attacks.

Hangman only had to look sideways at his father to see the truth written all over Shadow's face. He didn't contradict, but he didn't agree, either. He might even agree outright, but he would never follow it through. He would never humble himself to Hammer—ever.

Everyone migrated back to their shelters. Hangman worked for hours with the other men to carry all the dead Spiders out of camp.

The men had found a steep ravine across the valley where another deeper channel cut through the jungle. The men had gotten into the habit of throwing all the dead Spiders down there after every one of these attacks.

"It makes for easier hunting, too," Viking told Hangman on the way down there. "All the creatures go down there to feast on the bodies. All you have to do is go down there. The creatures are too busy eating to notice anyone sneaking up on them. You can take your pick."

Hangman grinned at him. "I guess that's one good thing coming out of this."

Viking got serious. "So what is he like?"

"Who?"

"Hammer. You saw him at the gathering. What is he like?"

"I didn't get to talk to him, but he and his people are all tall, strong, and healthy. All their wives and children look fantastic. The three young men were outstanding. They all got Godless wives. They're doing very well for themselves just like Kuvik says."

Viking turned away shaking his head. "I sure would like to see them again. They're good people. They deserve their success."

Hangman didn't answer. Hammer was becoming a sore subject for Hangman. He didn't want to talk about Hammer if Hangman couldn't see him at least once in a while.

He would have traveled with Hammer for at least a few days to and from the gathering if Shadow hadn't been there. Hammer and Hangman could have caught up on old times.

Hangman could have caught up with the younger men, too—the boys Hangman had watched grow up. He would have liked to see those men get married as if he had been their real Kral and taken responsibility for them at the gathering.

They shouldn't have gone with their brothers. Hangman couldn't find any fault with Hammer and Scarecrow, but Hangman wished he could have been the one.

He wished he could have brought the journey full circle from the early days when he and his cousins had taken those boys out of Ceon and made them the Godless men they were today. Those young men deserved that.

What a senseless shame it was to turn their relationship into a hostile mess like this—where Shadow refused even to let these people see each other.

Some of the girls who had become Hammer's men's wives still had family members in Shadow's band. Did he really plan to forbid them to see each other because of his own spiteful vendetta against Hammer? It made no sense at all.

Hangman didn't like to think of his own father that way, but Hangman found it impossible not to. He had been thinking this way for so long. Why did he even try to appease Shadow anymore?

He shouldn't. Hangman was rapidly getting to the point where he himself was in the wrong for defending Shadow and letting him get away with this—if Hangman hadn't already gotten to that point.

He returned to the shelter where Mora and the children settled into their former routine. The family slotted back into the same old camp life. Hangman sat down with them and the family relaxed together.

Hangman's eye inevitably wandered around the camp, but it wasn't as peaceful as he originally thought. Everyone kept their weapons handy, including the women and children. They constantly stopped their work to scan the surrounding countryside.

Neia's words rang in Hangman's ears. The Spiders attacked every day now. They would keep escalating their assaults until they wiped out the whole band. Hangman had to act for the good of the band.

His first gut instinct was to go talk to his father, but Hangman couldn't do that anymore. That window had closed.

None of the men considered Shadow their Kral anymore, either. Maybe it was time for Hangman to just step up and start acting as Kral without challenging Shadow. It could get a lot worse than that.

Chapter 14

Hangman waited for Mora to take the children into the shelter for the night. He caught her giving him one of those looks. It wasn't one of the looks about how far they had come together and how much they meant to each other after their meeting at the gathering.

This was the look that told him she knew he was planning something—something so big he couldn't even tell her what it was. She might never find out what it was, but she knew him too well not to know he was up to something.

She shut the door behind her. Of course she knew he wouldn't spend the night in there with the family—not tonight.

He immediately stood up and crossed the camp to Red's shelter. All of Red's children were old enough to occupy themselves nowadays. They didn't need him to step into Ena's place and put them to bed. They returned to his shelter when they felt like it.

He, Wildling, Prodigy, Butch, Carnage, and Creed stood around talking. They all stopped talking when Hangman showed up.

Creed broke the tense silence. "I sure wish I had gotten to talk to Hammer before we left the gathering. I wish I could have gotten to know the men my sisters married."

"They're good men," Wildling replied. "They grew up with us when they were boys. Hammer and his men will treat your sisters right."

"That's what Hangman says and I believe him," Creed went on. "I just wish I could have talked to them myself. It would have put my mind at rest."

Carnage glanced over at Hangman. "What's next for us?"

"We're going on another raid tomorrow morning," Hangman replied. "Spread the word to the other men."

"Um....what did you just say?" Red countered.

"I said we're going on another raid tomorrow morning. We need to spread the word. We're going to attack the Spiders' nest camp and wipe them all out down to the last man, woman, and child. This disaster has gone on long enough and we've already lost too many good people as it is."

The men exchanged glances. "Don't you need to consult with your father about that?" Prodigy asked.

"No," Hangman replied immediately. "We won't consult him about anything ever again. We all know what we need to do. We just have to go and do it. We have all the resources to do it. We don't even need to consult with Hammer. We can do it ourselves. We could have done it a long time ago and we should have. It's only my stupid love for my father that stopped me, but it won't stop me again."

"Um......" Red stammered. "Are you serious? This is a complete reversal for you."

"It isn't a complete reversal. I've been thinking it all along. I just can't live with this anymore. I'm in the wrong for not acting on it. That stops now—but I need all of you men behind me. I can't do it alone."

"You know we're behind you," Wildling countered. "We've been behind you all this time. We've all been waiting for you to act."

"So....do you plan to challenge your father after all?" Creed asked.

"I don't have to," Hangman replied. "You men say you're behind me. We can just start acting autonomously. We can do what we have to do. We don't have to ask him or challenge him or even tell him what we're doing—unless he finds out after the fact. It doesn't matter because he isn't involved in this anymore. We're the ones with wives and children on the line. I don't know about you, but I'm not going to sit around and let Mora and Zaedi and maybe even Thena take up arms to defend their lives when I have the tools to eliminate this threat in a few hours. Forget that."

"What tools will those be?" Red asked. "What tool would be as powerful as that?"

"The ants, brother," Hangman replied. "It's very, very simple if you think about it. All we have to do is go down the ravine and bring up a dozen of those fresh Spider bodies, tie them to harnesses around our chests, chop off the feet, and drop the bodies in front of the ants. The ants will try to chew the Spiders' legs and follow us. We lead the ants around the nest camp and they swarm the site and wipe out everyone there while we run away through the branches. It's that simple. The ants will kill all the Spiders—men, women, and children. We never have to worry about any of them coming back later."

The men gaped at him with their mouths open.

"Oh, my God!" Red whispered. "I knew you were our true Kral!"

"Hell yes!" Creed husked. "That sounds incredible!"

"Please challenge your father, Hangman!" Butch pleaded. "Please! We need you so bad!"

Hangman laughed at him. "You have me, brother. You have me as much as you need me. I don't have to challenge my father for anything.

He can keep living his life in peace with his wife. Leave him alone. He can rant and rave as much as he wants about being Kral. He can even be Kral. I understand now why he never challenged Butcher. Shadow never had to challenge Butcher. Just do as I say and we'll conduct this band as if I was Kral and you were all my loyal subordinates."

Gasps went through the group. "That's exactly what we need!" Carnage exclaimed. "That's perfect, Hangman."

Kuvik came over to them just then. "What's happening?"

"Hangman is taking over," Red announced. "We're going on the offensive. He's going to lead us."

Kuvik's eyes widened at Hangman. "Really?"

"You said you used ambush tactics against the Bounty Hunters on your journey," Hangman replied. "I want to know everything you did—or I want your ideas if you have any—anything like you did with the Coffincreep—all of that."

"I have a lot of ideas," Kuvik replied. "We used a lot of ambushes. We would have used a lot more, but the Bounty Hunters fled from us before we got a chance."

"He wants to use the ants," Creed interjected. "He wants to lead the ants to the Spiders' nest camp and wipe them all out."

"Good idea. I didn't think of that one." Kuvik frowned. "The question is how we would lead the ants up into the trees and then get away before we got wiped out, too."

"I'll explain everything when we get out there," Hangman replied. "Round up all the other men and tell them we'll go out in the morning as soon as it gets light."

The men spread out and went from shelter to shelter telling everyone the news—everyone except Shadow. Hangman didn't tell Mule, either. Maybe Creed and Maniac would tell Mule, but that was their business.

Hangman headed back to his own shelter for the night. He made up his mind on the way there to post the usual guards around the camp before he and the other men left in the morning.

The Spiders would likely have sent out more raiding parties who were already on their way to attack the Godless right now. Those parties wouldn't be in the nest camp when Hangman and his men attacked it.

The Godless would have to eliminate those raiding parties after the fact. They might even attack the camp while Hangman and his men pulled off their assault on the Spiders' nests.

Hangman didn't want to leave the camp totally unguarded and he wouldn't leave it unguarded. He might even have to hit the raiding party first to protect the band depending on where the raiding party was and how big it was.

He stopped outside the shelter. No sound came from inside. His family was all asleep. He was the last one left awake.

He cast one last glance over the camp—and in that moment, he knew something was wrong. He didn't know what it was. He just felt it in his gut.

His hands flew to his kukris, but not fast enough. A scream ripped out of the night and a crash echoed through the camp.

He took off running toward the noise—and stopped dead in his tracks when he saw another tidal wave of Spiders invading the camp in the middle of the night.

They surrounded Prodigy's shelter—or what used to be Prodigy's shelter. It stood on that side of the camp closest to the trees.

The Spiders had pulled the structure down on top of the family. The Spiders marauded through the wreckage killing everyone—Prodigy, Sida, and all their surviving children.

Those screams woke up everyone else, but not soon enough. Almost everyone was still asleep—all the women and children, at least.

Hangman charged forward with both kukris drawn. A dozen men surrounded him all armed to the teeth to meet the Spiders, but the men couldn't use their old tactic against the Spiders.

The Spiders' black face and body paint made them blend in with the night shadows. Hangman could only see the Spiders right in front of him. He became aware of countless Spiders flooding all around him to overrun the camp.

He met the enemy in a clash of weaponry, but too many of them pushed back against the defenders. Mora appeared at Hangman's side holding both her weapons.

"Take the children and get out, Mora!!" he bellowed over his shoulder. "Get out of the camp NOW!! Get everyone out! GO!!"

She hesitated a second and dove behind him on a dead run for their shelter. He didn't care if he lived or died as long as he held the enemy at bay long enough for her to get the children to safety.

He blamed himself for this. None of this would ever have happened if he'd only acted sooner. Prodigy and his family would be alive right now if Hangman had only pulled his head out of the sand and done what he knew he needed to do.

He fought his hardest, but the Spiders kept pushing forward. They brought countless fighting men this time. Hangman couldn't see the whole force to know how big it was. They surrounded him on all sides.

Someone grabbed him out of nowhere and pulled him away from the battle. "We have to fall back!" Red bellowed in Hangman's ear. "We have to go! Everyone is out except for us!"

Hangman paused just long enough to glance around. The Godless men stayed behind to defend the camp. None of the women and children were here anymore—except for the dead ones.

Hangman caught one glimpse of Katha lying face down at a distance from him. She didn't move. He turned away feeling sick and all the men charged away into the dark, shadowy jungle.

Chapter 15

Hangman and his men raced through the trees to put as much distance between themselves and their camp as possible. It wasn't even a camp anymore. It was nothing but a killing ground with a bunch of dead Godless women and children lying around.

The men pulled to a stop miles away in the shadowy canopy. "We have to catch up with the women and children," Carnage panted.

Butch looked around. "Not everyone is here. Kuvik is gone and so is Shadow. They both could have gone down."

"We won't know that until we meet up with the others," Hangman decided. "Did any of you see which way they went?"

"They went in a bunch of different directions," Wildling replied. "They could be anywhere."

"Then we'll just have to wait until morning and track them down." Hangman checked one man after another. "Is anyone injured?"

"I am, but I'll be okay," Red replied. He dug around in his bag, pulled out a bowl of leaf paste, and put it on a gash on his arm.

"Prodigy is gone," Butch murmured. "The Spiders got to his whole family first."

Hangman didn't mention Katha. Did Shadow even know yet? Then Hangman realized that Bantam and Lock were both with him.

Hangman only had to take one look at Lock to see the abject misery in the young man's face. Lock was barely sixteen. His features kept spasming and he blinked back tears.

Hangman squeezed his shoulder and turned to Bantam. "Mother is gone, Bantam. She fell in the camp just now."

Bantam's jaw dropped. "No!"

"I'm sorry, brother. We need to find the others and....."

"This is Father's fault!" Bantam fired back. "He got his own wife killed! He's been leading us into danger ever since...."

"If you want to blame someone, you can blame me," Hangman interrupted. "I should have stepped in a long time ago. She would be alive now if I had only done what I knew needed to be done. Now come on. We don't have time to point fingers at each other or anyone else. Our wives and children are in danger out there. Let's go find them. Come on. You show us where you saw any women and children leaving the camp, Wildling—any women and children at all. I don't care who they were as long as we find them."

The men backtracked to the camp. The Spiders still overran the area. The Godless men had to be careful to stay hidden.

Wildling led the way to a spot in the canopy where sets of women's tracks entered the jungle. Crowds of children's footprints surrounded the women—and then vanished when the women and children had climbed into the trees.

The men met up with a big crowd of women and children hiding together. Mora and the children weren't here and neither were Kuvik or Shadow.

The Spiders were already starting to spread outward from the camp to search the surrounding jungle. Hangman and his men took the women and children far out into the jungle east of the camp and hid them there under armed guard.

Hangman and his brothers went back with Red, Carnage, and Wildling. They tracked down another four groups, each one guarded by a handful of men.

The sun was already starting to come up by the time the men finally found Mora and the children in a much bigger cluster with Shadow and Kuvik. The men led everyone back to their hiding place where the band reformed—what was left of it.

"How long do we have to stay out here before we can go back?" Yoa asked.

"We aren't going back," Hangman replied. "Not to that camp, at least."

"What did you just say, my son?!" Shadow snapped.

"I said we won't go back." Hangman heard the silence settle over the group as everyone stopped talking to listen to him. "We'll either go north to the Angler Valley or we'll go west to meet up with Hammer's band."

"Over my dead body will we have anything to do with Hammer's band!" Shadow fired back. "Since when do you make decisions for this band? I am Kral of this band. I demand that you treat me with the respect due me...."

Hangman turned around extra slowly. "Do you even care that your wife is dead because of you? Do you even care that Katha is lying dead on her face in the middle of that camp you said was so defensible? When are you going to wake up? It's over. Whatever you decided to do is no longer a viable option for us. Look around you. We don't have a camp. We don't have a home. We just lost a lot of good people because of your decisions."

Shadow only faltered for a second when Hangman told him that Katha was dead. Shadow recovered his old bluster instantly. "Are you challenging me?!" he demanded and spun around to confront all the other men. "Which one of you has the backbone to challenge me?! I demand that you challenge me since you obviously don't want me as your Kral anymore!"

"You can't protect the band anymore or make decisions on what's best for us," Hangman murmured. "That's your first duty as Kral and you can't do that anymore. I don't want to challenge my own father, but I'll do it for the good of the band if you really want me to." Hangman lowered his voice a little more. He had to fight to control himself. "You and I both know you wouldn't win that challenge. If you were a true Kral, you would step aside and make one of your trusted warriors Kral in your place for the good of everyone. That's what a true Kral would do. You know this as well as we do. It doesn't have to be me, but it does need to be someone other than you. The time is over."

Hangman waited for Shadow to say something, but he didn't. Shadow just stood there staring at him in stunned shock.

Hangman couldn't wait any longer. He turned to his men. "We'll wait until daylight, go back to the camp, and make one last search. We'll make sure we find everyone and that no one is left alive in the jungle anywhere. We'll carry out this strike on the Spider Clan's nest camp and then we'll head north to the Angler Valley."

"Why not go back to the gorge camp if we're going to get rid of the Spider Clan?" Bantam asked.

"We'll be too close to all our enemy Clans if we stay here," Hangman replied. "We would constantly have to defend the gorge camp from someone. We won't have to do that if we go to the Angler Valley."

"We still have to get rid of the Anglers," Mora interjected.

"It will be much easier with all of us working together." Hangman turned back to his men. "I want you to keep all the women and children here until morning. We'll leave at first light and carry out our plan. Now everyone better settle down and see if you can get some sleep. We have a lot to do tomorrow."

It took a long time for everyone to relax enough to sleep. Shadow didn't say a word against Hangman's decision. Hangman didn't plan to speak to his father again, not even to invite him to take part in this campaign.

Shadow didn't exist for Hangman anymore. Lock and Bantam didn't talk to Shadow, either. How did it come to this? How did this whole nightmarish situation end with their family getting torn apart like this?

Hangman really wished he could go back and bury his mother—or do something for her. He hated leaving her lying on the ground like that, but he had no choice. He had no choice but to leave Prodigy and his family where they were, too.

A burning obsession started to eat a hole in Hangman's heart. He had to tell Cross about this. Cross should know that Katha was dead. How would he find out if not from Hangman?

Hangman considered sending Kuvik to Hammer's band to tell Cross the news, but Hangman needed Kuvik here right now. Hangman needed every man he could get who would support him.

Shadow was only one man. He couldn't go against the whole band—not if all the men stood together. Hangman couldn't afford for even one man to leave. They'd already lost Baron and Prodigy. Hangman couldn't lose Kuvik—not after all these years.

Hangman didn't turn around when he heard Bantam talking to Shadow in a low tone to one side of the group—at least they started in low tones.

Bantam escalated quickly and started going off on Shadow for essentially being responsible for killing Katha. Shadow tried to defend himself, but he didn't do a very good job. His reasons came out sounding more like pathetic excuses.

Hangman tried not to listen. Mora came over a few minutes later to sit down next to him. They shared one look before he looked away into the darkness.

"Are you okay?" she murmured.

"I will be." He turned to face her in the dark. "I want you to promise me something, Mora."

"Of course. Anything. What is it?"

"Don't tell anyone how to get into or out of the Angler Valley. Okay? Keep the secret to yourself—and tell the children not to tell anyone, either—not until we get there. I don't want the wrong person finding out how to get in or out."

She nodded. "Of course. I understand. I won't tell anyone."

He looked away. "Maybe we shouldn't tell the children to keep the secret. That could put too much pressure on them. They might feel they had no choice but to blab if we told them that."

She chuckled softly in the dark. "I can't think of anyone who would come right out and ask them—except for.....you know. But you did tell everyone that the only way in was to climb down the cliffsides. We can tell everyone we climbed out that way, too. That should be enough of an explanation for everyone."

"Then the question becomes whether all the enemy Clans will be able to climb down."

"That was always going to be a problem, but at least the cliffs will slow them down enough for us to prepare. We would see them coming long before they got to the ground. They won't be able to ambush us and they also won't be able to lower enough fighting men to put us in danger. You're right. It would be a much better position for us even than the gorge camp."

"I just hope it works," he breathed. "I hope it's worth the trip there."

"Look at where we are right now," she pointed out. "Can it really get any worse than this?"

He looked up and met her eyes. "Thank you—for everything. I'm glad someone here remembers what the valley was really like and still thinks it's a good idea."

"I think it's a great idea. It will take us longer to bring our young people to the gatherings, but that's a trade I'm willing to make considering how safe we'll be. No one will ever come into the valley and find out our secret except the women who marry into our band. If we really have to, we can blindfold them before we lead them through the tunnel. Even they won't find out the way in or out—not until they get old enough to take their own children to the gathering. We wouldn't have the same problem we had with Zyria and Aster."

Hangman nodded and took her hand. "I think you better get to sleep. I want you rested tomorrow. I need you to keep an eye on.....you know......while the men and I are away."

She squeezed his hand. "I'll go to sleep if you go to sleep."

Now he was the one who laughed and then got serious. "My mother is dead."

She squeezed again. "She was a wonderful woman. She was hard on me, but she also helped me. She helped me more than I could ever repay. She saved my life in more ways than one—and she helped me save you. She helped me when no one else believed in me. She taught me to fight and hunt and defend myself. I'll always remember her for that. I hope I can be someone's mother-in-law like that someday."

"I'm sure you will be. You're already a mother she would be proud of. I know she was proud of you. I know she thought you were a good wife to me and that I got lucky when I married you." He squeezed her hand back. "I did get lucky when I married you."

"I got lucky when I married you, too. I couldn't ask for a better husband. Now let's go to sleep or we'll be up all night."

Chapter 16

H angman surveyed the group of women and children hiding in the trees. "Stay here and don't leave. These men will stand guard. If the Spiders come in force, the men will move you somewhere else. Okay? You shouldn't get into a position of needing to defend yourselves again. The men and I will be back by the end of the day. Then we should be in a much better position."

All the women and older children nodded. Almost all of them still carried the same weapons these people had been carrying around for weeks.

Hangman couldn't wait any longer. He and his men had already scoured the terrain around the band's old camp in search of anyone left alive. No one was. The men had accounted for everyone—either living or dead.

He cast one last glance at Shadow standing in the back of the crowd. Shadow didn't look at Hangman or any of the other men. Shadow stood sideways looking off into the undergrowth.

The whole band had fallen asleep last night listening to Bantam and Shadow arguing. Now Bantam and Lock stood on the opposite side of the group from their father. Neither of the brothers would even look at him.

Hangman had assigned six men to stay behind and guard the women and children. All six men had explicit instructions not to leave Shadow alone with the women and children under any circumstances—or to let him do anything else.

Hangman said, "Let's go," to the other men and they took off through the trees. The men headed east from the camp, descended into the ravine, and came back with fifteen bodies—one for each man.

The men returned to the jungle west of their old camp. The Spiders had retreated in this direction after the attack last night. Hangman didn't trust them not to send out another force today to annihilate the surviving Godless down to the very last baby.

The Godless would just have to get to the Spider Clan first and that's exactly what Hangman planned to do.

He and his men scouted around and located two things they were looking for—a massive group of Spiders waiting in the trees and an even bigger army of ants a few miles away.

Hangman and his men stopped in the trees. Each man braided a length of rope, formed a harness around his chest, and tied the other end of the rope to his dead Spider's wrists.

He explained his plan to them and split the party into two. He put Viking in charge of the second group.

The ants were marching westward at the time—straight on course for the Spiders' nest camp. One group of men descended to the ground on one side of the ants and the other group positioned themselves on the other side of the ants.

The men hacked off the bodies' feet and dropped the bodies where the ants couldn't possibly miss them. The ants responded perfectly by trying to chew the bloody, hacked-off stumps of the dead Spiders' legs.

The two groups of men separated and the ants responded to that perfectly, too. The army divided. Half the ants came after Hangman's group and the other half went after the Viking's group.

Viking's men led the ants away to the east to intercept the Spider Clan's raiding party. Hangman and his comrades headed for the nest camp.

The ants followed the men every step of the way. The ants couldn't catch up enough to make a dent in the bodies. The bloody remains left a trail of gore to keep the ants interested.

Hangman spotted the nest camp from a long way off. "Separate!" he yelled to his men and they all split apart.

The men burst into a run and the ants sped up to keep pace. The men raced around the nest camp and converged from all sides. They entered the area at a dead run on the ground beneath the nests.

The Spiders jolted to high alert when they saw Godless warriors invading their camp from all sides. The Spiders rushed forward to attack the Godless. Then the Spiders saw the ants coming.

The Spiders charged back to their nests, but it was too late. The Godless made it to the center of the camp and scaled the trees as quickly as possible towing the bodies behind them. The ants swarmed up the trunks getting closer by the second.

The Godless paused just long enough to cut the bodies loose as close to the nests as possible. The men of the Spider Clan tried in every possible way to get their women and children out of the nests in time.

The Spider men were still trying to save their families when the ants overtook the men and started eating their way into the nests themselves.

The Godless men scrambled into the very highest canopy. The branches up here were barely thick enough to support the men's weight, but the ants didn't climb this high.

Hangman and his men rejoined in a clump of foliage and watched. The ants completely obliterated the nest camp in a matter of minutes. The ants tore the nests apart and even devoured the surrounding branches.

The ants left nothing behind and eventually climbed down to the ground to continue their migration westward.

"That should not have been so easy," Kuvik remarked. "It seems like it should have been harder than that."

"Let's meet up with Viking and see how his men are getting along. He might need our help."

Hangman climbed down to the stronger branches where he and his men could travel more easily. The men backtracked to where they'd found the Spider raiding force. It wasn't there anymore. The men did find Viking and the others.

"How did that go?" Hangman asked.

"Surprisingly easy," Viking replied.

"It was a brilliant trick," Wildling remarked.

"Let's head back to the band and get out of here," Hangman suggested. "I don't want to stick around any longer than we have to."

The men returned to the place where they'd left the women and children. Hangman found the men he'd posted as guards. They were searching through the trees, but the women and children were gone.

"What the hell happened?" Hangman demanded. "I told you not to leave the women and children unattended even for a moment."

"The Spiders attacked," Maniac explained. "At least...we thought they did. They....they were over there. We went over there to intercept them.....but....."

"Will you stop hedging around and just tell me what the hell happened?!" Hangman demanded. "Just spit it out. What happened?"

"Someone set up dead Spiders over there to make it look like they were coming through the trees," Creed explained. "We saw them and thought they were alive. We went to engage them—to defend the band the way you said. We realized they were already dead. They must have come from the ravine—and when we came back to the women and children were gone."

"And Shadow was gone, too, wasn't he?" Hangman demanded. "He was with them when you left and he was gone with them when you came back. Wasn't he? Tell the truth."

Creed squared his shoulders. "Yes, he was. I know you said not to leave him alone with the women and children. We thought the band was in danger from the Spiders. That's why we didn't think. We were too focused on the Spiders."

Hangman chopped the air. "I don't care about that. They're traveling along the ground, which means they can't be too far ahead. Come on. We have to track them down before something else goes wrong."

Chapter 17

M ora sat on a branch sharing the last of her food supplies with her children. She didn't have much and no way to get any more—not until the men went hunting for the whole band. That might not be for a while considering how things were going.

She caught some of the other women in the group casting questioning glances in her direction. The same question raced through every mother's mind. Mora couldn't answer their questions.

She tried not to think about it too much. Hunger would be the least of the band's problems on the journey north—and that was saying nothing about dealing with the Anglers. That would be a whole new nightmare.

Hangman would probably take the men into the valley first and leave all the women and children outside it at least until the men got rid of the Anglers.

She didn't picture Hangman taking women and children inside the valley—especially not this many women and children.

Creed yelled out just then. "The Spiders are coming! Here they come!"

He, Maniac, and the other men on guard charged away into the trees. Mora caught sight of a few Spiders at a distance from the band.

They were way too close. How did they get here so fast when the band was hiding so far away from their old camp?

Shadow sprang forward as soon as the men left. "Quick! Come with me!" He waved all the women and children toward him. "Follow me! Hurry!"

"We aren't supposed to go anywhere," Yoa pointed out. "Hangman told us to stay here no matter what."

"He told you to withdraw if the Spiders came in force! Come on!" Shadow herded the women and children away. Some of them cooperated.

Mora exchanged glances with Zaedi. She didn't see an overwhelming Spider force moving in. The men on guard must be holding the Spiders off.

Enough women and children obeyed Shadow. He could still flex his authority with enough people. Seeing them moving off got everyone else going, too. They would all leave Mora and her children behind.

Mora spotted some of the other women glancing in her direction again. She couldn't give them any answers, so she nodded to her children, got to her feet, and they went with Shadow, too.

He got them to descend to the ground and head south. Mora checked behind her. She didn't see the other men nor did she hear any sounds of battle. Was that possible if an overwhelming force of Spiders really had been coming after the band?

She couldn't go back alone. None of the men trusted Shadow any longer, but part of her still wanted to believe that he couldn't do something so blatantly underhanded as this.

Why would he do it at all if not to stick it to Hangman? Shadow was trying to steal the band right out from under Hangman's nose—and not just Hangman's nose.

All the women and children here were the wives, children, mothers, sisters, cousins, and nieces of all the other men.

Would Shadow really do something as vindictive as that—to steal the wives and children from a whole group of men while they were out there trying to save this band from certain death?

She found it impossible to believe that her kind, caring, protective father-in-law could really do something like this.

Shadow had always been kind to her. He'd never acted outright hostile toward her the way Katha did. He'd always been steady, reliable, reasonable, and welcoming.

She saw exactly what was happening. She just didn't want to believe it was real. She didn't want to believe he could have fallen so far off the train of rationality that he would actually go through with this.

Some of the other women seemed to be going through the same turmoil, especially the women who'd traveled with Hangman's band from Ceon to the northern mountains and all the way south to join this band.

All those people put their faith in Hangman and Hangman put his faith in Shadow. The whole group had dreamed, prayed, hoped, and wished for years that they could finally get to Godless country and rejoin Shadow's band. Did that journey really end like this?

The party stumbled through the jungle heading south. Mora kept glancing behind her. The group left a giant highway of footprints for the men to follow. It would take them a matter of minutes to catch up with the band.

Hangman would come back, find the women and children gone, and realize what Shadow was doing.

Hangman would be the one to decide if Shadow was doing something underhanded or if he really had saved the whole band from an overwhelming Spider Clan invasion.

Mora couldn't bring herself to do anything about that now. Doing something about it would mean confronting Shadow herself and rallying the other women to do the same thing.

She wasn't ready to do that. She wasn't ready to become an active participant in Shadow's downfall. He seemed to be in an awfully big hurry to get there all by himself without any help from anyone.

The group got farther and farther away from the place where Hangman told the women and children to stay. All the years of traveling turned everyone's brains off. They stopped thinking so much about where they were going.

Everyone fell into the old stupor of putting one foot in front of the other. This wouldn't be the first time the band had traveled without the men. They left the band all the time to scout the country, go hunting, or to reconnoiter suspected threats.

Mora felt the same thing happening to her. Shadow broke the illusion by encouraging everyone to walk faster. He kept repeating over and over that the Spiders would overtake the band and everyone had to hurry to get as far away from them as possible.

The band came to another wide river. He turned east to follow it. Did he even have a plan—or was his only plan to get the women and children as far away from the men as possible? Could he really be thinking that?

She noticed him glancing over his shoulder a few times, too. She could have explained this away by saying that he wanted to make sure the Spiders didn't overtake the party unawares. His behavior sure looked suspicious, though. She didn't like this at all.

The river wound for a few hours, crossed an open stretch of country, and reentered another patch of jungle. She almost didn't pay attention when the band passed a stand of trees with a bunch of drawings carved into the trunks.

She would have ignored them except that the drawings had a definite shape. They were stylized pictures of people with square heads, lightning bolts for bodies, and straight lines drawn at right angles pointing up and down to indicate arms and legs.

Each arm and leg ended in a small circle. Each figure's square head circumscribed another small circle to indicate the face.

"Do you know what that means?" Yoa asked.

"I've never seen it before," Mora replied. "It looks important, though. Look. There are twenty of them carved into twenty different trees."

The party passed on. Most of the women in the band either didn't notice the drawings or paid no attention to them.

The band kept going for a while before they saw some different carvings also etched into the tree trunks. These used three deep parallel gouges slashed in back-and-forth patterns to form another lightning bolt.

Each lightning bolt ended with a different shape at the bottom. One looked like a mountain range. Another looked like the side-to-side curving line of a river. Another used a bunch of circles stacked on top of each other.

"What do you think they mean?" Neia asked.

"I don't know, but I bet they mean something," Mora pointed out. "Someone went to a lot of trouble to carve these."

"Does that mean we're trespassing on another Clan's land?" Yonna asked.

"Every place belongs to someone," Mora pointed out. "Someone claims this area as their territory. The only question is if they'll consider it an act of war that we entered without checking with them first."

Yoa made a face. "I'm sure they won't appreciate it if we lead the Spider Clan here, either."

"Keep going!" Shadow called from the back of the group. "Don't stop! Try to hurry! We don't want the Spider Clan to catch up with us."

"What do those marks mean?" Nagana asked. "Does that mean we're encroaching on another Clan's territory?"

"Of course not!" he snapped. "They don't mean anything. Maybe children have been carving on the trees."

"Don't you think you better check?" Neia asked. "Don't you think you should scout the area?"

"I don't need to scout the area!" he countered. "Now get moving! You're all walking way too slowly."

The women exchanged another glance. Mora even noticed the older children exchanging glances.

The band turned another bend in the river and found a completely different set of marks. These were strange combinations of concentric circles with arrows through them, dots, parallel lines, and strange symbols surrounding the circles in obvious patterns.

"Don't you think this is a pretty obvious indication that some other Clan lives here?" Neia asked again. "I don't like this."

"We can't go back," Shadow countered. "I received a scout who told me that Hangman's raiding party was completely wiped out. The men aren't coming back, so we have to get away quickly. Come on! Keep moving!"

Mora's stomach dropped into the pit of her stomach at those words. When would Shadow have received any scout? The women had been with him every single minute since Hangman's raiding party had left this morning.

Creed and the other men on guard had left and then Shadow had taken the women and children away. The band hadn't seen another man since.

What if Mora was wrong about that? What if a scout had come up to the band while Shadow had been walking behind her where she couldn't see him? What if she made a mistake and he really was doing this for the good of the band?

The other women went through the same combination of confusion and trying to remember everything that had happened between now and when the band left their hiding place. Were the women and children really all alone now?

A deafening bellow erupted out of the trees right then and startled everyone out of their skins. The women and children screamed and sprang together. The noise surprised Mora so much she didn't think at first to grab her weapons.

She almost didn't believe it when she stared at a mob of huge men. She'd only ever seen one man this big and that was Alien. Now what looked like an entire army of them exploded out of the surrounding trees to attack the party.

She had one brief instant to realize that these men must have created the effigies she and the women had just seen on the trees. These men had huge shoulders and tree-trunk necks that actually really did make their heads look square.

They painted their heads, faces, necks, and bodies with some kind of red dye. It looked similar to the Spider Clan's black clay, but the red gave these men a completely different look.

The men wore thick, almost padded clothing made out of hardened animal skins tempered into some kind of armor. The padding made the men look even bigger and more powerful than they already were.

Each man wore an almost square tunic over the upper body. The upper corners of the square formed points that stuck out to the sides from each man's hulking shoulders.

Thick bands of hardened hide straps surrounded the man's chest and stomach under the arms to hold the tunic in place down to the waist.

The men wore pants made of the same armored hide strapped around the legs going all the way down to the legs. Red body paint colored all their clothes and a thin strip of hair running down the center of the crown of the skull.

Each man's hair came together in a long, thin braid hanging down his back. The paint saturated the hair, too, and even saturated the hide thong tying the end of the braid together.

The men had also painted shapes on their arms, legs, clothes, bodies, and faces in black paint. These shapes looked completely different from the parallel lines the Bounty Hunters marked themselves with before battle.

These people used the same combination of weird symbols they used to mark the trees. These symbols covered the attackers' cheeks and foreheads, ran down the sides of their necks, and dotted the men's huge arms.

The attackers came mounted on some kind of creature Mora had never seen before. They actually looked like a variation of the Blastidons she'd seen in the northern mountains. These looked slightly smaller but no less ferocious.

These strange men must be unbelievably tough to domesticate the Blastidons to act as mounts. The men could direct the Blastidons perfectly wherever they wanted them to go. The Blastidons posed a more direct threat to the women and children than the riders.

The Blastidons also wore a kind of hardened armor made out of animal hides painted red. The armor formed a sheet hanging down either side of the creature's back to shield it from attack.

The same thick straps held the armor in place under these sheets. The sheets protected the straps, too. That would make it harder for anyone to cut the straps and unseat the armor or the rider.

The men rode in saddles without stirrups. They held on with their knees. The saddle seemed to be fixed to this armored sheet, too.

Each rider carried a giant battle axe in one hand and steered the reins with his other hand. The men could strike right and left on either side of their mount.

The attackers charged their Blastidons into the center of the God-less party. The women screamed and the children scattered in all directions. Only a few thought to draw their weapons.

Mora finally remembered to pull her blades, but she didn't try to defend herself against these enormous men. One blow of their axes could shatter her blades. Then she would be defenseless.

One Blastidon charged into the band and trampled Shadow. The rider cleaved his axe down on Shadow's head and kept going. The Blastidon struck people down right and left if anyone got caught in its path.

Another Blastidon barreled straight for Mora. She couldn't stand up to it or the rider. The creature flailed its razor hoofs at her and sprang over her to keep on going.

She slashed her blade upward into its stomach and cut the creature enough to make it bleed, but the thick straps stopped her from doing too much damage.

The Blastidon knocked its hind hooves against Maeno as it vaulted over her. He sprawled across the ground and didn't get up, but she couldn't take care of him right now. She backed up and stood guard over him trying to face everywhere at once.

The whole jungle burst into chaos and confusion. The riders charged down women and children who tried to flee only for the children to run in different directions to get away. They wound up leading the riders away from the party and from each other.

Enough riders kept racing their Blastidons back and forth through the crowd. The riders would have wiped out everyone if the women hadn't kept dodging, hiding behind trees, and evading as much as possible.

Mora didn't see Zaedi and Thena anymore. Were they even still alive? She cast a hasty glance around, spotted Shadow lying on the ground, and at that moment, Hangman and the other men shot out of the surrounding trees to launch a counterassault against the riders.

The Godless men rampaged through the group killing the Blastidons first. The Godless ignored the riders until the men brought all the attackers to the ground. The women rallied, now that the men distracted the riders from attacking everyone.

Mora charged up behind a rider facing off against Viking. She stabbed the guy through the back of the neck and then hacked her blade across the neck of another rider threatening Bantam.

The other women responded the same way to the men's arrival. The whole band rallied until they brought down every rider.

The riders didn't retreat. They fought to the death down to the very last man. The Godless band surrounded the last survivors and brought them down one after the other until none remained.

Mora threw herself at Hangman and flung her arms around him. "Thank God you're all right! Shadow said you were all dead."

Hangman hugged her and then turned to his father. Shadow was the one who was dead. The band had lost a bunch more women and children in the fight, too.

Hangman squatted down next to his father's body. "I never wanted this," he croaked.

Red went over to him and gripped Hangman's shoulder from behind. "My Kral."

All the men copied Red and said the same thing. Even Bantam and Lock said it.

"We have to go, little brother," Viking told Hangman. "We can't stay in this Clan's territory. They're too powerful."

Hangman forced himself to his feet and turned around to face everyone. His eyes showed not the faintest spark of life. He had nothing left in him.

"You're right," he choked. "Everyone get back to Godless territory. Hurry!"

Chapter 18

The Godless band returned to the same valley where the Spiders had killed Katha and Prodigy's family. "Is it really safe for us to camp here?" Yonna asked.

"The Spider Clan isn't in the area anymore," Bantam told her. "We eliminated them—or enough of them. They won't come back for a while."

"We can stay here tonight," Hangman decided. "We'll leave for the Angler Valley in the morning. We'll hunt tonight and store as much food as possible for the journey."

"What can you tell us about the Anglers?" Creed asked.

"They're intelligent," Hangman replied. "They plan ahead and they understand more about human behavior than any other creature we've seen. The Anglers learn by observing us and they modify their strategies to attack us in different ways. They lay ambushes for us, track us, and they never use the same tactic twice. We'll have to use as much cunning to defeat them as we would use to defeat a human enemy—maybe even more."

"Tell me again while we're even going to this valley," Mule interjected.

Hangman hesitated for a split second when he remembered the battle against this new, unknown Clan of Blastidon riders. All the men declared him their Kral—all except Mule. He didn't step forward to declare Hangman his new Kral after Shadow's death.

Hangman made a split-second decision not to draw attention to it, but to keep an eye on Mule just in case. Mule never outright declared his support for Shadow, either. Mule stayed quiet on both sides.

Hangman didn't know anything about Mule—not really. Hangman and Mora had been gone when Mule's family joined Shadow's band. Hangman didn't know if Mule had outright declared Shadow his Kral then or if Mule just came to live here.

Shadow may not have asked for an outright declaration. It may not have occurred to him to ask for one.

Hangman also didn't know if Creed had given Shadow an outright declaration of loyalty and subordination. Creed was too old to have gone through either initiation or to go to the gathering under Shadow's authority.

Creed must have gotten married before Mule's family joined Shadow's band. Maniac was also too old for Shadow and his men to have initiated Maniac. Maniac's own father and older brother could have initiated him before they met up with Shadow's band.

Did Hangman really need every single one of his men to give him an outright declaration? He tried to remember if any of his supporters had failed to give him an outright declaration. He couldn't remember if Lock did it.

Red's men did and so did Viking. Kuvik didn't. He didn't have to. Hangman would never doubt Kuvik.

Hangman didn't need Mule to give in an outright declaration, but it did ring Hangman's alarm bells. He would have to keep an eye on Mule from now on.

That moment of doubt lasted a fraction of a second the minute Mule said those words. Mule's question on its own didn't indicate disloyalty or challenge. Any of Hangman's most loyal supporters could have asked the same question.

"We're going to this valley because it's the most defensible position against our enemies," Hangman replied loudly enough for the whole group to hear. "We're going because we have a lot of enemies—a lot more than a band our size can reasonably defend ourselves against. We came down to the gorge camp because the walls protected us on multiple sides. We thought we could retreat there from the Renegade invasion. We obviously can't. The gorge camp doesn't offer enough protection. Nowhere else does. We need a place that really is defensible—like the northern valley. The Angler Valley is even more defensible than that. There is no way in or out. We'll be able to completely eliminate the Anglers and then we'll have the valley to ourselves. Our children will be able to grow up there without having to constantly move around and defend against enemy Clans. We'll still have to deal with the normal jungle creatures, but we won't have all these enemies attacking us at every turn. We won't have to retreat and find new territory. We'll be able to build one camp and stay there for the rest of our lives—and our children will be able to stay there for the rest of their lives. It's a permanent solution. It's the only permanent solution."

"What about rejoining with Hammer?" Aliva asked. "That would be a permanent solution."

"Anyone who wants to go over to Hammer can leave right now," Hangman replied. "Just be prepared to fight your way through any stray bands of Spider Clan plus Renegades and Bounty Hunters between our territory and his. Just remember he's Kral of his band and you're going to face exactly the same problems of authority and leadership. Going to Hammer might be a solution for you, but it isn't for me. I'm taking my family north. Any of you who want to come with me are welcome. The more people come, the safer and better protected we'll be." He made a face at no one in particular. "I don't like your chances of making it back to Hammer's territory alive—not without the whole band going together."

That silenced everyone—for now, at least. The band got to work making camp. Hangman found himself watching literally everyone. Any two people talking to each other raised his hackles. Were they planning on questioning every decision that he made?

He was bound to face resistance after just taking over as Kral, especially when he made decisions so vastly different from Shadow's.

None of these people knew about the Angler Valley. It really did sound dangerous when he described it to his people—because it was dangerous. No one knew better than Hangman how dangerous it was.

He couldn't expect his people to just jump on board with that—not without at least asking a few questions. They had a right to ask questions. They even had a right to contradict.

He had to remind himself of that. He had fallen out of practice of being Kral these last few years. He had forgotten how hard it was to constantly explain himself to everyone and quiet their doubts and fears.

He had to constantly remind himself that not everyone had his stomach for risk and unusual behavior. Not even his bravest warriors understood why he did things the way he did. Even people who had known him for years struggled to accept his decisions.

It had been so easy to contradict when Shadow had been Kral and took all the responsibility for making those decisions. Questioning those decisions from the sidelines was always easier than actually making them and following them through to completion.

He went hunting with the other men, helped them kill two Stalkions, and returned to the band to help the men butcher and dry the meat overnight. He caught Mora giving him meaningful looks again. He didn't have to ask if she understood. She always did.

She was a Kral's wife again. That brought its own difficulties and responsibilities. The two of them didn't have to live under the weight of Shadow's hostility anymore. Now Mora and Hangman traded those problems for a whole new set of problems and concerns.

He found himself studying everyone in camp. He didn't have to worry about any of the people who had come south with him from the northern mountains. They'd traveled together for years and understood each other well enough not to question anything.

Besides Mule and his family, the band also included several people Hangman had rescued from the Bounty Hunters and all the people who had been part of Shadow's band before Hangman and the others returned.

He decided to keep an eye on Grizzly, Breaker, and Devil, too. They'd been making noise against Hangman before he ever separated from Shadow's band. Hangman didn't trust his three cousins not to try something now.

The band included half a dozen other men Hangman couldn't be sure about. Some of them had declared him their new Kral, but he still doubted them. Grizzly, Breaker, and Devil had done the same thing and he doubted them. Saying the words meant nothing.

The band also included a bunch of teenage boys not yet old enough to initiate. They would get there within the next year. Hangman would have to take care of that on the journey north, but at least he would be able to rely on those boys to take their place with the men.

Most of them had grown up on the journey south from the northern mountains. They understood the dangers and the boys would be ready to fight the way their older brothers did.

The band also included a cadre of younger boys Zaedi's age. These boys weren't close to the age of initiation, but they sure were growing up fast.

Zaedi ran with Wildling's son, Loso, and Butch's sons Kabi and Zakra. Hangman hardly ever saw the four outside each other's company. They were only twelve years old, but they were some of the fiercest fighters in the whole band.

The four of them never went anywhere without a weapon. They went on hunting trips together, sparred with their weapons, or practiced fighting trees and bushes and imagining the foliage was some creature the boys wanted to kill.

This was the best preparation anyone could ask for to teach the boys the skills they would need when they grew up. These boys had already faced their real enemies in combat and the boys had risen to the challenge.

Hangman didn't involve himself enough in their dealings to know if Zaedi was becoming their leader. Hangman had made up his mind a long time ago to let Zaedi grow up his own way without putting any pressure on him to be anything.

Becoming Kral all of a sudden sure changed the landscape. Hangman had to start thinking about a lot of things that could happen in the future.

Zaedi would initiate in two years. That was nothing. Then Zaedi and all these boys would become Hangman's men. His position as Kral would depend on them.

Maeno wouldn't be too far behind them. Hangman would have his own sons backing him up and carrying out his orders along with the other men. That would be something to see. It was a future worth fighting for.

Chapter 19

Mora woke up in darkness and peeled herself away from her children while they still slept. They hardly needed to sleep next to her anymore. They slept near her, but they needed space instead of the kind of constant body contact they used to need.

Mora arranged a few things in the rough shelter she had built last night. She had spent so much time moving around lately. She didn't really need to pack anything to get ready to leave again.

She went outside and found Hangman sitting up by the remains of last night's fire. He wasn't the only adult already awake and getting ready. Men and women moved all over the band's temporary camp.

"Did you sleep last night?" she asked.

"Some, but not much," he replied. "I had a lot on my mind."

She squatted next to him, put her arm around his shoulders, and kissed the side of his neck. "Thank you for yesterday. You don't know how relieved I was to see you."

"You don't know how relieved I was to see you," he countered. "I thought the worst when I came back and found all of you gone."

"Do you think that strange Clan will leave us alone, now that we aren't in their territory anymore?"

"I don't want to find out. I want to leave and get to the Angler Valley as quickly as possible."

She studied the side of his face. "Do you remember how to get there?"

He shrugged. "I think so." He squinted at her. "Do you remember how to get there?"

"Not very well. I could study the maps, but I guess I would have to see the country with my own eyes to know for certain."

He nodded. "That's what I was thinking, but anything is better than staying here. At least we know we won't be trespassing on another Clan's land up there."

"Maybe we should study the maps in the evenings on the way there. We can probably find some of the mountains and cliff country that led to the valley."

"That's a good idea." He frowned again. "Do you think it's a good idea for us to let the others see us doing it? They might lose heart if they realize we don't know where we're going."

"We know the general direction we're going." She held out her hand. "Show me the maps. Let me take a look right now before the children wake up."

He took the maps out of his bag and handed them over. She rifled through them and laid out the relevant sections on the ground just as Zaedi came out of the shelter.

"What are you doing?" he asked.

"We're reading the maps to find the Angler Valley," Hangman replied. "Maybe you could help us remember how to get there."

"I don't remember much about the journey," Zaedi replied. "I was too young. I remember what happened inside the valley, but everything that happened after we left just kind of blended together."

"I feel the same way," Mora replied. "I thought I would never go back there as long as I lived."

Hangman laughed. "I think we all thought that." He turned to his son. "I'm going to need you to help me on the journey, my son."

"How?" Zaedi asked. "I'm not initiated."

"I don't need you to be initiated for what I need you for. I need you to let me know if you spot any landmarks along the way—any interesting features you see that you recognize. I'm going to need you to help me and Mother guide the band there."

"I'll try," Zaedi replied. "I don't know how much good I'll be to you."

"You'll always be good to me." Hangman put his arm around the boy. "I'm proud of you. I'm proud of the man I see you growing up to become. I can't wait to initiate you and to make you one of my men. I know you're going to be great—you and all your friends."

Zaedi burst into a huge grin. "Could I help you in other ways, Father?"

"You and your friends can help me and the men guard the band on the march. You're already doing that with your weapons. You can help us keep watch and you can help us fight enemy Clans and creatures whenever they come around. That's the most important thing I need you to do."

Zaedi started to nod.

"I found it," Mora interrupted. Both Hangman and Zaedi turned around. Mora pointed to a spot on the map. "That's the mountain range Shadow's band was crossing when the flood washed us away."

"That doesn't tell us where the Angler Valley is," Hangman pointed out. "That mountain range has hundreds of valleys in it."

"None like this. Don't you remember? We came through the tunnel into another valley running north to south—and the Angler Valley runs north to south. The two valleys were right next to each other—and the Angler Valley had a square end with a waterfall at the

northern head and a narrow, V-shaped end at the southern foot. Remember? That's what made the valley so difficult to get into and out
of. It had steep cliffs instead of normal passes we could cross. The
mountain range has only one valley like that. See?"

Hangman and Zaedi both bent over to see what she was looking at.
They bent together at the same time and cracked their heads together.
They both yelled out and then burst out laughing.

Their noise woke up Maeno and Thena. "Mother!!" Maeno yelled
from inside the shelter. Mora went inside to help him. Thena sitting
up and getting ready to leave.

Maeno followed Mora outside and she gave the three children
something to eat. Hangman and Zaedi were already gone. Hangman
had taken his maps with him. He must not have wanted anyone else
to see him and Mora reading them.

That didn't matter because she knew how to get to the valley now.
She knew how to get to both of its cliff ends and she knew how to get
to the secret tunnel entrance.

She had plenty to do to get ready to go after that. Finding her way
to the Angler Valley would be the least of the band's problems for a
long time.

None of the Godless lacked motivation to pack up and leave. The
band moved out before the sun came up and traveled faster than usual.

Hangman followed a river through this part of the country. It
traveled north to south, too. Consulting the maps made traveling so
much easier. He and Mora knew exactly where to go to head straight
for the Angler Valley.

The band traveled for two weeks without incident. The Godless
didn't see any other people. Hangman kept sending out scouting
parties to check for other Clans so he could ask permission to cross
their land if the Godless needed to.

They didn't see anything or encounter anyone. Neither the Spider Clan, the Renegades, nor the Bounty Hunters seemed to be occupying this country. No one seemed to.

The band camped in another patch of jungle while the men hunted and stored up food for the next leg of the journey. Everyone in the band fell into the same easy rhythm as they had on the journey south from the northern mountains.

Anyone from Shadow's band who hadn't been with Hangman's party on that journey learned quickly enough and blended in with the rest of the group's routines.

The band stayed in that camp for four days and moved out on the fifth. Hangman sent out his usual scouts to survey the country. He used the uninitiated boys much more than Shadow did. In fact, Shadow didn't use them at all.

Hangman treated them almost as initiated men. He took them on hunting parties and let the boys sit in on the men's conferences.

The boys couldn't have been happier to be included. They responded to his leadership exactly the way Hammer and his men did in the past.

Hangman used the younger boys in Zaedi's group a lot, too. He sent them on their own scouting missions that didn't require them to travel as far or as fast as fully grown men.

He also sent them on hunting parties by themselves and constantly gave them independent assignments.

Kuvik seemed to take these boys under his wing. He told them stories about a boy he'd know who was only twelve. His name was Tren.

Kuvik said Tren could outhunt, outrun, and outfight any grown man in his whole band simply because he was bolder and put more energy into everything he did. Tren became something of a legend to Zaedi and the others. They all wanted to be like him.

Kuvik told them no end of stories about Tren's exploits. The boys always found Kuvik during their spare moments to ask him to tell them something Tren had done or what he would have done in a situation the boys had just dealt with.

Mora couldn't tell if Tren was real or not. His exploits sounded too outlandish and larger-than-life to be real. Kuvik insisted that Tren was very real. Mora didn't see any reason why Kuvik would lie about this.

He even insisted that Tren was real when none of the children were around to hear. Kuvik insisted that Tren was real when Kuvik talked about him only to adults. He had no reason to lie then.

Mora also noticed Kuvik sometimes getting thoughtful or going silent after he talked about Tren. She didn't think Kuvik would do that unless something bad had happened to Tren.

Kuvik never talked to anyone about what did happen to Tren. Kuvik always seemed to leave out that part of the story.

The boys responded to that with unholy energy, too. They threw themselves into everything they did, fought harder, ran faster, and worked a thousand times more enthusiastically to do everything grown men could do.

Chapter 20

The Godless band packed up all the new food supplies and entered another stretch of jungle.

Mora started to turn her brain off for another long trek. That was the problem with the men preparing so much extra food. The band wouldn't stop again for a long time—not for more than one night.

She didn't pay attention to what the men and boys were doing. They separated into scouting parties and disappeared in multiple directions.

The band traveled for a few hours before some of the men came back. Three different scouting parties met back up to give Hangman their reports on different parts of the country.

Mora happened to be passing near enough to hear Hangman and the others holding their conversation. Viking, Carnage, Maniac, and Breaker were all reporting to Hangman when Zaedi, Loso, and Zakra all dropped out of the treetops overhead.

"Father!" Zaedi gasped all out of breath. "The riders....they're coming.....the red riders.....coming from the south......"

Hangman spun around and grabbed the boy's shoulder. "Where?! Where did you see them?!"

All three boys pointed up into the trees. Hangman, the four men, and all three boys shot away into the branches just as fast. Mora actually stopped dead in her tracks at those words. The red riders......Zaedi could only have been talking about one group of people.

He was too smart to make a mistake like that. He wouldn't have reported seeing them if he hadn't been sure it really was the same people.

Mora wasn't the only person to hear the boys' report. A few other women stopped walking and exchanged glances. "Are the red riders really coming?" Neia asked.

Mora shook herself. "We better keep going. The men will come back and tell us...."

Hangman plummeted out of the trees just then. "All of you get into the canopy! NOW!!" he ordered. "Everybody up! Get off the ground and get as high into the canopy as you can! Get moving!"

Viking, Breaker, and Carnage all showed up to help the women climb. Hangman and the other men carried younger children. Zaedi and the boys helped as much as they could, too.

The younger boys couldn't do much. Hangman pointed to the tree boys as soon as the band got high enough. "Stay here and guard the band, my son," Hangman ordered. "Don't leave the women and children unguarded even for a moment. Understand?"

"Yes, Father," Zaedi panted.

Hangman squeezed his shoulder. "You did very well to warn us. I'm trusting you. Stay on guard—all of you."

He and the men raced away out of sight. Mora and the others couldn't see anything from up here.

"I want to go, too," Maeno chimed in.

"Wait until you're older," Mora told him. "I'm sure Zaedi will take you when you get big enough."

Zaedi gave his little brother a hard look, compressed his lips, and went back to surveying the surrounding jungle for any sign of a threat.

Dead silence fell over the jungle—or it would have if the women hadn't started whispering right then.

"Why would the red riders follow us this far?" Nagana asked.

"We killed their men," Yoa pointed out. "Or our men killed their men. They probably want revenge."

"They must have tracked us," Yonna squeaked. "They must have followed us out of their territory and all the way here. Maybe they'll never stop following us."

Mora opened her mouth to suggest that maybe the women shouldn't start imagining the worst possible disasters they could come up with.

Her throat seized up when she saw Kuvik coming toward the party at a dead sprint through the treetops. He came from the north—from the direction the band had been going before.

He didn't come directly toward the band. He dropped to the ground, passed the women and children, and kept going.

A few people gasped and had to silence themselves when they saw four enormous Krakelows dropped down right behind him. His speed distracted them from the band.

He barely came in sight before a mob of red riders burst out of the undergrowth mounted on their Blastidons. The riders must have been following the band.

The riders came at a gallop and would have overtaken the women and children if the band had still been walking defenseless on the ground.

Mora stared in stunned disbelief as Wildling, Bantam, Lock, and Hangman converged from both sides. Kuvik and those four were the band's fastest runners.

They also ran on the ground with multiple Krakelows pursuing each man. Bantam and Hangman crossed paths right in front of the

Blastidons and all their pursuing Krakelows collided with the red riders.

The Blastidons reared and tried to strike the Krakelows with their hooves, but the Blastidons only succeeded in shattering the Krakelows into dozens of segments. Kuvik, Lock, and Wildling ran past the conflict going in other directions.

The noise and commotion attracted the Krakelows to dive in and attack the thrashing riders and Blastidons while the five Godless men kept running to get clear of the confusion.

Lock and Wildling both got segments on them. The men rejoined on the ground to pry the segments off and treat the men's injuries.

The riders and all the Blastidons screeched, fought, and struggled to escape from all the Krakelows attacking them. None of them came after the Godless anymore. Hangman and his men didn't even have to climb into the branches to get away from the disaster.

Hangman watched from a distance for a while. The Krakelows were too busy devouring all their victims to notice the other men standing at a distance.

Hangman strode up to the tangle of bodies, grabbed one of the riders by his arm, and pulled him out of the pile. Segments covered him from the chest down.

He gasped, whined, and choked out anguished moans. He couldn't move his legs and he didn't have a weapon anymore.

Hangman dragged the guy to a safe distance and propped him against a tree. The noise brought all the other Godless men back in time to see Hangman bend over the guy.

"Who are you?" Hangman demanded. "What does your Clan call itself?"

"Red Riders!" the man spat. "Don't you know by now?!"

Hangman nodded. "It's as good a name as any. What do you want from us? Why are you following us? We never intended to trespass on your territory. It was an accident. We left it as soon as we could."

"You killed our men!" the helpless man fired back. "Any invasion of our territory is a death sentence—and you killed our men! We'll never stop until we track you down."

"Your brother riders will have to do that for you. You won't survive this."

The guy tried to snort and wound up grimacing in pain. "You're all cowards! You fight the coward's way! You'll all die—and your women and children will become part of our Clan."

"So that's how it is?" Hangman remarked. "You're nothing but another band of marauders. We know how to deal with you."

The rider spat at him and then burst into a hysterical fit of laughter that ended with him breaking down in sobs. "Throw me back in," he whimpered. "Throw me back in. Don't let me die like this. Let me die with my brothers."

Hangman straightened up. "Why would I do that when you just spat on me? I don't owe you anything."

The guy turned his face away and fought to control his features. He couldn't hide his anguish. He knew he was going to die.

Hangman finally took hold of the guy's arm, dragged him back to the pile, and hurled him close enough for the Krakelows to get to him again. They coiled around him, rolled him into the confusion, and the guy's body disappeared.

Hangman jumped into the treetops. "Get the band moving again, my son," he told Zaedi. "Take everyone to the ground and get back on the road north. Guard the band while the men and I finish scouting the area."

Zaedi murmured, "Yes, Father," and the men left again.

Mora gladly turned her back on the enormous mountain of Krakelows writhing on the jungle floor. The men were really taking this ambushing strategy seriously. Why fight a battle they couldn't win when they could turn the jungle against their enemies?

Chapter 21

H angman clambered up some high rocks and peered out over the mountainous country in front of him. The sun was starting to go down. It cast the mountains in a spray of soft colors disappearing toward the horizon.

He sighed, turned away, jumped off the rock, and ran downhill behind this mountain to the foot of the valley where he met up with the rest of his band.

The party snaked its way up a steep river course leading out of another valley system farther south.

"How does it look?" Viking asked.

"It's too far for us to travel tonight," Hangman replied. "We'll camp here and leave in the morning."

Groans broke out through the whole group. "How long will it take us to get there?" someone moaned.

"We should have gotten there a long time ago," another complained. "You never said it would take this long."

"I never said how long it would take," Hangman countered. "I only said we would have a more defensible territory once we got there."

"We can't defend ourselves now," Devil pointed out. "The Red Riders have attacked us the whole way here."

"Don't exaggerate," Hangman fired back. "They've attacked five times in the last year and we have never had to fight them again even once after that first time. We've ambushed them and finished them off without fighting. I call that a victory."

"We won't be able to ambush them once we go out into the open," Mule pointed out. "We'll be exposed with no way to defend ourselves."

Hangman fought down the urge to lose his temper. These grumblings and protests had been getting louder ever since he set out to lead the band north.

He took a deep breath. "This trip has taken a lot longer than I anticipated. I'll admit that and I should have foreseen this. Mora and I took over a year to make it back to Shadow's territory from the Angler Valley. This trip is taking even longer simply because we have more people this time. The men have to keep stopping to hunt to feed everyone. The Red Riders don't slow us down nearly as much as that."

"What's to stop them from following us all the way to the valley?" Red asked.

Hangman couldn't lose his patience with Red. Red and his men had been Hangman's staunchest supporters. They deserved to at least ask questions.

"Maybe the Red Riders *will* follow us all the way to the valley," Hangman replied. "I really don't know if they will and I don't care. We'll be able to defend ourselves there. We'll be able to get behind walls and at least slow them down. I know for a fact that they won't be able to bring their Blastidons into the valley."

"Why not?" Bantam asked. "What makes you so sure?"

"Because the walls are too steep," Hangman pointed out. "The only way down is to climb down hundreds of feet of vertical cliffs. I don't foresee the Red Riders using rope harnesses to lower their Blastidons down to the valley floor. We'll be able to attack and kill the Blastidons first if the Riders do that. I'm telling you the valley is our best option. Ask Mora if you don't believe me."

A few people turned to look at Mora, but no one asked her. The whole band had been having this exact same discussion almost every evening for the entire year.

Mora had explained a thousand times what the valley was like and she confirmed everything Hangman had been saying. No one had to ask her anything.

Sometimes he started to suspect that these people just kept questioning him to annoy him, but he knew that wasn't the case.

"How much farther is it to the valley?" Mule asked.

Hangman tried to shrug the question away. "It's a long way. I won't lie to you about that. I thought we would make better progress than we have, but we just have to keep going."

"Maybe there's another similar valley we could get to before that," Maniac suggested. "Maybe we can set up our territory somewhere closer—somewhere we don't have to keep traveling."

"Would you rather keep traveling or camp somewhere that really is indefensible—somewhere like that valley where Shadow told us to camp?" Hangman asked. "None of these valleys are like that one. That's the whole point. It's unique."

"Couldn't we at least look?" Grizzly asked.

"That will take even longer," Hangman replied. "You might find a valley you like, get all settled, and then the Red Riders could overtake us and attack us. Then we would have to flee anyway and probably lose some of our men in the process. We should just keep going."

"I don't think you even know where this valley is," Devil countered. "I think you made it all up and you're leading us on a wild goose chase through the middle of nowhere with no destination in mind."

Hangman didn't answer. He didn't trust himself to do it calmly enough. That was the very first outright challenge to his leadership he'd heard so far.

He'd heard a whole lot of doubt, naysaying, and quibbling about changing the plan to something easier with a closer destination.

No one had ever come right out and told him to his face that he didn't know where the valley was and didn't know what he was doing. He leveled Devil with a direct stare. Devil didn't look away. So this was how it started.

Devil hadn't said anything about supporting Shadow. None of the other men mentioned Devil being against someone challenging Shadow and maybe even deposing him.

Maybe Devil thought he would be the one to do it. Maybe Devil wanted to wait for Hangman to take over because Devil still thought of Hangman as a boy who wasn't strong enough to lead the band.

Silence answered Devil's statement. Hangman refused to answer first.

"Well?" Devil demanded. "What do you have to say about that? You don't know where this valley is and you don't know how to get there. Do you? Just admit it. I wouldn't be surprised if the valley didn't exist at all."

"Yes, it does!" Zaedi snapped from the edge of the circle. This was the first time he'd ever spoken in the men's council. "Thena, Maeno, and I were there with Father and Mother. We fought the Anglers together. We all saw the walls. It took us ages to find a way out of the valley."

"Keep your mouth shut, boy!" Devil fired back. "You have no business participating in this discussion."

"What happens to the band affects me, my sister, my brother, and my mother," Zaedi countered. "I have as much right to say what I know. I'm not going to stand here and let you call my father a liar. The valley is real and it's as solid as he says. Everything he says is true. I've seen it myself."

"Then how do we find it?" Viking asked. He turned to Hangman. "Tell us you know where it is and how to find it."

Hangman snapped his eyes back to Devil. "Are you finished yet? Is that all you want to say? I'm sure you have more things on your mind than that."

Devil hardened his features. "You still haven't said you know where it is."

"I don't have to justify myself to you, Devil," Hangman countered. "I would be very happy to explain it to Red or Viking or Bantam or Wildling. They would ask me out of respect so they could understand—not to challenge me to my face. I won't answer that. If you want to challenge me, go right ahead and do it. Don't pretend you're asking a question when you aren't."

The other men looked back and forth between Hangman and Devil. None of the men made a sound. Neither did Devil.

Hangman sniffed at Devil and made a show of turning back to Viking. "We know where the valley is and we know how to get there. We haven't been leading anyone anywhere except on the most direct possible route to the valley. I can prove it to you, but I give you my word we are traveling there as quickly as we possibly can. The Red Riders aren't slowing us down. The route isn't slowing us down. The band is. The women and children are. Traveling with this many people is slowing us down. You all remember what it was like when we traveled south from the northern mountains—and when we traveled north to get to them. The trip took years because we always had to keep stopping and starting. These things take time. Me showing you the route won't change that."

"What *is* the route?" Red asked. "Can't you at least show us that?"

Hangman took another deep breath and pulled the maps out of his bag. He forced himself to keep his temper in check, to stay calm, and explain himself in as much detail as his men needed him to—as much detail as his trusted men needed him to.

This was Shadow's mistake. He lost his mind over people just asking for a simple explanation. These people wanted to offer some input on matters that affected their entire lives and their families' safety. Every man had a right to do that.

Hangman had to work hard not to get defensive when his men questioned him. His memory of Shadow's madness helped Hangman rein himself in and explain the situation things to the men clearly and patiently.

Chapter 22

H angman squatted on the ground and laid out the maps. "Do you remember the maps we took from Ceon—the maps we used to find the ammunition store? These are the same thing. They show a diagram of the whole country. This is the gorge camp in Shadow's old territory. This is the valley where the Spider Clan attacked us and killed our people. The Red Riders' territory is here—southeast of that. The Angler Valley is here...."

"That's so far away!" Mule exclaimed. "We're barely halfway there."

"I already explained to you why." Hangman gathered up his maps and put them away. "The only alternative is that we don't stop as often. The alternative is that we send out hunting parties to kill and process our food for us while the band keeps moving without a break."

"We can't do that!" Yonna exclaimed. "Traveling like this is already hard enough. We need to rest sometime."

"We could always go back to Hammer's territory," Mule suggested. "It's closer than the valley."

Hangman had to stop himself from giving Mule a dirty look. He was easily the oldest man here and one of the few left over from Shadow's generation.

"We won't go back—and I can't let anyone else leave independently," Hangman replied. "You would never get there alive with all the enemy Clans running around and you would leave the rest of us completely unprotected. You would lead the Red Riders straight to Hammer's door if you survived to make it there at all. You followed me north so we could get to the Angler Valley. Now we have to just keep pushing until we get there."

"What if the Red Riders attack again on the way?" Yoa asked.

Hangman shrugged. "I'm assuming they will."

"How will you deal with that?" Grizzly asked. "How will *we* deal with it?"

"We'll deal with it the way we always do. We'll fight back. We'll use the resources available to us. We'll improvise and adapt to our circumstances." Hangman glanced around at Red and his men. "This country isn't that different from your home mountains. You survived there. We all did. We can do it again here."

Red brightened up. "You're right. I didn't think of that. It is a similar country."

"What does that mean?" Mule asked.

"It means we have resources that aren't immediately obvious on the surface," Hangman replied. "Now everyone better get busy making camp. We've talked about this enough for one night. We'll cross these mountains tomorrow and keep going into the next valley system. We'll be able to defend ourselves better there."

The group broke up. The women got to work making camp and the men helped them for lack of anything better to do. The men had already come back from their scouting trips. The country was empty.

"That's one thing about these mountains," Viking remarked an hour later. "We can see anyone coming before they get here."

Hangman lowered his voice. "Go around the camp and call up the men, Viking. Tell them I want to talk about our strategy for tomorrow."

Viking raised his eyebrows, but he didn't argue. He never did. He knew better than to question Hangman's fitness as a Kral.

The cousins parted, called up the men, and met at a distance where the women wouldn't overhear.

Hangman drew a sketch in the dirt of the pass over the mountains that he'd seen at sunset. "The way is narrow like the paths we followed through the mountains with Shadow. We'll position a handful of men at the front to lead the way. The rest of you will follow behind to meet the Red Riders if they overtake us in the middle of the pass. Red, I want you and your men to get up into the rocks if you see them coming. They won't be able to fight you up there as long as they're mounted on their Blastidons."

"How will we fight them if the way is so narrow?" Bantam asked.

"Don't fight them," Hangman replied. "Just knock them over the side. Don't think about killing the riders. Just take out the Blastidons at the knees and make them lose their balance. The Blastidons won't be able to come at us more than one or maybe two at a time. Forget about everything except their legs. Break or injure their legs and send them over the side. That's all you have to do."

Creed furrowed his brow at the drawing. "I didn't think of that. That's brilliant."

"We have resources here the same way we did in the jungle," Hangman replied. "We're switching to a different terrain. That's all. We can still use the same tricks to defeat our enemies. We aren't helpless."

"How do you want to deal with creatures?" Legacy asked. "Ridgebeaks and Boultars were a major problem last time."

"We're going to deal with them by not getting caught out on those paths for any length of time the way we did last time. We're going to deal with it by only going out on those paths when we have to cross a pass like we will be tomorrow. If you remember, the Ridgebeaks and Boultars didn't bother us at first. They only started doing it after they figured out that we would be there every single day for weeks on end. That's when they started coming around to attack us all the time. We won't let that happen. We'll cross each pass, descend into another valley, and travel through the jungle where we know how to deal with the creatures we're used to."

Legacy nodded. "That's true. That is how it worked back then. I forgot about that."

Hangman glanced around. "Any other questions?" He made sure not to glance in Devil's direction when he said it.

Maybe now all of these naysayers would learn the difference between asking a simple question for clarification and outright challenging Hangman's leadership.

No one spoke up, so he sent them all back to their families. Hangman returned to the camp and headed for Mora's shelter. Zaedi intercepted Hangman on the way.

Zaedi peered up at Hangman extra closely. "Did I do wrong by speaking in front of the men, Father?"

"Not at all, my son," Hangman exclaimed. "I'm proud of you and I'm grateful for your support. What you said was perfect. Thank you."

Zaedi looked away. "It's so hard to know the right thing to do."

"I know, but you're doing well. I know you're trying to hurry up and get to the age of initiation. I couldn't be prouder of you. You're an asset to our Clan even at your age."

Zaedi stopped in his tracks and studied Hangman again. "You're keeping the tunnel a secret from everyone, aren't you? I've never heard you telling anyone about it. You always say the walls are too steep. That's why I didn't say anything about the tunnel."

Now Hangman was the one who looked away. "You're right, my son. Mother and I talked about it. We think it will be better to keep the tunnel a secret until the last possible moment in case someone turns traitor or the Red Riders capture someone. Anything could happen. I understand if this is hard for you, but I would appreciate it if you could continue to keep it to yourself."

"Of course, Father. I've kept it to myself all this time. I haven't even told the other boys."

Hangman gripped the side of his son's neck. "Thank you, my son. Your loyalty and support is the greatest gift you could give me. I don't want to turn out like my father...."

"You aren't," Zaedi blurted out. "You're nothing like him. You're so patient. I wouldn't be able to stay as patient as you."

"I hope so," Hangman mumbled. "I.....You don't remember what things were like in the northern valley when I was Kral before. I had to explain myself to all the men. They have a right to know why I'm making these decisions and what we plan to do."

Zaedi hesitated and then blurted out. "Am I allowed to know what you're planning for tomorrow?"

Hangman laughed. "Of course, my son. What I'm planning for tomorrow isn't a secret—but you might not be able to do anything about it. You'll be in the middle of the group with the other children."

Zaedi grimaced in disgust. "I hate being a child. I want to be a man."

Hangman couldn't stop himself from putting his arm around his son's shoulders. "Enjoy it while it lasts, my son. You're going to be a man for a long time and being a man is a lot harder than being a boy. Even now, you have the option to go back to the band whenever you want to. You don't have that option when you're a man. Don't be in too big a rush to initiate."

"I can't help it. I want to help you."

"You are helping me, my son. You're helping me more than I could ever ask."

"So...what's your plan for tomorrow?"

Hangman gave Zaedi an in-depth explanation of his strategy.

Zaedi cocked his head and raised his eyebrows. "That's a really good idea. I didn't think of that."

"I might not be as young as I was, but I can still think, I suppose. Now let's get back to Mother and the others. She'll be worried about us."

Mora gave Hangman and Zaedi a strange look when they came back together, but she didn't ask any questions. She called Maeno and Thena into the shelter and left Hangman and Zaedi sitting outside alone.

Hangman felt himself settling into a different kind of relationship with his son. It would be like this in the years to come. They would share dangers, hardships, and responsibility. Zaedi would take over as Kral if Hangman outlived Bantam and Lock.

Hangman made up his mind right then and there to live long enough for Zaedi to become Kral. Zaedi deserved it after all the nightmarish trials he had gone through.

Hangman could think of a lot of other men who deserved it more—like Red. Maybe Hangman should just hand over the position to Red once Hangman got to be too old.

Then again, Red was even older than Hangman. Red might die first.

Zaedi would grow up. He would grow up to be a strong man in his own right. Hangman might stay Kral long enough for Zaedi to be old enough and strong enough. Hangman could only hope and do his best to make sure it happened.

Chapter 23

Mora woke up early the next morning and left Maeno and Thena sleeping. She found it harder and harder to sleep as time went on. Concerns for the day always made her get up early. She left the shelter. Thena was already awake.

Zaedi had curled up on the ground outside with Hangman. They looked so sweet together. She couldn't help but beam at the way they were getting closer. Zaedi couldn't wait to be one of Hangman's men. Zaedi essentially already was one.

The whole camp woke up pretty soon. No one wanted to wait around and delay the inevitable. Everyone got moving, left the safety of the trees, and started on the long, exposed, winding path to cross the pass.

Hangman assigned Mule to lead the band along with Lock, Maniac, Grizzly, and Kuvik. Hangman didn't give any of these men any direct instructions.

Mora spotted Hangman exchanging meaningful glances with Lock and Kuvik before they separated from the other men. Did Hangman want Lock and Kuvik to keep an eye on Mule and Grizzly?

Mora didn't think Hangman mistrusted Maniac. Creed and Maniac had been Hangman's strong supporters even though the two men were Mule's sons.

Mora didn't actually know if Hangman suspected Mule of any-thing. Mora didn't know if Hangman suspected Grizzly of anything, either, but Mora would have had to be dead or in a coma not to hear the way Hangman had spoken to Devil last night.

Devil stepping out of line like that cast suspicion on his brothers Breaker and Grizzly, too. They might just stand with their brother. Why wouldn't they?

She tried not to obsess about all the political ramifications of every single decision Hangman made—except that every decision he made did have political ramifications.

He had never faced resistance on the band's previous journeys. Everyone had followed Hangman without question.

He had never faced any challenges or grumblings or people insult-ing him to his face. That had never happened. The band had so many much bigger problems to deal with then. All their lives depended on Hangman's decisions and on the band's cohesion and cooperation.

The men surrounded the women and children in the usual way until the band got to the narrow pathways leading up to the pass. Then Hangman dropped back with the other men.

Red and his comrades climbed up the rocks the way they used to. Mora felt so much better with the men up there.

The band hiked up steep, winding, rocky channels before Wildling yelled out, "Here they come! The Red Riders are coming in!"

His warning electrified the band. The women and children walked faster, but no one could do anything with these steep walls around them. The party could barely walk two abreast.

The men stayed behind the group except for those five at the front. Mule and the others kept encouraging the women and children to hurry and get over the pass in time, but everyone was already walking as fast as they possibly could.

Hangman ordered Bantam, Creed, and the four uninitiated boys to climb up and help Red. The Godless couldn't face the enemy more than two at a time, either. The Red Riders would only be able to bring in two Blastidons at a time. This should get interesting.

The Blastidons' hooves echoed off the rocks long before the Red Riders got close enough to threaten the Godless. The endless vibration scared the women and children into racing through the channels as fast as they could go.

Their actions actually put them in danger more than they realized. Mule and the five men in front broke out into an open, exposed stretch of gravel leading to the top of the pass. The whole band burst into a run to cross this space as quickly as possible.

Hangman's voice rang out against the rock walls. He ordered the men to stay where they were and hold the Red Riders inside the walls until the women and children crossed.

Mora ran with the others. Her children flanked her all carrying weapons. Mule, Lock, and Maniac waved everyone forward and yelled for them to go. Kuvik and Grizzly charged ahead to lead the way.

The women and children crossed the pass and entered another steep, narrow, winding path winding around and around across a cliff face. The righthand wall stood straight up and down while the lefthand wall dropped thousands of feet to nothing.

The women and children flattened themselves against the walls trying to hurry without falling over the side. It was exactly the same situation that came so close to killing Bantam and Prodigy.

Mora glanced behind her. The men came racing up behind the party. The Red Riders weren't here yet, but the incessant pounding of the Blastidons' hooves announced the Riders' approach. The noise got closer by the second.

The women and children held onto each other for dear life while everyone hustled to make it down the other side of the pass to the jungle in time. They would never make it. The hoofbeats sounded like they were right on top of the party.

The tension among the men in the rear spiked off the charts. Creed and Rapid occupied the position in the far rear. None of the other men would be able to get near the Red Riders.

They came charging around one of the winding curves. Mora already saw the battle turning against the Red Riders. Only one Blastidon could barely fit on the narrow ledge.

The forwardmost creature kept stumbling and almost falling off before it got anywhere near the Godless men.

The Blastidon squealed and the Rider raised his axe to strike, but he couldn't swing on his right side closest to the wall. He could only hold his axe and wield it correctly on his left side—the side above the vertical drop-off to the gorge below.

Creed and Rapid struck at the same time. Rapid was much bigger than Creed. The two men switched places the minute they saw the Rider's predicament.

Rapid rotated to the outside, dove in, and raised his kukris above his head to block the Rider's axe swing. The Blastidon couldn't strike both Creed and Rapid at the same time.

Creed flattened himself to the wall and the Rider wound up driving the creature between the two Godless men.

Viking struck between Creed and Rapid at the same time and sank his axe head into the Blastidon's forehead. Creed sprang out of position, slammed his shoulder against the creature's shoulder, and his weight knocked the creature over the side.

The Blastidon would have taken Rapid with it, but he saw the situation unfolding before the Blastidon collided with him. He ducked down into a crouch and threw himself hard against the creature's legs toward the inside of the ledge.

His maneuver knocked the Blastidon's forelegs the rest of the way out from under it. The creature tumbled over him and vanished into open space down the side of the cliff.

Neither Creed, Rapid, nor Viking stood up in time to meet the next Rider. Carnage and Devil were the next two men in line. They met the next Rider before Creed, Viking, and Rapid recovered enough to take on their next victim.

Carnage and Devil had the same size discrepancy between them. Carnage was much shorter and nowhere near as bulky. They didn't have time to change places. Carnage got caught on the outside.

He reacted faster, dropped into a crouch, too, and scooted under the Blastidon's belly.

The path was so narrow and the battleground so confused and choked with combatants already that the Blastidon couldn't do anything to stop him. The creature couldn't even turn around.

Carnage chopped his blade across the thigh muscle of the creature's outer hind leg. The Blastidon shrieked in agony and reared all the way off the ground. Devil charged the creature and shoved it over the side, too.

Carnage barely yanked his blade out in time before the next rider barreled in. This one followed so closely on the second Blastidon's heels that the rider made it past Carnage and Devil completely.

The Rider engaged with Creed, Rapid, and Viking behind Devil's back while the fourth Rider tried to attack Devil and Carnage. Carnage never even got a chance to stand up. He stayed right where he was.

The Rider saw Devil standing up and armed in the middle of the ledge. The Rider tried to attack Devil and Carnage struck again.

The path turned a corner up ahead. Kuvik and Grizzly vanished around it leading the women and children farther away from the battle. Mora wouldn't be able to see the rest of the battle once she turned that corner.

She didn't want to see the rest of the battle. It wasn't even a battle. It was a bloodbath.

All of Hangman's defensive counterassaults on the Red Riders turned into bloodbaths. He used ruthless techniques to wipe them out en masse. He never gave them a chance to fight back. Today was no different.

One Blastidon after another fell over the cliff, never to return. The creatures screeched all the way down. Their Riders bellowed and screamed in terror as their voices faded out of sight into the bottomless chasm. Mora didn't envy those men one bit.

She hurried on her way to put as much distance between her and the Red Riders as possible, but at that moment, a different kind of scream broke out behind her.

She glanced back fearing the worst. Was one of the men going down right now?

She actually froze in her tracks when she saw another flock of Boultars attacking. They swooped through the valley, hurtled toward the cliff face, and snatched Blastidons off the ledge one after the other.

The Godless men surged away to catch up with the women and children. The Boultars completely ignored the Godless. The Blastidons offered too big a target.

The Red Riders' body paint and the Blastidons' bright red armor proved too strong a temptation for the Boultars to resist. They grabbed Blastidons and pulled them off the ledge in rapid succession, but the Boultars didn't try to fly away with them.

The Boultars dropped the Blastidons over the side of the cliff to kill them and eat them later. The Godless raced away in the confusion.

Mora turned the corner. The women and children in front of her made it to the edge of the cliff face. It widened, crossed another much narrower gravel field, and plunged into the jungle.

The women and children burst into a run and the whole band charged down the hill to the safety of the trees.

Chapter 24

T he whole band collapsed in the jungle panting, sweating, and gasping for breath. "I can't believe it!" Carnage choked. "I can't believe it actually worked!"

"What a way to die!" Viking murmured. "I would rather die just about any other way than that. Anything but that."

"The Boultars will eat well tonight," Red remarked in his dry, caustic way.

Hangman got to his feet and looked around. "Let's keep moving. We still have hours to go before dark. We can walk more slowly, now that we're under cover."

The band got moving and made camp that night. The families built fires and got comfortable. Almost everyone went to sleep while Mora and Hangman sat up talking. They were one of the only couples still awake when they both heard hoofbeats in the distance.

Hangman stiffened to listen. So did Mora. "Some of them must have come over the pass." Hangman got to his feet. "Stay here and try to keep everyone calm. I'll be back in a little while."

He didn't explain anything else to her. He darted away into the darkness, found Kuvik lying asleep with his arms around Yoa, and Hangman shook him awake. "Get up, Kuvik," Hangman whispered. "The Red Riders are coming back."

Kuvik's head shot up. He looked around him before he realized what Hangman meant. Kuvik got to his feet. Hangman woke up Red and no one else.

The three friends sprinted away into the trees. The Red Riders had never attacked at night before.

The Godless men had never carried out maneuvers against the Red Riders at night before, either. This would be a first for all of them.

Hangman didn't even have to explain what he wanted to do. The three men vaulted up into the trees and took off at their top speed to intercept the Red Riders.

They made themselves easy to find by riding with blazing torches. The Red Riders must not have been used to traveling at night, either.

Hangman grabbed a thick vine from the nearby undergrowth. He didn't have time to braid it into a rope. He didn't need to.

He pulled the vine across the Red Riders' path and they plowed their Blastidons straight into it. The vine hit the Blastidons in the knees and the first five went down hard.

Another seven following right behind them collided and fell over the first five. The other Blastidons stayed on their feet and the Riders pulled their mounts away from the confusion.

That's when Hangman and his men struck. All three burst out of hiding on either side, tucked, rolled between the Blastidons, and attacked their legs.

Hangman pivoted onto his knees and hacked his kukris into the knees of four different Blastidons before any of the Riders realized what was happening. The Blastidons screeched in pain and caused more havoc among the remaining mounts.

Some of the Red Riders tried to steer their mounts toward the three Godless men to trample or attack them. Hangman and his friends rolled out of the way and took off into the trees to hide in the shadows.

The three men doubled back once they made sure the oncoming Red Riders wouldn't get caught in the chaos. None of the Riders left the safety of their group. They stayed in their own torchlight.

A few Riders stayed on guard for the three Godless to come back, but this didn't last long. The squealing and thrashing of injured Blastidons blocked out any noise the three Godless men might have made blundering around in the woods.

Red, Hangman, and Kuvik rejoined in the undergrowth where they could watch the Red Riders try to straighten out the mess. They'd obviously never dealt with anyone attacking them like this before, especially not in the middle of the night.

Red elbowed Hangman and circled his finger in the air next to his head. Hangman nodded and the three men separated. They surrounded the Red Riders as well as three men could surround such a large group of much stronger, better-armed attackers.

The Godless pulled the same maneuver on them and took down another six Blastidons. The Riders figured out what the Godless were doing, dismounted, and posted more guards, but the damage had already been done.

The jungle's nocturnal creatures moved in on the sounds of struggling Blastidons and men bellowing in pain and rage. Krakelows started falling from the treetops. Hangman and his friends watched from the shadows at a safe distance.

The surviving Red Riders had to pull their uninjured Blastidons away from the wounded. The Krakelows even got to quite a few of the wounded Red Riders before their friends could save them from getting devoured.

The three men waited around for hours, but the Red Riders didn't get ready to leave until morning. They sent half their men back with the wounded.

Those Riders who stayed behind held a discussion about whether they should continue to attack the Godless considering how many devastating ambushes the Godless had wreaked on the Red Rider numbers.

The Red Riders surmised—correctly—that the Godless would continue to pull these maneuvers no matter where they went. Some of the Red Riders argued that they should leave the Godless alone and just let the band go on their way.

Other Riders countered that their Clan's reputation was on the line. They couldn't let some band of stragglers wander onto Red Rider land, kill a bunch of Red Riders, and get away with it.

These men wanted to track the Godless to the ends of the earth and make them pay for their crimes.

Still other Red Riders pointed out that the Godless had wandered onto the Red Riders' land unintentionally. The dead men had attacked an undefended party of women and children.

These Riders pointed out that the Godless had only killed these men to protect their families and that the Red Riders should have thought twice about going after any Godless in the first place.

The Godless had a reputation of their own. They weren't cringing, pacifist weaklings like the Followers.

The Godless were powerful warriors in their own right who could handle their enemies—as they had been doing ever since the Red Riders had started to follow this band.

The discussion turned into an argument that ended with quite a few of the able-bodied Red Riders calling it quits and leaving anyway. Those who wanted to go on were too few to go by themselves, so they wound up leaving, too.

Red, Hangman, and Kuvik watched them out of sight and then returned to the band. "I don't trust them not to come back," Red remarked on the way.

"I don't, either," Hangman replied. "Those who want to continue will just gather enough of their friends who think the same way. Then we'll have exactly the same problem."

"I don't see that we have a choice about continuing to the valley," Kuvik added. "You're right about that."

"I wish I could get everyone to see it that way," Hangman muttered.

"I think it's a good thing that not everyone agrees with you," Red pointed out. "This will give us a chance to flush out any traitors before they really show their hands."

"Something tells me they already are showing their hands," Kuvik countered.

"I agree, but I can't do anything to stop that now," Hangman replied. "I just have to keep going and wait for someone to make his move."

"Who do you think it will be first—Devil or Mule?" Red asked.

"Mule hasn't done anything—not anything as blatant as Devil," Hangman replied.

"Maybe Devil will be too stupid to actually do anything," Kuvik suggested. "Maybe he's just stupid enough to shoot his mouth off as loudly as he can with nothing to back it up."

"I've thought of that," Hangman replied. "We'll see if he took the hint the other night and keeps his comments to himself from now on."

"What will you do if he doesn't?" Red asked.

Hangman shrugged. "I might arrange for him to quietly disappear or I might have to call him out in front of everyone and make him publicly disappear. We can't afford to lose men if we can possibly avoid it. I'll bring him and Mule around if I can. Otherwise, they'll have to go somewhere else."

Chapter 25

Mora looked up from her work when she heard voices yelling across the camp. Zaedi and his boys happened to run past in the jungle at a distance.

The band had been traveling for two years suffering one disaster after another. The Red Riders kept coming, but they were the least of the band's worries.

The trip had taken much longer than anyone could have predicted. The band could barely move without something going wrong.

The journey dragged one inch at a time. The trip took even longer than the journey to the northern mountains and the band didn't have any pregnant women to slow the band down.

The landscape itself seemed to turn against the band. Every mile cost the band way too much time.

The boys had been growing up in the meantime. Everyone did. Hangman and the other men had long ago initiated the four teenage boys. The time was rapidly approaching for Zaedi and his friends to do the same thing.

Maeno had his own friends in the next age bracket down from Zaedi's. The two groups sometimes joined up to go on joint maneuvers, but Zaedi and his boys usually went out with the grown men.

Zaedi, Loso, Kabi, and Zakra stopped there to discuss something. Maeno and his boys came up to their older brothers and got involved in the discussion before both groups left together.

Mora turned back to her work and tried not to think about Zaedi going through initiation. She'd always known she would have to watch her beloved son walk out of her life forever and to meet a man when he came back.

She dreaded the day when Hangman came to her and told her it was time. She didn't want to be one of those mothers who sobbed all over the boy when he left and then sobbed all over the man again when he came back.

She wanted to be happy for Zaedi. He'd been looking forward to this day since....well since forever. He'd been planning his initiation since he was four years old.

She stopped her work when the boys returned. The men came with them. They brought the jointed limbs of a Gorlock with them, left the meat for the women to process, and Hangman came over to Mora.

He put his arm around her back and kissed her. "It's time. Say goodbye to your son."

Her head shot up. Zaedi had a few more weeks before he turned fourteen. Something must have happened to make Hangman decide to go ahead with the initiation now.

She didn't ask what it was. She glanced across the camp. Zaedi stood apart from everyone. He didn't come near her—or anyone—not right away. His eyes locked on her with supernatural power. He didn't look away.

He didn't get emotional. He just broke from everything he had been right up until this moment. He must not have been expecting this, either.

A buzz of excitement went through the camp, especially through his friends. Zaedi was the oldest boy in his age group. The other three boys would have to wait to go through initiation over the next few months.

They wouldn't have to wait years the way Hammer and his men did. These boys could wait three months each and still initiate on their fourteenth birthdays.

In the end, Mora was the one who crossed the camp to where Zaedi stood. He didn't come near her. She hugged him, but he didn't hug her back. He stood there in stiff, wooden silence until she pushed him back and held him at arm's length.

"You'll come home a strong, powerful man of the Godless Clan," she murmured. "I know you will. I'm proud of you and I love you. I'm so happy for you."

His eyes bored into her deepest soul. "Thank you, Mother."

She stroked his cheek once, but he didn't respond. He was already gone. He would only come back as a completely different person.

"You'll be fine with your father and the other men." She heard herself talking for no reason. He didn't need to hear any of this—not from her. "I'll see you when you return triumphant."

He only nodded. He didn't turn his back on her. She had to do it. She had to break away from him, turn aside, and steer him back into the camp to get him walking toward Hangman.

Zaedi joined up with his father and the others. The four youngest men went with them. Loso, Kabi, and Zakra had to stay behind.

They could join hunting and raiding parties, but not this. Initiations were closed to all but grown men. The initiating boy was the only boy allowed to attend.

A group of women gathered around Mora as the men filed out of the camp. Zaedi never looked back.

Mora didn't shed a tear. This moment turned out so differently than she'd ever expected. She expected it to be a lot harder on both her and Zaedi. Now he was just....gone.

Her little boy was gone. She would never call him by his childhood name again. She would almost have to forget it ever existed.

The men vanished into the jungle and everyone else went back to work. She had to do the same thing. The boys and a handful of men stayed behind to guard the camp. The band wouldn't go anywhere until the men returned.

This was just another interminable delay slowing the journey down. If it wasn't this, it would be something else. Something always happened to slow the journey down.

The band kept leapfrogging from one valley system to another and working their way north through the canyon country. Mora didn't have to consult the maps. She and Hangman had already read them enough times to memorize them.

She knew where the band was and how far the party was from making it to the Angler Valley. Hangman had shown the maps to the rest of the band many times. Everyone knew where they were. That didn't help them travel any faster. Nothing could accomplish that.

She joined the other women in cutting up the Gorlock, cooking the meat for everyone in camp to share, and drying the rest. There was always plenty for the band to do.

She tried to put Zaedi out of her mind, but she always wound up thinking about him anyway. Which creature did he choose to fight? Would he get injured? He might come home scared like Cross or Hangman. Zaedi might come home completely unrecognizable.

She could think of worse things that could happen to him. Katha had never acted too concerned about Hangman's scars. Everyone in the band treated them as a matter of course. Everyone had acted that way when Mora met him. No one even saw his scars anymore.

He wouldn't be the first boy to come home marked by his initiation. The men wore their initiation scars with pride. Some like Cross even took their names from their scars.

She had to wait for Maeno and Thena to come back from their own business before Mora gave them their food.

Thena and the other girls usually spent their time helping out the mothers with young children. Thena and her friends had become obsessed with babies and wanted to learn everything about how to take care of them.

The mothers couldn't be happier for all this help. Mora always saw Thena and the other girls carrying the babies around, playing with them, feeding them, helping them fall asleep, or just sitting in one place holding the babies while the mothers worked or bathed.

Mora wasn't one of those mothers anymore. She hardly had to take care of her children at all. Maeno spent all his time away from camp with the other boys. Zaedi wasn't a boy anymore at all.

The sun went down and Mora sat in front of her shelter watching the light go out of the world. Her children didn't come back. She saw them passing back and forth through camp on their own business. They left her to sit alone.

She had to remind herself that Zaedi wouldn't come back. He would build his own shelter after this. He wouldn't live with his parents anymore. She found it hard to believe that he would get married in a few years.

The band would have to travel a long way to take him to the gathering. The band would have to figure out a way to cover that distance more quickly. Maybe they would have to establish a different route—a safer, quicker, less treacherous route.

They wouldn't take pregnant women or mothers with tiny children. They could stay behind in the safety of the band while a small family group traveled faster and more easily.

Mora got ready to go inside her shelter and go to sleep. This would be the first time she'd slept alone in almost fifteen years—ever since she and Hangman first got married.

She sure wished he was here right now. She would have liked to share tonight with him. He was the only person she could share it with because he was these children's other parent.

He wasn't here and he wouldn't be here. He had to initiate Zaedi. She envied Hangman that he got to be there. He got to watch Zaedi fight his most important fight. Hangman got to be one of the first to congratulate Zaedi. Mora wished she could.

She turned around to go inside, but right then, a group of women came up to her. One of them was Celera, Mule's wife. She brought Creed's wife, Etiri, Maniac's wife, Laniza, Devil's wife, Steka, and Grizzly's wife, Turna.

Hangman had allowed Maniac, Devil, and Grizzly to marry on the journey. Maniac wasn't related by blood to Laniza's family. All these people would have had to live alone if Hangman hadn't allowed them to pair off.

Leaving women and girls of childbearing age unmarried was an even more unacceptable state of affairs than allowing them to marry within the band.

Steka and Turna's families had come from the freed Ceon captives or from freed Bounty Hunter captives. None of them was related by blood, either.

The band was too far away from the gathering and already traveling farther north by the day. The band would have had to retrace its route probably for years to take anyone to the gathering. That was going to be a problem in the future.

"Why haven't the men returned yet?" Celera asked.

Mora shrugged. "They might stay out all night for all I know. I wouldn't be surprised. They probably want to celebrate."

Steka cast a concerned glance toward the surrounding jungle. "They should have come back by now."

"I wouldn't worry too much about it." Mora frowned at each of the women's pinched, lined faces. "Why are you worrying about it? The men have stayed out longer than this before."

"You don't understand." The women exchanged glances like they were trying to keep a secret from everyone.

"We were supposed to meet up with them," Turna blurted out. "They were supposed to meet us at a certain point so we could....." She broke off.

A shiver ran up Mora's spine. "So you could what?" she demanded. "What's going on?"

"Hangman....he's going mad exactly the way his father did," Celera insisted. "We keep traveling around and around out here without end. Mule wants to lead everyone back to Hammer's territory. This trip is a disaster."

Mora gulped. "Your men....they actually plan to break away.....?" She thought fast. So Mule, Devil, and his brothers had been planning this behind the scenes all along. How long had they been plotting behind Hangman's back?

Now Hangman was out there alone with these men. Would they actually come to violence to leave the band?

She tried in every possible way to convince herself that Hangman would be okay. All his loyal supporters had gone with him this time.

His brothers had gone with him. He had Red's band with him. Viking was with Hangman and so were the four younger men.

They would protect Hangman. Mule and the others wouldn't be able to do anything against so many.

That must be the reason why Mule kept his plans a secret and didn't tell anyone. He knew he couldn't survive an open confrontation against Hangman, so Mule went behind Hangman's back to plan this.

"Hangman is not mad," Mora insisted. "Everything he says about the valley is true. You've seen all the disasters we've been going through. They could have happened to anyone."

"He said going to Hammer's valley was too dangerous," Etiri pointed out. "This journey has been even more dangerous. He isn't making decisions correctly on behalf of the band. He's putting all of us in danger. How much more do we have to go through before we get to safety?"

"And that's not saying anything about fighting the Anglers once we do get to the valley," Steka pointed out. "We might not even survive that."

Mora compressed her lips and tried not to lose her temper. "I've seen the valley with my own eyes. I agree with Hangman that it's our best option."

"We've been out here too long already," Celera insisted. "You should convince him to give up this plan. The journey back would be long, hard, and dangerous, but at least we would be with other Godless when we got there. We wouldn't be isolated up here by ourselves and in open confrontation against these deadly creatures."

Mora shook her head. "I don't agree with you and I won't say anything to change his mind because I think he is making decisions that are best for everyone. I think you should all use your influence with your husbands to get them to give up this plan. You've all heard what Hangman says. You'll leave the rest of us unprotected if you leave—and that's not counting the danger you'll be bringing to Hammer's band if you go there. I'm sure he won't appreciate that at all."

"He has the Ashtaws to help defend his people against the Red Riders," Turna pointed out.

"And that somehow makes it okay for you to knowingly put his women and children in danger?" Mora lost her temper. "I can't believe I actually have to tell you this. The Red Riders are our problem even if we never meant to antagonize them. Even if you're right and going to Hammer's band would be the best thing for us, then we should deal with the Red Riders on our own before we go anywhere near another band. It would be wrong to make the Red Riders Hammer's problem by asking him to help us. I can't believe any of you would even suggest that."

No one answered her. The women exchanged glances. Some looked at the ground. So there.

She decided to press her advantage. "Think for a second. Just use your brains for two seconds and you'll realize how foolhardy this plan is. You would only take a handful of men with you if you left the band now. That would weaken everyone against the Red Riders and all the other enemy Clans you would encounter on your way south. The Red Riders would overcome the men and take all the women and children as captives—including those of us who stayed behind. You would destroy the whole band. Don't you understand that?"

They still didn't answer, and when she didn't say anything else, they left.

Mora couldn't sleep now to save her own life. She stayed awake all night counting down the seconds until Hangman and the others returned. This was the last thing the band needed now or ever.

Chapter 26

Hangman stopped on the jungle floor and turned to his son, but Zaedi barely saw his father standing right in front of him. "Are you ready, my son?" Hangman asked.

"Yes, Father. I'm ready." Zaedi sounded a million miles away.

"Fight your best fight," Hangman told him. "You're going to be great. I'm proud of you, my son. Always remember that no matter what happens. You'll come out of this victorious and go home a man of our Clan."

Zaedi only nodded and got to work disarming himself. He took off all his weapons except for two battle axes he usually used for fighting. They weren't as big as Viking's huge axes. Zaedi wasn't big enough for them.

He'd fashioned these axes himself out of a different kind of stone than Hangman's kukris. Zaedi's axes weren't lightweight razor glass. He'd made his weapons out of a different kind of extremely sharp, razor flakes taken from these mountains.

Hangman said a few other things that Zaedi didn't hear. Hangman had to stop himself from reassuring Zaedi that he would succeed. Zaedi wasn't here anymore. He was already gone.

Hangman and his men retreated into the canopy. He became aware of Viking and Kuvik sitting extra close to him. Hangman was the anxious father this time. Was he about to watch his oldest son die in combat?

Zaedi turned away. He didn't acknowledge Hangman or any of the other men. Zaedi was all alone against the jungle now—the way it should be.

He set off heading westward. The men followed him through the canopy until he came upon a group of Demonex. Zaedi looked so small compared to them.

The Demonex were too busy gorging on a Stalkion carcass to notice him. Zaedi wouldn't be able to face the whole group and he didn't try. He waited for one enormous male to separate from the group and go down to the stream to drink.

Zaedi sprinted around the Demonex and approached the male from the other side of the stream. Zaedi stepped out of the trees where the Demonex could see him.

Zaedi bared his teeth and snarled in a deadly, feral challenge. The Demonex responded by flaring out all the spikes of his mane and the ridge of bristles stood up down his spine.

Zaedi flexed his knees and raised his axes. The Demonex reacted first, sprang across the stream, and charged Zaedi in a rush of pure muscular power.

Zaedi swung one of his axes and clubbed the creature hard across the side of the skull before the Demonex collided with him. The two combatants hit the ground rolling over and over each other.

Hangman had gotten used to seeing fully grown men go through their initiation fights. Hammer and most of his men had been grown when they initiated as had Kuvik.

These fourteen-year-old boys looked so small and helpless compared to the creatures they fought. The male Demonex completely enveloped Zaedi. He vanished under his opponent's much bigger body.

The Demonex attacked in fury, bowled Zaedi onto his back, knocked one of Zaedi's axes out of his hand, and pinned him there under the Demonex's massive weight.

The Demonex kicked out with his hind feet and scratched Zaedi all over his body. The long, brutal gashes immediately started pouring blood.

The smell of blood sent the Demonex into a murderous frenzy. The creature opened its mouth full of fangs and lunged for Zaedi to maul him to death. Zaedi moved his head out of the way just in time for the Demonex to sink its fangs into his shoulder.

Zaedi roared out in pain. Hangman had to hold onto the branch underneath him to stop himself from rushing down there and pulling his son to safety, but Zaedi wasn't finished yet.

He used the Demonex's close position to hack the creature with his one remaining axe. Zaedi hacked the creature's hind legs to stop it from kicking and then started flailing the Demonex in the head.

Zaedi roared out in battle rage. He pried himself around in the Demonex's grip. The Demonex couldn't move its head or the rest of its body as long as it held Zaedi down with its fangs sunk into his shoulder.

Zaedi reared off the ground as much as he could and delivered one crushing smash of his axe after another into the creature's skull. Zaedi grimaced from the effort and from pure wild rage. He vented all his pain and desperation through his weapons.

The Demonex felt the blows and tried to get away from them. The blows must have stunned the creature. He didn't completely let go of his bite on Zaedi's neck.

The Demonex lunged back and wound up carrying Zaedi with him. Zaedi's weight threw the Demonex off balance and they rolled back the other way.

The stream turned a bend there and the two combatants tumbled down a bank toward it without realizing where they were going. The Demonex lost control of his own weight. He couldn't check himself with Zaedi grappling onto him.

They both landed hard at the bottom of the bank and fell into a puddle of standing water at the edge of the stream. Neither of them could have known it was there and they were both so busy fighting each other that neither of them cared.

The pool turned out to be deeper and bigger than it looked. Both Zaedi and the Demonex plunged into a pit of black mud that submerged them both. The mud covered them from head to foot, but neither of them noticed.

The fall knocked the Demonex's fangs the rest of the way out of Zaedi's shoulder. The combatants broke apart and both of them surged out of the pit to attack each other just as hard. Zaedi bellowed in feral rage and so did the Demonex.

They met in the middle of the pit. Zaedi fought up to his waist in mud, but it didn't slow him down at all. He dove for the Demonex just as the Demonex dove for him.

The creature had to rear onto his hind legs to close with Zaedi. Zaedi took advantage of that position to tackle the Demonex backward into the mud.

They probably would have gone back to rolling and grappling if they'd landed on solid ground. The mud worked in Zaedi's favor. The Demonex submerged with Zaedi on top this time.

He seized a fistful of the Demonex's mane and used it to thrust the creature's head down into the mud. That part of the pit wasn't deep enough to actually submerge the creature.

Zaedi pinned the creature's head up to its ears in mud with its face sticking out where Zaedi could see it. He raised his axe and bludgeoned the Demonex right in the forehead. Hangman heard the skull crack even from this distance.

Zaedi had to wrench his axe free, but he was so out of his mind in frenzied rage that he didn't stop. He pried his weapon loose from the Demonex's cracked skull and nailed the creature again and again. Zaedi bellowed in fury every time he struck.

He hacked all the way through and pulverized the brain completely before he lost all his strength and collapsed to one side. He actually fell into the mud again before he floundered out onto the bank and sprawled there heaving with broken gasps.

Black mud covered him from head to foot. His own blood flowed into the mud and turned it into an even shinier, blacker coating than it already was. It covered his hair, face, body, and loincloth.

He didn't let go of his axe even then. Blood, gore, torn fur, hide scraps, and bone fragments covered his arms past the elbows. He looked like some kind of creature himself.

The men burst out of the trees leaping from branch to branch. They made it out of the canopy long before Hangman could bring himself to move. The men surrounded Zaedi, dragged him to his feet, congratulated him, and dragged the Demonex out of the mud.

The men gave Zaedi a hard time about how awful he looked. They recounted every phase of the fight and how well he'd done against a creature so much bigger than himself.

The men started building a fire and butchering the Demonex to eat. The four youngest men pulled Zaedi toward the stream to wash the mud off so they could start treating his injuries.

He laughed and blushed with pleasure at their attention and praise. He went with them to the stream—and stopped in his tracks when he came face to face with Hangman.

Hangman fought down the urge to get emotional. He would have liked to be one of the men congratulating Zaedi, hugging him, taking care of him, and making a big fuss about his bravery, strength, and determination to win even after he had gotten hurt.

"You're a man of the Godless Clan and your name is Blackjack," Hangman choked. "I couldn't be prouder of you, my son. You brought honor to your Clan, family, and band today. It's a privilege to welcome you into the company of men."

Blackjack had an equally hard time holding himself together. His lips screwed up in knots and tears sprang to his eyes. "Thank you, Father," he rasped. "I never wanted anything but to make you proud of me."

"I am, my son." Hangman allowed himself to squeeze the side of his son's neck, but the blood on the other side of it stopped Hangman from going any further. "Get yourself cleaned up and let's eat."

Hangman let Blackjack go. Hangman's closest friends surrounded him. The older men watched from a distance while the younger men washed all the mud and blood off Blackjack.

The men brought him back to camp, put leaf paste on his injuries, and settled down to cook the meat and brew Gooji juice for him. Kuvik spent the evening hacking six teeth out of the Demonex's mouth.

He charred the extra flesh off the teeth, fashioned handles for them, and made them into six identical blades for Blackjack as a present.

Blackjack copied Kuvik by taking one of the Demonex's claws, tying a piece of string around it, and wearing it around his neck as a trophy.

Blackjack sat next to his father and laughed and blushed with the other men while they told stories about his fight and their own initiations. Too many other people were already talking to Blackjack. Hangman didn't get a chance to say anything. He didn't need to.

Blackjack stretched out on the ground early that night. The men gave him another dose of Gooji juice and he passed out while all the other men sat around talking.

"He's a brave man," Kuvik remarked. "He did very well against such a creature."

"Did you see him when he reared out of the mud?" Red asked. "He went after the Demonex just as fast and hard as the Demonex went after him. That's how Blackjack won—by hitting the Demonex as hard as he did. He would have died if he'd hesitated for an instant. I'll never forget the look on his face. He shot out of the pool like anything. He didn't slacken in the slightest. That's what I call a man."

"Did you see how much bigger the Demonex was?" Viking added. "Fighting a creature that size would be like one of us fighting a Stalkion. It's one thing for a grown man to fight a Demonex, but he's so much smaller."

"He proved himself. That's for certain," Wildling added. "No one can accuse him of taking it easy on himself."

"He'll be unstoppable now," Kuvik remarked. "He's been waiting for this sanction for so long. Now he knows he can go out and conquer as much as he wants to. He doesn't have to hold himself back because he's a boy."

"Since when has he ever held himself back?" Bantam asked. "He's been a monster since the day he was born."

"He held himself back up here." Kuvik tapped his forehead. "He might not have held himself back, but his thinking did. He thought of himself as a boy who could only do the work of a boy. Now that's gone. He'll be even more driven to do the work of a man."

"Good," Hangman interjected. "He deserves it. He's earned the right to come with us and do as we do. He's never let us down yet and he won't start now."

Chapter 27

All the men woke up early the next morning, but Blackjack slept late. No one woke him up to tell him to get moving.

Hangman sent his men out to scout the area and to keep an eye on the band. They packed up the rest of the Demonex meat to take back to the others, but the men didn't take it with them—not yet.

They wouldn't take it home until Blackjack woke up and went with him. It was his kill. He would be the one to deliver it for the women and children to eat when he returned as a man of his Clan.

Hangman stayed behind alone and waited for Blackjack to wake up. He was still so small. Hangman had to stop himself from thinking of Blackjack as a boy.

He looked awfully young lying there asleep with leaf paste all over him. Hangman would have liked to cherish this boy and treat him like a baby. Blackjack's childhood had come and gone so quickly. Hangman didn't want to let it go just yet.

Blackjack woke up pretty soon, groaned, and dragged himself off the ground. He blinked at everything around him. "Where is everyone?"

"They're scouting the area," Hangman replied. "They'll come back in a little while to escort you home."

"You should have woken me up." He looked down and saw the six tooth blades lying there next to his knee. He fingered them for a second. "It's real. It really happened. It's over. I initiated."

"Yes, it happened," Hangman replied. "You acquitted yourself very well. All the men are proud of you."

Blackjack picked up one of the blades and turned it over in his hand. "These are so fine. I can't believe he made these for me."

"You deserve them. You'll get a lot of good use out of them over the years. You're a slayer."

"I thought I was going to die," Blackjack murmured. "I really thought I was going to die."

"We all do. Every man thinks he's going to die during his initiation. That's the whole point."

Blackjack looked up and his eyes widened. "It is? You never told me that."

Hangman shrugged. "The point is that you think you're going to die and you keep fighting. Some come closer than others to really dying and some actually do die. That's the point—that you actually look death in the face and keep fighting. You did that. That Demonex injured you badly—as badly as the Crusher injured me. You got back up and you attacked. That's how you won. You earned your place in the company of men. No one will ever take that away from you and no one will ever doubt your courage again. These injuries will heal. You'll carry the scars for life just like me. You'll wear them with honor as a mark of your victory. That's what initiation is."

Blackjack looked away. "I don't know how to feel about this. I don't know how to feel about calling myself a man. I don't know who I am."

"You'll learn. You'll grow into it. Today is the first day of you being a brand new person. You can't expect to know and understand everything today just like you can't expect to know and understand

everything there is to know about being a man. You've never been one
before. You have to learn that. That's what initiation is. It's the end
of one journey and the start of another." Hangman glanced down at
Blackjack's legs. "Do you think you can walk back to camp? I wouldn't
want one of the men to have to carry you home."

Blackjack snorted and pushed himself off the ground. "That's right.
Threaten me with public humiliation. That will make me walk back
if anything will."

Hangman laughed. The men came back in a little while. Blackjack
put all but one of the tooth blades in his bags. He kept the last one out
and used it to replace the stone knife he always wore in his waistband.

The scouts reported that another party of Red Riders was moving
into the area, but they were still dozens of miles away. They wouldn't
get here for another two days at the soonest.

The band never traveled fast enough to get away from the Red
Riders. The Red Riders always gave the men plenty of lead time to set
up an ambush in one place or another.

Hangman had been telling the truth. He and his men had never
engaged the Red Riders in open combat after that very first time when
Shadow had gotten killed.

Blackjack limped back to camp. He couldn't move any faster than
that and he couldn't move his right arm very well with the fang punc-
tures in his neck, shoulder, and upper chest.

Hangman and Kuvik accompanied Blackjack on the ground. Half
the men carried the Demonex meat. The others traveled through the
branches to keep an eye on the terrain.

The party made it back to the band by noon. None of the men
hurried, especially not Blackjack. He couldn't walk fast and didn't try
to.

The band erupted in noise when he came back and Hangman announced Blackjack's new name. Everyone gathered around exclaiming over his injuries and asking to hear the whole story. He blushed and tried not to look too pleased when the men told about his fight.

So many people crowded around that neither Hangman nor Blackjack noticed anything out of the ordinary at first. Thena, Maeno, Loso, Kabi, Zakra, and all the other boys and girls joined in the crowd to celebrate Blackjack's victory.

Hangman found himself looking around for Mora. Her absence became more glaringly obvious by the second.

Blackjack didn't notice until the crowd parted enough for both Hangman and Blackjack to see her. Hangman knew the minute he laid eyes on her that something was wrong—seriously wrong.

She finally came forward, hugged Blackjack with perfectly dry eyes, congratulated him, and told him again how proud she was of him. She stated in all sincerity that she had never doubted him.

Her flat expression and emotionless voice raised Blackjack's hackles, too. He scowled at her and peered at her extra closely. He knew her too well not to recognize when something was very wrong.

She played it off. The rest of the crowd started cooking up what was left of the Demonex, curing the hide, and talking about Blackjack's initiation. He got swept up in the general commotion.

Hangman had to choose his moment to pull Mora aside where no one would see or overhear them. She came willingly—like she had been waiting all this time to talk to him in private.

"What's going on?" he demanded. "Something happened while I was away, didn't it? Tell me what it was."

"Mule is planning to take his family and a few others back to Hammer's band. They may have been planning to do it yesterday or last night. The women got agitated when the men didn't come back sooner. They made it sound like they planned to leave right after the initiation—like they planned to slip out of camp, meet up with their men, and go."

Hangman's blood started to boil. "Which women got agitated? Which men are involved?"

"Mule, Creed, Maniac, Grizzly, and Devil for certain. I don't know who else. Those are the only women who came to talk to me. I tried to convince them that staying is the right thing for everyone, but they wouldn't listen."

Hangman compressed his lips to stop himself from blowing his stack right then and there. So these idiots were conspiring against him after all. He should have foreseen this—and he did.

What an underhanded trick to wait a whole year before they made their move. They had gone along with Hangman's plan at first. Maybe these conspirators didn't act or even say anything to make it seem like they planned to go along with him forever.

He wouldn't have expected Creed and Maniac to go along with this, but stranger things had been known to happen.

"Do you know their plans?" Hangman asked.

Mora shook her head. "I can't tell you anything more than what I just told you. They planned to meet up with the men. Maybe the women planned to slip out of camp when no one was looking—like by pretending to go fetch water. Then they would meet up in the jungle and leave from there. That's just my guess. I don't know for certain. You would have to ask them."

"I'm not going to ask them!" He heard himself snapping and tried to stop himself from expressing annoyance toward Mora.

She pretended not to notice. "What are you going to do?"

"I'm going to do what I should have done a long time ago." He turned away. "We have to go back out again as soon as everyone gets something to eat. Try to keep an eye on things while I'm gone, okay?"

She nodded and he left her alone. Of course Mule and Devil would be at the heart of this.

Hangman didn't say a word to anyone that evening. He relaxed with his family. Blackjack spent a few hours constructing a new shelter for himself. He held court with his friends and the younger boys. He didn't come back to Hangman and Mora's shelter.

Tonight should have been one of the sweetest nights of their marriage. They should have been able to enjoy it together, but Hangman couldn't even appreciate his own son's victory and rise to manhood. These rotten conspirators robbed him even of that.

The look in Mora's eyes told him she understood, but that only made the insult worse. He had to strike back and he had to be vicious. He couldn't wait around for Mule to take these people away from the band—especially not the women and children.

Hangman might have chosen to be merciful. He might have decided to maneuver these people into staying just so he could keep the men around to help defend the band.

He was all finished playing nicely and giving people chances. He'd been justifying himself to these men for years. He'd given them all the explanations and leeway they could possibly ask for.

Even their women had heard Hangman's explanations for why they had to do it this way. Mora had tried to convince them and it wasn't the first time.

He had no more reason to waste time on them. If they had heard all that and still persisted in undermining him—even going behind his back—then it was time to get rid of these fools once and for all.

He wouldn't let them leave. Their women and children were too valuable. They didn't deserve to die just because their idiot fathers and husbands couldn't think straight.

Creed had daughters Maeno's age. The band would need those girls in later years, especially since Mule's family wasn't related by blood to the rest of the band. Hangman didn't need any traitorous men around, but he wouldn't let the women and children go.

He simmered with rage and resentment all night long. At least Blackjack wasn't around to notice. Hangman's attitude didn't spoil Blackjack's victory.

Maeno and Thena didn't come back to the shelter until much later, so no one noticed Hangman's bad temper—no one except Mora.

Chapter 28

Hangman woke up all his men early the next morning. He woke up Blackjack, too. Blackjack still limped and favored his left arm, but he didn't complain. He brought his weapons and joined the men when they gathered to leave.

Hangman noticed Mule, Creed, Maniac, Devil, and Grizzly taking extra long to part from their wives. They all seemed to have a lot to say to each other all of a sudden.

Breaker didn't join them once Devil and Grizzly finally showed up. Breaker scowled at his brothers' delay. He acted as annoyed as everyone else that these men were slowing the whole party down.

Breaker wasn't married, so he didn't have a wife who could have spoken to Mora while the men were away at Blackjack's initiation. Hangman didn't know if Breaker was involved in the plot to abandon the band.

Hangman couldn't take the chance that Breaker might be one of the conspirators, but Hangman also couldn't retaliate against a man who might still be loyal.

Breaker had never spoken against Hangman—ever. Breaker had never doubted—not even once. He hadn't been Hangman's most vocal supporter, either, but Hangman could think of a dozen other men who hadn't spoken out in his favor. That didn't make them disloyal.

Hangman needed every able-bodied man he could get right now, so he took Blackjack's three uninitiated friends with the party, too.

Hangman threw caution to the wind and took Maeno and the younger boys, too. They needed to start moving up the ranks so they would be ready for initiation when the time came.

Most of them were as bold and skilled as Blackjack and his friends. Maeno and most of his friends were already eleven or twelve. They were old enough to get involved.

Hangman knew the boys were loyal. They were some of the most loyal members of his band. He would need them once he got rid of Mule and the others.

He assigned three older men from Red's party to supervise these boys on the march farther north toward the valley.

All the other men moved out and joined up with a scouting party that had located the incoming Red Riders. They were still far enough away for the Godless to ambush them.

Hangman stopped the party in a narrow draw leading up to one of the passes. The Red Riders had to travel through multiple valleys and cross a bunch of passes before they got to the valley in which the Godless had camped.

This was the exact problem that had been slowing the band down all these many long months. The countryside proved more treacherous than it seemed.

"The Red Riders will come this way to get to the pass." He pointed at the canopy overhead and at the jungle on both sides of the pass. "We'll set up our ambush here and come at them from both sides. Mule, Creed, Maniac, Grizzly, and Devil—you stand guard here. The

Red Riders will stop to confront you. That's when we'll spring our ambush on them."

Mule and the others stiffened, but they didn't show any sign that they suspected anything wrong.

Breaker grimaced in disgust, not just at Mule's family, but at his own brothers. He must have realized all along what they planned to do.

They may even have tried to recruit him to join in the plot. It sure looked to Hangman like Breaker expected and even approved of Hangman taking steps to eliminate these men.

Hangman split up the rest of the party. The simple fact that he had to take time out of his own mission to deal with these traitors gave him all the fuel he needed.

He had so many more important things to worry about. These men only made the band's situation more precarious than it already was. They deserved to die for that alone.

He divided the band in two. One party went one way and the other party went the other way. Hangman's group traveled deep into the jungle until they found another army of ants. The men gathered pollen and got the ants to follow.

The Godless only used a small amount of pollen so the ants would march faster to get to it all. The men kept increasing the ants' speed until the men had to run to keep ahead of them.

Blackjack and the younger scouts raced through the branches overhead. These men ran back and forth between the ants and the pass to deliver the message about how fast Hangman should be going.

He left the ants to his men, clambered up to join with the younger men, and charged ahead to see what was happening. Kuvik and another group of scouts headed another matching army of ants approaching the pass from the other side.

Both groups timed the ants' approach and even slowed the ants down so they didn't come on so fast. The Red Riders charged into the area and came face to face with Mule and the others blocking the way.

Hangman didn't want to watch the impending slaughter, but he did it anyway. These men's deaths were on his hands. The Red Riders charged their Blastidons at the five men, ran down Maniac right away, and then got into a furious battle against the remaining Godless.

Mule couldn't defend himself against so many much bigger, stronger, better-armed attackers. Three Red Riders teamed up on him and their Blastidons trampled him.

Creed, Grizzly, and Devil moved together, but that only made them easier targets. The Red Riders took down all three of them in no time—just in time for the ants to show up.

The men leading the ants raced into the area, threw the last of their pollen on the ground around the Blastidons' feet, and the Godless shot away into the treetops. The ants swarmed the Blastidons and pulled men and beasts down to the ground in seconds.

The whole party vanished under a tide of ants. The ants erased every last trace of the battle, including the Godless men standing guard to block the pass.

Their screams faded to nothing. Hangman turned to Breaker in the canopy. "Tell me you had nothing to do with this. Tell me you weren't planning to join this stupid conspiracy."

Breaker made a face that turned into more of a spasm. He looked away. "Devil and Grizzly tried to get me to go along with it. I couldn't tell you. I'm sorry. I know you'll say I should have and you're right, but I couldn't turn on my own brothers. I couldn't go that far—and they kept talking about it and never doing anything about it for a whole year. I hoped they would give up the idea, but they didn't. I....I guess I didn't know what to do. I couldn't win no matter what I did, so I did nothing."

"You've never spoken against me, Breaker," Hangman went on. "I want to believe you're loyal. We're five men down. We need you too much, but we need everyone working together even more. I need to know you're with us."

Breaker shrugged. "I don't see that we have much choice anymore, do we? We can't go back. I guess we aren't doing too badly out here—not as badly as we might be. It isn't easy and we don't make very good progress, but it's better than nothing. Going ahead is the best of all the bad options. That's the way I see it."

Hangman nodded. "I can accept that. Please don't make me regret this in the future."

"You won't." Breaker looked up and made eye contact with Hangman for the first time. "What are you going to do with the women—Mule's women, I mean? What are you going to do with Steka and Turna?"

"They'll stay in the band. They'll be free to remarry as soon as they're ready." Now Hangman was the one who frowned. "I'm only going to say this once, Breaker. You'll only be free to marry one of these women if they agree willingly—and that means you have to behave according to the law beforehand. I'll have no choice but to bar you from marrying at all if you break the law even once. Is that clear?"

Breaker looked away. Neither he nor Hangman had to explain any more explicitly than that. "Yeah, it's clear," Breaker mumbled.

"Let's get back to the band," Hangman ordered. "I don't like leaving the women and children unguarded."

Chapter 29

Mora glanced right and left. The uninitiated boys and a few men guarded the column of women and children hiking up the valley toward another pass in the distance.

Maeno occupied one of the places out there in the party of guards. He didn't walk near Mora anymore. He kept going back and forth to coordinate with the men and other boys about any potential threats in the area.

His absence gave Mora all the time in the world to think her own thoughts. She spent a lot more time alone these days when Hangman wasn't around. This was the most time she'd spent alone in her life.

She really couldn't wait for Blackjack to get married so she could have some grandchildren to help take care of. She needed a baby or young child to give her something to do and someone to take care of.

She wouldn't even have minded if Blackjack married a Follower girl. Mora would have liked to share that with another girl who had to leave her family to join a strange Clan.

Mora would have liked to be the mother-in-law the girl needed her to be. Katha had been the mother-in-law Mora needed her to be, but Mora wouldn't be so hard on the girl.

That would probably never happen. Blackjack would probably marry a Godless girl who already knew everything she needed to know.

Mora shouldn't even have been thinking about that right now. Blackjack wouldn't get married for another four years at the earliest.

He might not get married at all. He might go all the way south to the gathering and come home emptyhanded. He might be one of those many men who lived their whole lives alone.

Mora didn't think she could stand that, but she wouldn't be able to say anything about it. She had nothing to say about any of it anyway. She had nothing to say about who Blackjack married or which Clan the girl came from.

Movement caught Mora's eye just then. She looked up to check the position of the boys standing guard. That's when she noticed a bunch of other women talking with their heads together across the column from her.

Celera, Etiri, Laniza, Steka, and Turna leaned in close, exchanged a few words, and then faced front like they weren't doing anything wrong. They *weren't* doing anything wrong—not yet—but they obviously planned to.

All five of them kept glancing over their shoulders at the terrain behind the band. Everyone else in the group checked on both sides. Those five were the only women who looked behind them.

Yoa walked over there on that side of the column. She carried her two-year-old daughter, Uzima, in her arms while her four-year-old son, Danimi, walked next to her and held her hand.

Mora had gotten into the habit of helping Yoa and Kuvik as much as possible. Yoa had no other living relatives in the band, so Mora had adopted her as a surrogate daughter-in-law. Yoa and Kuvik welcomed all the help they could get, so everyone won in the end.

Yoa caught Mora watching the other women and Yoa made a face. Mora went over there just in time to hear Danimi complaining about being tired.

Mora picked him up and swung him behind her to carry him piggyback. That satisfied him. "Thank you," Yoa murmured.

Mora shot the five women a look. "Have you heard anything interesting?"

"Oh, yeah," Yoa replied. "It would be pretty hard to miss it."

The two women fell silent. Danimi rested his head against Mora's back and fell asleep there. She didn't have a wrap to tie him on, so she held him up with her arms.

The five women started talking again. Yoa was right. The women tried to keep their voices down, but they spoke in murmurs loud enough for Mora to overhear their conversation.

"How long should we wait?" Laniza asked.

"We shouldn't wait too long," Etiri pointed out. "Every minute takes us farther away from meeting up with the men."

"They could be coming to meet us," Celera suggested. "They could already be finished dealing with the Red Riders. The men could be coming this way. Then we wouldn't have to go very far to meet with them."

"How would we know?" Turna asked. "Mule didn't say when we should leave. He just said we should leave sometime on the march and rendezvous with them."

"Should we do anything?" Yoa murmured in Mora's ear.

"Like what—tie them up and carry them the rest of the way to the Angler Valley?" Mora countered. "I don't see that we can do anything to stop them from leaving if they really want to. That would make them our captives."

Yoa sighed. "I guess so."

The five women went back to walking without talking. They spent the next two hours pretending everything was fine and they weren't planning to run away from the band any second now.

Danimi woke up in a little while and wanted his mother to carry him. Mora tried to distract him by sitting him on her hip and offering him food, but he wouldn't listen, so she and Yoa switched. Yoa took Danimi and Mora carried Uzima for a little while.

She was a delightful little girl with a beautiful, glowing, friendly, cheery personality. She was the apple of her father's eye and everyone loved her to pieces, including Mora.

Mora entertained herself by making faces and getting Uzima to laugh. Then she got hungry, so Mora gave her food. Uzima didn't care who the food came from. She ate it anyway.

"You really need a daughter-in-law, Mora," Yoa told her. "You need grandchildren."

Mora laughed and blushed. "You can be my adopted daughter-in-law and Kuvik can be my adopted son-in-law."

"I'm pretty sure we already are."

"I can practice on you in the meantime." Mora cut herself off when the five women started whispering again. They kept getting more agitated by the minute. They wouldn't stop looking around everywhere.

The women couldn't get away without the nearby boys seeing them. That was the only thing stopping them, but in a little while, the boys reconvened to go check something again. They left that side of the column free.

The five women broke out of line to run for it. Mora and Yoa both jumped in front of the women to block them. "Don't you dare leave the band now!" Yoa snapped. "Don't you realize you're putting all of us in danger?"

"Hangman is the one putting us all in danger with this insane plan of his!" Celera countered. She grabbed her daughters-in-law and pulled them forward. "Get out of the way! You have no right to keep us here!"

Mora and Yoa had no choice but to let them go, but Mora didn't want to give up so easily. She dumped Uzima hand back into Yoa's arms and raced away to the other side of the column.

She found Butch and Lock consulting with Loso, Kabi, Maeno, and Zakra about something.

"Five of the women are breaking away to leave the band!" Mora blurted out. "They're going to join up with their men and head south to return to Hammer's territory!"

All the men and boys spun around fast. "Show us where they are!" Butch ordered.

Mora hustled back to the column and pointed out the five women getting farther away in the distance. They headed straight south down the valley toward the pass leading to the next valley.

Butch ordered the boys back to the column while he and Lock took off to catch up with the women. The men overtook the women in no time and another argument broke out. The party was too far away to hear exactly what Butch said to them.

The women must have used the same argument on the two men. The women split away and took off south again in the same direction. Lock burst into a run, raced ahead, and made it to the pass long before them.

Butch stayed with the women and accompanied them all the way. Mora could just imagine how this would go when Lock found Hangman and told him what was going on.

Hangman wouldn't be able to stop Mule and the others from leaving, either. They could all just claim they had a right to leave whenever they wanted to—which they did.

Mora thanked her lucky stars she wouldn't be around to deal with Hangman when it happened. He would be absolutely livid.

Mora turned back to the column. The situation had brought everyone else to a standstill while all the women and children watched the unfolding disaster.

No one got moving even after Butch and the women disappeared into the trees on their way up to the pass.

"Let's keep going," Mora ordered. "We need to make as much progress as we can before the men come back. You boys get back into position. We need you ready if anything happens."

Everyone obeyed her. She left Yoa alone with the children while Mora went up to the front of the column. She got everyone to follow her and then paced back and forth through the whole band encouraging and helping anyone who needed it.

The boys patrolled the way they did before. They organized their own scouting parties to check the area. They kept as close a watch on the surroundings now as they did when Butch and Lock were here to supervise.

Nothing else happened for the rest of the day. The band didn't make any other stops until Mora called a halt at sundown. The band started making camp.

Her gaze kept migrating behind her toward the southern pass. Hangman and his men would come back from there any second now. Then all hell would break loose if it hadn't already.

Chapter 30

H angman and his men met up after running a bunch of different scouting trips all around the area. He sent different groups
of men to different valleys and passes in the area.

He also sent a scouting party north to the valley the women and
children would be traveling through right now. He didn't predict that
they would cross another pass today—not at the speed they usually
traveled.

He opened his mouth to give new orders to his men when a crash of
breaking branches interrupted him. Everyone looked up to see Lock
hurtling down through the canopy to intercept them.

"What are you doing here?!" Hangman demanded. "You should be
back with the band. You better not have left the women and children
unguarded."

"Women....Mule....Mule's women....." Lock panted. "Breaking a
way.....they left the band.....on their way south....right now.....Butch
is with them.....the boys.....are back with the band....I just came to tell
you.....The women are heading over the pass right now......I gotta get
back....."

Hangman gripped his shoulder. "You did right to come and tell me.
Go on back and take Butch with you. I'll intercept the women and
......"

Another commotion interrupted him when another scouting party returned just then from a valley to the east. Carnage, Bantam, and one of the younger men dropped down on Hangman's other side.

"There's another party of Red Riders moving up through the eastern valley!" Bantam reported. "It looks like they're coming in multiple prongs to flank us from more than one direction. It looks like they're heading for the pass up there and planning to ambush us there."

He pointed at the pass behind Hangman—the pass Lock had just said Butch and the women were about to cross.

Hangman and his men spun away. No one had time to discuss what they would do or how they would do it.

The men charged away. They couldn't travel through the canopy for more than a hundred yards before the trees ended. The men raced along the ground to get to the pass in time. They crested the rise—and stopped there.

Hangman stopped in his tracks when he saw the Red Riders surround the party of women and children from Mule's family group.

The Red Riders were just in the act of cutting Butch down to the ground with their axes. He was the only man around to stand guard over the women.

Hangman's mind went into a tailspin. The Red Riders were too far away. They stood out there in the wide open and they had brought too many men. Hangman and his men wouldn't be able to do a thing to stop the enemy from taking these women and children.

Hangman and his men would have lost their lives if they tried. That would leave the rest of the band defenseless. Butch was already dead. Hangman couldn't do anything to stop that now.

He couldn't do anything to stop the Red Riders from throwing the women and children across their mounts and riding off with them.

The captives' screams echoed far and wide across the area. All the men stood and stared as the Red Riders headed off toward the south.

Hangman waited a lot longer than he should have. A thousand ideas raced through his mind and collided in a storm of different possible responses to this. Butch was dead along with Mule, Creed, Maniac, Grizzly, and Devil.

Today would go down in history as one of the worst days of Hangman's life—and it wasn't over yet.

He finally set off hiking down the hill and eventually burst into a run on his way back to the band. The women and uninitiated boys gathered to meet the men when they returned.

Everyone could see that Butch was gone. His wife started wailing her head off. Kabi and Zakra both fought back despair. Zakra eventually let tears streak down his cheeks, but he never left his post.

Hangman stormed through the camp glaring at everyone. "I hope you're all happy!" he roared. "Six men are dead out there and seven women are captives along with the same number of children! Are you all starting to take this a little more seriously now?! Do you think the men and I have been out there risking our lives for the fun of it?! The Red Riders could have taken the whole band! Do you realize that?! They could have put all the men and boys to the sword! Then all of you would be on your way into captivity right now! What will it actually take to get you all to pull your heads out of the clouds and start acting like a real band?! Huh?! What will it actually take?!"

No one answered him. No one made a sound.

He didn't stop pacing up and down. His eyes flashed and he curled his lips back from his teeth in a hideous snarl. "If any of you is even thinking about leaving, go ahead and do it right now! No one will stop you. You can find your way back south and good luck to you. Just walk away and leave now before you put the rest of us in danger, too. I won't tolerate any of you doing that—so just leave now. Go on. Go!"

No one budged. No one even breathed. Hangman had no plans to soften the blow.

"Now I have to divide our fighting men into even smaller groups to try to get these women and children back—and don't let me hear any of you suggest that we leave them to their fate," he went on. "I'm sure you would be singing a different tune if you and your children were the ones who had gotten captured. We're going after them—which means we'll have to leave fewer men and boys behind to guard everyone. I hope you're all happy now!!"

Hangman turned back to his men and divided them into two groups. He took his brothers, Red, Viking, and Red's remaining men. They didn't have many left, but they were the most experienced fighting men that Hangman had.

He left everyone else behind. "I'm putting Blackjack and Mora in charge. They know the way to the Angler Valley, how to get into it, and how to deal with the Anglers once you do get inside. The rest of you men will be responsible for guarding the party, but Blackjack and Mora will make the decisions about where the band goes, how you travel, and what you do. Keep going to the valley. Don't wait for us to get back. Get inside the valley and start eliminating the Anglers as best you can. We'll catch up as soon as we can."

He didn't want to wait around to discuss the situation any further. This situation couldn't possibly get any worse.

He and his men took off running into the night and left the band behind. Hangman didn't want to think about the band anymore. He wanted to get the captive women and children back as quickly as possible and return.

He and his men returned to where the Red Riders had killed Butch and captured the women and children. The men took a few minutes to lift Butch into the canopy, build a small platform for him, and to stand over his body in silence for a minute.

Hangman would have liked to say a few words over him, but Hangman didn't want to step on Red's men's toes. They'd known Butch all their lives and traveled all the way south with him to Renegade country before they met up with Hangman.

Red and his men didn't say anything, so Hangman and the others didn't say anything, either. In the end, Red was the one who turned away first and said, "Let's go," to the others.

The men left Butch there. He wouldn't be going on this mission with his brothers this time. He would never go out with them again. What a senseless waste of a perfectly good man.

The Red Riders' Blastidons had left a highway of hoofprints for the Godless to follow even in the dark. Hangman and his men had no trouble tracking the Red Riders, but the Godless didn't track the Red Riders—not yet.

Hangman led his men into one of the western valleys and scouted around until they found a different party of Red Riders coming up from the south. Bantam was right. The Red Riders were invading multiple valleys at once to try to get the jump on the Godless.

Hangman and his men searched the area until they found a group of Crushers hunting in the jungle. The men ran in front of seven and got the creatures to chase them.

The men sprinted back to intercept the Red Riders. The Blastidons panicked when they noticed Crushers charging toward them.

The Red Riders had to work their hardest to control their mounts—and then the Godless burst out of the undergrowth right in front of the Blastidons. The Godless streaked past the Blastidons and led the Crushers straight into the party of Red Riders.

The Crushers finished off mounts and riders in a few tasty mouthfuls while the Godless fled. The men spent the rest of the night locating and ambushing every other Red Rider group in the area.

"Why are there so many of them now?" Lock asked. "They're making a much stronger effort to catch up with us."

"They must be sending out a much bigger force," Hangman agreed. "These forward parties are just the first crest of the wave. They'll keep pushing forward until they catch up with us. They close the gap every time we stop."

"So what's the solution?" Bantam asked.

"Let's track the captives. The Blastidons are bound to lead us straight to the Red Riders' main force."

Chapter 31

H angman and his men crouched in the branches and looked down at another camp in one of the canyon country's many valleys. This camp was much bigger than any Godless camp.

The Red Riders had constructed round tents out of the same armored hides the Red Riders used to make their clothes and their Blastidons' trappings. The tents reminded Hangman of Thumion's tent in Ceon.

In fact, the whole Red Rider camp reminded Hangman of Ceon, but the resemblance ended there. The Red Riders had brought a whole army of captive-slaves with them.

Hangman and his men observed the Red Riders for a long time to try to understand their ways. The Red Riders brutalized their captives as badly as the Bounty Hunters did, but the Red Riders didn't do it as systematically as the Bounty Hunters did.

Hangman and his men saw the Red Riders bringing in new captives from multiple directions. The Red Riders didn't give everyone the usual introductory beatings. The Red Riders didn't seem to go around beating people for no apparent reason, either.

The Red Riders did use the men for hard labor. The Red Riders beat anyone who resisted, talked back, or tried to escape.

Hangman didn't see any women or children with bruises. He saw something much, much worse. Almost every woman here was pregnant.

The Red Riders kept chains locked around the women's ankles and wrists with the shackles attached by a short chain.

The chain allowed the women to walk in short, halting steps and to use their hands for certain kinds of work. The women were all obviously captives.

The disheveled, haggard, hunted look on every woman's face told Hangman loud and clear exactly what the Red Riders wanted these women for. He didn't see them doing any kind of manual labor—not the way they did with the Bounty Hunters.

He didn't see a single woman anywhere who wasn't visibly pregnant. The whole camp looked like a giant baby farm dotted with Red Riders here and there.

The Red Riders made a habit of handling any woman they chose whenever they chose. A woman being pregnant to bursting didn't stop the Red Riders from mauling her right out in public where anyone could see.

The Red Riders seemed to take special pride and delight in doing it in public. They usually laughed, applauded, and encouraged any of their brethren who did it, especially if it made the woman cry, scream, or struggle.

Lock turned away in disgust almost as soon as the Godless saw what was happening. "I can't watch this," he husked. "Tell me when you want me to do something."

He plugged his ears so he wouldn't hear the women screaming in the distance. Bantam watched a little longer before he moved away in the branches, too.

Hangman told himself not to look, but he couldn't look away. He somehow needed to see just how bad it was so he would be able to go through with this.

He and his men kept the camp under surveillance for twenty-four hours to find out the Red Riders' routine. The Red Riders slept at night and operated during the day—most of the time.

More Red Riders kept coming into the camp and going out of it. Some of these parties brought in fresh captives. Others didn't. Some brought in food or other goods they must have stolen from other bands.

"How do you want to do this?" Red asked on the second day.

"We need to come up with some other ambush," Wildling pointed out. "Something that won't put the women and children and other captives in danger."

"That rules out setting the tents on fire," Viking remarked.

"They have too many fighting men," Hangman began. "We can't engage them in open battle—not now. We need to reduce their numbers first."

"How do we do that?" Bantam asked. "It would take all of us working together to take down even one of those men. They're twice our size."

"They're distracted," Hangman replied. "It seems to me they're parading around their greatest weakness right here in front of us."

Red frowned. "How do you mean?"

"All these women. These men have a thing for women. None of them can go five minutes without getting their hands on some woman. I bet you every man in that camp takes a woman to bed with him every night. They have no reason not to. The men can do whatever they want with these women and the women don't dare to fight back. They can't. The men keep all the captives chained and unarmed."

"How does that help us?" Lock asked.

Hangman grimaced at him. "You're too young to have a wife of your own, brother, but take my word on this one. These men will be so distracted by their women that the men won't be able to fight anyone or even look around them to see if someone is about to attack."

Wildling rubbed his chin. "That's very interesting. I never thought of that."

"I say we take them one man at a time while their backs are turned and their pants are down. We'll wait until nightfall, get inside their tents, and take each man one at a time. We'll remove the women one at a time, too—or however many we find in each tent."

"That will tip off the others," Viking pointed out.

"I'll bet you anything they still won't be able to resist taking a woman to bed with them even knowing the enemy is hanging around. I bet you anything we'll still be able to do it. The Red Riders will post a guard around the perimeter so every other man in the camp can go home and enjoy himself without having to worry about anything."

Viking smirked and shook his head. "I know better than to bet against you, brother—especially about something like this."

"How will we take out the guards around the perimeter?" Lock asked.

Hangman shrugged. "We can ambush them and take them down first if we have to. Otherwise, we can just slip past them and carry out our attacks the same way. We'll just keep doing it until we eliminate them all—or until we remove all the captives. Once we do that, we can spring one of our more destructive ambushes to wipe out everyone left behind."

That decided it. The men relaxed until nightfall and then a little longer until full dark set in. Then the men separated to surround the Red Riders' camp.

The Red Riders confirmed Hangman's suspicions as soon as the sun went down and screams started echoing through the camp from almost every tent.

Hangman tiptoed to the nearest tent and peeked inside. The man whose tent it was knelt naked on his bed with a captive woman in front of him. She was already heavily pregnant, naked, and chained hand and foot.

Hangman couldn't enter through the main tent entrance without the Rider seeing him. Hangman snuck around the other side of the tent, crawled under the flap, and killed the guy from behind. His body fell over on the bed.

The woman spun around and started to scream. Hangman pounced on her, covered her mouth, and whispered low. "Be quiet! I'm here to take you away from the Red Riders. Keep quiet and I'll take you somewhere safe!"

She didn't make another sound after he let her go. She started crying, but she did it silently. He hunted around and eventually settled on wrapping her in a blanket from the dead Rider's bed.

Hangman led the woman out into the shadows and hid her in the jungle. "Stay here," he whispered. "I'm going back inside for someone else. I'll be right back. Okay? Don't try to run away. The chain will make too much noise."

She nodded and he left her alone. He worked fast for hours and brought seven women out of the camp, each one wrapped in a blanket and silently sobbing their eyes out.

They hugged each other and huddled in the dark until he rejoined them. He found a key to their shackles in one of the dead Riders' clothes.

Hangman squatted down in front of the women and tried to look at all of them at once. He'd never seen any more miserable women.

"I'm going to take you to a safe band," he told them all. "You're free now. You never have to go back, but I need you to do exactly as I say. Okay?"

"Thank you!" one of them sobbed. "Thank you so much!"

"Hush now." He got to work unshackling them. He had to look around before he found his brothers and friends.

They had all taken captive women out of the camp. The men amassed a huge group right outside the camp. "We can't stay here," Red pointed out. "The Riders will find us and retake us."

Hangman nodded and led everyone a mile away where the men helped the women climb into the canopy. The women didn't know how to climb and them being so heavily pregnant made the situation worse.

They did it in the end and eventually got to a place where the Red Riders wouldn't be able to recapture them.

The men spent the day catching up on sleep, giving the women as much food and water as the men could spare, and reassuring them all that they would be safe and no one would harm them after this.

The women wouldn't stop crying and continually expressing their gratitude over and over again. They wouldn't be quiet about it even when Hangman told them not to mention it anymore.

Hangman and the other men went on another killing spree the next night. Hangman's predictions came true again. The Red Riders posted guards around the perimeter, but they left enough gaps for the Godless men to get in and out easily.

Hangman worked faster this time, took more risks, and freed three times as many women. He also freed a dozen men.

Taking them out of the camp at the same time made it quicker and easier than removing the captives one at a time. He led them all out into the shadows, left them with other captives, and returned to steal a bunch of food supplies from the tents.

The party rejoined in the hidden canopy. The first group of captives welcomed the newcomers. The place was turning into a much larger band than any of the men could have predicted.

"I say we arm some of these men, go back in, and wipe out any Red Riders still alive," Red suggested.

"Okay, I agree with you, brother, but I don't want to send pregnant women into battle, not even against the Red Riders," Hangman replied. "Let's go back in tonight and concentrate on freeing as many men as we can plus stealing all the weapons we can carry. I'm sure the men will be happy to kill the Red Riders. Then we can free the rest of the women, raid the place for supplies, and leave."

The rest of Hangman's men agreed. They also discussed the situation with the freed captive men. They got over-the-top excited about taking revenge on the Red Riders and freeing all the women left behind.

Hangman and his men carried out their last raid and freed every male captive they could find.

The Godless went from tent to tent of all the Red Riders they'd already killed, gathered up every random weapon the men could lay their hands on, and took everything back out to the jungle.

No one slept the following day. Tension and excitement ran high among all the freed captives, both male and female. The women wanted to do things to help the Godless men at least run their camp, but the women didn't know how to do anything in the canopy.

Hangman and his men tried to explain things, but they had to pay attention to preparing for the battle. The Godless men hardly had to tell the freed men anything. They were all so hot to kill the Red Riders. The freed already knew what to do.

Hardly anyone could wait for the sun to go down. Hangman felt his nerves getting the better of him. He had to go off by himself more than once just to get away from the freed captives' electric energy.

The time finally came and Hangman spread all the freed men equidistant around the camp. He gave them orders not to invade until he and his men eliminated the guards. Then the freed men would use stealth and silence to enter each tent and kill the Red Riders inside.

The party agreed not to remove any women or children until the men executed every Red Rider in the whole camp. The freed men agreed to this. They agreed to every part of Hangman's plan.

Hangman had no choice but to trust these men. He would have preferred not to just charge into open battle against the Red Riders no matter how much the freed men might want payback.

The freed men didn't show themselves or even make a sound when he and his men slipped out of the shadows, hid behind certain tents, dragged the guards into the dark, and cut their throats. That left the way clear for the freed captives to invade.

They played their part to the letter, raced from tent to tent, and killed as many Red Riders as they could as silently as they could.

The party converged on the center of the camp, but some noise of scuffle inevitably broke out. A few of the captive women screamed when they saw armed men invading the tents and killing everyone.

These screams mingled with the camp's general noise, but it eventually and inevitably tipped off the surviving Red Riders. They armed themselves and came out in force to defend their camp, but it was already too late.

The army of freed captives had already eliminated too many Red Riders. The freed men moved in for the kill. Hangman and his men retreated while the freed men encircled their former oppressors and herded all the Red Riders into one cluster.

The Red Riders didn't last long after that. The freed men went through the camp releasing and unchaining all the remaining women and children. The Godless brought in the women they'd already freed.

The Godless men found Mule's wife, daughters-in-law, and Devil's and Grizzly's wives in the crowd. All five went into hysterical fits of weeping when they realized who it was who had freed them.

"You're all free to return to your own Clans and families if you want to," Hangman announced to the whole crowd. "We'll take anyone who wants to go north with us to rejoin our Godless band. You'll be safe and protected there. No one will harm you. You can give birth to your children there, marry if you want to, and raise your children in peace. These children will be welcome in our Clan as naturally born Godless. No one will hold their origins against them or yours. No one will ever mention it again. You have my solemn word on that."

The women exchanged glances. "We have nowhere else to go," one woman replied. "The Red Riders wiped out most of our family bands. We're alone. We would be stranded without you."

Hangman nodded. "You're all welcome to come with us. I just need you to arm yourselves and prepare to defend yourselves and your families as much as possible. Traveling with so many pregnant women will be hard. We'll need everyone to work together to protect ourselves."

Everyone agreed. The freed captives went through the camp and ransacked the place for everything they could find of any value. They took weapons, food, and clothes for themselves and their children.

Hangman eventually moved out a crowd of a hundred and fifty people including forty men and two dozen children. The rest were all pregnant women. Celera, Etiri, and Turna were the only women present who weren't pregnant.

"At least we don't have to guard all of them by ourselves," Viking remarked on the way back north. "These men are hardy and willing. It's good to see."

"They'll make good Godless men," Hangman agreed. "I just hope it doesn't take us too long to rejoin the band. I hope everyone is all right and not in danger."

Chapter 32

B lackjack glanced over his shoulder at the long line of Godless women and children stretched out behind him. His mother Mora walked at Yoa's side near the middle of the line.

She didn't step out of place to start taking over the band his Hangman's place. She showed no sign that he'd left her in any position of authority.

Blackjack faced front just as Loso, Kabi, and Zakra came up to him. "The western valley is clear," Loso reported. "We traveled all the way down to the southern pass. The Red Riders aren't there. No one is there."

"Here comes Oracle's group," Blackjack replied. "They can tell us if anyone is pursuing us from the south."

Oracle ran up to the party from the left and stopped in front of Blackjack. Oracle and his three friends had been the group of young men to initiate before Blackjack.

Oracle's three friends were named Pyro, Smash, and Chief. For some reason Blackjack couldn't figure out, all four of them had started treating him as their Kral ever since Hangman had departed with the other men.

"The south is clear," Oracle reported. "We'll wait a few hours and then go back out to check again. We planned to search it every few hours just in case."

Blackjack nodded. "Take Pyro and Smash to do that. Chief, I want you to follow the Blastidon track away from the place where the Red Riders killed Butch. I want you to send one man along that track just as often as you search the southern route to make sure no one is coming from that direction."

"Good idea," Chief replied. "I didn't think of that."

"Has anyone seen Maeno and the boys?" Blackjack asked.

"We just got back," Oracle replied. "We haven't seen anyone but you."

"We saw them on that ridge over there." Kabi pointed behind him toward the west. "They were still climbing. I guess they haven't crossed the pass yet."

"That's all right. They'll be okay." Blackjack surveyed the men and boys in front of him. "Do any of you feel like going hunting or do you want to kick back for a while?"

"We'll go," Kabi volunteered. "We aren't doing anything and we've been back the longest."

"Good," Blackjack replied. "Oracle, you might want to check in with Feather and see what he has to say."

Oracle nodded and he and his three friends went forward through the column to the very front. Feather and Banjo led the party up the steep hillsides to the next pass.

Feather and Banjo were the oldest men here and the last surviving sons of Silver's sons. Butcher's sons were all dead and so were Fang's. Viking and Hangman were the only other surviving descendants of Silver's line.

Feather and Banjo were both older than Hangman. They'd always stayed loyal to him and Shadow, but Blackjack couldn't trust Feather and Banjo to show *him* any loyalty. He wasn't Kral.

Having young men like Oracle's group treat him as Kral was one thing. The uninitiated boys could report to him, but Feather and Banjo were still technically in charge, especially of anything relating to the band's safety.

The boys and young men shouldn't have been reporting to Blackjack or taking orders from him. He shouldn't have encouraged them and he didn't. They did it on their own. He didn't ask for it.

He wasn't technically breaking any rule by giving them his ideas and telling them what he thought they ought to do. Any of them could refuse to follow his suggestions. He wouldn't be able to stop them or enforce any authority over them.

Oracle and the others stopped to talk to Feather and Banjo up there. Were the young men telling Feather and Banjo about Blackjack's decision to search the Blastidon trail? Either of these older men could overrule his decision. He was the youngest initiated man in the whole band.

He didn't feel like the youngest man in the band. He felt like Kral. He felt like he was stepping into his father's role and taking over this band in his father's absence. Blackjack shouldn't have thought that, but he did.

It was more of a gut feeling—an inner knowing that he really was Kral even if no one said so. Hangman wasn't here. The position of Kral would have transferred to either of his brothers if anything happened to him.

Lock and Bantam weren't here and neither was Cross. The position of Kral would therefore pass to Hangman's oldest son. He would become Kral no matter how old he was.

By law, it didn't matter if Blackjack had only initiated yesterday. He would still become Kral if none of his father's brothers could take over.

Hangman, Cross, Bantam, and Lock were all gone. Even Viking was gone. That made Blackjack de facto Kral.

He didn't say this out loud, but he found himself thinking it. He was Kral of this band. He was the most qualified to lead the party—though he couldn't explain to himself why he thought he was the most qualified. He just knew it in his bones.

Banjo and Feather didn't come back to tell Blackjack not to stick his nose into any more strategic decisions. The two men didn't come back to tell him anything. They finished their conversation with Oracle and Oracle and his men really did kick back after that.

They went off to one side and lounged in the shade under a tree while the column of women and children passed them by. The men waited an hour and then headed off south again. Did they plan to carry out their strategy after all?

Kuvik brought up the rear at the very end of the column. He happened to be walking close enough to overhear everything that passed between Blackjack and everyone who reported to him.

Kuvik never stepped out of line to tell Blackjack anything one way or the other. Kuvik didn't tell Blackjack to pull his head in and start acting his age. Kuvik wouldn't do that.

Their relationship had changed since Blackjack's initiation. He and Kuvik had been so close before. Kuvik had always treated Blackjack like the little brother that Kuvik never had.

Blackjack had always sensed Kuvik treating him as a stand-in for Tren, but that never bothered Blackjack. He considered it the highest compliment that Kuvik thought Blackjack could be like Tren.

All of that had gone out the window after Blackjack's initiation. Kuvik had withdrawn and hardly spoken to Blackjack at all. This would have bothered Blackjack except that Kuvik treated Blackjack as if he was Kral, too.

Blackjack had found occasion to ask Kuvik questions about the band's strategic position and what Kuvik may or may not have seen in the landscape. Kuvik had answered as if he was talking to his Kral. Kuvik had reported everything to Blackjack as if he really was in charge.

Breaker guarded the band on the opposite side from Blackjack. Breaker was Neia's son, so Breaker was Silver's grandson, too, but Breaker would never inherit the position of Kral. He didn't really count in the lineup.

He treated Blackjack with far more deference and respect than Blackjack's age called for. Blackjack didn't understand it and couldn't explain it—except for this nagging gut feeling.

Everyone acted like they already knew what he felt in his deepest being. Viking had once confided in Blackjack that Viking and Alien had both foreseen Hangman becoming Kral even as young as his initiation.

Now the same thing was happening to Blackjack. He would never unseat his own father, but Blackjack felt himself preparing and stretching into a role that would fall to him by natural right.

Maybe everyone already did know. Why shouldn't they if it was so obvious to him?

Loso, Kabi, and Zakra returned two hours later carrying the sections of a massive Coffincreep between them. The boys each carried a section, passed them off to different people in the band to carry, and left to bring back even more sections.

The boys were still bringing in the meat by the time Feather and Banjo called the halt for the night. Everyone got busy cooking, sharing, and curing the meat for travel.

Blackjack skirted the camp to check on everyone. Mora still sat with Yoa and Kuvik and helped them take care of their two children. Mora didn't need to get involved in all this strategic and political business.

Blackjack didn't need to, either, but he did it anyway. He was just on his way back when Oracle's party returned. They came up to Blackjack first for some reason. He was the closest on that side, but that couldn't be the only reason.

"The south is still clear and the Blastidon trail is clear," Chief reported. "We'll go farther south along both routes tomorrow. We'll just check to see if any Red Riders are coming north—just enough to give us time to prepare our response."

Feather and Banjo both came over just then. Breaker came with them. "Anything?" Banjo asked.

"Nothing," Oracle replied. "We were just telling Blackjack that we'll scout farther south along both routes tomorrow. That should give us enough early warning if anyone comes."

Banjo turned to Blackjack. "That was a really good idea to follow the Blastidon trail. None of us thought of that."

Blackjack opened his mouth to ask if his older cousins were okay with that and if they had a problem with him telling older men what to do.

He didn't get the words out before he heard a crackling noise in the nearby canopy. He looked up and saw Maeno and the other younger boys coming through the jungle to meet up with the rest of the band.

Maeno smiled when he saw Blackjack watching him. Neither Maeno nor any of the other boys noticed a massive tide of ants following right behind them. The whole carpet of black bodies headed straight for the band camped on the ground.

Blackjack didn't have time to warn anyone. He cast one desperate glance into the treetops and spotted a Krakelow traveling through the canopy. The Krakelow wasn't coming toward the band. Blackjack couldn't see what the Krakelow was doing and he didn't care.

He took off running. Maeno's smile slipped when he saw Blackjack running toward him. Blackjack sprang into the branches climbing fast.

He hurtled toward the Krakelow, cartwheeled past the creature, and delivered one swift blow of his axe across the back of the Krakelow's head.

The creature tumbled out of the branches right into the ants' path. They swarmed it and enveloped it. Maeno and the others saw and took off running straight for the band.

Blackjack couldn't waste a minute to talk to anyone. He grabbed a few vines from the canopy, twisted them into a noose, and descended into the branches right above the ants.

He looped the noose around the Krakelow and started to drag it away from the band. The ants followed the food and turned to head off in a different direction.

His quick reaction gave Feather, Banjo, Breaker, and Kuvik time to get the whole band off the ground. Everyone scrambled into the branches, but the danger was over. The ants kept walking away in their new direction. They didn't come back.

Blackjack stayed in front of them for a while to make sure they didn't turn off again. He didn't return to the band until later. None of the older men mentioned his actions. No one mentioned it at all until he went to sit next to his mother.

"That was excellent, little brother," Kuvik told him. "You saved the whole band."

Blackjack shrugged the comment away. "That's what I'm here for, isn't it?"

"That's something your father would have done," Mora remarked. "You reminded me of him just now.....only much better looking."

Blackjack laughed and found himself turning away so she and Yoa wouldn't see him blushing. "It was nothing."

"It was very brave and heroic," Yoa added. "I'm sure your father would be very proud. I know all the men are proud."

He didn't point out that they weren't proud. They hadn't even thanked him—not that he expected them to.

He did catch his friends and Maeno's boys staring at Blackjack in something like awe when he'd come back from leading the ants away. He didn't know what that meant except that he did.

He would have liked to ask Kuvik why everyone was suddenly treating him as Kral—but Blackjack already knew that, too. He would have liked to ask Kuvik if Feather, Banjo, and Breaker had a problem with him doing these things and making these decisions.

Asking that would have made Blackjack look weak and uncertain. Asking would have made him feel like he needed someone else to confirm what he already knew.

They didn't tell him not to. Kuvik didn't tell him not to.

Blackjack made up his mind to just keep doing it until someone told him not to. Someone would let him know if and when he overstepped his authority—as if he had any authority to overstep.

Chapter 33

Hangman climbed onto a high rock and surveyed the country to the south. He and his new band of freed captives had been traveling for four days since they'd left the Red Riders' camp in ruins.

He and his men had been keeping a sharp eye out on all sides, but on the south side especially. The men expected the Red Riders to retaliate and they didn't disappoint. He spotted a rising dust trail billowing into the sky in the distance. It was heading north.

He didn't say anything out loud. He didn't have to. Bantam, Lock, Red, and his men all stood on the surrounding rocks looking at the same thing.

Viking led the column of freed captives. The freed men surrounded the throng of women and children. The freed men had formed a cadre of some of the toughest, most resolute fighting men Hangman had ever met anywhere.

Hangman had never been in charge of such a powerful force before. These men could accomplish anything. Many came from warlike hunting Clans and knew how to provide for the band.

Mule's women were the only people here who came from the Godless Clan. Most of the others came from pacifist Clans. The Red Riders didn't care who they took as long as they got their hands on women of childbearing age.

The women also turned out to be a lot tougher than Hangman expected. They traveled faster, pushed themselves harder, and adapted much more quickly than the women Hangman had freed from Ceon.

Hangman dreaded the day any of these women started giving birth on the journey. He wanted to rejoin the Godless as quickly as possible.

The women seemed to be thinking the same thing. None of the men had to encourage the women to keep up. None of the women complained—ever—not even when their heavily burdened condition slowed them down and made traveling difficult.

The men turned away from the dust cloud. The Red Riders were still far enough away for the party to get out of the pass.

Hangman and the others followed until the band entered the jungle. The sun was going down. Hangman ordered everyone up into the trees.

"The Red Riders are coming for us," he announced after everyone had settled on their branches. "The men and I will spring an ambush on them tonight. All of you will need to keep still and stay extra quiet for this to work."

"You don't have to worry about us, Hangman," a woman named Raiba replied. She was one of the first women Hangman had freed from the Red Riders' camp.

She had made herself into some kind of liaison between him and the rest of the women. She reported to him about any concerns the women had and communicated his responses to them.

That saved him from having to talk to a hundred and fifty people about literally everything the band did. This wasn't even a band. It was more of a small city traveling through the wilderness.

The freed men had organized themselves, too. One man acted as their leader and liaised between the freed men and the Godless. This man's name was Yeoli. He came from the Whisperers Clan and he knew his way around both a weapon and the jungle.

He fit right in with the Godless. The men welcomed him as a brother and showered praise on all the freed men for their fortitude, effort, and outstanding attitude. Hangman couldn't have asked for better.

The children were all under the age of ten.

The freed children took to the Godless way as energetically as Hammer's band ever did. The boys all started carrying weapons and helping the men hunt and defend the band. Even the girls started carrying weapons.

The freed captives started to reorganize themselves as soon as Hangman made his announcement about the Red Riders coming in. The boys arranged themselves to stand guard. The women and girls pulled out their weapons to get ready to defend themselves.

Hangman retreated with his brothers, Viking, Red, and the others. Hangman didn't want the freed men to get involved in the actual ambush, so he posted them around the perimeter to help wipe out any survivors after the fact.

"What will it be tonight?" Red sneered. "Ants, Abnormits, Krakelows, Coffincreep, Crushers—take your pick."

Hangman glanced around. "I see two Abnormit nests in good positions. Thank you, Red. Excellent thinking."

Red snorted. "You're a bloodthirsty bastard, you know that?"

"I never said I was kind, caring, and considerate to my enemies. I didn't see them being kind, caring, and considerate to these captives." Hangman turned to the rest of his men. "I think some of us should stay behind and continue laying ambushes and booby traps for anyone who pursues us."

"Isn't that what we're doing?" Bantam asked. "This is the first group that's pursued us."

"I mean so we can widen a gap between us and them." Hangman shrugged. "I guess we won't need to. We're almost back to the place where we separated from the band."

"How far ahead do you think they've gotten?" Viking asked.

"I couldn't begin to guess. I suppose it depends on how many unforeseen obstacles the band comes across. They might not have gone anywhere."

"Let's hope they've gone at least somewhere," Lock remarked.

The men fell silent when they heard hoofbeats pounding in the distance just then. Every man strained to listen. The freed men all tightened their grips on their weapons.

"I have an idea," Red remarked and climbed down to a lower branch directly below the band's hiding place.

"What the hell are you doing?!" Viking snapped. "You're crazy."

Red cracked a grin at him. "You can't blame me for wanting a little taste of blood of my own. Let me enjoy myself while it lasts."

Hangman didn't argue and no one else made a sound as the Blastidons got closer. No one moved. The Red Riders thundered down the valley coming closer by the second until they burst out of the trees at a dead run heading north.

They all reined to a halt when they saw Red perched there in the branches. He was the only Godless the Red Riders could see. All the other Godless and all the freed captives stayed out of sight in the thick canopy.

"What are you doing here?!" one of the Red Riders demanded.

"I'm waiting for you," Red replied. "I came here to kill you. You're right on time."

"You—kill us—by yourself?!" another Rider fired back. "What are you going to do—blow on us?"

The other Riders laughed. Red smiled at them "I appreciate you coming," he remarked. "I always appreciate it when your people walk straight into my traps. Watching you die is becoming one of my most thrilling pleasures—so thank you. You men are going to make tonight so special for me."

"Too bad your wife isn't here to share it with you," one of the Riders sneered.

It was probably the worst thing any of them could have said to Red. His smile evaporated into a murderous glare, but it didn't matter in the end. Viking stood up on his branch and hacked his massive axe into one of the nearby Abnormit branches.

It cracked clean off and poured thousands of Abnormits onto the ground right on top of the Red Riders. Red's trick had brought them all to a halt right in the most dangerous spot. They had gathered around to talk to him and made themselves perfect targets.

Wildling cut through the other Abnormit nest. The two men flooded the area with enough Abnormits to take down the whole pack of Riders.

They and their mounts fell into the sea of grubs, larvae, and insects all eating as fast as they could. Blood-curdling screams floated out of the chaos until the screams stopped and silence fell over the jungle.

Red spat down at the Abnormits and clambered up to sit with his friends. "That was perfect, brother," Viking told him. "You positioned them in exactly the right place."

"That was the plan." Red glanced up at the freed captives. They all stared down at the Abnormits devouring the last remains of the Red Riders. "I guess it isn't exactly the Godless way."

"Getting ourselves killed isn't the Godless way, either," Hangman pointed out. "Anything goes if someone comes out to kill us, capture our families, or maraud the countryside. They get what's coming to them one way or the other. That's the way I see it."

"I agree with you," Red replied. "The Godless Clan is changing into something different."

"Something better," Hangman countered. "We're turning into something invincible—which is what we should be."

Chapter 34

B lackjack stopped at the edge of the cliff and looked down, down, down at the Angler Valley floor far below him. The waterfall pounded past him and plunged all the way down into the pool that fed into the river streaming south.

"I never thought I would ever come back here," he murmured.

"Neither did I," Mora exclaimed. "I don't know if I have the courage to go back in there."

"We have to," Blackjack replied.

"I don't remember anything," Maeno added from Blackjack's other side. "I don't remember the Anglers at all."

"You were too little," Blackjack told him.

"Be glad you don't remember," Mora chimed in. "I wish I couldn't."

Blackjack put his arm around his mother's shoulders. "It will work out. You'll see."

Breaker, Feather, and Banjo came up to them just then and peered over the side, too. "How do we get down these cliffs?"

"You would have to ask my father," Blackjack replied. "I didn't see what he did."

"Did you see?" Feather asked Mora.

"No, I didn't see, either. He came down by himself after we were already down there."

"How did *you* get down there?" Banjo asked.

"We got washed down there in a flood," Mora replied. "It's a miracle we survived at all."

"Father climbed down," Blackjack went on. "He fashioned ropes, secured them to these rocks, and climbed over the side. That's all I know. It took him days to braid enough rope to make it all the way down there—and I know he got attacked by Boultars on the way down."

Breaker furrowed his brow. "That's not good."

"We should camp up here while we figure it out," Blackjack decided. "We can start braiding rope, make sure we have enough to get all the way to the bottom, and start lowering people one after another."

"What about the Anglers?" Maeno asked.

"We'll lower some of the fighting men first," Blackjack replied. "They can defend everyone else—and we can hide in the caves for protection if we have to."

"What caves?" Banjo asked. "You never said anything about caves."

"They're indentations in the cliff walls that aren't big enough for Anglers to enter."

"You would have to go down first to show us," Feather suggested.

"I can do that." Blackjack walked away from the edge. "Let's get to work. Father said to get into the valley as quickly as possible."

Mora opened her mouth to say something, but she shut it when Blackjack gave her a look. He'd been acting so authoritative toward everyone, even men three times his age. She didn't contradict.

He led everyone back into the jungle behind the cliff edge. The band had just emerged from there after almost two weeks of travel.

Mora found it difficult to believe that the band had actually made it here after all this time.

Now everyone would be going into the Angler Valley. Could she really face that? She would have to. She was one of the very few people here who knew what the band would be facing and how to fight the Anglers when they did inevitably attack.

She could put it off a little longer while the band made camp. The men started braiding miles and miles of rope. Any of the women and children not occupied elsewhere joined the men to help out.

She didn't help out. She probably should have, but the band wouldn't need all that rope—not to climb down the cliffs or even to lower anyone down the cliffs.

She didn't know what circumstances would make Blackjack decide to use the hidden tunnel, but he would. He just needed the right opening before he revealed the secret to the whole band.

She didn't understand why she couldn't overrule him. It wasn't that he was a man or because he was her own son.

Something about him stopped her. She wouldn't have overruled Hangman if he had been here. She had somehow started to think of Blackjack as Kral in his father's place. She didn't understand why, but it somehow made sense that Blackjack would be Kral.

Everyone else seemed to have come to the same conclusion. None of the men ever contradicted his decisions about anything. He had just taken over the band and everyone went along with it for some reason.

She listened to him give orders to the men and boys to run scouting parties all around the area and into the neighboring valleys. They had all been following his orders since Hangman had left.

The band settled down for the night. The men kept braiding their rope and so did Blackjack. No one looking at him would ever guess that he knew of another way into the valley.

Thena didn't involve herself with these discussions or any others. She never revealed the secret, either, probably because she had other things on her mind besides whatever strategic decision the men made.

Mora helped Yoa for a few hours. Kuvik braided rope, too, but he did it with his family. He didn't join the other men. Mora caught him stealing sidelong glances at her throughout the evening. Did he realize that this rope-braiding exercise was just a delay tactic?

He could pick up body language and facial expression cues better than anyone else Mora had ever met. He seemed to have a preternatural ability to read people. It almost bordered on the supernatural—almost as if he could read their minds.

He must have noticed that Mora and her children weren't quite as enthusiastic or urgent about climbing down the cliffs as they should have been—especially considering the effort and danger the band had gone through to get here.

Everyone went to bed early that night and woke up the next morning excited for the project of finding a way down the cliffs. Mora kept quiet.

Blackjack spent the first part of the morning sending out scouting parties again. Then he posted guards in a semi-circle around the area so no one and nothing would approach the cliff edge while the men worked.

He went through an elaborate process of creating a bundle full of dirt, tying it to the end of the rope, and lowering it over the side to make sure it touched the bottom. The rope wasn't long enough, so the band had to retreat and braid some more.

Everyone helped out this time. Mora couldn't get out of it, so she joined in just because. She became more and more certain by the minute that Blackjack would never send anyone over the side like this. He wouldn't knowingly risk someone's life for no reason.

The band assembled for the second test. He tied on the bundle, lowered it, and bumped it against the dirt at the bottom to determine that it really was hitting the ground.

He turned around to face the other men. "We'll decide which men to send down first. I think we should send down Oracle, Pyro, Smash, and Chief. They aren't as heavy as some of you and they're strong enough to protect anyone else from a creature attack."

"I don't know about this," Smash murmured. "I don't want to go down there first."

"You wouldn't go down first," Blackjack explained. "Oracle would."

"Hold it right there, little brother," Oracle countered. "I don't want to go down first, either."

Blackjack made a face. "Since when are you four such cowards? Fine. I'll go down first. Does that satisfy you? Then you can send down Kuvik. I'm sure he won't have a problem with it, will you, Kuvik?"

"Of course not, little brother. You can send me down first if you want to."

Blackjack waved at Kuvik. "You see? This is how a real man faces danger. I'll go first—then Kuvik—then Breaker. You four can stay up here with the women and children."

Oracle flinched, but it was too late. Blackjack started pulling up the rope to retrieve the dirt bundle. He barely got it off the ground before Loso, Kabi, and Zakra came rushing up to the party.

"Red Riders...!" Kabi gasped. "Red Riders coming! They're coming right now!"

Blackjack dropped the rope, spun around, and seized his axes. "Why didn't any of our scouts see them?!"

"They're coming on the western side," Loso replied.

"What does that have to do with anything?!" Blackjack snapped. "We sent out scouts specifically looking for Red Riders!"

Loso opened his mouth and then blurted out, "Breaker is over there."

Blackjack shut his mouth in a hurry. "Get your boys and all the other guards back here immediately to defend the band!"

"Shouldn't we lay an ambush?" Feather asked.

"We're already sitting on one!" Blackjack countered. "We'll draw the Red Riders into attacking us and drive them over the side of the cliff. Simple."

The other men exchanged glances and gathered the women and children in one place.

Blackjack strode back and forth in front of the women and children giving orders to everyone. "All of you stay behind the men—over there." He pointed toward the cliff edge.

"We'll fall off!" one little girl wailed.

"Not that close," Blackjack told her. "Keep a good distance between yourselves and the edge. We'll back up to make the Red Riders think they have us trapped. Then all of you will dive out of the way and run over there." He pointed to one side farther down the cliff. "We'll double around you and drive the Red Riders over the side."

Some of the men frowned. "Will that work?" Feather asked.

"Do you have a better idea?" Blackjack asked.

No one got a chance to answer before the boys and guards came rushing back. Breaker didn't come with them. No one asked where he was.

Mora crowded in with the other women and children. She didn't like going near the cliff edge, but anything would be better than facing the Red Riders.

Danimi started crying. He wasn't the only one. She picked him up and held him while everyone listened to the Blastidons' hoofbeats coming closer.

The men assembled in front of the women and children and raised their weapons to meet the enemy. Mora had to hold onto Danimi with both hands. She couldn't hold even one of her weapons. She didn't like this at all.

The first hint of movement flashed between the trees. Her blood ran cold when the Red Riders thundered out of the trees riding full tilt to run the Godless down.

"NOW!!" Blackjack roared.

The women and children charged sideways. The Red Riders didn't have time to meet the Godless before the men dove out of the way, too. The Red Riders kept going. They saw their problem and tried to haul their mounts to a stop.

Blackjack sprang forward to circle the Red Riders on the inside, but he never got a chance before a colossal wave of people surged out of the jungle right behind the Red Riders.

Mora stared in mute shock as a whole army of armed men rushed the Red Riders and shoved the Blastidons closer to the cliff edge. Mora almost didn't believe it when she saw Hangman, Viking, Bantam, and all the others right there in the middle of the mob.

The Red Riders tried to fight back and strike these strangers with their axes, but the invaders' numbers confused and then terrified the Blastidons. The creatures tried to rear, but too many people blocked them in.

An even bigger tide of women and children lunged in behind the men just then and the whole force pushed and shoved the Blastidons toward the cliff edge. The first Blastidons tumbled screaming to their deaths and then the strangers pushed all the rest over, too.

Hangman didn't give anyone a chance to rest on their victory. "Everyone get to the tunnel! Blackjack! Mora! Lead everyone to the tunnel! Hurry!"

No one argued. Mora and Blackjack hustled away down the cliff calling all the Godless to follow. Mora didn't get a chance to ask Hangman who all these strangers were or why he was showing them through the secret tunnel entrance.

He retreated through the group and gave orders to Red and his men to follow and erase every track and trace of the band's route.

Chapter 35

Blackjack hustled to the tunnel entrance and waved everyone inside. "Go all the way to the other end!" he called. "You'll see some big machines! Get past them and go to the very end of the tunnel, but don't go out into the open. Stay inside where the Anglers can't get to you!"

The first Godless entered the tunnel. The strangers started to enter behind them. Blackjack couldn't help but notice that almost all of them were pregnant women. His father must have freed these people from the Red Riders.

More and more people streamed into the tunnels. He remembered them being extra wide and long. He didn't realize his father's party would come back with so many extra people. Blackjack sure hoped everyone fit in the tunnel.

They wouldn't be able to stay here—not indefinitely. They would have to camp somewhere—which meant the Anglers would find everyone.

The whole party eventually crowded into the tunnel followed by Hangman, Viking, Bantam, and Lock. Red and his men stayed outside to conceal the tracks of so many people.

Hangman had to shove his way inside. No one could move.

Hangman, Blackjack, and Mora rejoined somewhere near the valley end of the tunnel. "Now what do we do?" Blackjack asked. "We can't stay here. We have to camp somewhere."

"We'll camp right here outside the tunnel," Hangman decided. "We'll be able to retreat inside if the Anglers come."

"*When* the Anglers come," Mora pointed out.

Hangman didn't answer her. All three of them knew what was coming.

Hangman turned to everyone else. "Come on out, everyone!" he called. "We'll make camp right here in the open. We'll be able to get back inside the tunnel to escape from the Anglers."

The whole mob poured out of the tunnel. The band had tripled within a few minutes. The newcomers blended right in except that they wore different clothes and used different weapons.

The freed men stood guard and reported to Hangman as though they'd been with him for years. Blackjack didn't want to know what all these people had been up to while his father had been away.

Hangman and Mora met in front of their own shelter as the sun started to go down.

"We should attack the nest webs first," Hangman decided. "We should make regular campaigns to the Anglers' nesting grounds to destroy eggs, webs, and kill any young Anglers. That will make our jobs much easier. That will stop the young ones from growing up to replace the older ones we kill."

"There must be a way to ambush or trap them," Mora pointed out.

"They're too smart to fall for that, remember?" Hangman asked.

"I mean something we haven't thought of before," Mora replied. "We need to come up with new methods the Anglers have never seen before. They won't be able to anticipate it."

Hangman furrowed his brow in thought. "Let's see how far we can get with conventional methods first. One option is that the Anglers will fall back to their nesting grounds once they realize we're going after their young. That will stop the adults from coming after us. We'll be able to isolate them in one area and kill them there—plus we have all these extra people."

"We should tell them all how we killed the Anglers last time," Mora suggested. "We should talk to these people about getting onto the Anglers' backs and stabbing them in the head."

"The way *you* did last time," Hangman countered.

"Who cares as long as we kill them? If you're right, then we can just keep killing more and more of them. They won't be able to replace themselves without eggs and young coming up."

Hangman and Blackjack discussed everything in detail. Then the two men went through the whole camp and explained the strategy to everyone who might possibly one day have to fight the Anglers.

Hangman, Mora, Blackjack, and Thena spent a long time describing the Anglers and even drawing pictures of them in the dust so everyone would recognize the creatures.

Hangman spent an exceptionally long time explaining it to the freed men. Blackjack stood aside and listened. The men hung on Hangman's every word. All the freed captives treated him like some kind of god.

Blackjack found himself hovering close to his father. Blackjack didn't want to be Kral as long as Hangman was around.

Hangman returned to their family shelter—or the shelter he now shared with Mora. Blackjack didn't live there anymore. He'd been so busy that he hadn't taken the time to build a shelter of his own.

Hangman turned to Blackjack after they both sat down together side by side. "Loso told me about you leading the ants away from the band. I'm proud of you. You're becoming a strong defender of your people."

Blackjack looked away. "It wasn't all that."

"Tell me about what happened with the Red Riders. How did they get so close to you."

Blackjack cast a glance around. "That's what I want to know."

Hangman frowned. "I don't understand."

"I posted guards and ran scouting parties the way I should have. I scouted the country every few hours from the time you left until the time you came back. We kept the country under surveillance around the clock. I swear it, Father."

"I believe you. So what happened?"

Blackjack opened his mouth to answer and then shut it again. "I'm not sure. I never found out. We were planning to climb down the cliffs—or at least we were talking about it. We braided a rope and I posted a guard to protect the band while we tested it out. We were just negotiating who to send down first when Loso came along and told me that the Red Riders were coming in from the west. He said...he said Breaker was over there. I planned to use the cliffs as an ambush point. I planned to use the women and children to lure the Red Riders close to the cliffs and then push them off—but you got to them first and did it for us."

Now Hangman was the one who looked around. "I haven't seen Breaker since we came back."

"Neither have I. He didn't come after the Red Riders attacked. He may be dead up there. They may have killed him. I don't want to say anything against him if he died fighting the Red Riders to hold them off."

"That doesn't explain how they got past your scouts."

Blackjack looked away. "I don't understand that, either...unless...." He trailed off and didn't say it.

"Never mind about that," Hangman interrupted. "You did very well. I'm proud of you."

"Can I ask you a question?" Blackjack blurted out.

"Of course. You can ask me anything."

Blackjack lowered his voice. "You'll think I'm being arrogant. You'll think I don't know my place and that I'm too young...."

"Just ask, my son," Hangman insisted. "It can't be so bad if it's only between us."

"I wish it was," Blackjack murmured.

"You better tell me what it is. Were the other men displeased with your conduct?"

"No, not at all. That's the problem."

Hangman scowled even more darkly. "I don't understand what you mean."

"Viking says you were different when you were young—different from other men your age and even different from men much older than you. He says men treated you like you were already Kral even when you were barely initiated."

Hangman looked away again. "Oh, that. Yes, they did."

"Did you.....did you sometimes feel as though you *were* Kral when you weren't?"

Blackjack turned around to face his father. Now he knew he absolutely had to get this out. He had to come clean to his father before Blackjack did or said anything else.

"Please don't think I'm trying to overthrow your authority, Father," Blackjack insisted. "I would never do that. I would never set myself up as Kral in your place. I would never betray you like that."

Hangman actually laughed at him. "Is that what this is all about? You feel like you're Kral already?"

Blackjack squirmed. "I never said that.....but sometimes it seems like the other men and boys treat me like I am......I mean they treat me like I am a lot....like all the time....except when you're around, of course."

Hangman laughed again and clapped him on the shoulder. "I'm proud of you, my son. Yes, I felt that way a lot when I was young—and the other men treated me that way a lot. They always just sort of assumed that I was in charge as long as Butcher and Shadow weren't around. I could say things to them that no other man my age would be able to say to his Kral. Much older men told me all the time that I would be Kral one day—or even that I was Kral already because Butcher took my ideas as his own." He shrugged that away. "That's the way it is, I suppose."

"But I could never be Kral as long as you're here. You would never take my ideas as your own."

"I might use your ideas. In fact, I know I would. I would just tell you that what you said was a good idea and that we would do it your way. That's how a young man takes over as Kral after the older man isn't around to do the job. The young man wins the respect, trust, and support of the other men. Then the old Kral dies or gets killed and the young man takes over because all the other men know he's already Kral."

Blackjack couldn't hold his father's gaze. "I don't want to talk about you dying or getting killed."

Hangman faced front and talked in a low undertone as if he was talking to himself. "Everyone thought Shadow was the real Kral while Butcher was still alive. Everyone thought Shadow could have taken over from Butcher anytime Shadow wanted to. Shadow never challenged Butcher or even contradicted him—not ever. Butcher didn't like anyone speaking up against his orders. He would have retaliated against me or anyone else suggesting that he should do differently. Shadow did retaliate even when I didn't suggest that he should do differently. He retaliated for no reason. I don't want to be like either of them. If you step up—if you have something to say—if you even tell me that I'm doing wrong—I want you to. I want you to move in as Kral in my place. That would be my dream come true—if you became Kral in my place and everyone followed you because they trust you, respect you, and support you in my place. That would be the best I could ask for. I would step aside and let you become Kral. I want you to—especially if the men already treat you that way."

"I don't know what to think about it." Blackjack heard his voice shaking. "It goes against everything I've ever been taught about showing loyalty to my Kral."

"No one has been more loyal to me than you have, my son. I could never ask for a better man to take over for me as Kral."

"There are so many men here who would be better. I'm almost still a boy."

"So what? What does that have to do with anything as long as the men follow you? I was younger than Viking and Alien the whole time we were out of the territory. Even Red and his men are older. They told me to take over as their Kral. They wanted me to. That's why I did it. I did it for the good of the band. It can never be wrong if that's the reason you're doing it." Hangman studied the side of Blackjack's face. "That is the reason you're doing it, isn't it?"

"Of course. I wouldn't do it at all if the band didn't need me to—or if the men didn't act like they need me to."

"Exactly. Then you have nothing to worry about."

Chapter 36

Hangman came out of Mora's shelter. He'd posted men on watch around the camp overnight to keep an eye open for Anglers. The band didn't have to worry about human pursuers anymore. Now the band had a much, much bigger problem.

He met up with Kuvik near the mouth of the tunnel. "Are we going Angler hunting today?" Kuvik asked.

Hangman nodded. "I want to talk to you about something before the others wake up."

"What do you want to talk about?" Kuvik asked.

"I want to talk about my son and how he conducted himself while I was away."

Kuvik snorted with laughter. "Do you even have to ask? Didn't he already tell you everything last night? I saw you two talking about the fate of the universe."

Hangman ignored that. "He's worried because he sees himself acting as Kral when he's still so young."

"Why is he worried about that? He is Kral." Kuvik raised both hands. "You know what I mean."

"So the men didn't have a problem with it?"

"Of course not. He came up with some great ideas. They all fol-lowed him—and then he saved everyone from the ants. Who else would we follow—Breaker?"

"Where is he? I haven't seen him."

"Neither have I. He didn't come down from the cliffs with us. I assumed the Red Riders must have killed him."

"Would you please go check?" Hangman asked. "We won't leave without you. I promise."

Kuvik took off running through the tunnel. Hangman didn't question Feather or Banjo about Blackjack's conduct. Hangman didn't have to question the other uninitiated boys. They already couldn't stop talking about what a champion Blackjack was.

Loso had already filled Hangman's ears with more information than he needed about how Oracle and the other young men had acted around Blackjack.

Hangman didn't know why he felt the need to ask at all. Blackjack himself had admitted that the other men didn't tell him he did wrong. One of them would have told him real quick to step back in line if they didn't want him to actively step out of it.

No one understood this process better than Hangman did. He didn't want to be Butcher and definitely not Shadow. If Blackjack stepped out, more power to him.

Hangman would have felt the same way about anyone stepping out, especially someone everyone else respected—like Red. Hangman had been telling himself that for ages.

It was no less true now simply because the man in question was his own son. That only made it even more important that Blackjack stretch into this role if everyone else supported him in doing it.

Kuvik came back an hour later and said he'd found human remains on the west side of the clifftop along with the stone head of Breaker's axe. Kuvik couldn't tell what had killed Breaker, but he was definitely dead from one cause or another.

Hangman decided to take a page out of Blackjack's book and let the matter drop. Hangman had no reason to think that Breaker had died doing anything other than defending the band. No one had any reason to criticize him for that.

The rest of the band woke up, started moving around, and Hangman gathered all the men into one place. He also called Mora and the boys to join them.

He assigned Mora to lead the boys and younger men to the Angler breeding ground to destroy as many eggs, webs, and young Anglers as they possibly could. He planned to lead the rest of the men on a killing campaign from one end of the valley to the other.

He planned to sweep the entire valley until the band completely annihilated every last Angler inside the walls.

Then he ordered all the pregnant women and mothers with children to go back inside the tunnel for the day. He would be taking all the men away and leaving no one behind to guard the band.

The men returned to the head of the valley where Hangman had first descended to search for Mora and the children. He and his men lined up across the area.

Operating in this valley felt so different with all these powerful, armed men. This was nothing like how it had been with just him and Mora trying to defend their family.

The men started walking south. They had to spread out a little wider as the valley widened. The men had to put more space between them.

They walked for a mile before a commotion broke out on Hangman's left. A dozen freed men converged and flushed out a whole nest of young Anglers. The creatures barely came up to the men's thighs.

The men attacked in a flash. They had to run the Anglers down through the jungle and other men closed in from either side to trap the Anglers where the men could kill them all.

The men spent some time there talking and catching their breath before they went on. They only made it a dozen yards before exactly the same thing happened.

The men scattered another clutch of young ones about the same size—and then the rest of the men in that patch of jungle scared out another three dozen Angler young.

Hangman and the others rushed over to help the men exterminate all the young. The process took a long time. The Anglers kept breaking through the Godless line, but enough men gathered around to finally circle and eliminate all the creatures.

Hangman called a halt as soon as the killing stopped. He and his men regrouped, doubled back, and reestablished their line at the edge of that patch of jungle. This seemed to be a nesting ground for young Anglers.

The men made pass after pass of the same area, each time driving more and more young Anglers into the open. The men killed dozens of them and eventually decided to drag the bodies backward out of the undergrowth and make a pile of them there.

The pile kept getting bigger by the hour. The men always retreated to the edge of the trees. The men no longer tried to cover the whole valley. The men surrounded that patch of jungle and converged toward the center.

They could kill more Anglers this way. The party killed hundreds of them and removed them all. The men were still at it when a deep roar echoed out of the distance.

Hangman barely looked up before a dozen huge adults charged the men from the south and scattered everyone.

The men had to regroup back at the tunnel entrance. "I guess the adults know what we're up to," Red pointed out.

"Good," Hangman replied. "Let's get back into position, but we'll be ready to engage with adults this time."

"What if they overwhelm us with numbers?" Banjo asked.

"Fall back if the tide turns against us. We aren't here to throw our lives away. We can win just by chipping away at them from the bottom up. If the Anglers are too powerful and we don't have enough people to kill them, we'll retreat and go after them another way. The important thing is that we keep hitting them as often as possible and taking out as many as possible. The women and boys will stop the Anglers from reproducing. They won't be able to survive as long as we keep doing that."

The men returned to the head of the valley and formed the same line. The adult Anglers didn't come back. The men passed through the same patch of jungle, but they didn't find any young Anglers.

The men kept going until another alarm went up from the left again. Hangman went over there to see what the problem was. The men on that end of the line had discovered another Angler breeding ground with dozens of webs loaded with eggs and little Anglers running around.

Hangman gave up on the line. He and his men spent the rest of the day building fires to destroy webs and killing every young Angler the men could find. The men had to run away multiple times to avoid adult Anglers who saw and came after the men.

Hangman hoped Mora and the boys were having equal success. This project couldn't fail as long as the Godless kept doing this.

Chapter 37

Mora and the boys crept through the jungle undergrowth and observed the Angler breeding ground from a safe distance.

"My God, look at them all!" Kabi breathed. "There must be hundreds of them right here alone."

"That's why we have to eliminate them while they're young," Mora replied. "See those webs up in the branches? The webs are full of eggs. All those little Anglers on the ground should be easy to kill. We just have to be careful not to alert the adults who are standing guard. They didn't stand guard when I saw them last, but they're doing it now."

"How do we do that?" Maeno asked.

"You boys start a fire out here away from the breeding ground where the adults can't see you. Loso, Kabi, Zakra, and I will start killing the young ones. We'll kill as many as we can before the adults notice us. As soon as the adults do notice and come after us, you and your boys will sneak in from the sides—over there. Set fire to the branches around the web and destroy each one. Get back under cover as soon as you start the fires so the adults don't see you. Just ignite the branches and disappear. The older boys and I will run and hide from the Anglers until they go back to what they were doing. Then we'll do the same thing over again while you ignite the next web. Understand?"

The boys nodded. Maeno and his friends retreated and started building a small fire at a distance from the breeding ground. Mora and the older boys crept closer.

The adult Anglers had to guard a large area with countless small Anglers scuttling, playing, and exploring all over the place. The small Anglers covered the ground as thickly as the last time Mora had seen them here.

"Just kill the young Anglers as quietly as you can for as long as you can," Mora murmured. "Don't make any unnecessary noise that will tip off the adults."

The boys all acknowledged her instructions and drew their weapons. Maeno and his friends divided up burning sticks from their fire.

The boys positioned themselves at strategic points around the area. The boys would be able to get to as many nests as possible before the adults realized what was happening.

Mora, the older boys, and the young men stepped out into the open and started swinging their weapons at all the little Anglers. They made it easy for Mora by raising their heads up to examine her.

The young Anglers had obviously never encountered people before and didn't recognize the danger. They made themselves perfect targets.

She swiped her blade back and forth chopping off all their heads as fast as she possibly could. She kept an eye on the adults just in case.

Maeno and his friends saw their opening and tiptoed out of the jungle on both sides. The boys didn't wait for the adults to notice and go after Mora and the others.

The older boys and young men copied her. They hacked their way through dozens of young Anglers and left the bodies carpeting the ground. Mora and the older boys must have killed two hundred young Anglers before the adults noticed.

Maeno and his friends positioned themselves under one web each. Mora barely glanced up there to see what the boys were doing. They had taken her instructions and run with them much further than she suggested.

The boys had collected branches of leaves from a certain tree in the surrounding jungle. Volatile oils in the leaves made them especially flammable. The boys packed handfuls of these leaves into the crooks of the tree limbs holding up the webs.

The boys set fire to the leaves and they woofed upward in sheets of fire. Flames enveloped the webs. The webs' fiber threads turned out to be extra flammable, too. Five webs exploded in flames.

The boys had to scramble to get out of the branches in time and retreat. They raced away just as the adult Anglers turned around and noticed their webs in flames.

The adults went into a frenzy, but they couldn't do anything about it. They didn't even see the boys scampering away into the under-growth.

The boys' ingenuity gave Mora and the older boys plenty of time to maraud their way through even more young Anglers. The adults raced back and forth, around the burning webs, and roared in fury. Then the adults started hunting around for the culprits.

The adults searched the surrounding jungle and found the scent trail leading them to the younger boys. Mora couldn't wait any longer.

She and the older boys turned tail and fled, but the adults didn't stop. They kept hounding the party until both groups joined up. They took off running through the jungle with the adults in hot pursuit.

Mora glanced behind her and saw ten enormous adult Anglers closing in on her and the boys. She almost gave the order to split up and head back to the tunnels when the party collided with Hangman and the men coming the other way.

Hangman took one look at the adults closing in and everyone bolted for the tunnels. The pregnant women and mothers with young children were already in there. Everyone had to crowd in as tightly as before.

The Anglers stormed up and down in front of the tunnels roaring and snarling. The creatures kept rushing the tunnel entrance, smashing their heads and bodies against the rock, and trying to stretch their limbs into the entrance to capture someone.

No one dared to move or breathe for a long time. The Anglers didn't go away. They stayed hour after hour.

The pregnant women and mothers with young children eventually settled down on the tunnel floor. This wasn't the most comfortable place to camp, but it was safer than going outside.

"Maybe we can find other tunnels or caves the Anglers can't fit in," Mora suggested. "That will at least give us some more space where the families can get comfortable."

"That means going outside," Maeno pointed out.

"I mean we would look the next time we can go outside," Mora replied. "These rocks have a lot of indentations and false walls. Some of them could give us protection, too."

"That means breaking up the band," Hangman countered. "I don't want to separate anyone, especially not someone who might be defenseless and need protection."

"It would be a temporary measure until we can eliminate the Anglers," she told him. "Each family or group of families would have a designated cave or hiding place where they can retreat for protection if and when the Anglers come around. The families can sleep there.

They won't need anyone standing guard to defend them because the Anglers won't be able to get to them."

Blackjack came up to them in time to hear the rest of this conversation. "We're going to need to hunt for food soon. People are starting to run low. We should run some hunting parties outside the valley to bring in kills."

"No, we don't have to," Hangman replied. "We already have enough."

Blackjack frowned. "We do? Where are they?"

"I'll show you, but we have to wait for the Anglers to leave first, obviously."

Maeno peered out through the tunnel opening. "What if they don't leave? What if they stay there all the time?"

"They have to eat, too," Hangman replied. "We just have to be patient for a while."

"This is going to be an ongoing problem," Mora pointed out. "You realize that, don't you? This first killing campaign tipped them off. Now they know we're here and that we're killing young Anglers. The adults will start hunting us from now on."

"Then I guess it will be even more important that we have safe points where we can withdraw and take shelter." Hangman glanced around at the people nearest him. "You're right. It's too cramped in here. We need more space."

No one could do anything about that right now. No one had a choice but to do anything but wait. In the end, the family settled down on the floor, too. Everyone did.

Thena and the teenage girls had gotten into a similar habit of helping the mothers with young children. Thena came back later and sat with Mora, Hangman, and their two sons.

This was the first time all of them had spent any time together as a family since Blackjack's initiation. It didn't feel the same, though.

Blackjack was growing up fast and now Maeno was helping out with the campaign against the Anglers.

Mora saw Thena racing to grow up and have her own family. She would get married one of these days. She might even leave the band to go to another Clan. Mora had to prepare herself for that.

Then again, all these pregnant women brought in new blood. The women and their babies' fathers weren't related to anyone in the band. Half of these babies would be boys and half would be girls.

The band's children might not have to go to the gathering anytime soon. That would give the band enough time to figure out how to get to the gathering in good time without the trip taking two years like it did this time.

Those problems sure looked a long way off with the Anglers storming up and down outside the tunnel. All five members of the family dug in their bags and shared out what food supplies they had left. No one would get anything else until the Anglers left.

Chapter 38

Hangman woke up and listened to the silence. The Anglers were gone—but not gone. They no longer patrolled the area outside the tunnel, but they would come back. They would always come back.

He got to his feet. Blackjack was already awake. A bunch of the freed men were also awake or just waking up. The whole band would wake up in a minute.

"Go down the cliff walls, my son," Hangman told Blackjack. "Try to see if you can find any other caves, fissures, or tunnels into the rock that are small enough to protect people from the Anglers. If you find any, you can start moving families down there to give us some more space."

"Where are you going?" Blackjack asked.

"I'm going to get food to feed all these people. We can't go on without food."

Blackjack left and came back in a little while to tell each family about caves and hiding places along the cliff walls. He took them out five to ten families at a time. The tunnel started to empty.

Hangman got the freed men to go back to the jungle and start carting all the young Anglers back to the cliffs for food. He organized the boys and able-bodied women to bring in as much firewood as possible.

The men delivered dead Angler young to every cave. The women butchered the creatures out in the open while the children and teenagers built fires in the caves to cook the food.

The band was in the middle of this operation when the adult Anglers came back with a vengeance. Everyone had to flee back into their hiding places.

The adult Anglers smelled the offal from the butchered young. The smell drove the Anglers into another tempest of rage. They attacked the cliffs again, but the Anglers couldn't get inside.

Blackjack got trapped in one of the other caves. The Anglers stayed much longer this time. It was a good thing Hangman had brought in the food when he did. The Anglers stayed all day and didn't leave until night fell for the second time.

Hangman and Mora wound up with Maeno and the younger boys in a cave thirty feet down the wall from the original entrance tunnel. The Anglers' constant roaring and attacks put everyone on edge and made the children cry.

The cries of babies and children hiding in the caves electrified the Anglers into fresh bursts of charging the rock and trying to claw their way into the caves.

Eventually, all the hiding Godless got too bored and exhausted to pay attention anymore. There was nothing left to do but cook the food, eat it, and go back to sleep.

The band woke up early the next morning—or Hangman did. He left the cave without waiting for Mora and the others to wake up.

He went down the line of caves and roused every man over the age of initiation, including Yeoli, all the freed men, Oracle's group,

Blackjack, Red's men, Viking, Kuvik, and every other man Hangman could find.

He led them all away from the caves and assembled in the canopy where they could all observe the Godless camp—for what it was worth.

"What's the plan?" Yeoli asked.

"We've eliminated a lot of the eggs and young Anglers," Hangman replied. "Now it's time for us to start getting rid of the adults."

"How do we do that?" Oracle asked.

"We could always lay some more ambushes for them," Legacy suggested. "I suppose ants, Krakelows, and Abnormits can eat Anglers the same way they can eat everything else."

"The Anglers already know how to deal with those," Hangman replied. "We'll have to overwhelm the Anglers with our numbers. That's our advantage."

"How does that work when there are so many Anglers?" Yeoli asked.

"We'll kill them one at a time if we have to," Hangman replied. "All of us working together could bring down one Angler easily. We have no reason to take them on all at the same time. That would be stupid."

"So what are we doing out here?" Feather asked.

"We're waiting for the Anglers to come back. Then we'll strike."

A few people asked some more questions. Hangman answered them as patiently as possible, but the Anglers answered all the men's questions as soon as the creatures showed up.

The families hidden in the caves offered an irresistible temptation for the Anglers. The families emerged from their caves as long as the area stayed clear. The children ran around playing in the sunshine. Their laughter and yelling attracted the Anglers like nothing else.

Another ten adults showed up to storm and rage outside the caves
the way they did yesterday. The Anglers had to spread themselves out
to attack all the caves. This made the Anglers perfect targets for the
men.

Hangman split his force into two. He took half the men to one
end of the line of cliffs and sent the other half to the other end of the
line. The men had no choice but to step out into the open with no
protection.

The Anglers saw the men instantly and turned to attack—or the
Angler on that end of the line did. The men swarmed in and overwhelmed the Angler in seconds. The creature couldn't fight this many
people.

Men on one side of the creature stabbed it, slashed it, and impaled
its body. The creature whipped around impossibly fast, dove for the
men, and made them jump out of the way to save their lives.

The creature's actions exposed its other side for the rest of the
party to leap in and attack the creature while its back was turned. The
men cleaved the Angler across the legs, brought it to the ground, and
hacked it to death.

The other group of men did the same thing from the other end of
the line and brought down another Angler over there.

The Anglers in the middle of the group realized what was happening and turned outward to gang up on the men.

Mora and a few other women and older children darted out of
the caves, jabbed the Anglers with weapons, and distracted them into
turning back to the caves.

The Anglers roared in fury, charged back to assault the cliffs, and
the men swarmed in to bring the creatures down.

The men worked inward dropping one Angler after another. If the
Anglers ever thought to team up against the men, the men either fled

back to the safety of the jungle or the women got involved enough to distract the Anglers away from the men.

The two groups of men met in the middle of the field with all the dead Anglers lying bleeding on the ground. "This is working out so much better than I expected," Viking remarked.

"That was only ten of them. We have a long way to go." Hangman turned back to the caves and called out to all the women. "Come on out here, butcher these creatures, and take the meat back inside the caves before more Anglers come."

He posted a guard in front of the cliffs, but he gave orders for the men just to keep watch for more Anglers. He had to pace himself and not go on a killing rampage across the whole valley right now.

The Anglers would keep coming back. The creatures were too smart not to figure out by now that these caves housed a fighting force that was waging war against all of Angler kind.

He had to be smarter than the Anglers. He had to choose his battles and also choose the time and place to wage them.

These caves bought the group some much-needed time and protection. They needed it. The Godless couldn't protect themselves from the Anglers any other way.

Everyone worked together to butcher the ten Anglers. Two hundred people ate a lot. Hangman had never been Kral of a band this big.

He and everyone else worked nonstop until sunset to bring in as much firewood as possible and supply everyone with water for the night. The dead Anglers gave the band enough food to last a long time as long as the Godless preserved the meat in time.

The band retreated inside the cave for the night only for Hangman to get the news that some of the freed women were giving birth in other caves. He went to check on them, but he couldn't do anything the other women weren't already doing.

He returned to the cave he shared with his family. Blackjack, Thena, and Maeno made a point of coming back here at night whenever possible. None of the family wanted to stay anywhere else.

It somehow seemed more appropriate for Blackjack to stay with his family even though he'd initiated. No one in the band had their own shelters. Everyone lived right on top of each other.

"It will be like this all the time from now on," Hangman murmured once he sat down. "These women are going to be giving birth one after the other for a long time."

"This band is going to get even bigger," Blackjack added. "We're going to need even more space and even more food."

"We'll have that as soon as we get rid of the Anglers and move out of these caves," Hangman replied. "We'll have a real camp out in the jungle somewhere."

"We might have to have more than one," Mora pointed out. "We might decide to split up the band into three or four smaller bands to live apart from each other. This is a big valley. It has enough space for everyone to spread out with different territories and different hunting grounds. That could solve the problem of the young people finding husbands and wives."

"We'll need to get out of these caves before we can do that." Hangman turned back to Blackjack. "I want you to go out with Oracle, Pyro, Smash, and Chief bright and early tomorrow morning before the Anglers come around. I want you to start at the head of the valley and search the whole area for any other breeding sites—anywhere with webs and young Anglers running around. Don't engage the adults and don't do anything to hit the sites. Just locate them so we can go back and hit them later. We'll probably have to wage isolated campaigns as long as the Anglers keep us locked up in these caves. That may be their strategy—to stop us from going out. We'll leave first thing in the morning, carry out our strikes on them, and then retreat back here—but we need to know where the breeding sites are so we can get to them quickly."

"Yes, Father," Blackjack murmured. "That's a good idea."

"You and the men can keep ambushing the Anglers when they attack the caves," Maeno suggested. "You can keep killing the adults the way you did today."

Hangman found himself smiling at his sons. Maeno was growing up to be as much of a badass as his brother. "We could do that. We'll need to keep killing the adults. Killing the young and destroying the eggs is important, but we will still need to keep killing the adults."

"What about rigging up the booby traps you used last time?" Blackjack asked. "If you send out teams to carry out operations in the early morning before the Anglers come, then you could send out teams to set up the booby traps, too."

"I have an idea," Thena chimed in.

Hangman looked up. His daughter hardly ever got involved in these conversations. She was too interested in babies, children, and what her life would be like after she had some of her own.

"What is it?" Hangman asked.

"Do you remember how you ambushed the Red Riders on the cliffs when they could only come at you one at a time?" Thena asked. "You could do something like that. You could find someplace where the Anglers can only come through one at a time—maybe in one of these rock fissures or something like that. Then you could kill them one at a time with all your men."

"We would have to search the whole valley before we found some-place like that," Blackjack pointed out.

"You could build one. You could set up two fences in a funnel like this." Thena brought her hands together into the point of a V. "You could send out a team of your fastest runners and get the Anglers to chase them into the funnel. The runners would be able to get through the point of the funnel easily because the point would be big enough for one Angler. The Anglers would all crowd into the funnel trying to follow, but only one could get through. Then your men could kill that one and all the others as they come through one at a time."

"How would you stop all the others from coming through while the men are fighting that one?" Maeno asked. "That one would leave a gap big enough for the next Angler to come through."

"The men could build the funnel narrow enough that the Angler would have to stop and wedge itself through. That would slow it down long enough for the men to attack it while it's still wedged into the opening. Then it would come through and the men would kill it. The opening would slow down the next one so the men would get to it in time before it came through."

"It's a good idea," Hangman replied. "We could definitely work on something like that."

"You would have to find the right location for the funnel," Maeno pointed out. "You would have to build it somewhere that the Anglers couldn't just walk around the funnel and come after you. There would have to be no other way out."

"Good point," Hangman replied. "This is all really good thinking. I'm proud of you all."

A few of the women who had been working on the cooking fires came around and delivered a share of the Angler meat to the whole family. Everyone settled down and started eating. No one talked about how to kill the Anglers again after that.

Chapter 39

B lackjack skimmed through the jungle with Oracle, Pyro, Smash, and Chief. The group crisscrossed the valley in wide swaths without staying in one place for more than a few seconds.

The men never stopped running. They didn't have to look very closely to sweep the area for Angler breeding sites. The men could see webs a long way off.

Adult Anglers stood guard over the breeding sites all the time now. Blackjack and the others only had to look out for Anglers. No Anglers standing guard meant no breeding sites.

The men traveled a long way and spotted five different sites, but the men didn't go near any of them. The men stayed clear the way Hangman told them to.

They kept going and weaving back and forth in wide patterns to cover more ground. They didn't have to search any open grassy areas. The Anglers only built their webs in trees.

The men came to another patch of jungle and closed together to search the area more thoroughly. They had to travel through denser canopy here and actually blundered straight into another breeding site before they realized it was even there.

Blackjack and the others froze in place. Their sudden arrival alerted the adults on guard. Five huge female Anglers turned around to glare at the men standing there.

Blackjack thought fast. He and his men couldn't fight this many Anglers. The men couldn't even get out of the area without the Anglers following them.

The Anglers advanced on the men. Blackjack didn't stick around to think twice about what to do. He and his comrades shot away into the branches and took off heading back the way they'd come.

He realized a second later that he probably should have kept going, but he didn't think of it in time. His one thought was to put the Anglers behind him.

They followed anyway. They moved fast and sure through the tree-tops following the men's scent trail. Blackjack and the others couldn't slow down or stop at all. The Anglers kept gaining by the minute.

He glanced behind him only once. All five females came after the party, so the men couldn't split up.

Blackjack turned back toward the caves. "This way! Come on!"

The men didn't argue. Blackjack would have liked to race ahead and warn the rest of the band, but the men had to run their fastest just to stay alive.

He expected Hangman to have posted guards around the caves to at least keep watch. Blackjack felt terrible about leading the Anglers back to the caves this early in the morning. He didn't want to be responsible for that.

Another group of Anglers was already there attacking the caves as usual. All the men crowded inside the caves, but they didn't passively wait for the Anglers to leave.

Blackjack saw it all in a flash. Hangman and the other men stood at the cave mouths and used the Anglers' own attacks to wound, weaken, and even kill the creatures.

The men stabbed and hacked the Anglers every time the creatures smashed their heads into the rock. The men stabbed out the Anglers' eyes, slashed their throats, hacked at their limbs and faces, chopped the creatures' heads off, and impaled them through their mouths.

Blinded, wounded Anglers blundered around, collided with each other, tripped over each other, and even attacked each other right there in front of the caves.

Blackjack and the others were running too fast to stop. All the healthy, uninjured Anglers kept attacking the caves and didn't turn around to see the men approaching.

Oracle checked himself, but Blackjack never stopped running. He didn't say a word to encourage his friends to keep going. He didn't want to alert the Anglers.

The men dodged around the injured Anglers, had to spring out of the way more than once, and skidded into the cave. Hangman and the other men pulled Blackjack and his comrades to safety just as the fresh group of pursuing Anglers charged in to attack.

The men sprang forward to retaliate. Hangman impaled one Angler through the roof of the mouth and the giant body collapsed right there across the cave entrance. That one Angler would have blocked the others from getting inside.

The Anglers who had followed Blackjack's party here went into an even more frenzied rage, ripped the body out of the way, and the rest of the Anglers plunged in all over again.

Blackjack rushed back to the cave opening to help the other men. The Anglers shoved their faces close to the opening trying to snap every man within range.

Too many men crowded the cave opening. Blackjack and Oracle's men could only get near the Anglers from the sides, but this turned out to be the best place to attack them without putting the men in danger.

Blackjack and the others stabbed and hacked the Anglers in the eyes and heads, slashed their throats from the side and underneath, and brought them to the ground while the Anglers kept trying to attack the men right in front of them.

The same thing happened again and again. Dead Anglers fell across the cave mouth and blocked other Angers from attacking. The noise of enraged, wounded, and dying Anglers attracted even more Anglers to the spot.

One hour passed another and the attack didn't ease. The men exhausted themselves by fighting for so long. Some dropped back to rest while others came forward to carry on defending the cave.

Blackjack caught glimpses outside in those brief moments when the Anglers left the cave opening clear before another Angler dove in to collide with the rock.

The rest of the band defended their own caves in the same way. The band brought down one Angler after another. More still showed up to continue the assault.

A woman started wailing, screaming, and crying in the background. Blackjack barely glanced over his shoulder to see another group of women surround the person. All the men backed away and turned their backs so they wouldn't see.

The woman's cries and all the other women talking sent the Anglers into another frenzy. They almost seemed to understand what was going on inside. Were other women giving birth in the other caves right now?

The Anglers didn't stop attacking no matter how many died. They assembled from all over. Blackjack couldn't see outside well enough to know where they were coming from or how many might be out there.

The attack went on and on. Children cried and their mothers tried to comfort them. Then the children passed out from exhaustion. The sky darkened and no one lit a fire in the cave.

The men stayed on watch killing Anglers as the night wore on. The men tired and collapsed against the walls and on the floor while other men took their places. The Anglers didn't leave.

Blackjack finally couldn't fight anymore. He couldn't raise his weapon. He crawled away from the opening and let the other men take over. Some who had been sleeping through the pounding noise woke up, came forward, and started killing Anglers again.

The Anglers' furious roars, their constant smashing into the rock, their dying shrieks, the bellows of wounded Anglers blundering around outside, the screams of women in labor and children crying—all those sounds drifted into Blackjack's brain while he slept.

This was his life now. Hangman had been right. Blackjack's initiation had marked the end of his childhood—a childhood he hadn't even realized he was living at the time.

He thought at the time that he was doing everything a grown man would do. He and his friends had been going out every day, scouting, hunting, and standing guard over the band on the journey and in camp.

He had always been free to go sit or lie down whenever he wanted to. He could have even when he chose not to. That was the difference. He had never actually taken personal responsibility for the band before.

He woke up sometime in the middle of the night and heard the Anglers roaring outside. He got to his feet, picked up his weapons, and went straight back to killing Anglers.

He fought with different men this time. They were all freed captives who had come back with Hangman's party. Blackjack didn't know any of these men, but that hardly mattered.

They fought as bravely as any Godless men—or any naturally born Godless men. It sure looked like these men were Godless now.

Hangman and the others slept a little longer. They stayed back and got themselves something to eat. A different woman went into labor back there somewhere. Blackjack didn't take the time to see who it was.

He went into a trance of killing, collapsing, dreaming about killing Anglers, and then waking up to go straight back to doing it again. He lost track of how long the assault went on. The Anglers seemed to have an endless supply of adults to throw at these caves.

He felt his vital force draining away from him. He might keep fighting like this until he died.

He woke up in silence on the third day. He barely opened his eyes before he saw his mother bending over him. "Drink a little water and eat some food, my son," she murmured. "Then you can lie down and go back to sleep. You don't have to get up."

She helped him sit up and drink from one of her water skins. Men lay sprawled in senseless, unconscious sleep on the floor all around him. None of them moved even as some of them still gripped their weapons in their hands.

Blackjack glanced toward the cave opening. Dead Anglers lay all over the open ground out there. Some showed the unmistakable signs of having parts of their bodies carved off.

A few people had built fires in the cave to cook the Angler meat. The savory, juicy smell drifted into Blackjack's nose. Mora pushed a bowl into his hands. Roasted Angler meat piled it high with more food than he could reasonably eat by himself.

She smiled at him. "Get some food into you and then rest. You're exhausted. No one will be going out there for a while."

She stroked his forehead, petted his hair, and left him alone. She went through the cave talking to every man as he woke up, helping them drink, and passing out food to everyone.

Quite a few people did go outside, either to butcher the Anglers, to gather firewood, or to get water. Blackjack didn't think too hard about any of that.

The silence unnerved him. The constant noise and danger of the last few days shattered his mind. He had a hard time thinking about everything that had happened and everything that was currently happening.

Why did the Anglers break off their attack? Maybe they needed to rest the same way the people did. Maybe the Anglers were out there planning their next assault.

Blackjack found it difficult to believe that the Anglers really wouldn't be able to get into this cave. His first nightmarish experience in the valley had convinced him that they would always find a way to attack no matter what the defenders did.

He propped himself up on his elbow to eat, but even that felt like too much of an effort. He stretched out on his back and ate lying down. Men and women went into and out of the cave for a while. He heard his mother talking in her low voice.

She spent some time tending to Hangman and then moved on to helping everyone else. She didn't stay with any one person for long.

Blackjack didn't hear any women in labor. Maybe everyone in the whole cave was too exhausted to do anything right now.

Some of the people who went outside went to different caves. People from different caves came in here and talked to others they knew. Almost everyone here was a stranger to Blackjack.

He ate half the food in his bowl and passed out again. He woke up in darkness except for a single fire burning in the center of the cave. A bunch of people sat around it, including Hangman, Mora, and Chief. Everyone else was asleep.

Blackjack went over there and sat down near his parents. "How long do you think this reprieve will last?" Chief asked.

"I don't plan to wait long enough to find out," Hangman replied. "We'll go out again tomorrow morning and hit one of their breeding grounds."

"That will probably provoke another attack," Mora pointed out.

"I hope it does. We'll just keep provoking them. We can kill more adults like this without putting our people in danger. We'll keep eliminating Anglers—but I don't think it will provoke another attack. They're too smart to keep throwing themselves into certain death like this. I don't think they'll attack again—not like that."

"What do you think they'll do?" Blackjack asked.

"It will be something we haven't seen before. We need to be more careful after this."

"How can we be more careful than we already are?" Chief asked. "We haven't left these caves."

Hangman pointed to the cave opening. "One of the Anglers could cling to the cliff wall above the cave opening and drop on someone the minute they go outside. The Anglers could hide in the jungle and ambush us when we try to go for water. Then we wouldn't be able to go for water at all."

"We can go back out into the outer valley for water," Mora pointed out. "We aren't trapped in here."

"I know that, but the Anglers don't. They probably think we are trapped in here—and we don't want to go into the outer valley if we can avoid it. The whole point of us coming here was so we would never leave. Going out there will alert our enemies that we're here. Our tracks will lead them straight to the tunnels."

"We have to go out in one direction or another," Chief replied. "We have to get water from somewhere. We'll have to go to the outer valley if we can't go inside."

Hangman turned to Blackjack. "I want you to run a scouting party around the valley's outer rim tomorrow, my son. I want you to find out if the Red Riders or any of our other enemies have followed us here. Stay in the trees to conceal your tracks and don't engage them. Conceal that you were ever there if you can so you don't lead them back to the tunnel."

"Yes, Father," Blackjack replied.

"The rest of us will mount another attack on the breeding sites. We'll hit as many of them as we can before the Anglers attack again."

Chapter 40

Hangman peered extra closely into Mora's face. "Are you sure you want to do this?" he asked. "I don't feel right about letting you go out there."

"Someone has to do it," she pointed out.

"It doesn't have to be you. You should stay here. The men and I will destroy the Angler breeding sites."

"It will work better if more people go out," she argued. "We'll be able to eliminate more sites if we send out more than one team. We might only get one chance. We should send out as many teams as possible. It isn't like I'm needed here."

He snorted. "Of course you are. I see you taking care of everybody."

She beamed at him. "I'm not doing anything anyone else couldn't be doing and you need as many people as you can get."

"I have all these men. You're my wife. I don't want to send you."

"Obviously I won't go if you absolutely forbid me to, but I'm one of the only people here who knows how to destroy the breeding sites. Just let me go. I'll be fine."

He made a face. "Now I really don't like the sound of that."

She laughed, but he got distracted just then by Blackjack, Oracle, Pyro, Smash, and Chief gathering to leave the cave. Hangman hadn't let anyone else leave yet this morning, not even to get water.

He went over there to give the scouting party their last instructions, but it was the same thing he'd told Blackjack last night. The five men inched to the cave opening, peered around in all directions including straight up at the cliffs, and then stepped outside.

Nothing happened. Anglers didn't drop from the walls to pounce on the men. Blackjack and the others took off running for the jungle.

Hangman spent a little more time assigning armed men to guard any women and children who went outside to get water. The band had enough food to last a long time.

Insects, Abnormits, and other creatures were already starting to gather to devour what was left of the dead Anglers. Then an army of ants came through and erased all the dead Anglers from existence.

Hangman gathered three teams to go after the breeding sites. He assigned the seven uninitiated boys to go with Mora. "Don't try to hit more than one site. Destroy one and get back here alive and unhurt. Don't come near the cave if the Anglers are here. Stay in the canopy until the attack clears."

The others asked a lot of questions about how Hangman wanted them to carry out the strikes, but Mora didn't have to ask. She already knew what she had to do.

Each team took a bowl of live coals from the cave fires. That would save considerable time once each team made it to the target site. The attackers wouldn't have to light a whole new fire.

Mora's nerves strained listening to the others talk and ask Hangman about everything. She wanted to leave and get it over with.

She and the boys wound up leaving first. Hangman made them check the cliff walls and surrounding terrain before they ran off into the jungle.

Mora and the boys climbed up into the branches and raced through the canopy to where Blackjack had reported one of the breeding sites.

This one must have been new. It didn't have as many young Anglers running around on the ground.

The site did have a lot more webs, each one packed to bursting with eggs. Mora and the boys didn't have to discuss their strategy first. They split up.

Mora, Loso, and Kabi went down onto the ground and started killing the young Anglers as quickly as possible.

Zakra, Maeno, and the other boys divided into two teams and snuck around the site from both sides. Four adult female Anglers stood guard all around the site. The boys couldn't get near the webs.

Mora worked her way through the young Anglers and realized the boys weren't setting fire to the webs. She had to change something to draw the adults away from the webs.

She, Loso, and Kabi stopped on the other side. Only a few young Anglers still ran around and played at her feet. She decided to get the adults' attention.

She stepped on one of the young Anglers, pinned it to the ground, and pressed her foot against it to make it squeal. The sound got the adults' attention in a split second. All four spun around and glared at Mora.

The four females stalked a few steps closer and the boys darted in behind the adults' backs.

The boys crouched under the webs, packed flammable leaves into the branches, and raised their coals to ignite the leaves. The adults didn't notice what was going on behind them.

Mora pressed her foot down into the little creature's body one more time. The creature blared louder and squirmed and thrashed to get away.

That sound set off a murderous response from the four adult Anglers. Maybe these four were the young ones' mothers. They sure acted like it.

They charged Mora and the boys. All three bolted into the trees and had to keep on running as the Anglers picked up speed coming faster and faster. The Anglers launched into the treetops, too.

Mora glanced behind her to see how close the Anglers were getting. That was the moment when she saw smoke and flames billowing out of the canopy behind her. Maeno and the younger boys had the breeding site to themselves.

Mora had to keep running to get away from the Anglers. Loso and Kabi raced ahead and then doubled back to distract the Anglers from getting too close to her. Then all three had to sprint for their lives to put more distance behind them.

The three Godless didn't pay attention to where they were going. Mora didn't realize until a few minutes later that she and the boys were running away from the caves where they could take refuge.

Mora didn't know if the adult Anglers would be attacking the caves again by now, but right then, she and the boys blundered into another breeding site they didn't know was there.

The three of them wound up racing straight into another crowd of young Anglers running around on the ground.

Five enormous adult females stood guard over the little ones. Mora and the boys almost collided with the adults.

Mora and the boys skidded to a halt, but it was too late. The Anglers spun around to attack—and that delay gave the pursuing Anglers enough time to catch up with the three Godless.

The pursuers' arrival distracted the five guardian Anglers into turning the other way for a second. Mora and the boys dove back into the jungle and scaled into the treetops to safety.

The three of them crouched there panting and sweating while they peered through the undergrowth at the Anglers around the breeding site.

The newcomers entered and went through a process of sniffing and making noises at the creatures standing guard. All nine Anglers took extra time to get acquainted before they started looking around for the Godless.

"We should get out of here," Kabi whispered. "We should get back to the caves."

"Let's destroy the site first," Mora suggested.

"We would have to disobey Hangman's order if we did that," Loso pointed out. "He told us not to go after a second site."

"We didn't," Mora told him. "We stumbled on it accidentally when we were running away from the Anglers. We didn't go looking for this site. We should destroy it now while we have the chance."

Loso squinted through the undergrowth. "I don't know about this....."

"I'll do it alone if you don't want to," she went on. "Hangman can get mad at me if he wants to get mad at someone. You boys can go back to the caves."

"We are NOT leaving you out here alone!" Kabi fired back. "Hangman would skin us alive."

"Then distract the Anglers into following you or at least leaving the site," Mora replied. "I'll go in and ignite the webs. Here. Give me your coals. You won't need them."

Both boys handed over their coals. Neither looked happy about this, but Mora paid no attention. She couldn't waste this opportunity to kill another generation of Anglers.

She retreated to one side. The boys clambered higher into the canopy and rustled the branches far enough out of sight that the

Anglers wouldn't be able to see the boys. Then the boys darted away to another area to hide.

The Anglers went after the rustling leaves. Mora sprinted for the site the minute the Anglers left the webs unattended. She would have liked to kill the young ones, too, but the webs were the easier target.

She jammed the flammable leaves into the bend of a few branches and ignited the leaves. The flames licked up and the web caught fire. She had to race from one web to another doing the same thing to all of them.

She shortened the process by taking branches from the flammable trees, igniting the leaves, and carrying the whole branch to the next web. She used these homemade torches to ignite the fibers themselves. She didn't need to use the coal each time.

The flames distracted the Anglers. They glanced back—and the boys rustled the leaves again—louder this time. The boys even made whooping and cackling noises.

Their voices sparked the Anglers' fury. They charged into the undergrowth to hunt the boys down, but Loso and Kabi weren't there anymore. They led the Anglers on an obstacle course of misdirection while Mora set every web on fire.

She ignited them all, jumped down to the ground, and looked around. The mother Anglers—if that's what they were—kept crashing around in the undergrowth. Mora couldn't see them and they sounded like they were getting farther away.

Some of the young Anglers raised their heads to peer up at her. She couldn't resist. She drew her blade and mowed down dozens of them with every pass. She marauded back and forth across the site slaughtering every young Angler in her path.

She didn't stop until she'd killed them all. She tracked the mother Anglers' movements through the jungle. They were coming back.

She launched into the branches and raced back toward the caves. She met up with Loso and Kabi on the way. They retraced their steps until they found Maeno and the other younger boys on their way back to the caves, too.

The party rejoined and sprinted for the cliffs, but Mora slowed everyone down when they got close enough to see across the open stretch of ground. There was nothing there. The Anglers didn't come back to attack the caves.

Mora and the boys could walk across that space and reenter the caves whenever they wanted, but Mora kept casting glances over her shoulder. When would the Anglers come back?

Would they come back at all? What if the band had already eliminated enough of them to actually make a dent in the population?

Chapter 41

B lackjack sprang into the treetops as soon as he left the tunnel leading out of the Angler Valley. He took Hangman's warning seriously. No one wanted to leave a highway of footprints for the Red Riders to follow to the valley's secret tunnel entrance.

Oracle and the others followed Blackjack. No one had to give orders to anyone on this trip. They all knew what they had to do and they traveled as friends. No one was in charge.

They moved through the branches to the head of the valley. The men had to come out into the open to cross rocky, exposed terrain to the cliff edge and the top of the waterfall.

The five men stopped there, looked down at the valley spread out below them, and then turned backward. Another stretch of jungle covered the mountainside behind this point and climbed to more peaks farther away.

"This is where the Red Riders came at us before," Chief pointed out. "It stands to reason that they'll come back here if this is the place they last saw us."

"None of the men who saw us are still alive anymore," Smash countered. "How would the others know to come here?"

"The Red Riders have been doing the same thing ever since our first encounter with them," Blackjack interjected. "We kill the entire pursuit party and leave no one alive, but the next party comes right back to exactly the same spot."

"How is that even possible?" Smash asked.

"I don't know, but I'm with Chief on this one," Blackjack went on. "I think we should assume that the next party of Red Riders will do exactly the same thing. They'll come back here and then try to track us wherever we went next."

"Then the Red Riders will come out of this jungle," Chief added. "We should assume they're coming straight for us right now the way they did last time."

Blackjack nodded. "Let's spread out and search the area. Don't engage if you find them. Just locate them and we'll meet back here and compare notes."

The men climbed back into the branches and streaked away in opposite directions. Blackjack got a sinking feeling about everything Chief had just said. The Red Riders had attacked the Godless at the cliff edge, but the Red Riders hadn't come from directly in front.

He headed off to the west—toward the place where Breaker had been standing guard when he died. The Red Riders had come from there. They had either killed Breaker or he had been conspiring with them for some reason.

Neither Hangman nor any of his men had found any fault with Breaker's loyalty or his behavior. He had been strong in Hangman's corner against all the traitors, including Breaker's own brothers. That said a lot.

Blackjack wasn't about to start questioning the guy's loyalty, now that Breaker was dead and couldn't defend himself. The fact remained that the Red Riders had come from this direction for whatever reason.

He heard their voices long before he got near them. The Red Riders were too used to living in their own camps where they could make as much noise as they wanted.

They had pitched tents in the jungle. Blackjack hid in the undergrowth and observed the Red Riders at their leisure. They didn't look like they were planning any kind of assault or campaign at the moment.

He only saw men moving back and forth from one tent to another. They rode in on their Blastidons or came in on foot carrying their kills. The Red Riders tethered their Blastidons at a distance from the camp.

The Red Riders took off their Blastidons' trappings as soon as the Rider dismounted. The Riders left their mounts on long tethers so the creatures could browse in the jungle. The Riders had to tether their mounts far apart from each other so their tethers wouldn't tangle.

Then each Rider took his mount's trappings back to that man's tent with him. The Riders left their mounts relaxed and unprepared for any kind of battle. The Riders would take a long time to put the trappings back on each mount before anyone left to do anything.

Blackjack watched for a long time before he could bring himself to leave. He wanted to keep watching and get as much information on these men as possible, but he'd delayed too long already.

He returned to the cliffs and told the other four men what he'd found. None of them had found anything.

"It looks to me like they're getting ready to use this camp as a base to search the area," Blackjack told them. "Either that or they already are—or maybe they're planning to use this camp as a staging area to send out their next party."

"Could you tell if they know where to look for our band?" Smash asked.

Blackjack shrugged. "I couldn't tell. The Riders I did see looked very relaxed and at home. They didn't look like they were doing anything or getting ready for anything. They even took off all their Blastidons' gear so the Blastidons could graze and relax, too."

Oracle frowned. "How odd. Don't the Red Riders understand that they're in a war zone and that we might attack them at any time?"

"Apparently not. They didn't act like they were in a war zone at all. Maybe we haven't attacked them in so long that they've forgotten what it's like. Maybe we need to remind them."

Chief's head shot up. "Now you're talking. What should we do? We would have to hunt around to find the right creatures to use against them."

"Maybe we don't need to use creatures," Blackjack suggested. "Maybe we could do something a little more subtle."

"What's more subtle than creatures?" Smash asked.

"There's always poison," Blackjack pointed out. "We haven't used that against them yet—and they would never have to know what was happening to them."

Oracle frowned. "How do you say we should do that?"

"I'll show you."

Blackjack led the way deeper into the jungle. The friends had to search for miles before they found a certain vine growing in the highest canopy.

The Godless never went near this vine or used the vine for anything. Its leaves, stems, and sap were poisonous even to the touch.

Blackjack and his men sat up in the treetops for hours whittling countless tiny, sharp darts. "What are we even doing with these?" Oracle grumbled. "This isn't the Godless way."

"Using the ants or Abnormits isn't the Godless way, either, and neither is pushing the Red Riders off a cliff," Blackjack pointed out. "It looks to me like my father is taking us in a different direction."

"Which direction is that—the direction of cowardice?" Oracle demanded.

Blackjack chose not to glare at Oracle for calling Hangman a coward. "It isn't cowardice to use alternate methods against a superior force you couldn't possibly beat in an open confrontation. It isn't cowardice to protect your families and other helpless people the Red Riders might kill or capture." Blackjack finished one of his darts and put it aside. "My mother told me about this. She learned about it from the Followers. The warrior dips the dart or arrow in poison, shoots his target, and the poison kills the target."

The men whittled over a hundred darts. Then the other four stood back well out of the way while Blackjack used the darts to handle the vines. He didn't dare to handle them with his hands.

He used the sharpened point of one dart to slice open one vine stem. The sap oozed out and he rolled the tip of each dart in the sap as it ran down the stem. He laid all the poison darts on a piece of clean hide.

He led his men back to the Red Rider camp. The Godless gathered in the undergrowth near the Blastidons' grazing area.

Blackjack took out the long, hollow stem of another tree he knew. Water usually moved up and down the tree through the inner column. Water gushed out the minute anyone cut that stem.

It left the inner chamber hollow and perfectly straight and smooth. He dropped one of his darts into the tube and raised it. "We'll test the darts on the Blastidons first. Then we won't alert the Red Riders if it doesn't work."

"It better work," Oracle muttered. "We should have reported to Hangman already."

"Let's find out if it does work. Wouldn't you rather report to him that we found the Red Riders and killed them all than just that we found them?"

Blackjack didn't wait for anyone to answer. He raised the tube to his mouth and puffed a strong, sudden breath of air down the tube. The dart flew out, pricked the nearest Blastidon in the rump, and the creature snorted and kicked out its leg in annoyance.

Its movement dislodged the dart. It only penetrated a fraction of an inch and dangled there sticking out of the creature's skin for a second before the dart fell out. It hit the dirt.

The Blastidon kicked a few more times, snorted, and tossed its head. Nothing happened for another minute except that the Blastidon didn't settle down.

It had been passively browsing in the nearby undergrowth. Now it started pacing around and around at the limit of its tether. The creature snorted a lot more and eventually worked itself into an agitated frenzy.

A few other Blastidons looked up at the creature, but they couldn't do anything. All the Red Riders were too far away in their tents to hear or notice anything wrong.

The poison took effect in a matter of minutes. The Blastidon eventually stopped pacing, stood there shivering and trembling violently all over, and then buckled at the knees. It hit the dirt heaving for breath—and then that eventually stopped, too.

Blackjack and his friends watched from the treetops. "I can't believe it actually worked!" Smash whispered. "It's dead."

"The same thing would happen to us if we touched that sap." Blackjack loaded another dart. "Let's finish off all the mounts. Then we can start working on the Red Riders themselves."

The other men spread in a circle around the Blastidons' grazing area. Each man took a tube and a supply of darts. The five men darted each Blastidon and finished them all off in no time.

The men barely had time to complete the project before another Rider came back from hunting somewhere.

He rode in on his Blastidon, took his mount to the edge of the camp to tether it there, and discovered all the other Blastidons either dead or rapidly on their way there.

He raised the alarm and all the other Riders came running to see. None of them could figure out how their mounts had died. Blackjack and his men shrank away into the undergrowth and regrouped in the canopy to watch.

Now would have been the perfect time for Blackjack and the others to dart all the Red Riders in one place. Doing that would almost certainly have alerted the Red Riders to what was going on and how the Godless were attacking.

The Red Riders stood around the dead Blastidons talking endlessly about what might have killed the creatures. The man who had discovered the creatures pointed out that his mount was perfectly fine while all the rest were dead.

The men speculated if some herb or plant in this area might have poisoned all the Blastidons. The men made a detailed study of all the nearby plants, but the men knew them all. The Blastidons had been grazing on these same plants for years.

The Abnormits eventually discovered the dead Blastidons and the Red Riders couldn't do anything to bring their mounts back to life, so the men returned to their tents. The newcomer tethered his mount somewhere else far away from the dead creatures.

"Now what do you want to do?" Oracle asked Blackjack.

"I think we should wait until nightfall when the Red Riders return to their tents. They'll be even more relaxed and unguarded. We can dart them in their tents and they'll die in their beds. That will stop them from alerting each other that anything is wrong."

Chief shook his head. "You're as devious as your father, you know that?"

"Thank you," Blackjack exclaimed. "I hope I can grow up to be like him."

"You already are."

"Don't tell him that!" Oracle countered. "Don't encourage him!"

"Well, it's true," Chief returned. "You know it is. They're cast from the same mold."

Blackjack looked back and forth between the two friends. "Are you finished yet?" Blackjack asked. "Can we go kill some people now?"

The friends split up again and surrounded the Red Riders' camp this time. The men didn't have to wait long before night fell.

The Red Riders lit up almost every tent with a fire even when only one man lived in that tent. Blackjack couldn't imagine what the Red Riders were doing in there alone.

He found out when he snuck to the first tent. The man inside had stripped to the waist. He went through a series of ritualized movements with his axes. The routine resembled combat training, but it wasn't. It was some kind of ceremony.

The Rider performed the whole sequence in front of a shelf loaded with trinkets. Some were carved stone figures while others had been fashioned out of clay or carved out of wood.

Each one represented the effigies of people the Godless band had seen etched into the tree trunks in the Red Riders' own territory. Blackjack didn't understand the significance of the figures or this man's ritual.

Blackjack didn't need to understand it. He darted the guy in the back. He felt it instantly, spun around, and then swiped his hands back and forth across his back trying to dislodge the dart.

He knocked it loose and stared at the dart on the floor for a second. Then he picked it up and fingered the tip for a minute while he thought the matter over. He actually touched the tip where he would get the poison on his skin.

He waited too long, grabbed his weapon, and stormed away to leave the tent, but the poison acted much more quickly on him than it did on the Blastidons. He took two steps, buckled at the knees, tried to stagger to his feet, and toppled across the floor.

He made a few more writhing, pathetic efforts to crawl to the tent entrance to warn his comrades, but he never made it that far before he collapsed and fell unconscious right there on the floor.

Blackjack skimmed away to the next tent. The man inside must have already finished his ritual. He sat down on the edge of his bed with his shirt off and started doing something to his axe on his lap. He laid another axe aside on the bed next to him.

Blackjack darted this man straight in the chest from the front. The dart lodged in the muscle above his heart and acted on him almost immediately. He looked down at the dart and then up. He looked straight at Blackjack.

The guy grabbed his axe, lunged to his feet, and folded at the knees. He still lay on the ground convulsing all over by the time Blackjack slipped away to the next tent.

The others went much more quickly. He didn't stick around to watch how the poison affected each man in turn. Blackjack darted them one after another and raced away to the next tent to do the same thing.

He spotted the other Godless men sprinting from tent to tent to dart everyone as quickly as possible. The Godless didn't have to be careful anymore, now that so many Red Riders were already dead.

Blackjack entered a bunch of tents with only dead bodies in them. He met back up with his friends out in the middle of the camp. Night had fallen completely by now.

"Is that all of them?" Blackjack asked. "Are you sure we haven't missed anyone?"

"Let's go tent to tent and check," Smash suggested.

The friends reconvened at the edge of the camp where they'd started. The men went from one tent to the next working their way systematically across the camp to its other side. All the Red Riders were dead.

Blackjack darted the last remaining Blastidon and left the whole camp exactly the way it was. He wanted any follow-up party of Red Riders to find the camp if they happened to come along before the jungle creatures got to this place first.

The men retreated. Blackjack wrapped all the remaining darts in their hide bundle and buried the whole bundle in the jungle before the men took off running back to the tunnel entrance to the Angler Valley.

Chapter 42

H angman took Red and his men on a trip to scout the area. They searched for hours and didn't find any Anglers anywhere.

The Godless teams had razed all the breeding sites Blackjack had found. None of the sites remained. The teams had wiped out all the little Anglers, too.

The men had made another sweep of the whole area and annihilated all the older, bigger juveniles. Hangman started to get a bad feeling about this when he didn't find any adults in the area, either.

"What do you think it means?" Red asked on their way back.

"I think it means they're planning something. They're trying to lure us out into the open so they can strike again."

"Maybe it means we've killed enough of them," Carnage suggested.

"We haven't killed enough of them because we haven't killed all of them. Some Anglers are still alive, so we haven't killed enough of them."

"How can we find them if they're this well-hidden?" Wildling asked.

"I know the perfect way," Hangman replied. "We'll tell everyone to come out of the caves and start building a permanent camp. That will bring the Anglers out of hiding if nothing else does."

"Do you think it's wise to use our own people as bait?" Red asked. "They won't like it."

"They already don't like staying in those caves. We have to come out sometime. Besides, I have a plan."

Carnage snorted. "Since when have you ever not had a plan?"

"Never," Hangman agreed. "As soon as we get back, I want you to organize all the men to stand guard while the women build their shelters. We'll also build fortifications around the camp to stop the Anglers from getting inside or at least to slow them down."

The men returned to the caves. The women and children fell over themselves in excitement when they found out they could finally leave and go outside.

Hangman spent a long time warning them that the Anglers would come back. The women barely paid any attention to that.

The freed men stood guard over everyone, but no Anglers showed themselves. Hangman led the band back to the rocks where Mora and the children had first camped in this valley.

Hangman showed the band into a much wider place with a flat, sandy floor and high rocks all around it. The area had three different entrance points where the rocks came together to create bottlenecks like the one Thena had suggested.

Hangman got some of the stronger, more able-bodied women to construct sturdy fences across two of these gaps. That left only one entrance and exit point for the whole camp.

Even that was a narrow entrance barely big enough for a fully grown man to pass through. It would act as a choke point if the Anglers tried to get in that way.

"What a good idea," Mora exclaimed. "I wish I had thought of that." She laughed when Hangman gave her a look.

"We still have to worry about them coming down from above." He turned back to the rest of the band to give a different order, but he broke off when Blackjack came back with Oracle, Pyro, Smash, and Chief.

Blackjack gave Hangman a brief description of everything he and the other men had been doing up on the clifftops.

He also related the conversation he and his men had held about how the Red Riders kept following the Godless band after the Godless eliminated so many groups of Red Riders and left none alive to tell the tale about what had happened.

"Another group is bound to come along soon," Blackjack finished. "These men must have been part of a much larger horde coming behind them. The Red Riders may be planning to move into this area permanently.

"And they only had men in the camp?" Hangman asked. "No women or children?"

"No, none," Blackjack replied. "Every man lived alone in his tent. We didn't see a single woman in the whole camp."

Hangman only nodded. "Thank you, my son. You and your men did very well. I'm pleased."

He walked off and rounded up Red and his men. Hangman didn't notice Blackjack following him.

"What are you going to do?" Blackjack asked. "You're going after them, aren't you? You're planning to eliminate them, aren't you? I want to go with you this time. I can help you."

Hangman turned around to face his son. Blackjack had grown as tall as Hangman now and Blackjack wasn't even fifteen yet. He grew more and more by the day. He might even get as big as Viking once Blackjack stopped growing.

"You can help me by staying here and taking care of the band, my son," Hangman murmured under his breath. "The band needs a strong leader and that's you. If anything happens to me and I don't return, then you and your men will have to step in to lead the band. That will be hard enough because someone older than you might challenge you for being so much younger than they are. You'll be helping me by handling that. I know you can do it and you're the only man here that I trust to lead this band in my place even if I'm just out of the area. That's the best thing you can do to help me."

Hangman turned away to meet Red and the others who had accompanied Hangman to confront the Red Riders on their last trip. Hangman started talking to them about making another campaign against this latest incursion.

He became aware of Blackjack standing behind his back listening. Hangman wouldn't have felt right about any of the other young men listening to his conference with older men about a campaign that didn't concern him.

Hangman didn't hesitate to talk about all his plans in front of Blackjack. Hangman trusted Blackjack more than any other man here. The band would be in the best possible hands while Hangman, Red, Viking, and the others were away.

The other men who would be going on this campaign spent a few hours helping their families build shelters and get comfortable in their new camp. Hangman did the same thing. This site looked better and better the longer the band stayed here.

Certain features of the surrounding cliffs made them more defensible than he originally thought. The Anglers would only be able to approach the cliffs and pounce on the camp from certain points. The band would be able to defend those, too.

He did see one potential problem right away. The band was too big. Mora had been right about that, too.

No other family band had ever stayed together when it got this big. Human bands stayed small, light, and mobile for a reason. A band this big would attract too many creatures.

He would have to address that at some point and raise the possibility of splitting everyone up into four or five much smaller family bands to occupy other areas of the valley.

The human population might get too big for the valley to support everyone. Then someone would have to leave and find territory elsewhere.

He didn't want to do that now. He needed everyone to help defend the band at least until they eliminated the Anglers. Then everyone could think about what to do and how to live after that.

He spent another two hours scouting this end of the valley, but he didn't find what he was looking for. The valley was too big. He would have to travel for days to get to the other end of it.

He finally rounded up his men for the second time, gave instructions to everyone that Blackjack and Mora would be in charge based on their prior experience with the Anglers, and Hangman left with his party. He couldn't think about the band or the Anglers anymore.

He and his men picked up speed the farther they traveled away from the tunnel. Hangman got another surge of pride in his son when Hangman saw that Blackjack and the others had erased their footprints from the landscape.

Hangman and his men returned to the cliff tops. Blackjack and his men hadn't made any effort to conceal their presence here—or not as much of an effort. They didn't have to. The Red Riders already knew the band was here.

Blackjack and Chief had been right about one thing. The Red Riders always seemed to find out where their last party had disappeared.

They could only do that if they had some central organized command keeping track of where all these groups went each time and where each one disappeared.

Hangman didn't think too hard about why the Red Riders would go to so much trouble over one Godless band who happened to accidentally stumble into their territory or even killed one of their parties in self-defense.

This obviously wasn't about that anymore. Hangman and his people must have killed hundreds or maybe thousands of Red Riders over the years since the band had first left Shadow's territory.

Whoever was in charge of the Red Riders sent out more and more and more men for Hangman's people to do exactly the same thing.

Maybe every Red Rider patrol that Hangman eliminated spurred the Red Riders to retaliate harder. Maybe the Red Riders had already committed so much to destroying this band that the Red Riders couldn't quit now even if they wanted to.

Maybe raiding the Red Rider camp, killing all the men, and stealing so many women and captives had been the final insult to trigger the Red Riders to retaliate with everything they could throw at the Godless

Hangman would never understand why the Red Riders did what they did and he didn't need to. The Red Riders were coming after his people. He didn't need to understand anything more complicated than that.

Chapter 43

H angman and his men didn't have any trouble tracking back to the Red Rider camp that Blackjack and his men had destroyed with their poison darts. The ants and Abnormits had already wiped out most of it and were still working on the rest.

"He's as ruthless as his father," Viking muttered under his breath.

"You're going to have to come up with something pretty spectacular to beat this one," Red added. "I can't wait to see this."

"It isn't a competition," Hangman countered. "I'm not in competition with my own son to see who can be the most ruthless to our enemies."

Red grinned at him. "Are you sure about that? It sure looks to me like he's trying his hardest to be exactly like you."

Hangman looked away. "He isn't like me. He's his own man."

"Maybe that's the problem. Would you have used poison darts to kill your enemies?"

"I wouldn't have thought of it. I didn't even know you could do that. I don't have to think too hard to find out who gave him the idea."

"He learned from the best," Viking chimed in. "You can't fault him for that. He's a combination of the best of both worlds. That's what we all want, isn't it? That's exactly why we're doing this. We've been using Mora's information against our enemies for years. Why wouldn't he do the same thing?"

That finished the conversation because Hangman and the rest of his men had no argument against any of that. Hangman couldn't even fathom all the tricks Mora might know that the band hadn't even tapped yet.

He really needed to take some time to talk to her about all of this. He could be utilizing her information so much more effectively than he currently was.

The men also had no trouble tracking the Red Riders back to their original source. Their Blastidons left glaring trails of foot traffic heading south. They led to a much larger camp the way Blackjack had suggested.

Hangman and his men hid in the jungle and observed this camp. The Red Riders had set up everything exactly the same as before except that this camp didn't have any women or other captives in it, either.

The Red Riders came and went the same as always, but they didn't bring in captives. They brought in kills and they brought in goods. They didn't bring in people.

A different air hung over the camp. All the Red Riders acted much more serious and ferocious without their women around. They talked to each other much more harshly.

"I guess they aren't distracted," Red remarked. "We'll have to come up with some other way to eliminate them."

"We won't be able to eliminate all of them," Hangman pointed out. "They don't have their females here. That means this isn't any kind of permanent base or established site. We would have to track all the way back to Red Rider country and wipe out the whole Clan. That would be the only way to completely remove the threat."

"Not all the booby traps and ambushes in the world could do that," Wildling argued. "We wouldn't be able to take all the captives anyway. We have too many people already."

"Exactly," Hangman replied. "This is going to be an ongoing issue. We'll just have to keep the valley under watch and eliminate as many of our enemies as possible so none of them find the tunnel entrance."

"If Chief is right, then the Red Riders will keep coming back to the same place," Red suggested. "They'll always come back to the top of the cliffs. We would never be able to push them farther back from there."

"Maybe there's a way we can do that, too," Hangman replied. "We can start training our younger men to go out on raiding parties to push the Red Riders back."

"I don't understand what you mean," Carnage countered. "How would they do that if each raiding party kills all the Red Riders?"

"One raiding party would hit the Red Riders wherever they're camping," Hangman explained. "Then the next raiding party would go out before the Red Riders have a chance to bring in their next patrol. Each raiding party would report that they've eliminated a Red Rider camp. Then we would send out the next raiding party before the next patrol has a chance to move forward. We would keep pushing back and back and back working our way through the patrols until they couldn't get near the valley anymore."

"The raiding parties would have to travel farther and farther away from the valley to do that," Red pointed out. "You could conceivably push the Red Riders all the way back to Shadow's old territory if you kept up this campaign for long enough."

"We might not have to go as far as that," Hangman replied. "We'll eliminate the Anglers from the valley. Then we won't have to worry about any enemy Clans attacking our people, razing our camps, and marauding the countryside. We'll need to find creative ways to test our young men once they initiate. What better way than to send them out to attack enemy Clans farther away? The young men will get the experience without putting the band in danger."

"So what do you want to do about this group?" Viking asked. "Do you have some deviously creative way to kill them all or will we just go from tent to tent killing everyone the way we did last time?"

"Going tent to tent probably isn't the best way—not the way we did it before—not when these men aren't as distracted as they were."

"So what's the solution?" Red asked. "Something tells me it will be something bloodthirsty, painful, and cruel."

"I think we should do what Blackjack did but without the poison darts."

"Of course not," Viking muttered. "You wouldn't want to steal his thunder."

Hangman laughed. "I don't need to steal his thunder. He has enough already."

"So do you," Red prompted. "So what's the plan?"

"I was thinking we get some Abnormit grubs and turn them loose on the Blastidons."

"That will alert the Red Riders that someone is trying to ambush them," Carnage pointed out.

"That's the point," Hangman replied. "They'll know someone is doing this. They just won't know who it is. The Red Riders will consolidate in their camp and not leave it. That will make them easier to eliminate."

"I knew it would be something bloodthirsty, painful, and cruel," Red added. "You couldn't just walk up to your enemies and stab them with a blade like a normal person."

"I couldn't get near enough to do that," Hangman pointed out. "I didn't come here to throw my life away."

"You came here to throw the Red Riders' lives away," Wildling corrected.

"Yes," Hangman replied and everyone laughed.

Viking shrugged. "I guess we better do this. How do you want to start?"

Hangman and his men spent an hour hunting through the jungle until they found an Abnormit nest in a hollow tree. The men spent another hour very carefully carving a hole in the side wall under the bark.

Hangman pried the thin wood out of the way and exposed one of the nest chambers inside. He didn't want to release the whole larvae horde. That would put him and his men in danger.

He put his hand inside, took hold of one Abnormit grub by its waxy, stark-white thorax, and pulled it out of the nest. The creature squirmed and squealed in his grasp. The larva tried to twist its body around to get its mouth near him.

He held the grub out to Viking, who opened one of his shoulder bags. He'd emptied it just for this. Hangman dropped the grub into the bag and then did the same thing for each of his men. Each of them took a grub and Hangman took one for himself.

The sun was already going down by the time the men retreated back to the Red Rider camp. The men stationed themselves in the treetops above the Blastidons, and each man dropped his Abnormit grub on top of a Blastidon's back.

The Abnormits latched onto the creatures right away and started chewing. The Blastidons screeched in pain and tried in vain to thrash around and throw the Abnormits off. The Abnormits only chewed faster and bored deeper into the Blastidon's bodies.

The sound of their mounts in distress brought the Red Riders running. They all raced out and discovered the problem, but not fast enough.

Most of the grubs had already eaten their way so far inside the Blastidons' bodies that the Red Riders couldn't remove the grubs—not without killing the Blastidons even faster.

Some of the Red Riders actually broke down in emotional despair when they saw what was going on. A few Red Riders had the presence of mind to kill their Blastidons then and there to put the creatures out of their misery.

The rest of the Red Riders went into a shocked daze watching the Abnormit grubs devour the Blastidons from the inside out.

The Red Riders held a heated debate about how this had happened. Hangman saw so many parallels between this scene and the one Blackjack had described after he and his men poisoned the Blastidons at the previous camp.

Hangman felt absolutely no qualms about copying his son's techniques. Blackjack was the one copying Hangman's techniques.

The Red Riders searched the area, but they didn't find the nest with a hole carved in the side. All the Blastidons collapsed and died while the Red Riders were still trying to figure out what to do about this.

The Red Riders eventually had no choice but to go back to their camp and go on with their business. They gathered in groups to discuss the situation. Hangman and his men eavesdropped from the canopy.

The stories of the Godless band ambushing Red Rider patrols had somehow traveled back to the whole Clan. All the Red Riders knew about the Godless ambushes even though no Red Riders had ever survived to make it home and tell the tale.

The Red Riders figured out pretty quick that the Godless must be doing this, too. The Red Riders had come this far and built this camp to track down the Godless. What else did the Red Riders think was going to happen?

Knowing who was killing their Blastidons didn't help the Red Riders retaliate against the perpetrators.

"Now what do you want to do?" Red asked. "How exactly do you plan to distribute Abnormits to the whole band without anyone seeing us?"

"We'll do it the same way we did last time," Hangman replied. "We'll go into their tents while they sleep and deliver the grubs to one man at a time. We'll have to make sure to attach the grubs to some body part that the man won't be able to get it off when the grub starts chewing on him. Go for the back or the base of the neck."

Viking shook his head. "I really think you're starting to enjoy this."

Hangman pretended not to hear. "We'll just keep eliminating them one or two at a time if we have to. Deliver as many grubs as you can before the alarm goes up. Then get out and hide in the jungle. I don't care if the Red Riders find out we're doing this as long as they don't catch us."

The men worked for the rest of the day to weave baskets to carry dozens of grubs. Then Hangman carefully and cautiously removed them from the nest in readiness for tonight.

The men had to wait a long time for the Red Riders to go to sleep. They followed the same pattern as Hangman's last campaign against them. The Red Riders posted guards around their perimeter. The Godless men had to sneak into the camp.

Each man could only carry two baskets at a time, but this many men added up to almost thirty grubs. The men scattered and each one ducked into a tent.

Hangman worked fast. He found the first Rider asleep on his side with his back to the room. This couldn't have been more perfect if Hangman had planned it in advance.

He used the basket to maneuver the grub into the right position so it would attach right at the base of the man's skull. The grub latched on and the man screamed out in pain and surprise.

Hangman didn't stick around to see anything else. He bolted to the next tent. This man slept on his back. The first victim's shrieks and pained bellows had already started to rouse the second Rider.

Hangman tipped the second grub onto the man's neck from the front and bolted for his life. He sprinted out of the camp and into the shadows before any of the Red Riders made it out of their tents.

Screams and roars echoed out of dozens of tents. The noise woke up everyone else. The Red Riders all raced to check on their comrades. Hangman couldn't see what was happening inside the tents and he didn't want to.

The Red Riders went into a frenzy when they realized their enemies had struck right here inside their camp. The Red Riders raced through the camp arming themselves and searching the area.

The screams didn't stop. They escalated. The silence that fell afterward somehow made the attack seem so much worse. None of the injured men survived to come out of their tents.

Chapter 44

A group of young men and uninitiated boys followed Blackjack through the camp while he checked on every family. Oracle, Pyro, Smash, and Chief hovered around Blackjack.

Loso, Kabi, and Zakra went everywhere with Blackjack and the other young men now. Blackjack's three friends included themselves in his councils and acted as if they'd already initiated.

The young men treated the three uninitiated boys as their own. Blackjack couldn't think of them as boys anymore. They were only a few months younger than he was. They would initiate as soon as Hangman and the other older men returned.

Maeno and his friends did the same thing. They followed Blackjack around and included themselves in everything the men and older uninitiated boys did, but everyone really did treat Maeno and his friends as boys because they were.

They were still some of the most capable warriors Blackjack had ever known. Maeno and the others had grown up hearing Kuvik's stories about Tren and everyone else's stories about what Hangman had been like when he was younger.

The boys copied all of this by being far bolder than their age required them to be. They threw themselves into everything with maximum energy, volunteered for the most dangerous scouting missions, and absolutely refused to let anyone leave them behind.

The boys didn't even ask if they could come most of the time. They just invited themselves and went. They sometimes went anyway even if someone told them not to.

It usually turned out to be safer for the boys if the men just took them along instead of trying to order the boys to stay only for the boys to follow on their own.

Blackjack made it to the other side of the camp and spotted Banjo and Feather working on their own shelters. Neither of them had wives, so the two men had to build the shelters themselves.

Blackjack pretended not to see the two older men. Banjo and Feather had never caused Blackjack any problems before, but there was always a first time for everything.

Banjo and Feather didn't get involved with his and his men's maneuvers. Banjo and Feather held themselves apart as though they were too good to associate with men so much younger than themselves.

Banjo and Feather definitely treated the boys as if they weren't good enough to get involved in defending the band. Banjo and Feather even treated Loso, Kabi, and Zakra that way.

Blackjack didn't have to think too hard to figure out why Hangman had left Banjo and Feather behind. Hangman had left those two behind both times he'd gone out to wage war against the Red Riders. Why?

Hangman had taken the men he trusted the most—Red, Viking, Red's men, Bantam, and Lock. Hangman had been waging these campaigns with Red's men for years. Bantam and Lock were Hangman's brothers.

That left Banjo and Feather out in the cold even though they were so much older than the younger men. Banjo and Feather were even older than Hangman. They were almost Viking's age.

Hangman could have left either Banjo or Feather in charge of the band. Hangman could have left Oracle in charge of the band—or Chief.

Blackjack turned away and headed back to the other side of the camp. He didn't want to deal with Banjo or Feather. Blackjack's gut already told him he would have to deal with them eventually—either separately or together. They would be his first project as Kral.

He got another overwhelming feeling that he was Kral in every way that counted. He had gotten that feeling in the marrow of his bones the minute Hangman left the valley. Who else would take over as Kral if not Blackjack?

The freed men helped work with the women. Most of the freed men had paired off with someone or other. All these new people started living together as families, including the pregnant women and mothers who'd recently given birth.

Blackjack and his men got halfway across the camp before they heard shouting coming from the far end of the enclosure. The shouting voices sounded like children.

Blackjack and the men ran over there just as a crowd of children rushed through the bottleneck to enter the camp. Blackjack spotted Anglers moving through the jungle behind the children's backs.

The children kept running through the camp yelling out that the Anglers were coming. Blackjack and his men and boys got to the camp entrance first, drew their weapons, and braced themselves to defend the camp from the worst.

The Anglers charged the opening and smashed into the rock trying to break their way inside. Hangman's genius saved the band this time, too. The narrow entrance gave Blackjack and his comrades all the time they needed to cut the Anglers down one at a time.

The same situation unfolded here as played out at the caves. The Anglers tore the dead out of the way so more Anglers could rush in and meet their deaths.

The Anglers didn't keep it up as long this time. They didn't go for days or even all night. They stopped after only a few minutes, prowled around, and some climbed up the surrounding rock cliffs to peer down at the camp from above.

The Anglers jumped down from strategic points, but as Hangman predicted, few enough Anglers invaded that the freed men could overwhelm them and bring them down, too.

Blackjack, Oracle, Chief, and Loso defended the camp entrance alone. Everyone else went after the Anglers that jumped down from the cliffs. The band killed twenty of them before the Anglers figured out that they couldn't get in that way, either.

The Anglers stopped jumping down. They swarmed all over the cliffs for a little longer and then shrank back into the jungle. "At least we can defend ourselves," Chief pointed out.

"And we have plenty of food now," Maeno added. "These Anglers are so considerate providing for our Clan. We should be really grateful."

Loso and the other older boys laughed. Kabi hooked his elbow around Maeno's neck and the two of them got into a wrestling match on the ground.

Blackjack posted a guard outside so the women and children could start butchering the dead Anglers.

"We're going to have enough food for the rest of the year," Oracle exclaimed.

"We might need it if the Anglers launch another extended assault to trap us here." Blackjack stood up. "Let's go see about hitting some more breeding sites."

"Aren't they all gone?" Smash asked.

"Not all. Anyway, I want to mount an offensive even if we do it against the adults. I don't want to wait for them to come to us."

He took the freed men, the four young men from Oracle's party, and left the boys to guard the camp. They were good at that.

Blackjack didn't know where to find any more breeding sites or pockets of young Anglers, so he organized another sweep down the valley from the top end.

The band had already cleared enough of the valley. The men didn't find a single trace of Anglers for a long way south. The men traveled for hours before they found a completely different nest site for the older juvenile Anglers.

Ten huge adults stood guard over them this time. Blackjack and his men stayed off at a safe distance and eyed the site.

"Those adults are going to be a problem," Oracle remarked.

"They know better than to leave their young unguarded," Blackjack agreed. "The Anglers are learning and adapting to what we do."

"All the more reason to hit this site," Chief countered. "The fact that they're guarding it means we should definitely hit it."

"So they can kill us all?" Smash asked.

"No, so we can kill them all," Chief returned. "That's what we're here for—to eliminate all the Anglers. Someone would have to come along and kill these creatures. Are you saying we should retreat and let someone else do that? That's the coward's way."

"I'm saying we should come back with enough men to defeat them," Smash replied. "I'm saying we have no reason to throw our lives away when we could defeat these creatures so much more easily with more men."

"More men would tip them off that we're going after this site," Blackjack pointed out. "I'm with Chief on this. We can kill the adults without putting ourselves in danger. Then we can go after the...."

"How would we kill ten adult Anglers with only five men?!" Smash demanded. "You're out of your head."

"Watch your mouth," Chief fired back. "When has Blackjack ever let us down before?" He turned back to Blackjack. "You have an idea, don't you?"

"My mother killed a bunch of Anglers when we were trapped here alone. She jumped onto one of their heads and stabbed it in the back of the skull. Then she jumped to the next creature and did the same thing. We would only have to kill two Anglers each if we all attacked at once."

Chief raised his eyebrows. "Wow. I knew Mora was resourceful. I didn't know she could do something like that."

Blackjack pointed to the trees around them. "Let's get into position."

"The Anglers will see us if we go out there," Smash pointed out.

"Then let them see us. They won't be able to stop us. Come on. Grow a spine and be bold. Remember you're making this valley safe for your future wife and children to live and your descendants to grow up. Let's go."

The men spread out. Each man selected a different tree above the nesting site. The Anglers all saw the men, reared onto their hind legs, and tried to grab the men out of the branches.

The Anglers couldn't get that high without climbing into the branches and leaving the nest site unguarded. The adults eventually dropped back down onto their feet.

Blackjack took advantage of this to jump onto one of the Anglers' backs. He hacked his ax into the base of the creature's skull just as the Angler nearest him came down onto its feet, too.

He leapt clear of the falling body and landed on that Angler next. His comrades all plummeted out of the trees one after the other. They carried out the operation perfectly until Smash landed on his Angler.

Pyro landed first and struck hard to kill his first Angler. The creature went down hard and the Angler next to it wheeled to attack Pyro just as Smash landed on the creature's back.

He stabbed, but the creature's quick movements threw him off balance. He missed his first strike and impaled the creature through the shoulder instead.

The Angler screeched in rage and pain, reared again, and threw Smash down onto the ground. Smash sprawled onto his back and hit his head. The blow stunned him, but not enough to stop him from seeing the Angler turn around and stalk him down.

Blackjack took a flying leap, landed on the Angler, and hacked his axe through the back of the creature's head. None of the other Anglers were close enough for him to jump to any of them, so he rode the creature to the ground.

He stood over the dead Angler gripping his axes and looking around for any other Anglers to come after him. He spotted one just as it moved in to annihilate him. He stood on the ground exposed with just his two axes to defend himself.

The Angler's attention riveted on him in an unbreakable glare. The creature prowled closer to finish him off. Blackjack braced himself for the showdown of his lifetime. This would be even harder than fighting a Demonex.

Right then, Oracle launched out of the trees from somewhere, landed in a teetering balance on the Angler's back, and brought it down in seconds with a well-aimed strike to the back of the head.

The Angler thudded onto the ground with Oracle still wobbling there. "Thank you, brother," Blackjack exclaimed. "I owe you for that."

"Not at all. That was outstanding. Now we can go ahead and kill all these young ones. Let's get to work."

The men had to retreat to the other side of the site and wait for the young Anglers to calm down after the battle. The young Anglers didn't notice their enormous relatives missing. The young ones went back to exploring the area. Some even decided to gnaw on the bodies.

Blackjack and his men lined up on that side and started mowing their way through all the young Anglers. The men killed a hundred before the young ones scattered and fled from the attack.

The men retreated, watched, and waited. The young Anglers didn't know enough to protect themselves. They all eventually migrated back to the place they believed they would be safe.

The men started in again and the same thing happened. They made pass after pass killing dozens of young Anglers before the creatures realized what was wrong, fled, and then came back to the same spot as soon as the men backed off.

The project took a long time, but the men eventually killed every last Angler in the area. The Abnormits, Krakelows, and a few Demonex heard the commotion and discovered the dead bodies, so Blackjack and his friends left for home.

Chapter 45

Mora sat in front of her shelter holding one of the babies that had been born in the caves just a few days ago. Mora tried not to listen to the mother sobbing inside Mora's shelter.

The mother's name was Zoana and she had been an emotional wreck ever since giving birth to a baby fathered by one of the Red Riders. Not even knowing that her captor was dead and that she was now free could take the sting away.

Zoana struggled even to look at her baby son, much less hold him, nurse him, or take care of him. She had been coming to Mora ever since the baby had been born. Zoana hadn't even named the baby yet. She couldn't face it.

Mora loved taking care of the little boy, but he really needed his mother. She usually broke down in wretched sobs every time she had to nurse him. She white-knuckled it through every feeding and immediately handed him off to someone else as soon as it was over.

Mora sat with her legs stretched out and close together, laid the baby in the channel between her thighs, and used her legs to bounce him up and down while she moved his arms and hands around and made faces at him.

He stared up at her like she had three heads. He actually got an expression on his face like he really thought she was out of her mind.

His expression and reaction to her antics made her laugh. She tried to do it quietly so Zoana wouldn't hear.

Zoana was still inside the shelter when Blackjack came over to Mora's shelter and sat down next to her. "I didn't know you were carrying another child, Mother," he teased. "Why am I only finding out about this now?"

Mora laughed again. "You'll be getting married soon. Then you won't be able to make fun of me anymore."

He bent over and examined the baby boy. The baby's attention immediately switched to Blackjack. The baby didn't look away. He extended one of his hands toward Blackjack's hair.

"He likes you," Mora remarked. "Maybe he sees that he'll be fighting alongside you when he grows up."

"He's a fine boy. I'm sure he'll grow up well."

Mora got serious. "I have to tell you something, my son."

Blackjack's features turned dark. "Wait. Don't tell me. Let me see if I can guess."

She smiled at him. "It was only a matter of time. You're young. That on its own makes you a target."

He looked away and gritted his teeth. "Don't tell me anything else. I don't want to know."

"Okay. I won't. How did it go today?"

"It went very well today. Father is a genius for choosing this spot. It's so defensible."

"Did you and your men find anything out there?"

"Yes, the Anglers are adapting and protecting their young better—but your information about ambushes and booby traps is always the best way to deal with our enemies. It works every time."

"I'm glad I've been able to hand that down to you. I'm glad your father sees the value in fighting this way and doesn't view it as cowardice."

"Winning isn't cowardice, especially against an enemy this much more powerful than we are. The point is not to make a statement about how foolhardy we are. The point is to protect our Clans and make sure we survive."

She smiled at him. "Your father is the one who made it possible for the Godless to learn that lesson. He saw the value in using other skills besides size and strength to accomplish his aims."

Zoana came out of Mora's shelter just then. Zoana tried to wipe the tears off her cheeks, but Blackjack saw them anyway. She hustled away and vanished without taking her son with her.

Mora sighed and turned back to the baby. "It looks like you have a grandmother after all, little brother."

"He's lucky to have you," Blackjack remarked. "I'm surprised more of these women aren't turning their backs on their own children."

"So am I. I thought more of them would have a problem with it. I guess the women's new husbands are convincing them to make it work. The new husbands don't care, so that makes it more acceptable for the women."

"Doesn't this woman have a husband? I don't know her name, but I think I've seen her with one of the new men."

"Yes, she has a husband and he's been kind and supportive. That doesn't help her get over her feelings. The baby being a boy doesn't help at all to be totally honest with you. She would probably have an easier time if the baby was a girl."

"I don't see why," Blackjack countered. "It isn't the baby's fault that his father was a Red Rider and it isn't the baby's fault that he's a boy. He deserves a mother."

Mora smiled at him. "You're going to be a good father one day."

Blackjack looked away. "At least I have a few more years before I have to start thinking about finding a wife. Heaven only knows where I'm going to get one."

"You might be surprised. A lot can happen in four years. We would be able to travel to the gathering much more quickly now, especially if you went with just your father and a few key relatives. The trip wouldn't take that long without the whole band tagging along."

"I sure hope you're right," he murmured.

Mora opened her mouth to say something else, but one of the free men came up to them just then. The man's name was Kavis. He was one of Yeoli's main lieutenants and a staunch defender of the band.

Kavis was one of the youngest of the freed men. The freed men all wore their hair short and a different combination of clothes made out of a mixture of woven fabrics and the hardened animal skin armor that the Red Riders wore.

None of the freed men had a very good build. The Red Riders hadn't treated the men well or fed them as much as the men needed to stay in good condition.

The men had been putting on weight since they joined the Godless, but the freed men still had a long way to go before they regained their condition.

Kavis had stolen a thick, stiff belt from the Red Riders after Hangman and his men had wiped out the camp. Kavis had also stolen two Red Rider axes for himself. He wore these tied to his belt by their handles.

Someone must have told Kavis about Mora's technique of pulling the slip knots on her blade handles when she wanted to draw them. Kavis had copied the design and used slip knots to lash his axe handles to his belt.

Two straps around his thighs secured the axe heads so they didn't bump into his legs when he wasn't using them.

He had to release these thigh straps first before he could actually wield his weapons, but he still managed to do this in a matter of seconds whenever something threatened him.

The axes were too big for him to use as effectively as he might have. He would have had an easier time if he used something smaller, but he never took anything smaller even when the other men offered him different weapons.

He seemed to take it as a matter of personal pride that he used stolen Red Rider weapons against all his enemies, both Red Riders and everything else. He seemed to want to make a point to himself and the world by using these weapons instead of any other.

"Um.....can I ask you something?" Kavis asked Blackjack.

"Of course. You can ask me anything."

"It's just......" Kavis glanced over his shoulder. "Banjo just came around and told a bunch of us to build another fence across the camp entrance. We weren't sure if we should do it until we heard from you—and then he went over to the other side of the camp there and told a bunch of people they had to move their shelters away from the cliffs."

Blackjack's features closed up in a mask of grim determination. "I see. Thank you for telling me."

"So....should we do it?"

"You don't have to. You can go on with your business as though it never happened."

Kavis looked behind him again. "What should we do about moving the shelters?"

"Don't do anything," Blackjack replied. "Just leave them where they are."

"What about....what about Banjo? What should we tell him if he insists?"

"Tell him I told you not to move the shelters. Tell him he should come and talk to me about it if he has a problem with that. He and I will straighten it out. You don't have to do anything until we agree."

"But you're....you're just a kid. I know this is the Godless way and everything and that you're technically Kral in your father's place...."

"I'm not Kral because my father is still alive." Blackjack's voice strained from the effort of keeping his composure. "My father went on a hunting trip. He isn't dead, so he's still Kral. Banjo isn't Kral any more than I am. If you don't want to tell Banjo that I told you not to do anything, tell him you'll wait to hear it from Hangman. Tell him you're still learning the Godless way and you won't make any strategic decisions until you hear exactly who is taking over as Kral in my father's place—assuming we don't have reason to believe he'll come home in a couple of days."

"I didn't mean to offend you," Kavis stammered. "I'm just trying to learn all of this."

"You didn't offend me at all, Kavis," Blackjack growled. "I'm angry at Banjo, not you. I'm grateful that you came to tell me what he said. None of this has anything to do with you. You don't need to get in the middle of it. No one will blame you for staying out of it."

Kavis nodded and scampered away. Mora had to chuckle. "I wonder what he'll do. I wonder if he'll do what Banjo told him to or not."

Blackjack stood up. "I have to go, Mother. I can see you have your hands full with your new baby grandson."

Mora laughed. "Let's hope it doesn't turn into that."

"He could do a lot worse than to be raised by you. No one knows that better than I do. I'll see you later."

He walked off into the camp. Mora watched him go in between checking on the baby. Blackjack sure was growing up fast. He had just initiated and he was already facing his first challenge. That's what this would turn into.

Chapter 46

Mora stood up, put the baby boy on her shoulder, and patted him on the back while she walked across the camp to find his mother. Mora had decided to call the little boy Eco since his mother didn't show any inclination to name him or treat him as a real person.

Mora found Zoana at her shelter. Her new husband's name was Kuri and he was unbelievably kind and patient with Zoana's troubles. Mora couldn't imagine a better man for Zoana than Kuri.

Kuri would be the best person for Eco, too, as soon as Zoana dealt with all the bad memories associated with the little boy's birth.

Mora found both Kuri and Zoana outside their shelter in the sunshine. Mora stood there waiting while Zoana nursed the baby.

She couldn't even bring herself to look at him once he attached to her breast. She looked away in the other direction and grimaced in disgust that her own baby was touching her so intimately.

Mora talked to Kuri while she waited. She'd been going through this ever since Zoana had come to Mora for help in dealing with the child. Mora told Kuri about giving the baby a name.

"It's a good name," he remarked. "I like it. It suits him."

"I figure he'll grow into it," she replied. "It might be too big for him now, but he'll only change it at initiation. It doesn't matter if he doesn't like his childhood name."

"I don't think it's too big for him at all," Kuri countered. "I think it's great. Thank you."

She smiled at him. He started to smile back, but his smile drained away when he saw something behind her. Mora almost dreaded turning around, but she had to. She had to see this for herself.

Blackjack squatted across the camp next to Oracle's shelter. Oracle, Pyro, Smash, and Chief had all built their shelters on that side of the camp closer to the cliffs. Kavis and a bunch of the other single freed men had built their shelters over there, too.

The shelters of certain families dotted the area. No one had specifically decided that the single people should all live in one place because they didn't. They lived all jumbled up with families and everyone else.

Oracle sat on the ground next to Blackjack while they held a conversation between the two of them. The two men were minding their own business not paying attention to anyone else when Banjo strode over there.

"I told you to move these shelters away from the cliffs," he snapped at Kavis and some of the others. "You should have already done it by now."

Blackjack got to his feet before any of the new people had a chance to say anything. He squared his shoulders at Banjo. "I told them not to. I told them to leave the shelters where they are."

Banjo spun around. "*You* told them?! You don't have the authority to tell anyone anything. You're barely initiated. You have no business throwing your weight around."

"You don't have any authority to tell anyone anything, either, Banjo," Blackjack murmured. "My father is still Kral of this band until we have some credible reason to think he's dead and won't come back from his trip. He went out for a few days. He didn't die. No one in this camp has acknowledged you as Kral, so you have no business issuing orders to people behind my father's back."

Banjo swiped his hand at the shelters. "It's for their own protection! Any moron can see that! They're right under the cliffs where the Anglers could jump down on top of them."

"These shelters are under the part of the cliffs where the Anglers *can't* jump down on top of them," Blackjack went on in the same measured tone. "There are too many shelters here to move them somewhere else. These people would have to crowd at the center of the camp which would put everyone in danger. Everyone is safer and more comfortable where they are."

Banjo narrowed his eyes at Blackjack. "Are you challenging me?"

Blackjack shrugged. "I'm not challenging anyone because neither of us is Kral. You're a man and I'm a man. If you have a problem with me, then we'll settle it like men." Blackjack dragged his gaze down to Banjo's feet and back up to his face. "I think we both know who would win that fight. I might be smaller, but we both know what the outcome would be."

Oracle got to his feet just then and stood next to Blackjack. "Blackjack is my Kral until Hangman comes back," Oracle declared. "No one gives orders to this band except for them."

"The boys and I are for Blackjack, too," Loso interjected from the other side of the area. "You might win, Banjo, but you'll never hold any authority in this band. We'll initiate one of these days and we won't forget what you did here today."

Chief sauntered over from his shelter and stood on Blackjack's other side. "You don't have the influence to lead this band, Banjo. You're older than Blackjack. That's the only thing you have on your side. He's smarter, braver, more cunning, and he knows how to defeat all of our enemies. You don't have any of that. You can't protect the band. You can't lead us at all. You'll never be the warrior he is no matter how long you live. He's his father's son and he's our only Kral as long as Hangman isn't here."

Smash and Pyro came over just then. The young men gathered around Blackjack. He never took his eyes off Banjo.

Banjo fumed as his temper kept rising. His eyes darted from one man to the next. "You call this boy your Kral?! That's outrageous!"

"*You* don't call yourself our Kral," Chief countered. "No one is our Kral unless we say so. I don't hear anyone calling you their Kral. Go back to your shelter where you belong."

Banjo raised his arm and pointed in Blackjack's face. "You call yourself a Kral?! I challenge you, then! I challenge any claim you have to be a Kral!"

"I've never called myself Kral, Banjo," Blackjack replied. "I told you that."

Chief stepped forward. "I call him Kral. You can challenge me for saying so."

Blackjack grabbed Chief's arm and pulled him back into line.

"I'm not challenging *you*!" Banjo snapped at Chief and then turned back to point at Blackjack again. "I'm challenging *you*. It doesn't matter if they call you Kral or you call yourself Kral. I still challenge you. You will never be Kral of this band. You don't deserve even to walk around in this band if you call yourself that."

"Very well," Blackjack replied. "Choose your weapon and meet me over there." He pointed to the center of the camp. It was one of the only places not occupied by shelters.

Banjo stormed off to the other side of the camp, drew his weapons, and paced back and forth glaring at anyone who dared to make eye contact with him.

Banjo fought with axes, too, but his were much bigger than Blackjack's. Banjo had all the advantage of size and strength on his side.

He didn't have brains and cunning. Chief was right about that. Banjo didn't think strategically. He couldn't be thinking strategically if he didn't see the tide shifting in Blackjack's favor a long time ago.

Maybe Banjo did see it. Maybe that was why he felt the need to act now to stop it before the groundswell of support in Blackjack's favor became overwhelming and unstoppable.

Feather stood off to one side and didn't go near Banjo to support him. Feather must have realized the foolishness of this course before Banjo stuck his neck out and said something he couldn't take back.

Blackjack's friends surrounded him. "Let me fight him on your behalf!" Chief murmured. "Let me get rid of the bastard."

"You know I can't do that," Blackjack replied. "I have to face him. He's obviously been planning this for a while. He's taking advantage of Hangman's absence to get rid of me while I'm young."

"He's a traitorous coward," Oracle muttered. "He wouldn't dare to say anything like this to anyone else."

"All the more reason why I have to face him." Blackjack pushed past his friends. "Don't intervene. Let me handle this."

"He's a dead man either way," Chief muttered. "We'll kill him if he wins this fight."

"What happens if he wins this fight doesn't concern me." Blackjack pulled his axes. "Just stay out of the way and don't get involved. This is between me and him—no one else."

He didn't stick around to say anything else. He strode out into the middle of the camp to face Banjo.

Mora should have felt more misgivings about her son facing a man so much bigger and stronger than himself, but she felt no tension or nerves at all. It never crossed her mind that Blackjack would lose.

Right at that moment, Zoana shot to her feet, shoved Eco into Mora's arms, muttered, "I can't watch this," and darted inside the shelter.

Eco must have just finished nursing because he didn't fuss or make a sound at suddenly being passed off to a stranger. He knew Mora. He was already starting to get used to the routine of nursing from Zoana and spending all the rest of his time with Mora.

She put the baby on her shoulder and turned her attention back to the fight brewing between Banjo and Blackjack. Blackjack halted in the center of the camp while Banjo kept pacing back and forth.

"It doesn't have to be this way, Banjo," Blackjack told him. "We're cousins. We can just wait until Hangman comes back—or one of his men comes back. We can settle this amicably for the good of the band. We don't have to fight."

Banjo pointed one of his axes at Blackjack and raised his voice so the whole camp could hear him. "This boy calls himself Kral over our band! This boy elevates himself to a status above the rest of us!"

"You're a liar!" Chief snapped. "He never called himself Kral! *We* said he was Kral! We called him our Kral and anyone who knows what's good for this band will do the same thing! We sure as hell will never follow you, Banjo! You would be the last man we ever made our Kral."

Banjo didn't answer. He raised his axes and flexed his knees to confront Blackjack. Blackjack heaved an almighty sigh and raised his weapons, too. He didn't move forward to engage.

Banjo scooted forward one foot at a time and circled from one side to the other. Blackjack didn't move except to turn around so he would continue facing Banjo. Blackjack didn't make the first move.

Banjo struck hard and fast, lunged forward, and swung his axes one after the other in a blur of movement. Blackjack reacted even faster, sidestepped, and brought his axe down in one swift backhand across the back of Banjo's skull.

Banjo crumpled into the dirt and didn't move again. The whole fight lasted less than thirty seconds before it was all over.

Blackjack's victory left even his closest friends and allies absolutely stunned into silence. They gaped at him with their mouths open.

Now he was the one who paced back and forth to glare at everyone. He turned his back on Banjo's dead body.

"I'm Kral of this band until my father or one of his men returns!" Blackjack roared. "Anyone here who disagrees or wishes to challenge me, step out now and declare yourself! I won't tolerate any other challenge after this! Choose your leader now and then be silent! You can call me a boy. You can call me anything you want, but no one will challenge me after today—not until my father returns! He's still alive and he will return. He's fighting our enemies right now! Do you understand that—all you would-be traitors?! My father and his men are out there fighting to defend your lives and your freedom—and this is how you repay him—by going behind his back and sowing dissention in the band!" Blackjack pointed down at Banjo's body. "This traitor waited until my father left the area and then undermined his authority by picking a fight with me. My father is the only Kral of this band and he left me in charge while he's away. If anyone disagrees with that, step out now!"

No one stepped out. Blackjack paced back and forth with his black eyes flashing. He especially glared at Feather, but Feather didn't say a word or make a sound.

Blackjack finally stopped next to the body and waved his axes at it. "Get this piece of trash out of here."

Oracle, Pyro, Smash, and Chief came forward. They each picked up one of Banjo's arms and legs, hefted him off the ground, and hauled the body out of camp.

A deadly silence hung over the area after they left. Blackjack stormed off back to Mora's shelter and threw himself down to sit on the ground. Kuri gave Mora a pointed look and went inside his own shelter to see about Zoana.

Mora had nothing else to do, so she took Eco back to her shelter and sat down next to Blackjack. She would have smiled at him, but he refused to look at her. He went through an elaborate process of cleaning the blood off his axes and putting them back in his waistband.

She busied herself by taking care of the baby. He settled down and eventually fell asleep on her shoulder. She didn't dare to move him, so she left him there.

She considered breaking the silence and talking to Blackjack, but one of the teenage girls came over to him just then and handed him a bowl of freshly roasted Angler meat.

The women had been butchering, preparing, and distributing all the meat from all the dead Anglers the men had killed since the band had moved here.

The girl smiled at him, blushed when he thanked her, and retreated. He stared down at the food in his hand. He took a long time before he started eating it.

Mora kept an eye on him on the side. Hangman had never faced a challenge like this. He'd never really faced any challenge at all. Everyone had always accepted his leadership and even asked it of him when he didn't want to accept it.

Blackjack wasn't even technically Kral and he was already facing challenges from his older relatives.

Oracle and the other young men returned without Banjo's body. No one asked what the young men had done with it.

They spotted Blackjack, came over, and squatted and sat around him. They started talking to him about going after the Anglers again and he started eating.

The tension crept into his voice while he talked, but that strain faded the longer he talked of other things. The young men went on as though Banjo's challenge had never happened.

Chapter 47

Hangman used a big rock to pound a long stake into the ground at the top of the cliff. Viking, Bantam, Carnage, Burn, and Lock did the same thing.

The men drove the stakes in a long way to make them secure, shaved the flattened tops into points, and impaled a bunch of severed Red Rider heads on top of the stakes.

The men had spent the last three days feeding the Red Riders to the Abnormits. The Red Rider numbers had dwindled to the point where they couldn't stop the Godless from killing more and more Riders while they slept.

Hangman and his men staked twenty heads along the top of the valley where future Red Rider patrols would be sure to find them. Hangman stood back and admired his handiwork.

"That will definitely get their attention," Red pointed out.

"They already know we're here," Hangman replied. "Maybe some of them will take the warning and leave us alone."

Viking turned away. "That will never happen, brother. They'll never leave us alone."

"Then we'll stake their heads around the entire valley. We'll announce this valley as the place where Red Riders come to die."

Red laughed and the whole party headed down the hill toward the tunnel entrance. The men traveled through the canopy for most of the way to conceal their line of travel.

They made it back to the band's new camp by midmorning and met up with Oracle and his men. Hangman didn't see Blackjack or the boys anywhere around.

"What's the news?" Hangman asked Oracle.

"Banjo is dead," Chief blurted out. "He challenged Blackjack like the fool that Banjo was. End of story."

Hangman raised his eyebrows. "Why would Banjo challenge Blackjack when I'm still Kral?"

"Because Banjo was an idiot," Oracle added. "Banjo tried to throw his weight around and give orders to these people. Blackjack stuck up for you and said you were still Kral and neither he nor Banjo should be telling anyone to do anything. Banjo decided to pick a fight with Blackjack...."

"And we told Banjo that Blackjack was our Kral until you came back," Chief cut in. "We told Banjo we would never accept him as Kral."

"Let me guess," Red remarked. "He didn't take it very well."

"That's when he challenged Blackjack," Oracle went on. "Banjo made a big noise by saying that Blackjack called himself Kral when he didn't. We were the ones who did it."

"Anyway, they fought and now it's all over," Chief finished. "Feather has been keeping quiet and minding his own business far away from us and Blackjack."

Hangman had to bite back laughter. "So is everything else under control?"

"We've been making runs out into the jungle to eliminate more Anglers, but that's all," Oracle replied. "They haven't come back here."

"What do you mean when you say, 'we've been making runs out into the jungle to eliminate more Anglers'?" Hangman asked. "Do you mean just the four of you?"

"No, Blackjack leads us," Chief replied. "He's a devious bastard when it comes to killing them. He's always coming up with new ways to kill them. He says they learn too fast so he always has to keep changing his methods."

"I don't believe it," Viking muttered. "I didn't think it was possible for any other man to be as hard and tenacious as Hangman. Now I find out there are two of them."

"It looks to me like there are a lot more than two," Carnage murmured. "Here they come now."

Hangman and the others turned around to see Blackjack and the seven boys coming through the jungle to enter the camp. They dropped out of the trees and walked the rest of the way.

The boys looked taller just since a few days ago when Hangman and his men had left the valley. The boys surrounded Blackjack and they all talked on their way through the entrance opening. Where had Hangman seen this before?

Blackjack reminded him in that moment of Hammer. These boys would form their own internal nucleus band. They would rise to take over this band after Hangman and his men got too old to protect anyone.

Blackjack already had Oracle and the others behind him. All four of them had already declared him their Kral until Hangman came back.

Blackjack spotted Hangman and the others standing there watching. Blackjack and the boys crossed the camp to join the older men. "Welcome home, Father," Blackjack exclaimed.

"Thank you, my son. Have you been out there killing more Anglers?"

"We weren't killing them," Kabi replied. "We just scouted the valley to the south and located some of their nesting grounds for our next strike."

"The Angler numbers are dropping," Blackjack went on. "We have to travel farther and farther south to find more sites to attack. We're succeeding in reducing their population. We can finish them off if we keep going like this."

"We start at the top of the valley and work down every time," Maeno interjected. "To make sure we don't miss any of them and they don't get around us. See?"

Hangman studied him and then all the other boys. "I see, my son. Thank you. You've been doing great work."

"Oracle and his men have been doing the most," Blackjack added. "We couldn't have done any of it without them."

"Have you been taking the freed men with you?" Hangman asked.

"We've been leaving them to guard the camp," Blackjack replied. "Most of them need to spend time with their wives and new families anyway. We can travel faster without so many people—and the freed men don't move so well in the trees. It isn't anything personal. It's just easier when we go alone—and we wouldn't be able to go at all if we didn't leave someone to guard the camp."

Hangman nodded. He tried not to show how delighted he was with his son's conduct—and with all the boys' and young men's conduct.

"Kabi is coming up for initiation, Father," Blackjack went on. "The men and I were planning to initiate him if you didn't come back in the next few days."

"Go ahead and initiate him now," Hangman replied. "You're men. You can initiate anyone you want to. You don't need our permission for that."

"Don't you dare initiate him without us being there," Carnage snapped. "Don't even think it. He's Butch's son and Butch is dead, so we have to be there. We have to stand in his father's place."

Blackjack opened and closed his mouth a few times. "I'm....I'm sorry....I should have thought of that. I never meant....."

"Don't worry about it, little brother," Red interjected. "We're back now so we can all go."

"We just didn't know when you would get back," Blackjack blurted out. "We thought....."

"You don't have to explain," Hangman interrupted. "You boys can all go back to your families. We'll meet later to discuss our next moves. You can let us know what you found out about where the Anglers are nesting."

The group started to break up, but right at that moment, a massive stampede of Anglers rushed the entrance from outside. They attacked the same way they did before, smashed into the rock, and swarmed all over the cliffs.

Hangman and his men leapt into position and all the freed men rushed to the entrance and side walls to defend the camp from the invasion. Children screamed and all the women retreated deeper into the camp to get out of danger.

The men killed as many as they could get, but the Anglers played it much smarter this time. They didn't come within weapons range.

They paced up and down in front of the entrance so no one could go outside.

More Anglers climbed over the surrounding walls in all the places they could get to without actually dropping to the ground inside the camp itself.

The men had to constantly stay on watch. The Anglers kept everyone on edge by screeching and squealing all the time, rushing close to the entrance, and then dodging out of the way before the men could harm them.

The Anglers on the walls did the same thing. They darted downward and came close enough to make all the men brace themselves. Then the Anglers sprang away and left the men tense and watchful.

Hangman guarded the entrance for more than three hours before he started to see a pattern here. He backed off and let his men take over.

He met up with Blackjack, Yeoli, Kuvik, and Viking in the middle of camp where the men could see the defenders on all sides.

"How are there so many more of them now?" Blackjack asked. "We reduced their numbers. I swear we did."

"Wait until nightfall," Hangman told him. "Then sneak out with Oracle and the other men under cover of darkness. Head south and see if you can find them. Don't worry about sweeping the valley or locating any other nesting sites. Just find out where they're hiding. They must have another population cluster somewhere to the south—somewhere we haven't explored yet. Just find it. Don't do anything else. Find it and come back and tell me. Then we'll know what to do."

They didn't get a chance to talk any further. Hangman went back to the entrance, but he only stayed another hour.

He strode through the camp and divided all the men into three watches so they could relieve each other and get enough rest.

The Anglers still didn't attack when Hangman sent the first watch away. He ordered all the men to go inside their shelters so they wouldn't see the Anglers prowling around. The men would still be able to hear the creatures screeching, though. Everyone could hear that.

The men on watch had to stay alert, but the Anglers still didn't do anything—not really. They kept making these rushes, but the Anglers never actually entered the camp.

They couldn't enter through the gap. They could only get inside the camp by coming down the cliff walls and the Anglers never did that. The men on watch couldn't maintain the same level of tension all the time. They started to relax and just kept watch.

Some of the men even lowered their weapons. Hangman didn't correct this. This wasn't really an attack. The Anglers might just be trying to intimidate the Godless into halting their extermination campaign.

Hangman didn't care about much of anything at this point as long as Blackjack and the others made it out of the camp tonight. Nothing mattered except finding out where the Anglers were consolidating their numbers. It obviously wasn't anywhere near here.

The sun started to go down. The watch changed twice before Blackjack and the others went off duty. Hangman walked the five men to the other end of the camp where the fences blocked the other two entrances to the area.

"Take care of yourselves and come back in one piece," Hangman murmured. "We need this information so we can mount our final campaign to finish these creatures off."

Blackjack nodded. "We will, Father. We won't come back without it."

Hangman would have liked to hug his son, but Hangman couldn't do that in front of the other four. Blackjack and the others climbed over the fence and disappeared into the dark.

That left Hangman and the others to defend the camp until Blackjack returned. Hangman only hoped and prayed Blackjack would find out something that would tip the balance in the Godless' favor once and for all.

Chapter 48

Blackjack and his men raced through the dark, sprang into the shadowy treetops, and took off heading south. The men traveled much faster than usual. None of them looked out for Anglers anywhere.

Blackjack traveled a long way until he came to the last site where he'd seen Anglers. The place was deserted now. Nothing remained of the webs, the young, the adults, or any other sign that the Anglers had ever been here.

He and his men traveled for hours until they came to the edge of the jungle. Blackjack didn't trust going out into the open in the dark, so he and his men hunkered down in the canopy and got some sleep until the sun started to rise.

They climbed down to the ground and made their way out into the open on foot. All five of the friends could see for miles in any direction. No Anglers would be able to come up on the men unawares.

Blackjack spotted the steep mountains ahead. He knew from listening to his parents talk about getting out of this valley that these mountains were not the end of the valley. They only looked like it.

The mountains came to a pass there and the valley continued south beyond that. The Anglers must be taking shelter there. Hiding there wouldn't save them forever. The Godless would eventually work their way that far south and eliminate the Anglers there, too.

The Anglers might not have realized that or maybe they did. Blackjack had to find out, but he and his men had to travel a long way even to get to those mountains.

The men camped in the open a few times, reentered the jungle, and finally made it to the top of the pass. They looked out over a hundred miles of territory. It was a good thing Hangman's family had never tried to walk out this way. They never would have made it.

Blackjack spotted the Anglers right away. Spending so much time in the valley fighting these creatures had tuned his senses to pick up the slightest trace of their movements.

He picked out a dozen breeding sites with countless webs full of eggs. Movement in the jungle told him where the Anglers kept their young hidden in the undergrowth.

Herds of adults stood guard over all their young and ranged farther afield to hunt and patrol their end of the valley.

Blackjack saw a lot of things there that he didn't voice to his friends. Their group could go back to the band now. They had found out what Hangman wanted to know.

The men turned back and set off running. They didn't have to be cautious. The Anglers had completely retreated beyond the pass. The men didn't see a single Angler anywhere on the northern side.

They must have sent out that one swarm to target the Godless camp. Those Anglers must have come over the pass specifically to launch this attack. No other Anglers came this far north.

The men made it to the jungle and vaulted into the branches. "You go ahead!" Blackjack called to his friends. "Tell Hangman where the Anglers are!"

"Hey! Where are you going?!" Oracle demanded.

"I have to check something! I'll see you back at the camp!"

"What should we tell Hangman about where you are?" Chief called after him.

"Tell him the truth! Tell him I went to go check on something and I'll be back soon."

Blackjack didn't wait around any longer to explain. He didn't have time for that. Enough Anglers lived south of the pass. They might decide to bring in hundreds more next time and make a real assault on the camp. Then the Godless would be sitting ducks.

Blackjack wouldn't have moved the women and children out of the caves so soon, but he wasn't Kral of this band no matter what his men might say.

He raced through the jungle putting more and more distance behind him. He plunged through the secret tunnel, came out in the next valley, and turned left to head south.

He didn't slow down or stop, not even when night fell. He kept running until the following morning.

He made it to the other end of the valley by the time the sun came up. He stopped at the very southern end of the Angler Valley where he could look down at the creatures from the opposite direction.

He couldn't see them as clearly from this distance. The end of the valley was too far away from the Anglers' breeding grounds. The adults stayed there to guard their young.

Memories flooded his mind of his early childhood in this valley with his parents and younger siblings. Hangman had searched the valley rim for days before he finally had to admit that there really was no way in or out.

The cliffs across valley's the northern end presented a sheer, flat wall of stone plunging hundreds of feet to the valley floor.

The southern end of the valley came to a point. It narrowed from the valley's widest sections to a narrow channel flanked with equally high vertical walls. The two walls eventually came to a crack embedded in solid stone.

Blackjack stood there staring at it for a long time. He remembered a lot from his first stay in the Angler Valley. His brain seemed to have become acutely aware of every detail of this valley and how it related to the Godless' interaction with the Anglers.

He stayed a lot longer than he should have. Fatigue and sleep deprivation were starting to get the better of him.

He wouldn't get any more sleep until he made it back to the camp, so he took off running again. He ran through another night, staggered through the secret tunnel, and finally made it back to the camp. The Anglers were gone. They'd broken off their siege.

Blackjack collapsed in front of his parents' shelter and shut his eyes. His whole body trembled with exhaustion. He needed to crawl inside and pass out for a week, but he couldn't do that yet—not until he talked to Hangman.

Mora came back and found him first. She still carried that baby boy around on her shoulder. Blackjack didn't see the baby's mother anywhere.

Mora frowned at him. "Are you okay?" she asked. "Where have you been? Your father and I have been worried sick."

"Where is he, Mother?" Blackjack croaked.

"I don't know. I think he's over there somewhere talking to someone." She waved behind her.

Blackjack dragged himself off the ground, sat up, and swallowed to get his parched throat working again. "Could you please go get him, Mother? I need to talk to him. It's important."

She gave him a hard look and walked off in the other direction. He was already sitting up, so he crawled into the shelter and sprawled on his parents' bed. He couldn't talk to Hangman in public anyway.

Blackjack found some of his mother's water gourds and some dried food in the shelter. He guzzled down all the water in one of her gourds and stretched out on her bed to eat.

He was lying there starting to feel somewhat normal when his father came in. Hangman started by giving Blackjack a hard look, too. "Where have you been?" Hangman snapped. "Oracle came back telling me that you ran off by yourself."

"I did. Did he tell you that the Anglers are all south of the pass?"

"Of course he told me. I knew they would be somewhere."

Blackjack opened his eyes and pushed himself up on his elbow. "Did he tell you how many there are?"

Hangman's expression slipped. "Yes, he told me, but that's nothing I didn't already expect." Hangman frowned. "What is going on? Where have you been? Answer me."

Blackjack sat all the way up. "Listen to me, Father. The Anglers are planning something. They have enough adults over there to come at us in force. They could get inside the camp and we wouldn't be able to stop them—not if they really came at us. These rocks won't protect us. I think you should move everyone back to the caves. I didn't want to say so before, but I think we left the caves too soon. We still need that protection. We need it now more than ever."

"That would only be a temporary solution. You saw what happened. The Anglers can block us in and stop us from leaving. We would be stuck there."

"That's exactly what I'm saying. It would be a temporary solution to keep everyone safe while we launch our last campaign to finish off the Anglers for good."

"How would we do that? We would have to send all our men south and then we would be exposed with nowhere to take shelter."

"No, Father. I have another idea. Do you remember Thena's plan to create a bottleneck or choke point to trap the Anglers? We can kill them one at a time without them being able to ambush us in return."

"Of course I remember, but it would take us days to create something like that."

"It might take us days, but I have the solution. You went around the valley on all sides to try to find a way in. The whole valley is surrounded by these cliffs. Nothing can get in or out."

"I already know that. How does that help us?"

"You've seen the southern end of the valley. You know it comes to a point—like this." Blackjack drew two lines on the ground to form a V. "All we have to do is construct two high walls—here and here." He created another V above the first one to show where the walls would come together, but they didn't meet. He left a gap at the top.

Hangman furrowed his brow and scowled at the drawing. Blackjack could just see the wheels turning in his father's head.

"We can go around the valley on the western side," Blackjack went on. "The Anglers are all on the eastern side protecting their webs and young. We can get to the southern end of the valley and build these walls in a way that the Anglers won't be able to climb over the top. We'll also create some much smaller holes either under the wall or at the sides that the Anglers can't get through. Then we'll sweep the valley and lead the adults to attack us. They'll follow us through the opening here. They'll only be able to get through one at a time. That will give our people time to get out. The Anglers will all wind up inside this enclosure. They'll only be able to get out through the bottleneck—which is where we'll kill them. Mother and the other able-bodied women can follow behind us once we've cleared out all the adults. The women can set fire to the webs and kill the young. That will end the Anglers for good. They won't be able to come back from that."

Hangman stared at the drawing and then sank down on the bed next to Blackjack. Hangman stared into space for a long time thinking it over. Blackjack relaxed back on the bed and ate some more. He needed rest before he did anything.

Chapter 49

Blackjack and Hangman were still sitting in silence in Hangman and Mora's shelter when Mora came back with baby Eco. Hangman used his foot to erase Blackjack's drawing before Mora saw it.

Thena came with her and fussed over the baby as much as Mora did if not more. Mora let Thena hold the baby as much as she wanted.

Thena left with the baby to go walk him around the camp. Mora stayed behind and talked to Hangman about something one of the new families needed.

Hangman didn't mention Blackjack's idea. He answered Mora in his usual calm tone. A minute later, another couple came over and entered the shelter. They sat on the floor with Mora while the couple talked to Hangman.

This couple included a heavily pregnant woman and freed man from Hangman's first raid on the Red Riders. The couple wanted to adopt Zoana's baby. The woman was already lactating and they wanted to give the little boy a family.

"We don't want to intrude on you, Mora," the woman insisted. "You probably want to raise him yourself."

"Not at all," Mora countered. "He's a sweet, innocent child. He deserves a family and he won't get it from his mother. I've only been taking care of him because she couldn't."

"I should talk to her," Hangman interjected. "It isn't the Godless way for parents to turn their backs on their children, especially at this young age."

"There must be some leeway for special circumstances," Mora pointed out. "You can understand why she would have a bad association with this child considering what she's been through."

"That's no excuse to abandon her child," Hangman countered. "It isn't the baby's fault. Why should he suffer because of something his father did?"

"He wouldn't have to if he came with us," the woman insisted. "He might never know the difference. We would raise him as our own. We want to."

"I'll allow it, but I'm still going to talk to her," Hangman told her. "She should understand that she'll be relinquishing all claim to this child. She'll never be able to take him back or make any claim that he support her in old age or any other obligation she might be able to place on him for being his mother. She would have to completely let him go."

The woman winced. "I'll have to leave that up to you."

"Don't do anything until I talk to her," Hangman went on. "She might come around once she hears what I have to say. I don't want you to get attached to the boy as long as there's a chance she might take him back."

The woman nodded. She could barely control her voice when she said, "I understand," and left.

Hangman sent Mora to get the child's mother. Zoana entered the shelter next and Kuri came with her. They held hands during their meeting with Hangman.

"Another couple in the camp wants to adopt Eco and raise him as their own," Hangman began. "I want to hear it from you that you really don't want to have anything to do with this child. I want to hear you tell me to my face that you really don't want to be this child's mother. I can't believe that. I could never believe that about any woman."

Tears sprang to Zoana's eyes and she looked away. "I do want to be his mother!" she choked. "I just don't know how to!"

"You be his mother the same way you would be a mother to any other child you had. Why should you treat him differently than you would treat a child you had with Kuri here? You're married. You will have children with him. Are you telling me you would love them more than you would love Eco? Do you not realize how unfair you're being to your own child? Do you not realize how unfair it is to him that some strangers are giving him the love and care he needs—the love and care he should be getting from you? What's wrong with you? What kind of mother are you?"

"I....I try....."

"Stop trying," Hangman snapped. "Just treat him as though he was born from Kuri. Eco *is* born from Kuri. Kuri is the only father Eco will ever have. That's all you need to know. Eco is part of your family as much as his brothers and sisters will be."

Zoana sat there struggling to control her lips while tears streaked down her cheeks.

"I brought you here to tell you one thing," Hangman went on. "If I give this child to the other couple, you'll never see him again except as someone else's child. You'll have no claim on him. You won't be able to come back later and say you want him back. Some other woman will cry over him when he goes out for initiation and when he comes back a man. He'll care for some other woman in her old age. Another couple will go with him to the gatherings. Another man will stand next to him and negotiate for him to take a wife. You'll never be able to call

him your son again. You'll lose him forever. You'll become a stranger
to him. You won't even be able to call yourself his relative because
you won't be. He'll call another woman, 'Mother' and another man,
'Father'. Is that what you want?"

"No!" she wailed. "Of course not."

"Then be his mother. Be the mother he needs you to be. Do you
think it's easy for any woman to raise a child? Do you think it's so different for all the other women I brought out of Red Rider country?"

"No," she moaned.

"This woman who wants to adopt him is pregnant from the Red
Riders. She's in exactly the same situation you are and she's planning
to raise your son as her own to give him the family he deserves. I don't
know how you can live with that."

She broke down sobbing into her hands. She had to let go of Kuri's
hand to cover her face. "I can't! I can't live with it! I can't live with any
of it."

"Maybe this child can be the way you can live it," Hangman suggested. "Maybe you can see him as one of the people the Red Riders
hurt the same way they hurt you. He didn't ask for this. He only asked
to live a good life with a family that loves him. Someone else will give
it to him if you don't. I can't stand by and allow him to suffer because
of you. He's as much a victim of the Red Riders as you are. Maybe he
can be the way for you to come out of this. Maybe you can see yourself
going through it with him and healing alongside him. Maybe he can be
that for you the same way you can be it for him. He needs you to show
him that he isn't wrong because he got stuck in that situation through
no fault of his own. Kuri accepts you even though you went through
that. You should give Eco the same consideration. Heaven knows he
deserves it as much as you do if not more."

She nodded still sobbing her eyes out. Thena came back just then. She clutched the baby and glanced around in terror when she saw so many people crowded into her parents' shelter.

Mora stood up, took the baby out of Thena's arms, and gave him back to Zoana. She clutched him close and cried hard into his little shoulder.

Blackjack found himself staring up at his father. This man in front of Blackjack right now—this was the only true Kral this band would ever have. Blackjack could only dream of being a Kral as good as his father.

Hangman was it. This was the reason everyone accepted Hangman and never challenged him—because of moments like these.

He could say these things to a distraught woman and she would listen to him. He could turn her life around with a few well-chosen words. He could do the same thing with any of his men. He could do it with the whole band.

Zoana and Kuri finally left and took the baby with them. Blackjack would have been very surprised if Mora ever took care of that baby again.

Hangman left for a while to go inform the other couple that Zoana wanted to keep her baby for now. Hangman left Mora and Thena in the shelter with Blackjack, so none of the three talked about anything important.

He relaxed on his mother's bed for a long time and then both women left. He fell asleep there and woke up alone hours later.

Chapter 50

H angman stood off to one side and shot flinty glances at the surrounding jungle. The women and children filed through the trees on their way back to the caves.

They grumbled a lot about having to move, but they finally had to accept Hangman's promise that they could all come back to their homes very soon if the operation against the Anglers went well.

Two long lines of armed men and boys flanked the women and children all the way through the jungle. The men and boys created a protected column with the women and children filing between them.

Hardly any of the men watched their wives and children walk past. All the men faced outward into the jungle keeping their eyes open for Anglers. They hadn't come back since the siege, but Hangman had taken Blackjack's warning seriously.

Hangman had heard all the stories from everyone in the band about Banjo calling Blackjack a boy. Hangman probably would have felt inclined to treat Blackjack as a boy, too.

Hangman couldn't think of any other Kral in the history of the Godless Clan who would take the recommendation of such a young man. Blackjack was hardly a man at all. He'd barely initiated.

Hangman would have had to be bone stupid not to see the sense in Blackjack's recommendation. Hangman would have had to have his head so deeply buried in the sand that he no longer cared about the band's wellbeing—exactly the way Shadow had.

None of that mattered now because the band was going ahead with Blackjack's plan to the letter. Hangman hadn't said a word about it to anyone.

He'd let Blackjack announce it to the rest of the men and those able-bodied women who would carry out the second prong of the attack on the Angler breeding sites. Hangman pushed Blackjack to the forefront in preparing the whole operation.

Blackjack had been the one to organize a party of men to travel south through the pass, sneak around the Anglers on the west side of the valley, and construct the walls to create the bottleneck.

Blackjack had been the one to divide the men into teams that would enter the southern part of the valley and lure the Anglers into the trap.

Blackjack had also been the one to organize the able-bodied women into teams to go after the breeding sites while the Anglers were busy trying to run down the men.

Hangman had sat back and watched and listened to his son take command of this band. Blackjack did everything so expertly.

He held the men in the palm of his hand and they obeyed him to the letter. Hangman couldn't have been prouder watching and listening to all of Blackjack's speeches, encouragement, and explanations. He was a born leader.

Now the day had finally arrived for the band to put his plans into motion—starting with moving the women and children into the caves.

The men would leave these people unprotected. No men would be around to kill the Anglers if they made it back here to attack these people.

All the dried Angler meat the band had been preparing would have to keep everyone going until the men came back. The band had enough food to last a month. That should be plenty of time.

Blackjack didn't plan for the men to be gone longer than a week. The whole operation should take less than two days if he had planned this the right way.

The women and children flooded the caves. Everyone knew the drill. The band also brought extra stockpiles of water so they wouldn't have to leave the caves at all.

They didn't bring firewood. Everyone agreed not to light any fires until the men came back and told the women it was safe to leave the caves.

The men took a long time to get their families situated and for the women to be ready to take over. Most of the women had no problem staying behind. They already understood life in the caves.

The men didn't leave until close to noon. Then they had to hike for two days down the valley to the pass.

Mora led a group of thirty women of various ages. None of them was pregnant or had young children to take care of. Most were the wives of Red's men plus Nagana, Viking's wife, and a few others.

A group of older girls came with them including Thena. Almost all of these girls were at least fifteen years old and had no other family obligations to keep them in the caves.

The women traveled in their own cluster separate from the men. Hangman didn't listen to what the women talked about back there.

They had never traveled apart from the men during all their journeys together. Hangman could already see these women forming their own little army all to themselves. They would wage their own private battle against the Anglers. The men wouldn't participate in that.

Hangman thanked his lucky stars that Mora, Thena, Nagana, Yonna, and the others were there. He and the other men didn't have to worry about these women doing their part. Hangman didn't have to worry about these women at all.

They all knew how to defend themselves. Mora had fought the Anglers enough times to know what to expect. All these women knew how to get up into the branches if they needed to.

The men just had to lead the Anglers to the bottleneck. That was it. The rest would be easy.

He still found it nearly impossible to imagine this valley without Anglers in it. He couldn't picture what his life would be like once he didn't have to fight the Anglers anymore.

He would still have to stay on constant watch for the Red Riders and any other enemy Clans that came around. At least the Godless would be able to fight these enemies outside the valley. The enemy Clans would never find their way inside.

An air of calm certainty and deep warmth spread through the group when everyone camped at the edge of the jungle. The affection, connection, and closeness in the group hung heavy over everyone.

Hangman had never felt closer to these people than right now. He'd gone through hell with them and made it back to fight another day. He would gladly go through all of that and a hundred times more as long as he could go through it with them and not someone else.

He wouldn't trade his connection with these people for anything. He couldn't think of any better reward for all his years of hardship than to sit around these fires with these people and feel what he felt for them.

His affection and even love for these people—it was the purest joy of his life. His wife, his sons, his daughter, his brothers—they were all here. They had shared the darkest times of his life and now they were here with him when it really mattered.

His heart burst with pride for every member of his family. Mora. Blackjack. Thena. Maeno. Bantam. Lock. He couldn't have asked for better than this right here.

He felt the spirits of his dead comrades and relatives hovering around the fires that night. They were all here. None of them was lost. They traveled with him. Alien was here. Baron was here. Even Cross, Hammer, and their comrades were here.

Nothing was lost. It all kept growing. Everything that mattered in the world kept growing and expanding.

Hangman read the same truth in his comrades' eyes. He saw it glowing in his wife's and children's eyes, his brothers' eyes, and the eyes of their closest friends and relatives. They all understood. No one had to explain it to anyone.

This was the moment that made them a Clan. They should by rights have taken a new name for this Clan—the Clan born in this valley. They were still Godless, but they became something new when they came here.

It wasn't even new because it had been growing and struggling for years to come into existence. Hangman couldn't explain it to himself except that this band was like no other in the whole Godless Clan. This band had evolved into something much, much more.

Mora stretched out with him when the time came for them to go to sleep. He put his arm around her shoulders and she rested her head on his chest. They hadn't slept together like this in public for years. He couldn't even remember the last time.

It seemed so fitting now. The feeling between them had grown beyond anything he could ever put into words. He never would have wanted to come on this campaign without her and Thena—without all of them.

The party woke up in the same state of deep calm the next morning. Everyone got up, shared their food and water, and set off for the top of the pass. The party stopped there and looked down in silence at the Anglers in the distance.

Blackjack and his men had come back telling Hangman how many Anglers lived in this part of the valley. Hangman didn't quite believe it until he saw it for himself. They had amassed the bulk of their remaining population into certain areas.

The Anglers must have started organizing themselves so much better than before—or maybe he just didn't understand enough about their ways to fully grasp how organized they were.

No one had really been talking on the way up here, but the sight of all those Anglers cast a pall over the group. Hangman wasn't the only one to feel it.

Blackjack got everyone's attention by turning around and facing the whole group. "You know what you have to do. Split up into your teams. You women will stay here while the men skirt the west side and get beyond the Anglers. You should be able to see when they start moving off toward the south. Don't enter their breeding grounds until you see the adults leave the area. You men station yourselves where I told you. We won't act until everyone gets into position. Is everyone clear?"

Everyone nodded. They'd already gone over this more times than Hangman could count.

"All right," Blackjack breathed. "Let's do this."

He and the men set off down the hill. Hangman cast one last backward glance at Mora and Thena. He wasn't the only man to do it.

They all made eye contact before the men slipped away down the other side of the pass and reentered the jungle. Hangman didn't look back. He and the men took off running, broke out of the jungle on the west side, and skimmed along the cliff walls heading south.

Chapter 51

Blackjack veered hard into the trees and all the men scattered into their teams. Each team would carry out the same operation in different parts of the valley.

The men had to make sure they antagonized all the Anglers to follow the men and left no one behind to guard the breeding sites.

All the men split up and scattered through the jungle. Blackjack didn't see any of his comrades again. He ran for a long way and headed back north toward the breeding sites.

He didn't stop until he charged straight into the site. He even trampled a bunch of young Anglers. He did it on purpose to make them squawk. His ploy worked. Twelve adults spun around to glare at him.

He twisted the knife by pulling his axes and hacking off the young ones' heads right in front of their parents. The Anglers roared and stomped toward him. He actually threw the dead young ones at the adults to make them really enraged.

They picked up speed to tear him apart. He turned and ran for it. He had to run his fastest to get away from them in time. They launched through the jungle coming faster and faster to hunt him down.

He ran for his life. He hadn't run this fast in a long time. Sheer terror made him run faster. Adrenaline charged his veins and wiped out all thought. He was nothing but prey to these creatures.

He came to his senses when he saw Kuvik ahead. He stood fifty yards beyond Blackjack's position. Kuvik's eyes widened when he saw the Anglers coming. Blackjack launched into the branches with all the Anglers right on his tail.

They all lunged up to try to grab him. Kuvik charged forward and hurled a bunch of large rocks at the Anglers to get their attention.

It worked. They turned on him in a rage and took off to chase him next. The Anglers completely forgot about Blackjack hiding in the canopy.

Kuvik vanished out of sight along with the Anglers. Blackjack didn't have a second to catch his breath. He set off through the canopy on Kuvik's trail.

The Anglers outpaced them both and eventually overtook Kuvik. He vaulted into the branches just in time to save his hide and Oracle took over from there. Blackjack and Kuvik met up and traveled together until Oracle bailed out and Chief took over.

Deafening screeches echoed through the jungle on all sides as more and more crowds of Anglers converged from all sides. They all came together as the men led the Anglers closer to the bottleneck.

Blackjack and Kuvik met up with Chief and Oracle. More men assembled in the branches from all the other teams. The Anglers gathered into a massive horde of pure venomous fury. Blackjack wouldn't want to be the man leading them right now.

The men finally broke out of the trees and had to descend to the ground the rest of the way to the bottleneck. Hangman, Wildling, Carnage, Pyro, Yeoli, Kavis, and five other freed men led the Anglers the last stretch to the walls.

The men vanished inside the bottleneck. The Anglers slammed into the opening and charged inside to annihilate the men.

Blackjack and the others dropped to the ground and rushed into the open just as the first men squirmed out through the side openings in the bottleneck's outer walls.

The walls hid the men so Anglers didn't see them escape. The Anglers crushed each other against the opening trying to get inside as fast as possible. It never crossed their minds that this might be an elaborate trap.

The Anglers who first entered the bottleneck saw the men escaping through the gaps. The Anglers rushed in to try to catch the men only for the men to skim away just in time. The Anglers left plenty of room for their friends to get in behind them.

The Anglers' own bloodlust kept driving them into the bottleneck trying to catch the men who weren't in there anymore.

The Anglers who entered first obviously couldn't communicate the situation to their friends. All the Anglers packed inside and found the men gone.

Blackjack and his men rejoined with Hangman's party. They all gathered around the gap and met the Anglers there just as the Anglers figured out that there was only one way out of this place.

Blackjack drew his weapon and prepared for the last stand. The Anglers wouldn't and couldn't get away. None would survive to bother the Godless ever again.

Hangman, Viking, and Red approached the bottleneck first. All the men closed around the gap for the final blow.

The Anglers surged back to the opening and the first one came through. The men struck in force from all sides and cut the creature down just as the next Angler broke through.

Too many men crowded around the first Angler already dying on the ground. The men automatically split into two teams and then again into three to meet all the Anglers coming out one at a time.

The first team attacked an Angler the minute it got through the gap. The same team followed that creature to the ground just as the second team finished off another Angler and moved back into position to take on the next Angler coming through.

The men arranged themselves without discussing it first. One team attacked the Angler while another brought down a second Angler and the third time was just slaughtering the third Angler in time to meet up with the fourth.

The process sped up. The Anglers saw and understood the situation now. They shoved and butted each other to get out of the bottleneck faster. They must have been thinking they could overpower the men if the Anglers only got enough of them outside at the same time.

So many Anglers fell right there in front of the bottleneck that they wound up blocking the opening. The men couldn't move the Anglers out of the way as easily as the Anglers themselves could move their own dead.

The Anglers still trapped inside the bottleneck must have finally realized the predicament they were in. They stopped rushing to get out there and meet their enemies. The Anglers pulled back. They still couldn't get away. Thirty Anglers remained trapped inside.

Hangman lowered his weapons and cast a glance over all the dead Anglers. "It sure does seem a terrible waste not to use this meat."

"We could butcher them, move the meat out of the way, and clear the way for the others to get out," Oracle suggested.

"I don't think the others will come out even if we open the way," Blackjack suggested. "They won't come out unless we drive them out."

"How do we do that?" Maeno asked.

"We can use fire," Blackjack replied. "We can crawl in through the side gaps and set fire to the grass inside the enclosure. That will drive the Anglers out, but we need to clear this space first. Let's get to work."

"Take a look." Kuvik pointed behind the party toward the distant jungle. Columns of smoke rose from the treetops where the Angler breeding sites used to be. The women were attacking the breeding sites according to Blackjack's plan.

The sight energized all the men. They started butchering the Anglers one after another starting with those farthest away from the bottleneck.

"We'll be going home as heroes after this," Viking joked. "We'll be eating so much that we won't be able to walk."

"Speak for yourself," Wildling teased. "You could probably eat one of these Anglers by yourself."

The others laughed. An air of celebration broke out among the men even though they hadn't finished off the Anglers yet. Everyone helped section the carcasses and drag the skeletons and offal into the jungle for the ants.

Blackjack kept an eye on the surviving Anglers as the men worked their way closer to the opening. The gap cleared as the men removed one dead Angler after another. The surviving Anglers paced back and forth in there. They didn't come near the opening.

The men had all the time in the world to wash the blood off their hands and weapons and stand around studying the Anglers from a safe distance. The Anglers knew better than to come out of the enclosure.

"Well, I guess there's nothing to do but try it," Blackjack remarked.

He and the uninitiated boys went out into the jungle, came back with a bunch of tinder and branches, and lit a fire to one side where the Anglers wouldn't see it. Blackjack put two large branches into the flames and ignited the ends.

Then he and Loso took a branch each and returned to the side openings at both ends of the fence. Blackjack ignited the grass inside the enclosure before he crawled through. The flames spread outward in both directions, including toward him.

He stamped them out before they could get too big. They kept growing and spreading inside the enclosure. They eventually burned a big enough space for him and Loso to crawl in.

The flames produced an instant effect on the Anglers. They panicked, crashed into each other, and crowded closer and closer to get away from all the smoke and flames.

Blackjack and Loso moved in from the sides. Blackjack held his burning branch out in front of him to herd the Anglers toward the gap. He and Loso moved together to get behind the creatures.

The Anglers didn't wait long enough for the two friends to get into position. Blackjack couldn't be sure in the end if the Anglers even saw him and Loso. The creatures were too scared of the flames licking closer through the grass.

The Anglers roared, squealed, shrieked, and bellowed. They kept colliding with each other when they realized they had to run through the gap to get away from the flames.

The Anglers held their ground a lot longer than Blackjack expected, but they eventually caved when the flames got right around their feet. The Anglers screeched in terror when they felt the heat.

The whole pack charged the opening and wedged there trying to shove their way out fast enough. The creatures kept casting terrified glances behind them. A curtain of flame blocked the creatures from seeing Blackjack and Loso.

The Anglers pushed through the gap one at a time and fell to the men waiting outside. The flames ate through the rest of the grass inside the enclosure, but the grass didn't provide enough fuel to ignite the enclosure walls.

The fire eventually burned out everywhere except right there behind the gap. Blackjack and Loso advanced and watched the men slaughter the last Anglers. The two friends stepped on the flames and put the fire the rest of the way out.

The men broke out in thrilled laughter once they took down the last Anglers. Dead Anglers lay all over the grass as the men jumped up and down, hugged each other, and some even blinked away tears of pure elated joy.

Hangman grabbed Blackjack in a huge hug. All the men gathered around talking loud and fast. Everyone present congratulated Blackjack on the success of his campaign.

The men were still grabbing each other, shaking each other, and laughing when the women came running up. They charged out of the jungle and stopped in their tracks when they saw the men standing around all the dead Anglers.

"Is it finished?" Mora asked.

"Yeah!" Hangman croaked. "It's over. They're all dead. Did you finish off all the breeding sites?"

The women nodded. "It took a long time to kill all the young ones, but we got them all."

The men rushed the women and the whole group spent the next half hour doing nothing but celebrating and talking everything over. Then the party spent another few hours butchering all the remaining Anglers.

The party couldn't carry all the meat, so they strung the haunches up on ropes in the jungle where the creatures couldn't get to it. The friends loaded up with as much as they could carry and headed back north to the caves.

The friends ate and talked a lot on the way back. The atmosphere around the fire that night couldn't have been more different. Everyone talked and laughed much louder than usual. No one tried to be quiet.

The friends cooked an insane amount of food and stuffed themselves silly before everyone crashed.

The spirit of celebration stayed with the group all the way to the caves. Then things really got out of hand when the men rejoined their families and everyone celebrated together. The party carried all their Angler meat back to the camp in triumph.

Everyone stayed up late that night to feast, laugh, joke, and enjoy themselves. No one stood guard over the camp entrance.

Godless voices echoed off the rocks. Firelight lit up the camp as everyone relaxed and enjoyed themselves in ways no one had in all the years since they'd left Shadow's territory.

Blackjack enjoyed himself as much as everyone else. The men would travel back to the south and retrieve the rest of the meat tomorrow. No one would let all those dead Anglers go to waste.

Their meat belonged to the Godless band by right. Blackjack and his comrades had killed those Anglers. No one could take the meat away from them. The band would need it to feed all these people.

No one would take this valley away from them, either. If the band could defeat the Anglers, they could defeat anyone. Anyone who came around to mess with the band would wind up just as dead as the Anglers. Blackjack and his fellow Godless would make sure of it.

End of Book 7.

Keep Reading

Rise of the Giants Series: Book 8: Rise of the New Race

Hangman and his men aren't young anymore. They can't move as fast or fight as hard as the younger generation. With the brutal Red Riders moving in on the Godless Clan's territory, a new breed of warrior must rise to protect the next generation. Hangman's oldest son, Blackjack, takes over as Kral of the band while Hangman's second son gets thrown into a deadly game of cat-and-mouse that could decide the fate of the human race.

With time running out and everything they hold dear on the line, the Godless must make the ultimate sacrifice in one last-ditch gamble to save their home and their people. Nothing can stop the march of time. The old generation doesn't belong in this world anymore. It's time to rewrite the rules and forge a new path that will carry the younger generation into a world of hope and promise.

You can find it at your favorite book retailer.

Sign Up Once--Get all Theo Mann's free books including brand new releases

S ign Up Once--Get all Theo Mann's free books including brand new releases

In a world where everything is out to kill you, humans must fight for survival every day against huge dangerous creatures and enemy Clans. The Godless Clan has enough to worry about already. They don't need to fight their own.

Sixteen-year-old Shadow knows exactly what to do when he discovers a girl from an enemy band hiding in the jungle. He takes her captive as a prisoner of war, but the Godless have a strict code of honor when dealing with women—even enemy women.

He and Katha will have to fight for their very survival and overcome generations of mistrust before they make it back to their people—who just might be the most dangerous enemies either of them has ever faced.

Sign up at www.theomann.com to read it for free

About Theo Mann

I write 70 books per year—and yes, before you ask, all these books are my original creative work. Nothing written under my name is AI-generated or ghostwritten because I write better than AI and any ghostwriter out there.

People don't read fiction for entertainment or to escape from reality. People read fiction to see their humanity reflected in another person's character and story.

This is my promise to you. When you read my books, you'll see your own humanity reflected in the characters and stories. I take this commitment to my readers very seriously. My books are an intimate form of communication between us. I would never disrespect my readers by turning that over to a machine or another writer. This is my bond between me and you as my reader.

I write 20,000 words per day as my daily work output. If anyone with a public platform would like to challenge me to prove this in a controlled environment, feel free to contact me on this website's contact page.

I worked as a professional ghostwriter for fifteen years. Now I'm on a mission to set a Guinness World Record by writing 700 books over the next ten years and 1400 books over the next twenty years, all originally written by me. See my website for the full book list.

I'm also the author of *Proof for the Existence of God* and the *Crimes Against Fiction* blog. You can find all my nonfiction work at www.crimes-against-fiction.com.

If you have a story idea, or if you would like me to explore a series in more depth, or if you'd like me to explore a character by writing a spinoff series about that character or world, leave me a message on my website's contact page. I answer all reader emails, so ask me anything, tell me what you liked and didn't like, and let me know where you'd like your favorite series to go. I would love to hear your ideas and find out what you'd like to read next.

Find out more at www.theomann.com.